DATE DUE

D1132357

NIGHT
ROAD

BRENDAN DuBOIS

OTHER WORKS BY BRENDAN DUBOIS

THE LEWIS COLE MYSTERIES

Dead Sand

Black Tide

Shattered Shell

Killer Waves

Buried Dreams

Primary Storm

Deadly Cove

Fatal Harbor

Blood Foam

OTHER NOVELS

Resurrection Day

Six Days

Final Winter

Betrayed

Twilight

Amerikan Eagle (as Alan Glenn)

Dark Victory

SHORT STORY COLLECTIONS

The Dark Snow and Other Stories

Tales from The Dark Woods

NON-FICTION

My Short, Happy Life In "Jeopardy!"

NIGHT ROAD

BRENDAN DuBOIS

MIDNIGHT INK
WOODBURY, MINNESOTA

FIRST EDITION
First Printing, 2016

Book format by Teresa Pojar
Cover design by Kevin R. Brown
Cover Illustration by Dominick Finelle/The July Group
Editing by Nicole Nugent

Midnight Ink, an imprint of Llewellyn Worldwide Ltd.

Library of Congress Cataloging-in-Publication Data (pending)

ISBN: 9780738746395

Midnight Ink
Llewellyn Worldwide Ltd.
2143 Wooddale Drive
Woodbury, MN 55125-2989
www.midnightinkbooks.com
Printed in the United States of America

This novel is dedicated to my brother Stephen,
who knows and traverses many night roads indeed.

ACKNOWLEDGMENTS

The author wishes to extend his thanks and appreciation to his fantastic editor, Terri Bischoff, as well as Beth Hanson, Teresa Pojar, and other members of the Midnight Ink publishing team. Thanks, too, to my wife and first reader Mona Pinette, as well to my friends and relatives in my state's true North Country.

AUTHOR'S NOTE

This is a work of fiction. There is no Washington County in New Hampshire, nor is there a town called Turner. There is no resemblance between any characters or locales in this book and the good people and towns of New Hampshire's North Country.

Daily Threat Assessment Task Force Teleconference Call
April 10th

Homeland Security representative: "… could you repeat that again, Jerry?"

CIA representative: "Yeah, our counterparts in Canada report—"

State Department representative: "Canada has counterparts? Who knew."

[[Laughter]]

FBI representative: "Some fucking diplomat you are. Go on, Jerry."

CIA: "Like I said, our friends in the Security Intelligence Services up north received a tip-off that there was a shipping container coming in at the St. Lawrence Seaway that might be of potential interest. Said to be identified as a Mextel Lines container, off-loaded from an Algerian-registered vessel."

FBI: "Potential interest like smuggling maple syrup to avoid duty fees, or something more explosive?"

CIA: "The latter. They got intel via cellphone intercepts and the usual chatter. Thing is, they located the shipping container. Next day, they went back to tag it so they could track it … it was gone."

[[Cross-talk]]

FBI: What now?"

[[Cross-talk]]

Homeland Security: "… we'll take the lead in notifying the appropriate authorities, once Jerry can get us a better description of that shipping container and what might be in it."

FBI: "That's it?"

State Department: "What else, then?"

FBI: "Christ, if the Canadians think this is a threat, once we get an ID on what the damn thing looks like, let's go public. Let the people know. Do it that way, we'll get the damn thing in twenty-four hours."

[[Cross-talk]]

CIA: "Plus letting our jihadist friends know about the SIS's techniques. No, I like the low-key approach. It'll work better."

FBI: [[Expletive deleted]] "Thought our job was to protect civilians, no matter what."

Homeland Security: "One would think that, wouldn't one."

ONE

Forty-five miles south of the Canadian border, Andre Ouellette checked the hip holster underneath his leather coat to make sure it was in place. His driver, Pierre Bisson, maneuvered their black Lexus into the dirt parking lot of the Flight Deck Bar & Grill in Turner, New Hampshire. His piece, a Sig Sauer 9mm P226 with a 15-shot extended magazine, was where it belonged. Good. It had been a long drive from west of Montreal. When they left this crappy joint later tonight, the guy they were meeting was either going to roll over and present his ass up for a good reaming, or was going to get his brains blown out.

The guy's choice. Andre was just here to deliver the message and get it done, one way or the other.

Pierre put the Lexus in park, switched off the engine. The place looked like somebody's creaky one-story wood frame house that had two or three additions tacked on, satellite dishes on top, with motorcycles, pickup trucks, and a couple of shitbox cars with rusted out fenders and bumpers parked in two rows. Pierre draped his beefy arms over the steering wheel. "My uncle, he was in the biker wars, ten years back, you remember? When the Hells Angels tried to take over our territory in Quebec? Was ex-Army, expert in demolitions, rolled a couple of homemade bombs into a clubhouse and a motor home, took out a couple of the Hells Angels. Told me he was just helping 'em go to where they belonged, that being hell."

Andre said, "Were they IEDs?"

"The fuck is an IED?" Pierre asked.

"Improvised explosive device," Andre patiently explained.

Pierre snorted. "Shit, weren't nothin' improvised about them, like I said, he was an expert. Thing is, I'm looking at this shitbox and wish my uncle was here. We could toss a couple of loads into the windows, take care of business without any bullshit talk going back and forth. Be back home before you know it."

Andre reached for the door handle. "Too much of a bang, Pierre. Don't want to bring outside attention to what we're involved with."

Pierre opened his door first. "Hell, look at the dump. Pretty much could blame anything blowing up on the propane tanks back there."

Andre stepped out onto the dirt lot, stretched his back, felt the pleasure as muscles popped back there. About the only joy he had experienced in the long dull drive south through the farmlands in Quebec, through the main border crossing in Derby Line, Vermont, and now over here to New Hampshire. Pierre ambled over, a large fellow whose arms were so long he could almost scratch his kneecaps without bending over. But he was also a fast shot when you needed your ass covered. He and Pierre were dressed alike: black sneakers, clean blue jeans, and short black leather coats. But there the resemblance ended. For the past five or six years, Andre kept his head bald—no fag Rogaine or drugs rubbed in his scalp once his hair retreated north—while Pierre had a permanent five o'clock shadow and had a thick unibrow running across his sloping forehead.

Andre went up wide wooden steps and checked his Tag Heuer watch. Five p.m. Windows were on either side of the pub's front door. A handwritten sign, black marker on cardboard, said: NO COLORS WORN INSIDE. Beside him Pierre said, "We're an hour late. Think it's going to make a difference?"

"Going to do something," Andre said. "You remember the set?"

"Yeah," Pierre said. "You tug at your right ear, first clear opportunity, I cap the guy."

"Yeah, but this time make sure I'm far enough away. Last time my sneakers got splattered, had to buy a new pair. You know how hard it is to get sneaks in my size, my feet being so damn wide."

Once Pierre opened the door and they walked in, Andre gave the place a quick scan. It was another dreary roadhouse joint, like so many he had been in before. It was like there was some central distribution center that dumped places like this up and down rural roads and forgotten intersections throughout this part of the world: bar in the back, short-order cook working to the side, two pool tables with rectangular lampshades hanging over them, three hi-def televisions suspended from the wall showing a Red Sox game, a NASCAR race, and a golf game. The men and women inside gave them a look as he and Pierre walked in. Photos and prints of warplanes and ships hung on the cheap paneled walls.

The guys were all of a type, too. Dirty jeans or green work chinos, sweatshirts, a couple of fellows playing pool and wearing colors despite the warning sign outside: cut-off jean vests with big emblems on the back showing a mountain peak with the letters W.C.M.C. underneath. One squirrelly-looking guy, better dressed than the others, was sitting in the corner, reading a newspaper. The girls had jeans on as well, some of them rough looking, most with tattoos on their arms or tits. Andre remembered when girls with tats got his rocks going. Now he liked going to the pubs outside of McGill University, where sweet tight young things enjoyed being with older guys who knew their way around and didn't put up with any bullshit. Maybe Andre didn't know the latest *American Idol* star but he knew how to spend money and make pretty college girls feel special, especially when they got the extra thrill of being around somebody dangerous.

He and Pierre went up to the bar and sat down on round cushioned stools. Before they could order a beer, one of the scraggly guys wearing colors and carrying a pool cue came up to Andre, his beard down mid-chest on his Harley Davidson T-shirt.

"You're late," he said, his brown hair long. "Plus, I don't like your look."

"Can't do anything about the time," Andre said, swiveling around on the stool. "And my look is the way it is. Are you Duncan?"

The biker shook his head, pointed his pool cue to the guy reading the newspaper in the corner. "There's Duncan," he said. "Go on over."

Pierre gave Andre a look, and Andre shrugged. Slid off the stool and went to the corner of the bar, Pierre pacing him. The guy in the corner seemed to be in his late thirties, with a folded-over newspaper in his left hand, his right hand holding a fork. A half-eaten salad was in front of him. He was bulky about his shoulders but he had a funny little smile, like being here was one big joke. He had on a tight-knit blue sweater and his black hair was cut short. Reading glasses were perched at the end of his prominent nose. Andre scoped him out, thought he really didn't need Pierre to put this little fuck down, but Pierre was a good driver. Andre hated driving long distances, except when he was on his bike, but it was still too damn early in the season for long hauls on his Harley.

Andre sat down without an invite, and so did Pierre. The guy said, "You two gentlemen are from the Iron Steeds. I'm Duncan Crowley. And you are …?"

Andre just stared at Duncan. This was going to be easy. He kept on with the look and said. "I'm Andre. This is Pierre. This is how it's going to be. We're gonna come to—"

Duncan speared a little cherry tomato, popped it in his mouth. "Must have been a long drive from Montreal. Need something to drink? Nice selection of drafts on tap, not much of a menu, but before he got hooked on smack, Tony in the kitchen used to—"

Andre scraped his chair closer to the table. "Don't need a drink, don't need a fucking cheeseburger. This is how it's going to be. You got a nice little deal here in these north woods. Some weed. Some loan-sharking. Little cross-border smuggling. But you got something big stirring up in our neck of the woods, coming through our turf. You haven't shown us the proper consideration. So you're going to have to pay us a toll."

"A toll," Duncan repeated.

"That's right. A tribute. A levy. Call it what you want."

Duncan considered that for a moment, put his fork down. "Just to make sure I got this straight: the whole border up here, that's your turf, anything to do with Quebec. So if I was moving stuff through Ontario, maybe go through upstate New York, you guys would be fine with that?"

"Not going through Ontario, are you? You're going through Iron Steeds turf."

"Once it used it to be Hells Angels turf."

"Long fucking time ago. Had a little war before your time to straighten things out. Wars are like that, you know? Give peace all the fucking chance you want, war tends to settle things permanently."

Duncan picked up his fork, stirred the lettuce around on his plate. "Funny thing, I thought our meet was going to be at four p.m. My watch is a bit off but it looks like you're an hour late. What, a long line getting through Customs? Moose get in your way? Lord knows, I've seen moose wander on the road some mornings or nights, they're hard to pass and—"

Andre interrupted, "You not hearing what I'm saying? I'm saying, we don't give a shit when you're crossing cigarettes or Labatt Blue over the border, but this is different. We don't know what you got, but it's worth something. Even got the Canadian Security Intelligence Service sniffing around."

"Really?" the man asked, surprise in his voice. "I'm impressed that you found that out."

"Yeah, well, motorcycles don't have boundaries, right? So the deal is, you pay a toll—ten percent of your load's value, once we inspect it and figure out its worth—plus a couple of our guys go along as security. Paid details."

That seemed to get Duncan's attention. "Security? Really? Will be they as nicely dressed as you two, or will they be in Iron Steeds colors, riding hogs, long hair streaming out, 'Born to Lose' tattoos across their chests? That your idea of security?"

Pierre shifted his weight, causing the chair to creak. Andre said, "Not your worry. Your worry is, we come out of here with an agreement in the next five minutes, or there's going to be some serious shit trouble."

Duncan took his glasses off, rubbed at his long nose. "Like Marlon Brando, hunh? Making me an offer I can't refuse?"

"The fuck you talking about?"

"Marlon Brando. *The Godfather.* Good book, great movie. Making me an offer I can't refuse."

"Yeah, sure, what the fuck ever. I'm making you an offer you can't refuse. So what's it going to be?"

Duncan put his glasses back on and said, "Ask you a question first?"

Andre felt his hands tingle. He wanted to throttle the little bastard, all this dancing around. He said, "Sure, yeah, ask me a question."

"Just how the hell did you fine gentlemen find out about my connection with this particular matter? Was it through the Security Services from your fine country? I find that very concerning."

Andre said, "The fuck this is, an interview? Look. We're done talking. All right? We come to an agreement right now or we'll take it another step further. You, your friends, your family. You think you can go through our turf and not show us the proper respect? Do you?"

It was like an overhead light bulb had just flickered. Something seemed to shadow Duncan's face. Just for the barest moment, Andre wondered what was going on behind that odd man's steady gaze. But a smile quickly returned and he said, "I understand. Proper respect. You've made your point. Several times, in fact. But I'm afraid I'm going to disappoint you. That shipment is of tremendous value for me. The only people accompanying it are going to be people I trust with my life. Not members of a Quebec biker gang."

"I didn't come all the way from Montreal to be disappointed," Andre said, glancing at his watch. "Looks like your five minutes are up, sport."

Duncan removed his glasses again. "What do you say we go outside and wrap this up."

Andre nodded firmly. "Yeah, let's do that."

As he got up Pierre looked over, and Andre tugged his right ear. Enough was fucking enough. He was tired of sparring, tired of wasting his time. A waitress came over, dropped a check on the table. She was plump, in a long black skirt and white blouse, black hair, and she spoke strange, like she had a mouth full of marbles. "Here you go, Duncan."

"Thanks, Tiffany," Duncan said. "I'll take care of it when I get back. Do me a favor, wrap my salad up, all right?"

"Yeah, okay," she said, picking up the plate. She turned and Duncan said, "Sweet kid. She's deaf. But she can read lips just fine."

Pierre laughed. "Bet she can do other things with those pretty lips."

Again, that little flicker across Duncan's face. He joined Pierre and they went through the bar, out to the main door. Andre made sure that Duncan went first, followed by Pierre and then himself. He couldn't tell what came next because something slammed into the back of his head.

———

Cold water was thrown at his face and Andre coughed, choked, and shook his head. The rear of his head ached and his nose burned, like some chemical had been pressed up against him, ether or something. His mouth was stuffed with a rag. His wrists hurt. He flicked his eyes open, looked around. His wrists hurt because they were stretched overhead. He peered up, saw a length of chain going from his wrists to an eyebolt set in a wooden beam. The rest of the room was small, with cement floor, cement walls, a couple of storage lockers and a sink. In front of him was Duncan, who held an empty plastic pail in his hand. He was now dressed in white paper pants, jacket, and little blue booties over his shoes. His hands were also covered with bright yellow rubber gloves.

Andre tried to talk but he couldn't move his tongue around what was shoved in his mouth. He started breathing hard through his nose. Duncan stepped back. "Take a look to the left, on the floor."

He did as he was told. His breathing increased. Heart thumping hard. On the floor was Pierre, stretched out in an X-formation, mouth gagged. Chains leading from each wrist and ankle were bolted to walls. Overhead fluorescent lights flickered and hummed. Pierre's face was bright red, his eyes were wide, and his nostrils were flaring like a horse running for its life.

Andre started grunting against the gag. Duncan said, "Right about now is when you're going to beg for mercy, or say it's all a mistake, or that you take it all back. I don't think that's happening. So tell me this. You ever see *The Godfather* movie?"

Andre frantically nodded his head up and down. Duncan said, "You ever read the book? Now don't lie. I don't like lying."

Even with his heavy breathing through his nose, Andre felt like he was suffocating. He shook his head, left to right, left to right. Pierre started moaning.

"Fine, you didn't lie, glad to hear that," Duncan said, stepping behind Andre. He closed his eyes, thinking frantically, trying to think of what he could do, what he could say. Duncan came back in front and Andre opened his eyes. "Maybe you should have read the book. A great book. Maybe not particularly well written, but sweet Lord, the sheer force of the story. Mario Puzo really knew how to grab you, right from the start. But only about eighty percent of the book made it into the movie."

Duncan stepped away and Andre started howling against the gag. Duncan held an axe in his hand, the head shiny and sharp looking. "Remember Luca Brasi? He was that heavy-set fellow, looked like a wrestler who could tear your head off. He was Don Corleone's enforcer, a loyal soldier who'd do anything for the Godfather. He played a much more prominent role in the book, the twenty percent that didn't get filmed."

Duncan tossed the axe from one hand to another. "You see, part of the book described Vito Corleone's rise to power. As he was expanding his criminal activities in the New York City area, Al Capone in Chicago sent two of his associates east to seize control from Don Corleone. As you might imagine, the Don didn't appreciate the attention. So Luca Brasi took care of business for him."

Andre started screaming, tugging at the chain, as Pierre started grunting again, making *oomph, oomph, oomph* noises. Duncan went over, raised up the axe, and Andre looked away.

Thump!

Through his gag, Pierre let out a muffled scream. Andre started yelling himself against his own gag, so he couldn't hear what was going on next to him.

Time passed.

Pierre mercifully fell silent. A rubber-clad hand was on his face. Andre opened his eyes. Duncan stood there. "Well. You're still alive. That's impressive. You see, in the book, when it came time for the second Chicago hood to be attacked, he was already dead. Poor son of a gun had swallowed his gag and had choked to death when his pal fell under the axe."

Andre slumped down, legs fluttering, chains cutting into his wrists. Duncan shook his head. "Mistakes, my Lord, the mistakes you made, right from the beginning. First, thinking I owed you and your fellow bikers a single dime. Or a loonie, depending on your point of view. Second, to think I'd invite two of you fellows to be on in my next major shipment, serving as bodyguards. Please. A nonstarter. Why not send up flares as the delivery's moving south, announcing to any law enforcement officials what was going on? Then, to wrap it all up, you insulted me by coming an hour late. Plus, you were stupid. Oh, so stupid."

Andre suddenly realized his crotch was wet, started sobbing. He had just pissed himself. "You see, Tiffany, my sweet waitress that your recently deceased companion insulted, reads lips quite well. So when you and your friend came up to my place, she saw what you said through one of the windows. About clipping me after you tugged your ear. So here we are."

Andre lifted his head, tried to put some sort of emotion, pleading, anything in his eyes. Duncan said, "To quote someone you know quite well, this is how it's going to be. I'm going to take your gag out. You answer a few questions from me, the axe stays in the corner. Deal?"

He nodded, up and down, up and down. Duncan stood the bloody axe in the corner and poked his rubber-gloved fingers into Andre's mouth, pulled and tugged. Andre nearly vomited and then spat, as the rag was taken out. He moved his swollen tongue and whispered, "Please, for the love of God . . ."

"Shhh," Duncan said. "First question. How did you find out about my shipment?"

Tears came from his eyes. Andre quickly said, "A contact in the Quebec provincial police. I swear to God, I don't know his name. All I know is that our president or his deputy, they've got him by the balls. So he came to them with the tip about the shipping container. Then we found out the Security Services were sniffing around so we knew it had to be worth a lot."

"You know what's in the shipment?"

"Only that it's coming from one of the docks on the St. Lawrence Seaway. That's it. And that it's worth a fuckload of money."

"Your president's name?"

"Francois Ouellette."

"You related?"

"He's my uncle."

"What was the plan for the shipment?"

Andre coughed. "We find out what's in it and where it's going, and then we'd hijack it, kill your crew."

"Tsk, tsk," Duncan said. "Not a very friendly business arrangement on your part. So where do we go from here?"

"Please … let me go … I swear to God … I'll leave here, I won't go back to Canada, I won't bother you or—"

Duncan said, "Shhh, you keep on insulting me like this, and the axe comes back. You know and I know, I can't let you go. Oh, maybe if your little visit had gone a bit more politely, I would have considered it. But no, Andre, that didn't happen. You threatened my family. That's the beginning and the end. The alpha and omega. I'm sure you understand. My family comes first, last, and forever. After you made threats like that, I can't risk having you out there, no matter how many promises you make."

Andre closed his eyes, knew with ice-cold certainty that it was over. Duncan said, "No more agony for you. Questions answered."

There was a *click-clack* as a pistol's action was worked, chambering a round. Andre opened his eyes. Duncan held up a familiar object: his own 9mm Sig Sauer pistol with extended magazine. Duncan said, "Your deceased friend over there was carrying the same piece. Good thinking. You both get in a firefight, you can pass each other magazines without worrying about the caliber of the other fellow's rounds. But your last mistake?"

Andre said, "Please …"

Duncan stepped forward. "You underestimated us. From the start. Thought we were backwoods idiots, making moonshine and humping each other's cousins. Far from it. So now your mistake bites you back. Hard."

"Witnesses … lots of people saw me and Pierre back there."

Duncan shrugged. "Man, you just don't get it, do you. We knew when you were going to show up. Everybody back in the Flight Deck either works for me or is related to me. People around here, they take loyalty real seriously. So I'm not going to stay up late tonight, worrying that some cop from away is going to ask questions about whether or not the two of you came to my pub."

Andre coughed. "My Uncle Francois … I don't come back, he's coming down on you like a fucking load of bricks."

Duncan said, "Thanks for the warning. But I sort of figured that out on my own."

Andre's last sensation was feeling the cold barrel press up against his forehead.

TWO

DUNCAN CROWLEY PULLED THE Sig Sauer's trigger and Andre's head snapped back, a blossom of bone, blood, and brain spewing out from the rear. The chains squeaked as his body slumped, and he looked at the Sig Sauer. A fine weapon. A pity he couldn't keep it. He dropped it to the floor and got to work.

He first unlocked the chains to Andre and to Pierre, and from a storage locker in the far corner, took out two rubberized body bags. Working by himself took some effort, but in an hour he was done. The bodies of the Quebec biker gang members were bagged, with the chains and the Sig Sauers in each of the bags, along with the axe, which Duncan placed in next to the biker named Andre. The floor was stained with blood and fluids, but somebody else would clean it up.

He then stripped off his soiled paper trousers, jacket, and booties, and crumpled them into a Shaw's Supermarket paper bag. The plastic gloves joined them, but only after he took a cigarette lighter and melted the palms and fingers so any trace evidence was permanently destroyed. That bag also went with one of the dead bikers. Overhead one of the fluorescent lights flickered again. He'd have to tell his older brother, Cameron, to get it fixed.

Speaking of Cameron, the outside door opened and his older brother came in. He had on the same rig he was wearing from before at the Flight Deck Bar & Grill: boots, jeans, and dungaree colors that announced W.C.M.C.: Washington County Motorcycle Club. But his long hair was now tied back in a neat ponytail and he nodded to his younger brother

"Fucking bloody mess," his brother said, shutting the door behind him, glancing down at the stained concrete floor.

"Had to go medieval on their asses," Duncan said. "I didn't have time to take the usual interrogation route. I needed the second guy to answer questions in a hurry, and that he did."

"Didn't think the axe was too much?"

"Not at all," Duncan said.

"You sure?"

"They threatened my family," Duncan said.

"It was just business, bro. Not personal. You know that."

"No, I don't know that," he said, walking over to a waist-high metal sink, where he washed his hands in the cold water. It felt good after being tucked in the rubber gloves.

Cameron said, "I know it's your family, but—"

Duncan wiped his hands on rough brown paper towels. "Cam, m'boy, the time you stop boffing waitresses and lonely housewives, get married, and settle down, then I'll listen to you when you talk about family. And not till then."

He tossed the paper towel into an empty metal wastebasket, turned, and rubbed at the bridge of his nose. "Sorry. Uncalled for. A long day. You and Lenny did good, ambushing them after they left the pub. Nice to know ether still works for knocking out folks."

Cameron said, "What do you want next?"

Duncan gestured to the two body bags. "Get them into their Lexus, take them up to ... let's see, what quarry would be good this time of year?"

"Walker Quarry, I'd guess."

"Not Palmer? That's closer. Less chance of something getting screwed up. Bored State Trooper pulling over a Lexus with Quebec license plates, that sort of thing."

Cameron said, "Palmer's getting kinda of crowded, bro. We had two dumps there last year, remember? The guys from Boston and their friends from Providence. We could try Palmer but I'd hate to have the tail end of the Lexus poking out and bobbing in the breeze this time tomorrow. Bird-watchers might find it. They're pretty damn focused on working on their lifetime sighting list, but I think even the densest birder would notice a half-sunk Lexus sticking out of a flooded quarry."

Duncan said, "Good call. You got the right guys to do it?"

"Yeah," Cameron said. "Dickie Leighton and his cousin Tom."

"You sure?" Duncan said. "I don't want them taking the Lexus for a joy ride, or have them root around in the body bags, take out the pistols or wallets. Crap like that we don't need. You understand?"

"Heard you twice the first time."

"Glad you did. When they're done cleaning in here, I want you to come in and I don't care if you can eat off the floor, I want them to clean it again."

"Take some time."

"Time we got," he said. "But half measures will put us in Concord, with long time on our shoulders."

Cameron's eyes narrowed and Duncan was angry with himself. Cameron was a good sort, a bit too quick with the fists and a lousy dresser, but boy, what an older brother. Cameron always had his back, except for a couple mistakes years ago, one of which sent Cameron to prison and another that had derailed Duncan's first career choice. But still, he had to stop pushing the poor guy. Duncan cleared his throat. "Sorry again. Getting cranky today."

Cameron smiled slightly. "What did you find out?"

He sighed, looked down at the body bags. He didn't have regrets, didn't have any deep philosophical debate over what he had just done. They had threatened his family, had insulted him, and before they even came into his place—one of the several pieces of property he owned in Washington County, the northernmost and emptiest county in New Hampshire—they had plans to put two rounds in the back of his head. He didn't think his head was particularly better or handsomer than other heads, but it was his and he liked it. As it was, they were in the body bags and he wasn't, and that was just fine.

"Some snoop up in Quebec found out about our shipment. Word went to a provincial cop and then to the Iron Steeds. From there, they decided to come down to get a piece of the action."

Cameron gently nudged one body bag and then the other with a booted foot. "Iron Steeds took some heavy shit from the Hells Angels, back when they tried to take over their turf. So I'd give them a day before their organization realizes their two guys ain't coming back. Add another day or two as they check hospitals or cops down here, see if their guys are hurt or in custody. When they come up empty, then they're gonna come back at us with some heavy shit."

Duncan said, "Chance we've got to take. Shipment's coming in less than a week. Something that will set us up for life. If we're lucky, by the time the Iron Steeds send down another, uh, negotiating team, delivery will be made and they'll be out of luck."

"Hell of a chance."

"Didn't see any other choice."

Cameron said, "Surrender, but I guess that's not an option."

"Nope." He checked his watch and said, "Damn. Running late. Don't want Karen chewing my butt when I get home."

He walked outside and Cameron followed, closing the door. The concrete shed was set adjacent to a fake log cabin building that was Washington County Weapons & Surplus, another one of Duncan's businesses. A sign dangling from outside the shed said it was SEASONAL DEER BUTCHERING: BEST PRICES GUARANTEED. With the concrete floor, sinks, cleaning equipment, and drains inside, it was a good place to take care of challenging business without the fine State Police CSI guys getting all excited about finding blood trace evidence, if anything up here ever did get their interest.

But Duncan doubted that. The State Police were based in Concord, the state capitol, a very long way down south.

He walked to his maroon Chevrolet Colorado pickup truck with an extended cab, parked next to his brother's own dark green Honda Pilot. It was still too cold in April for bikes, though he and his brother would take out their own Harleys soon enough. His right leg ached as he walked.

Duncan pulled out his keys and suddenly stopped. His brother almost bumped into him.

"What's wrong?"

He stayed quiet, looking at the shed and the darkened windows of the gun store. There was nothing else here except a wide dirt and gravel lot, and beyond that, tall pine trees and a few oaks, and farther away, the near range of the White Mountains. He knew the back roads and trails and logging cuts through all of these woods and peaks, and he never tired of looking at the wooded mountains.

"Nothing's wrong," Duncan said. "Everything's wrong. I just got the feeling we've gotten some people's attention."

"Sure we have," Cameron said. "A fucking motorcycle gang from Quebec."

"No, more than that."

Cameron said, "Who, then? Local? County? State? Federal?"

"Don't rightly know," Duncan said. "But I want everything smooth tonight, okay? In fact, make sure Dickie and Tom clean the place a third time. Take out the drains, give 'em a good steam bath as well. You do that, all right?"

Cameron put his right hand on his younger brother's shoulder. "You can count on me."

"Damn, that's the truest thing I've heard all day."

————

The drive home took forty-five minutes, about thirty minutes longer than it should have. But Duncan took a couple of side roads, turned around in the dirt lot of the American Legion Hall outside of Turner, and sat and listened to the truck radio for a few minutes while parked in front of Jackson's Old Town Deli and Service Station. He picked up a National Public Radio station from Vermont with an earnest discussion about the current recession, the longest and deepest in American history. Next to him on the truck's leather seat was the Styrofoam container with his leftover salad. Karen was nagging—she would say gently reminding—about his weight again, and he wanted to show her that at least in this, he was listening to her.

He shifted the truck into drive, got back out on Route 117. Clear. Nobody following. Nothing in the air.

Time to go home.

————

Home was a simple country-style two-story structure up on the crest of a hill off Old Mill Road, with a wraparound farmer's porch and attached two-car garage. On the front lawn were a bicycle belonging to his son Lewis and a tricycle belonging to his daughter Amy. Their home was stained dark brown and as he went up the driveway, he recalled the home of his first real boss. Ronnie Gibbons, down near Milan. Ronnie was the biggest weed dealer in this part of the state and had a sprawling McMansion with a big pool and a collection of ATVs, snowmobiles, and bass fishing boats on trailers scattered around the yard. Even one year out of high school, Duncan knew that Ronnie Gibbons was an idiot. His day job was working as a janitor at Turner Regional High School—where Duncan had attended—but he was suddenly rich because of his expertise in setting up light systems to grow weed in abandoned barns around the county and finding scores of willing customers, some who even moved the stuff to Montpelier, Manchester, and Portland.

So instead of putting his money in bank accounts or sticking it in a safe or even shoving it under a damn mattress, Ronnie dropped his weed money on a huge house, toys for him and his wife and in-laws and out-laws, bringing the whole Gibbons clan down to Aruba twice a year. Duncan thought it was like painting the roof of his house in bright orange and with black letters a story high, saying DRUG DEALER LIVES HERE.

Duncan stayed with Ronnie until he knew his contacts, his operations, and where he bought his lighting and fertilizer supplies, and then left, saying his bum leg hurt too much to keep working for him. About six months later, the DEA, the State Police, and the county sheriff's department descended onto Ronnie's McMansion with SWAT teams, a helicopter, and enough police cruisers to outfit a medium-sized Mexican city, and that had been that.

Duncan parked in front of his two-car garage, hesitated. A light blue Toyota Camry sagging to one side with lots of rust was parked in the driveway, a car he didn't recognize. His wife's Toyota RAV4 was in the garage. He reached under his seat, where a Bianchi holster was secured, holding a Smith & Wesson Model 5906 semiautomatic. His hand was grasping the butt of the 9mm pistol and he relaxed when his wife Karen came out the front door. She was carrying a dish towel in her hands. That was the all-clear signal. If the dish towel was over her shoulder, that meant trouble.

Duncan stepped out, carrying the Styrofoam container. Karen smiled, came up to him, and he still felt a little flip in his belly as she approached. It was an old story but a good story, of the prettiest and most popular girl in high school and the star baseball player getting together after graduation. The story had been preplotted—they were both going to UNH, she on a scholarship set up by some New York financier, he on a baseball scholarship because of his skill at tossing change-ups and curve balls—but like lots of stories, theirs took a few detours along the way. His was first, when his knee and lower leg got nailed in a drunk driving accident, where he was the pissed-off passenger, trying to talk sense into a drunk older driver. A year later, her detour came when the New York financier got his picture on the cover of *Newsweek* and *Time* after being revealed as one of the biggest Ponzi schemers Wall Street had seen since Madoff.

So goodbye scholarship for Karen. She came back to Turner, and a year later, they were married.

Tonight she was dressed in white sneakers, tight jeans, and a buttoned yellow sweater showing off a hint of freckled cleavage, her long red hair about her shoulders. She kissed him on the lips and said, "Do me a favor?"

"I'm yours to command," he said.

"Hah," she said. "Keep on deluding yourself. Monica Ziff is in your office. She needs some help. I do her hair twice a month."

"What kind of help?"

"She got caught up in that mess when Tyson Heating Oil went bankrupt. She pre-bought her winter's supply and now she and her kids are going to be out in the cold later this year. Literally."

"I thought the State AG's office got a settlement from Tyson Oil for its customers."

Karen wrinkled her nose. "They sure did. If you call getting a fifty-dollar voucher to use at a nonbankrupt oil company of your choice a settlement."

He handed over his Styrofoam container. "Sweetie, you do know if that you keep this up, when we get to our final reward, Lewis and Amy are going to inherit a mortgage and your collection of Hummels."

Another kiss on the lips. "I trust you more than that." She opened up the container, frowned. "Honey, you should know better than this. A salad like this won't last. The lettuce will get soggy and the dressing will make everything slimy."

"Maybe I'll have it for dessert," he said.

She gave him an impish grin. "If you take care of Monica, maybe I'll have you for dessert."

———

Inside he greeted Lewis and Amy—ten and eight years old—who both said, "Hey, dad," as they turned back to watching an old Jonny Quest cartoon on television, sitting on one of the couches. Behind them were sliding glass doors that led to the rear deck. Duncan had watched the same cartoons as a kid, and one day, a couple of months ago, was horrified to see that the cartoons had been heavily edited, taking out explosions, fist fights, and other acts of violence. What the hell was that about? Wasn't anything sacred anymore? He decided then that if he could find them, he'd get his kids the unedited versions of the TV series as Christmas gifts.

As Karen stayed in the kitchen, he passed through the living room, down a hallway that had doors leading to the kids' rooms and the master bedroom, then to a spare bedroom he had converted into an office once they had moved in. It was small but cozy, with built-in bookcases, two black metal filing cabinets with sturdy locks, a high-speed shredder that turned documents into dust, and a nice old wooden desk Karen had picked up for him at an estate sale some years back.

A woman sitting in front of his desk stood up. She was in her mid-fifties, thickset, wearing black stretch pants and a black sweatshirt with a Disney World logo on the front. Her brown hair had little auburn streaks at the ends, no doubt from Karen's handiwork. She stuck out her hand and he gave it a quick shake.

"So happy you could see me, Mr. Crowley," she said.

"Please call me Duncan," he said, going around the desk and taking his own chair. "What can I help you with?"

She sat down heavily. "I won't keep you, 'cause I know you're busy and all. And I won't take charity. Too damn stubborn for that."

"All right," he said, folding his hands together, "Go on."

Monica sighed. "Things have been tight ever since I got laid off, when the paper mill down in Berlin closed. Fucking Iranians, excuse my French. They came into town, made lots of promises, got Federal loan guarantees and grants, and then they robbed the place blind and skipped town. Living someplace in the Caribbean, I hear, on some island that don't have a treaty with the United States to extradite them. So me and about six hundred others are out of a job. Still, I get by, doing housework, some babysitting... but Tyson Oil, they had a good deal for the oil pre-buy late last year. I don't have to tell you what happened next."

"You and the other customers got a fifty-dollar voucher from the state of New Hampshire. I know it won't go far."

That made her tear up. "Won't go far at all. So … here I am. It's just me and my three girls, and last year, oil ran out early so I had to heat the place up by keeping the stove open. Before putting the girls to bed, I warmed up the sheets with a hair dryer, and made them share a bed. Anything to keep them from shivering. I swear, I'm not going to let them go through that this year."

Duncan nodded, not wanting to press the woman, but he was getting hungry and his shoulders ached from his earlier work.

Monica said, "I'm keeping you, I'm sorry. I'll wrap this up. Whatever you give me, whatever you can, I'll make it worth your while."

He unlocked the top desk drawer, pulled it out. "Don't worry about it."

She took a deep breath. "I do worry about it. So here's what I'm offering. I love gardening, landscaping. I've already talked to your wife and she said I could help her with the flowerbeds and shrubbery … if you agree."

Duncan tried not to grin. "With my wife negotiating on my behalf, how could I not agree?"

That earned him a smile from his visitor. He took out his ledger-style checkbook, opened it up. "All right. How much do you need?"

Her face struggled and he sensed the fight that must be going on within her overworked and stretched and proud soul. "Would … would five hundred dollars be all right?"

Duncan took a fountain pen in hand—a real fountain pen, not one of the knock-offs that had ink cartridges—and wrote her a check for one thousand dollars. In the memo section, he wrote "Advance for landscaping" and tore it out, blew on the ink, and passed it over.

Monica took the check, brought a hand to her mouth, gasped. Tears trickling down her cheek, she said, "I owe you something big, Mr.... er, Duncan. I really do."

"You might change your mind when you're digging through the dirt this summer, yanking up weeds."

"The hell I will change my mind." She folded the check in half, slipped it into her purse. She took a deep breath. "One other thing, before I leave."

"Oh?" Duncan asked, really feeling his shoulders tighten up, wondering how he could easily push her out of the house before his dinner got cold. "Go ahead, then."

Monica snapped the purse shut, wiped at one eye and then the other. "Thing is, my girl, she babysits the kids next door. The woman there, she has a boyfriend, and my girl, she overhead him talking. His name is Gus Spooner. This Gus, he claims he works for you."

Duncan said carefully, "Maybe. I've got a number of people working for me. I'm afraid I don't know all of their names."

Her eyes narrowed and got tight. "Now Duncan Crowley, I have a piece to say, and do me the favor of not interrupting, all right? I know you and I knew your parents, God bless 'em, before they died in that airplane accident. So I've got that on my side, all right?"

He nodded. She firmly went on. "I even watched you in high school, when you made those baseball records. I know about your scholarship, about how you hurt your leg, how you didn't leave Turner. I know how you kept busy since you graduated. Lots of us do. I could rightly give a shit for what you do besides running your stores and your gun shop and other things. None of my business. Me and so many others are just so goddamn thankful that you're here." She patted the purse, as if for reassurance, and went on. "So I'll wrap this up. My girl, she overhead Gus Spooner say he had a plan to make some real good money, real quick."

He no longer cared dinner might get cold. "Did he say how he was going to get this good money, real quick?"

Her hands were tight about her purse. "Gus Spooner, way I found out, he works at one of your convenience stores. Somehow there was a screw-up in delivery and a case of cold medicine got dropped off. Instead of shipping it back, he kept it and now he's going to use his Daddy's hunting camp to cook meth."

Duncan slowly leaned back in his chair. "Do you know where the hunting camp is?"

Monica said, "I checked it out. Before I came over here. Up on Town Road Twelve. You go up five miles, you'll see a wooden sign on the left, nailed to a birch tree. Name there says Williams, the previous owner. Go up that side road, it's right there. Dumpy piece of shit on concrete posts, the front porch is falling down."

"I see," Duncan said. He took out his wallet, passed over five twenty-dollar bills. "Thanks for the information. I appreciate it."

She got up, the twenty-dollar bills in her hand. "Now I'm keeping you from your lovely bride, your sweet kids, and your dinner. I owe you more than you know. I hope what I told you about Gus Spooner is worth something."

"It is," he said. "Can I ask you a favor, Monica?"

She smiled, revealing a dimple on her left cheek. "Of course."

"Have my wife come in when you pop out."

———

He swiveled his chair around, looked out the floor-to-ceiling windows that gave him a great view of the back lawn, the thick green sprawl of pines and other evergreens, and the distant peaks. He never tired of the view, which was so fine, even though the glass was particularly thick. Such thickness impeded the view some, but also made it safe to sit here, without thinking of some disgruntled customer or potential rival sending a copper-jacketed .308 round through the back of his skull at about twenty-five hundred feet per second.

But the windows didn't keep prying eyes away. There might be somebody out there with a spotting scope, keeping track of visitors, keeping an eye on what was going on here, the center of the Duncan Crowley empire. So what. They would see a woman come in, and a woman leave. As for electronic surveillance, he had the house swept once a week. With Karen here most of the time, and one of her sisters babysitting the kids, there was no way anyone could get in to set a bug.

Still, he had that nagging feeling. Even before Andre had confessed that Duncan's upcoming shipment had reached someone's attention, he had the sensation he was being watched, that he was under some sort of unexpected observation.

Damn.

That shipment was going to set him up well, so he could finally leave the day-to-day running of his businesses and give it up, take his wife on some trips, be able to go through life without looking over his shoulder all the time. Oh, they had squeezed in an occasional visit to Bermuda or South Beach in Miami, but long trips were out of the question. You go on a long trip and sometimes things go to hell, or knuckleheads who worked for you thought it was a good idea to start cooking up meth in the back woods.

Crystal meth. A great way to catch the attention of everyone from the DEA to the FBI to the State Police. His own activities were highly illegal, no doubt about that, but hardcore stuff like meth or Oxycontin would show up on law enforcement radar like a damn Boeing 747 coming onto approach at the single skinny runway at Milan airport.

So to have this new shipment come through unscathed was vital. It'd give him breathing room, a chance to start getting out of the business, do something fun with Karen and the kids.

Karen came in and put her strong hands on his shoulders. "You did good."

"Thanks. Just don't make it that much of a habit."

She kissed the top of his head. "I've made you so many promises, sweetie, but you know I can't keep that one. I'm always here to help our neighbors. But can I ask you another favor?"

"Go right ahead."

"My uncle, Hubert Conan. He's still bugging me about you. Being a stringer for the *Union Leader*, his stories are usually about the moose lottery or lost hunters. But he thinks a story about you, a successful businessman in a county that has twice the unemployment rate of the rest of the state, would be great."

"I thought we'd agree we'd say no. You know publicity is something we don't need."

"I can't say no to him, hon. He's my Uncle Hubert. You're going to have to do it."

"Right, your Uncle Hubert who got fired from the *New York Times* for being a drunk."

His wife kept her hands on his shoulders. "He was fired because he was drinking. Big difference."

"Care to explain?"

"He got drunk one night in the newsroom and said he had voted Republican all his life, that he supported the Second Amendment, and thought Ronald Reagan was the greatest president of the twentieth century. Right there and then, he committed career suicide. They didn't care he was a drunk. They cared that he was a right-wing knuckle-dragger."

"So much for celebrating diversity," Duncan said. "All right, I'll try to take care of it. Mind telling me what's for dinner, or is it a surprise?"

"Stuffed pork chops. But you get the smallest one."

"Swell."

She started kneading his shoulders and he sighed with pleasure. Her fingers worked his muscles and tendons expertly, and he felt himself relax and unwind. He'd have to talk to Cameron in a bit, set up a session to take care of Gus Spooner and his new business. Most of the time he admired entrepreneurship among his workers, but this wasn't going to be one of those times.

"My, your shoulders are so very, very tight," Karen said, again kissing the top of his head. "How was your day, hon?"

He recalled the two Quebecois bikers, one with dismembered limbs, the other with a 9mm round through his forehead, the blood and spatter that had to be cleaned up, the stench of death, the sharp smell of burnt gunpowder. Karen knew some of what he did, but not everything—a good arrangement.

Duncan reached up, patted her right hand. "Routine."

THREE

Tom Leighton followed his older cousin Dickie as the old buck drove the Lexus with Quebec license plates up Route 15, keeping it under the speed limit, coming to a complete stop at every stop sign, which were few and far between. Even though there wasn't any goddamn traffic on the road this time of the night, his uncle drove like he had just gotten his license. Tom was driving his cousin's Jeep Wrangler, a ten-year-old piece of shit that had duct tape holding up the passenger-side window, and lengths of wire keeping the muffler from dragging on the pavement. Tom wanted to drive the Lexus—a sweet, sweet piece of drivability that he would have loved to put through its paces—but Dickie grunted, "hell no," and that had been it.

But damn, what a waste, he thought, as he got off on an unmarked dirt road to the right. That car should be driven by someone who appreciated the fine seats, the purring engine, and damn, the whole clean-smelling interior. Not like this Jeep, smelling of stale cigarettes, spilt beer, and grease.

The dirt road narrowed, tree limbs whipping along the fenders as they climbed up and up. The Lexus lights spilled out, lighting everything up, and when they spun around one corner, a deer startled, leaping into the side of ferns and low brush, the white tail flicking up as it raced into the woods. The road got bumpier and dust was kicked up behind the Lexus, and then the brake lights popped twice as the Lexus came to a stop.

Tom pulled the Jeep up next to the Lexus, the lights illuminating the dirt lot, blending into exposed rock, blending into a dark opening. He had a brief shiver of fear, knotting in his guts and balls, knowing a slip of his foot on the accelerator would propel him off into the dark oblivion of the quarry before him. He carefully set the parking brake, turned the engine off, and got out, leaving the headlights on.

His older cousin came over and said, "Okay, we're going to—"

"Hey, cuz, got an idea."

"Sounds dangerous," Dickie said with a sigh. "Make it quick."

Tom looked around. "Look. This is a fucking waste and you know it."

"Know what?" his cousin said. "What the hell are you talking about?"

Tom knew what he was talking about but wasn't sure how he could explain it. He was just two years out of high school and it seemed like everything he touched turned to shit. He had worked as a dry waller and a roofer and had gotten fired from both. Now he worked as a clerk at an Irving service station, making sure customers paid for their gas instead of driving off and ensuring there was enough coffee, doughnuts, and pastries for the worker bees to get before going off to their drudge jobs and drudge lives.

Shit, come to think about it, about the only excitement he'd had since getting out of high school was last winter, when he was at Sparky's Pub, and somebody asked him if he was interested in working at the new super Wal-Mart that had opened up, about an hour's drive south. He had said, shit no, he wasn't going to work for a bunch of assholes like that. He had heard once that before each shift, crews had to hold hands and chant stuff like some religious cult, and down at the other end of the bar, some college cutie that was with some of her friends, heading up to one of the ski areas in Quebec, had overheard him. Funny thing was, she was half drunk and thought that Tom didn't want to work for Wal-Mart because of its antiunion activities, and she bought him a drink and they got laughing. For about an hour she talked his ears off about something called Marxist labor theory and the oppression of the underclass and the rights of workers to organize. He didn't give a shit about any of that, but later on, she took him to her BMW and as the car warmed up, she gave him a blow job before she had to leave to meet some friends.

A fun night, even though the phone number she gave him proved to be fake, and—

"Damn it, Tom, what did you want to tell me?"

Embarrassed, Tom said, "Look, cuz, we're about to drop a thirty-five-thousand-dollar piece of fine machinery into this quarry. That's a goddamn waste and you know it, just as well as I do. So what I'm thinking, we just take those two body bags out and toss 'em into the quarry, and then we take the Lexus down south. Head to Manchester, maybe Boston. Sell it for cash, right up front. Might get ten grand, something like that. We split it, fifty-fifty. What do you think about that?"

His cousin glared at him. He had on a dirty sheepskin coat, dark green chinos, and work boots. He used to work for a timber company up by the Canadian border until a tree fell the wrong way and nearly took off his right foot. Disability should have set him up for life, except the insurance company sent an investigator to check up on him, and got pics of him shoveling out his driveway some months ago after a nor'easter. Christ, of course he was going to shovel out his

34

driveway, what did they expect? But the insurance company convinced some judge to take away the disability, and since then, like his younger cousin, Dickie had been scraping by.

"No," Dickie said. "Forget it."

He turned and Tom stepped forward, grabbed his arm. "Oh, come on, what's the deal, hunh? The two body bags get dumped here, that's fine, and the Lexus gets dumped, too. Except the Lexus gets dumped someplace where we get some good money for it. Hell, we'll split sixty-forty, you get the bigger chunk, and—"

Dickie violently shrugged off his grasp. "I said forget it. So let's get this thing done."

His cousin limped back to the front seat of the Lexus, shifted it into neutral, and then switched off the engine. He left the front door open and went to the other side, popping open the front passenger's-side door. The dome light lit everything inside up, and a couple of curious night bugs started banging around the light.

Dickie grabbed the doorframe and called out, "Get over here, Tom. Not going to push this bastard by myself."

Tom swore under his breath and went over, grabbed the smooth and cold doorframe. He dug in his heels, grunted, pushed. Dickie said, "C'mon, Tommy, put your goddamn back into it!"

He kept his mouth shut though he wanted to say if Dickie didn't kiss Cameron Crowley's ass so much—Jesus, they had to clean that place three times, even though after one go-through it was clean enough—they'd be home by now. With a crunch of gravel, the car started rolling. There was a slight decline to the open stone maw of the quarry, and once the Lexus got moving, it picked up speed. Tom stepped back and so did Dickie, and Tom felt sick watching thousands of dollars in cash roll out into the darkness.

Stupid cousin Dickie, he thought. Why was he so pussy around that scrawny biker?

The Lexus crunched its undercarriage on exposed stone and flipped over, and in seconds, was nothing but a hard splash. Fuck. That would have been some payoff.

Tom quietly put his hand into his coat pocket, felt the cold metal of a watch. The Tag Heuer he had robbed off one of the stiffs.

When Dickie had been in the shed, steam-cleaning out the grates, he had been struggling with the body bags, trying to make them fit in the trunk of the Lexus. One was particularly lumpy so he had unzippered it enough to move the arms around, and under the trunk light, he had spotted the fancy watch on the dead guy's wrist.

Not as good as the car, but not bad.

Dickie said, "Let's make sure it's sinking."

Tom walked with his cousin close to the edge of the quarry. The lights from the Jeep illuminated the far side—showing the gouges and cuts where the stone had been taken away—and the light bounced off the stone and lit up the water, maybe fifty or sixty feet down. Tom peered over and sure enough, the Lexus was bubbling its way under.

Tom said, "Looks good from here, cuz, and—"

Something punched him hard in the back, he waved his arms and screamed as he fell over into the darkness.

———

And he suddenly stopped, hanging over the abyss, his feet barely holding onto the edge of the cut stone. Somebody strong was holding the collar of his jacket. He moved his arms, tried to hold onto something, found nothing, choked, cried out, "Dickie, Dickie, please, please…"

The collar twisted tighter around his neck. All he could see was the lit stonework across the way and the dark tree line. Dickie said, "You stupid little shit, take it out. Take it out now and toss the fucking thing into the water!"

Tom felt like he was going to crap his pants and with one shaking hand, tried three times to find his coat pocket before he succeeded. He found the watch and held it out so Dickie could see it. "It's right here, it's right here!" he screamed. "I'm gonna toss it now, cuz, just you watch!"

He tossed it and waited, wondering how cold the water was. Would he pass out when he hit it, or would he hit a rock—

Dickie grabbed his shoulder and pulled him back. Tom couldn't help it, he sobbed, and then his cousin threw him to the ground, kicked his ribs. "You numbnut, I saw you back there at the gun shop, saw you open the trunk and unzip the body bag … what, you think I didn't know you were doing something? Did you?"

Tom rolled, held his hands up around his head. "I just wanted to score something, that's all! Who'd miss it? Hunh?"

Dickie reached down, grabbed his coat, pulled him up so he was standing. His breath stank. He said, "Cameron Crowley told us what to do, what exactly to do, and I'll be goddamned if I'm goin' to let you fuck it up. You understand?"

Now that he was off the edge of the quarry, Tom felt bolder. "Why do you have to kiss his ass so much, hunh? Jesus Christ on a crutch, you know that place was clean when we finished it the first time. But he made us do it twice more! The fuck is he, the pope?"

His cousin shook him. "No, you moron, his younger brother's the fucking pope. He's the senior cardinal, and I'm just a goddamn deacon. He tells me to do something, I do it. You know why? 'Cause I get paid, right away, and it's cash. Look at me, bum foot and all. Where am I gonna get work? Food stamps is gone, unemployment ain't there no more and job training is for folks with computers, which I ain't got. What I got is that Cameron trusts me to do a job. So I do it right, no whining, no questions, and I get paid. He trusts me … and what you did tonight … Jesus Christ, Tom, why ain't you thinking?"

Dickie dropped his hands and wiped at his face, took a deep breath. "Let's say you hawk that pricey watch. Somewhere along the line, maybe it gets spotted in a pawnshop. Or some nosey cop wonders why a guy who works at a 7-Eleven is sporting a such a fine piece. Then it comes back to you, and me, eventually gets traced back to that guy down there. If you think Cameron and his brother Duncan are gonna stand up for us after we screwed them over, forget it. There's enough quarries in this part of the state … oh, forget it."

Tom thought his uncle was about to cry. He didn't know what to say. Christ, all right, maybe it was a dumb thing to try to score that watch, but still, what a sweet, sweet payoff.

His older cousin said, "You know, down there in Massachusetts, in Quincy and other places, there are quarries bigger than this one where morons go swimming every summer, even though it's against the law. They got rivers and streams and fucking public swimming pools, but they gotta go swim and dive in the quarries. Each summer, one or two of them drowns."

Dickie stepped closer and flung his right arm around Tom's shoulders, squeezed him hard. "You're my cousin, Tom, and part of the family, but I swear to all that's holy, you ever try to dick around with my line of work doing stuff for Cameron and his brother, I'll fucking dump you in this quarry myself. Got it?"

"Got it," Tom whispered.

"Good," Dickie said. "Let's get going. I don't want to miss *SportsCenter*."

FOUR

In Purmort, New Hampshire, Zach Morrow stood out in his dirt driveway, ready to put more windshield wiper fluid in his Ford F-150 pickup truck, when trouble came up the driveway in the guise of a dark blue Crown Victoria, bearing white US government license plates. Well, what do you know, he thought. He went around to the front of his truck, reached in past the grille, undid the latch, and pulled the hood up with a satisfying squeak. It was morning and his big plan for the day was to write yet another letter to his congressman, and then cut some brush in the rear yard, and then read John Keegan's latest work on World War II.

The arrival of someone from the Feds wasn't entirely unexpected, but it sure promised to break up his day.

The Crown Victoria pulled up in front of his white double-wide. The car's sides were stained white with road salt. They had come a long way. He unscrewed the top of the Wal-Mart wiper fluid container, opened up the near-empty reservoir in his truck, topped it off, and then he was done. The hood came down with an equally satisfying *thunk*. He looked to his double-wide, remembered a time early on when this was going to be just a temporary shelter, until something better could be built on the fifty acres he owned here. The double-wide was old, used, leaked in a fine drizzle, and although Zach couldn't prove it, he was sure its provenance included being temporary housing for muddy refugees in Louisiana after Hurricane Katrina.

During the past several rugged months, temporary was unfortunately beginning to look more and more permanent.

The left rear door of the Crown Victoria snapped open and a woman stepped out. She had on sensible black shoes, tight black slacks and a buttoned dark gray coat. She was petite, looking like she was barely out of high school. Her fine hair was blond and was sculpted around her slight head, cascading just a bit over her shoulders. There was a sprinkling of freckles across her small nose. In one hand she carried a bulging manila folder. She was a Fed, no doubt, but she was the most attractive Fed he had seen in a very long time.

"Zach Morrow?" she asked in a soft voice. "Chief Petty Officer Zachary Morrow?"

"The same," he said, leaning across the hood of the truck. It was five years old, six months overdue for an oil change, and once upon a time it was light red. Now it was the color of muddy clay.

Her voice quiet, she said, "Tanya Gibbs, Department of Homeland Security."

"Good for you," he said.

She stood across from him, put the folder down on the truck's hood. As she was doing that, her driver got out and stared at Zach, eyes not blinking. He had on a long belted black trench coat, black trousers, and shoes. The woman's driver looked like a hockey player who had been released for skating too little and fighting too much. His biceps seemed as thick as his boss's thighs. Zach stared right back at him and then turned away. It was too early in the day to get into a pissing contest.

"I need to talk to you about something," she said.

"Lucky for us, my afternoon is free."

She opened up the manila folder. "From what I've seen, you've spent most of your career serving in the Coast Guard, all across the world, mostly in Africa and the Middle East, in rivers and ports. Mind telling me how you ended up in this little village, so far away from the coast?"

"Finally got tired of being in and around water all the time."

She looked to his home. "Seems pretty remote. What do you do all day long?"

He said, "Cut brush. Write letters to my congressman. Read a lot of history books."

"So why Purmort?"

Zach said, "When I got discharged, I left First District Headquarters in Boston, started walking. Not hitchhiking, mind you, but walking. Over my shoulder I carried an oar. First time somebody asked me what the hell I was carrying on my shoulder, I knew I had gone far enough from the Atlantic."

Tanya smiled and flipped through another page. "I think I've heard that old tale before. Did you like the Coast Guard?"

"Had its moments," he said.

"Why did you join up with them? Why not the Navy? Or the Air Force?"

Zach didn't like being asked all these questions, but he found it hard to be angry with her. With her size and soft voice, she seemed like somebody's daughter who had stolen a government vehicle during "Take Your Daughter To Work" day. Despite the fact she was probably ten or so years younger than him, she was still good-looking in a sort of fresh-washed, enthusiastic-government-employee kind of way.

"Figured with the Coast Guard, if something bad was going to happen, I could always wade to shore," Zach said, trying hard not to smile. "Look, this is nice and all, but why are you here?"

Her driver drifted over, not walking fast, not moving with a purpose, but getting closer, barely out of Zach's field of vision. Zach found it hard to keep his eye on the both of them. In his double-wide he had a variety of weapons, and he was out here with this bruiser, unarmed. He didn't like the sensation.

"Funny thing about your records, Zach, is that you belonged to an outfit that hardly anybody knows anything about," she said, flipping through another set of pages. "Coast Guard Special Forces. Sounds very odd, like killer nuns or obese ballet dancers." She offered him a slight smile. "Very elite, very small. Just how small are you?"

"Staff meetings were held in the nearest phone booth," he said.

"And what did you do for Coast Guard Special Forces?"

"You look like a smart young woman. I'm sure you know already."

"You would think," Tanya said, her voice sounding distressed. "But your record's been mostly redacted and the originals are in a classification level so high even I can't access it. About the only thing I found was one case of insubordination from your last covert mission that got you dishonorably discharged. Someplace in West Africa. Which means no pension. No benefits. No nothing. Am I right?"

Zach felt something stirring inside of him, something he hadn't felt in a long time. Hope? Anticipation? The chance to make it all right? He wasn't sure.

"So what's the deal?" he asked.

"Excuse me?" she said.

He tried to smile at her with some sort of grace, not sure if he was doing it right. "Once upon a time, the Coast Guard was under the jurisdiction of the Treasury Department. In case of war, like Korea or Vietnam, it was controlled by the Navy. Now, because of a bureaucratic clusterfuck of epic proportions that took place after 9/11, it belongs to you busy ladies and gentlemen of Homeland Security."

"That's quite observant of you, Chief Morrow, but—"

"Lady, wanna come around the truck and give me a kiss and a pat on the ass?"

Her face flushed. "I'm sorry, I don't know what you're talking about."

"Ma'am, when I'm getting screwed, I like getting kissed and having my ass patted. I know you're not up here to console me on my bad discharge. So you have something to offer me, something you want done for the greater glory of the Department of Homeland Security, so cut to it. Save us both a lot of time and aggravation."

Face still flushed, Tanya lowered her head to her folder and said, "You grew up in Turner."

"A fair number of people did," he said, now regretting his earlier words about a kiss and a pat on the ass, but that regret left the moment she started speaking again.

"Your dad was an executive councilor for the state. What does an executive councilor do?"

Zach said, "Should have read up a bit more on this state instead of me. Around here, people don't trust the government that much, Miss Gibbs. Governor is only elected to a two-year term. The legislature is the biggest in the world, with more than four hundred representatives. Executive councilors serve as a brake on the governor. Left over from Revolutionary War times. There's five of them, from different districts in the state. My dad was from the one up north."

"Was he much of a brake, then?"

Zach felt the old shame, the old embarrassments. "He was what was known in somewhat polite society as a horndog. Balled anything in skirts, from lobbyists to state reps. In what little spare time he had, I guess he did his job."

"After your mom passed away, says here he was placed in a nursing home in Carroll County."

"Been there for ten years. Alzheimer's."

Tanya returned to her papers. "I take it you know a man named Duncan Crowley."

"Went to school with a Duncan Crowley. Turner Regional High School. He was star pitcher two years in a row for the varsity team. Big man on a small campus. So I knew him a bit, but not well. What's going on with Duncan?"

Tanya passed over a color photograph of Duncan, standing in front of an Irving gas station. Even with the twenty years that had gone by, Zach recognized the prominent nose, the cocky grin, the bulked up shoulders. In the photo he had on a simple EMS blue outdoor jacket and it looked like he was talking to some biker guy with long hair, beard, and leather jacket. He recognized the other guy as Duncan's brother Cameron.

"Your buddy Duncan—"

"Not my buddy," he interrupted. "Just knew him a bit."

"All right, your classmate Duncan has built himself up a nice little criminal empire up in Washington County."

Zach couldn't help it, that this slight woman and her beefy driver—still hovering around the rear of Zach's truck—had come all the way here to talk about Duncan Crowley. He burst out laughing. "The shit you say, really? What does he do up there? Sell illegal moose pelts?"

"No," she said sharply, her voice stronger than one would think from someone so small, and, let's face it, cute. "He's involved in marijuana cultivation and sales, the smuggling of cigarettes and liquor, loan-sharking, and a variety of other unlawful activities. About everything and anything illegal that goes on up in Washington County, either he's active in it or gets a cut of the proceeds."

"If you know all these naughty things about him, then why isn't he in jail?"

"You look fairly smart, Chief Morrow," she said. "It's one thing to know if some skell is doing something outside of the law. It's another thing to prove it in court. You know the budget situation in Concord and in D.C. Unless it's a slam dunk, resources aren't going to be used in something that's too hard, too difficult to prove. He's also an expert at being discreet. It's not like he's shooting up banks or beheading his competitors."

Zach folded his hands on the truck's hood. "All right. So he's managed to skate on being a bad boy, but now he's gotten the interest of Homeland Security. What's he smuggling that has your attention? It can't be booze or cigarettes. So what is it? Illegals?"

"Not a bad guess," Tanya said. "Most everyone—including Congress, the editorial board of the *New York Times,* and about ninety percent of the American public—forget we have a northern border. Sure, all the bad news and coverage and interest is on our failing friends to the south. Which means the northern border is practically wide open for criminal minds, terrorist minds, and everything else in between."

"Duncan? Terrorism? What the hell do you mean by that?"

She pulled out another photo. "This is what we mean by that. Check this out."

He looked down, recognized it instantly. A rectangular cargo container, like hundreds of thousands afloat at any time during the day on the Atlantic and Pacific, either coming in or going out. Containers holding everything from car parts to rubber duckies to jet engines. Structures like this were off-loaded from ships, stacked up in ports, then dropped onto tractor-trailer truck frames and driven around the world. This particular container was half-sized, bright yellow, and marked with a shipping company logo in blue and red: MEXTEL LINES.

"For some reason, your friend Duncan—I mean, acquaintance —has a business interest in this particular container," she said. "It arrived last week at a terminal on the St. Lawrence Seaway. We believe this container is under the control of people either working for Duncan or cooperating with him, and that it's headed to the New Hampshire border with Quebec. But now it's disappeared."

"Disappeared as in kidnapped by aliens, or disappeared as in the surveillance was screwed up?"

"Disappeared as in the Vice President last month said something stupid about our Canadian friends, and to retaliate, they've been dragging their snowshoes on helping us out in certain investigative matters," Tanya said. "Like this container, which we believe is going to be smuggled into northern New Hampshire sometime over the next several days, into the waiting arms of Duncan Crowley."

"What's in the container?"

"Which is where you come in, Zach," she said, ignoring his question. "You have certain skills, you're from the area, and you even know him. We'd like to have you go back up to your hometown, quietly and gingerly poke around, find out what you can, and pass it on to us."

"What's in the container?" he repeated.

"A matter of national interest," she said.

"That's not enough."

"I'm afraid it's enough for you," she said.

"My security classification access was pretty high up when I was on active duty, and—"

"That access was taken away upon your dishonorable discharge," she said.

He said, "Something bad is in that container, isn't it. A dirty bomb. VX gas. Vials of anthrax. Not immigrant Inuits, looking for day labor."

"I can neither confirm nor deny, Chief Morrow."

"But it's important, then."

"Vitally."

"So why is Homeland Security coming to me?"

She shuffled some papers about, kept her head down. "There was something in your paperwork that stuck in my mind, that hadn't been redacted. That even faced with disciplinary action, you said you were going to do what was right. No matter what. So here you are. And here I am."

"Meaning what?"

"Meaning I'm also going to do what's right, no matter what."

Zach pondered that. "Seems like you're going off the reservation, there, Miss Gibbs."

"So far off that I'm not sure I can get back in," she said, looking up. "But it's extremely important that this container get intercepted. Officially, unofficially—I don't care."

"So why isn't the full force and fury of the US government coming down to bear on this rogue trailer? Why is Homeland Security pinning its hopes and dreams on me?"

She took a deep breath. "Because with the trailer missing, my higher-ups have decided it'd be easier to say there was nothing there to begin with. The official story is that the original concern of what was in the trailer was wrong. A glitch, an oversight, a mistake by the Canadians when they were high on huffing maple syrup. Nothing to worry about. But I've managed to see some of the original intelligence. I don't think it was a mistake. I think it's still very much something to worry about."

"My, you certainly are off the reservation," Zach said. "I bet if we stay here long enough, we'll hear the hoofbeats of the cavalry coming after you."

"Perhaps."

Zach said, "What's driving you, then?"

"My professionalism."

Zach laughed. "No, seriously. What's driving you? And tell me the real deal, or I walk back into my home there, and you can find somebody else to go up there and play around in Turner."

She seemed to sigh. "You ever hear of Colby Consulting?"

"No, can't say that I have."

She said, "Colby Consulting was a business firm in New York City. My college roommate, Emily Harrison, my best friend in the whole world, worked there. Went to Simmons together in Boston. We shared secrets, troubles, the state or non-state of our love lives. We could go a month or two without talking, and then one of us would pick up the phone and we'd start up the conversation like only a day had passed. She entered business because of her father, who ran a hedge fund in Manhattan. I took up law enforcement because of my dad, who was a small-town police chief in New Jersey. We used to laugh that our fathers had planned our lives right from conception. You ever have lifelong friends like that, Chief?"

"Can't say that I have."

"Colby Consulting was in the ninety-fourth floor of the South Tower of the World Trade Center. She was at her desk, bright and early, on one September Tuesday morning. Need I say more?"

"More than a decade has gone by," Zach said. "Bin Laden is dead. We're pulling out of Afghanistan. Most people have forgotten."

"Not all of us," she said, her voice suddenly sharp. "Some of us think the threat is still out there, no matter what other people say or wish for."

He waited. Looked at the photo of the container. Looked at her. The hulking driver was now near the right rear fender of his pickup truck. "What are you offering?"

Tanya smiled, still looking like a sixteen-year-old pretending to be a grown-up. "Your dishonorable discharge is reversed, to honorable. All back pay and benefits are restored. You'll also get a generous stipend over the next several days, until the moment we intercept that container through your investigative efforts. Say, one thousand dollars a day."

"Pretty generous," he said. "Being as you practically said this little adventure isn't authorized, how can you make it right for me when the time comes?"

She said, "Let's just say I have someone on my side."

"Who is it?"

"Can't say."

"Legally, how do you do this? Am I a contractor? Freelance?"

She said, "After the World Trade Center went down and my best friend was murdered, a lot of laws got passed. There's one that allows those who've been dishonorably discharged to be placed in the inactive reserve list, whereupon they can be reactivated in the national interest. Consider yourself reactivated."

Zach looked at the steady gaze of the attractive woman standing across from him, again having the deep feeling that he always knew something like this was going to happen. Even after his dishonorable discharge, he knew his days of working in the shadows were going to continue, one way or the other.

Like now.

"Just to be clear, then," he said. "You want me to go back up to Turner, quietly snoop around, meet old friends and acquaintances, and find out when and what Duncan Crowley is doing with this shipping container. In return, I get the stipend of one thousand dollars a day, and if the container is intercepted by you or your associates, I get my back pay, pension, and discharge status changed."

"Correct," she said.

"What if I don't find the shipping container?"

She shrugged. "Keep your stipend as payment from a grateful Homeland Security administrator. Alas, everything else—your dishonorable discharge and all the rest—remains the same if we don't grab that container."

Zach again felt that sense of anticipation tingling inside of him. It had been a very long time since he had been excited about doing something.

"Lady, you got yourself a deal," he said.

———

In the next few minutes, Tanya went back to her car and returned, passing over a brown business-sized envelope. Zach opened it up and saw the placid face of Benjamin Franklin looking up at him. He flipped through the bills, counted out ten.

"Your first day's stipend," she said. "The following daily stipends will be deposited into your checking account."

Zach folded the envelope, stuck it in the back pocket of his Levi's.

"I take it you already have my checking account number," he said.

"Of course," she said. "Here, take this."

She passed over a cellphone. It was silver and simple-looking, with the standard numeric keypad and a few other switches. "Encrypted and untraceable," she explained. "Any calls coming to you will be from me or someone working for me. You press the speakerphone button there, it doesn't bring up the speakerphone. Instead, the phone dials directly to me or to my voice mail. Either I'll access the voice mail or someone who works for me will. I'll want a daily report. If I don't get one, the deal is off."

He took the cellphone. "All right," he said. "Anything else?"

"You know everything else," she said. "The container, Duncan Crowley, and you have under a week. Oh, and not to tell you how to do your job"—and with that, she offered another shy smile—"go in quiet and subtle. Duncan didn't get to where he is without being very, very cautious."

"I'm sure," he said, putting the exotic cellphone into his coat pocket.

She started putting her papers and photographs back into the manila folder. "Then here's something to make you more sure. Among the other information we've received about Duncan Crowley is this delightful tidbit: Last year, in two separate incidents, emissaries visited Duncan from what passes as organized crime outfits in Boston and Providence. Seems like they were interested in getting a piece of Duncan's businesses. They went up to the northern woods armed with weapons and bravado, and they never came back. Disappeared. Vanished. So your friend plays for keeps."

"Not my friend."

"Whatever," she said. Manila folder back in her slim hands, she said, "Ask you a question?"

"Go ahead," Zach said. "Won't guarantee an answer."

She said, "So what did you do to get a dishonorable discharge, Chief?"

Flash of memory, of standing shin-deep in a warm and muddy river up the ways in Sierra Leone, a dark-skinned man and his wife and children patiently looking at him from the riverbank, waiting and waiting, while behind them, a village burned and gunfire roared and screams were going on and on and on …

"Instead of following orders, I decided to stand up for the honor of the United States," he said.

Tanya said, "Bet you learned your lesson, doing a silly thing like that."

"Learned something, that's for sure."

———

He watched her walk back to her car, seeing a fine butt wiggle underneath her long coat. When the Crown Victoria had maneuvered its way out of his gravel driveway and disappeared, he let his breath out, rubbed his cold hands. Lots of things raced through his mind but as he had learned so long ago in Cape May, New Jersey, during Coast Guard basic training, it was time to focus on the mission.

But first, just a little check of the situation.

He went to the rear of his truck, where Gibbs's driver had been hanging around. Zach got to his hands and knees, peered up at the underside of the truck. Right there. Little black box stuck next to the gas tank, little trailing antenna sticking out. No doubt the cellphone had a tracking device, but Homeland Security—at least this particular part of it—was being more efficient than he thought possible. Whaddya know. Not a particularly trustworthy group, but that was to be expected.

Zach got up, brushed the dirt off his knees, and went back up into the double-wide. Looked around. This place was a shelter, but definitely wasn't a home. Some years ago he had bought these fifty acres sight unseen with the romantic notion that he would build a cozy retirement home when his service was completed. But his service was completed ahead of schedule, against his wishes, and instead of a home, he had this dump. Inside he spent a few minutes packing a change of clothes in one black duffel bag, and some personal items and books in another duffel bag. He didn't waste much time checking anything else out inside the creaky building. The kitchen was tiny and looked grimy, no matter how much he cleaned it, and the furniture was old and smelly, picked up at the local Goodwill and Salvation Army stores. The bathroom had collections of mold that looked like they had been developed at a secret Soviet Union germ warfare outfit before the Gorbachev era. Having spent the past twenty years in the service of his nation, he didn't have much in the way of possessions. With the two black duffel bags, everything he cared about could be carried out in his hands.

Three more things to do before it was time to shove off.

At the rear of the double-wide was a crumbling wooden deck where he kept a barbecue grill. He opened the squeaking sliding glass door and dragged it in, sliding the door closed afterwards. In the narrow living room, he undid the hose to the propane tank and turned the valve wide open. Propane gas started hissing out.

He went outside, closed the door behind him. Carrying his two duffel bags, he went into the front seat of his Ford pickup truck. Unzipping the nearest duffel bag, he took out a disposable cellphone—not trusting the super-duper cellphone for his own calls—and dialed a memorized number from down Boston way. So it had happened after all, he thought. Now it was time to get to work on something else.

The phone rang and rang, and was picked up, an older man answering. "Yes?" the man asked.

"It's me, Zach," he said, saying the practiced words with ease. "Can't you help me out?"

"I'm afraid I can't."

"Please," Zach said. "You know what happened to me wasn't fair."

The older man said, "Please don't call me again," and then hung up on him.

Zach sighed. The answer was totally expected but the call had to be made. He waited. Looked at the double-wide, and then called his landline number.

The phone rang until a spark was generated from the phone and the near windows of the double-wide blew out in a blossom of red and orange flame. In a matter of seconds, the place was burning merrily along. Even though he was anticipating the explosion, it still made him sit back hard against his truck seat.

But not enough to cause him to ignore the last of his three tasks.

One more phone call. When it was answered on the second ring, he said, "Hi, my name is Zach Morrow. I'm calling from 10 Timberswamp Road. Holy Christ, my house is on fire."

Zach hung up, turned the key to the Ford, and after a few seconds of a horrible grinding noise, it started up. Zach turned the truck around and went down the gravel driveway, and about three miles down the road, a bright red American LaFrance fire truck belonging to the Purmort Volunteer Fire Department roared by him, heading up to his burning home.

He didn't look back.

FIVE

BACK IN THE COMFORTABLE interior of her government-issued Crown Victoria, Tanya Gibbs crossed her legs and let out a deep breath. A close run thing, but it had gone well. She had gone in and dangled the bait, and Chief Morrow had eventually snapped it up. Like most government workers who had spent decades in its employ, he was desperate to do something, anything, to get his precious bennies back.

Not a fair fight, but she didn't care. She thought about her best friend Emily for a moment and pushed the painful memories away, remembering that Tuesday morning more than a decade ago, those frantic, choking phone calls from Emily as she slowly smothered at her desk…

Tanya looked out the rear window of the Crown Vic as Henry drove down the dirt driveway, seeing the disgraced Coast Guardsman staring at her. She felt a warm feeling start in her lower chest. Something about him was intriguing, attractive. He had carefully trimmed brown hair and his face was worn from spending a lot of time outdoors, and he had a strong, unyielding look about him. His steady gray eyes seemed to stare right through her. For years she had been around men of action, men who thought they were God's gift to women, but Zach Morrow was different. He seemed to move slow and methodical, like he was carefully evaluating everything and everybody around him.

Like her.

She looked out the window at the passing trees. Another memory came to her, making her shiver again. Back in New Jersey, as a kid. Mom pushed her to join the Girl Scouts, though she really didn't care to do it, and Tanya had asked Dad to intervene, but Dad being Dad, he had gone along with whatever her mother wanted, just so that screechy voice didn't rise in anger. So into the Girl Scouts she had gone, and it had been dull and all right, save for the first time she had gone on an overnight camping trip, somewhere in the Pine Barrens. Bad enough that her troop leader had agreed to let the older girls tell ghost stories, it got worse later, when two older girls led her into the woods, promising to show her a magic cave that had rocks that glowed in the dark. Of course, the magic cave was a secret, so she was blindfolded. After what seemed to be a long time in the dark woods, they ran way, giggling, leaving her alone. Tearing off the blindfold in terror, she had wandered through the night, a nine-year-old girl, scratching her face and arms, bumping into tree trunks, until she finally saw the glow from the campsite's stone fireplace.

That night, she didn't say a word to the two girls—who had smirked and giggled behind their hands all evening long—but a month later, when her troop went out on another overnight, she waited until everyone was at a neighboring campsite, making s'mores with another troop. She had sneaked away back to her own camp, went to the nearly-dead campfire, blew on it until it burst back into flames, and grabbed a burning pine branch. She had tossed the branch on the tent belonging to her tormenters and it burst into a blossom of fire. She then scrambled back to the s'more cookfest, and that had been that. Still, since then, she had never much liked the woods.

To her driver, she said, "Henry, you've spent time in this part of the state, haven't you?"

"Yes, ma'am," Henry Wolfe said, driving in the right lane, keeping the speed at a constant fifty-five miles per hour. Another useless government program, all of the fleet vehicles now had little black boxes that spied on you and reported if you went over the speed limit. A cute little snoopy program put in by the current First Lady, who apparently assumed her mission in life was to make people lose weight and get stuck in traffic.

"Then tell me," she said. "Why do people stay in these poor little towns? What's the point?"

Henry said, "Truth is, ma'am, most of 'em don't have a choice. They're born poor, in a rural area, and the only way out is through a good job, the military, or a quality education. Most of the good jobs are gone, the schools are struggling to teach the basics, and the military is so choosy now, they only select the best."

Tanya looked out at what passed for scenery. They were on a two-lane highway heading south. To the left were trees, and to the right were trees. Up ahead were trees. Despite the importance of her unauthorized mission, boy, she hated being up here.

"Then how did you make it out?" she asked.

"Was born out," he said. "Grew up in North Quincy, south shore of Massachusetts. Only reason I know anything up here is that my grandparents, they had a dairy farm near the Connecticut River. Spent a lot of summers there as a kid, before I joined the Army."

She looked at the back of Henry's strong neck, thought about other administrators in her office, back in Boston. On road trips like this, most of them insisted on being up front with their driver and armed escort, thinking it was the just and democratic approach, showing their solidarity with someone with less education, fewer skills, and a hell of a lot lower salary. But she was different. She liked sitting in the back, talking to her driver without having to figure out his facial expressions, and also knowing she could shut her mouth without having to explain herself.

Tanya said, "I see all these small towns, all these damn trees … still find it hard to believe anything criminal, anything evil goes on up here. Like this Duncan Crowley character."

Henry didn't reply for about a mile and then carefully said, "For most of his neighbors, I bet they don't think of him as being a criminal. From what I've learned from you, ma'am, in some way he's providing a service to the residents up there. Cheap booze and cigarettes from Canada. Marijuana to whoever wants it. Loans to people would never make it through a background or credit check from a bank or a credit union."

Tanya laughed. "You defending that crook, are you?"

"Not defending, ma'am. Just explaining. If most of his neighbors don't think he's a criminal, even fewer would think he's evil. Oh, evil's up here in these woods and small towns, but usually, it comes from some darkness, some outside influence."

"Like what?" she asked.

"Like a few years ago, these boys got together in a gang. They loved violent video games, ninja movies, that sort of thing. So they broke into a quiet rural house in Mount Vernon, not more than an hour from here, found a mom and her ten-year-old daughter sleeping, and took machetes to them both, just to see what it was like to kill. A few years before that, two teenage boys, all screwed up in the head, decided to steal money so they could start a new life in Australia."

Tanya said, "If I was a teenage boy, I'd think about starting a new life in Cancun, not Australia. What did these two punks do? Rob a bank or an armored car?"

Henry said, "They went to a house up near Hanover, knocked on the door of two professors from Dartmouth. They claimed to be high school students doing research for a school project. Being the polite and liberal professors that they were, the boys were invited in. Can you imagine that? Two Dartmouth faculty members, cultured and privileged and living in one of the safest states in the nation, invite two teenage boys in without question. The husband answered their questions. The wife made them lunch. And later these two boys slit their throats."

The car stayed silent for another mile. Tanya said, "Outside influences, you said. So how do I fit into the equation?"

"I don't understand what you mean, ma'am."

Tanya said evenly, "You know exactly what I mean. You heard my discussion with Zach Morrow back there, about his role in nailing Duncan Crowley and getting that shipping container. You saw the expression on his face, thinking I had the power and the authority to make it all right for him, get his dishonorable discharge reversed, get all of his benefits back. Simple soul bought the entire story. Didn't even ask for a signed agreement."

Henry's voice sounded just a tad reproachful. "Perhaps he was relying on your word being your bond. People in these parts, they take another person's word very, very seriously."

"Having spent all these years in government service, the saltwater must've rotted out his brain. He should have known better."

"But you told him you had somebody backing you up who could make it right for him."

"I do."

"Your uncle, Warren Gibbs, am I right?"

59

She sighed. "The senior senator from Ohio has more important things on his mind."

"Like running for president?"

"Exactly. So if Morrow does succeed, maybe I will make that call. And maybe not."

Henry kept quiet for a bit and said, "A thousand dollars a day seems to be a lot."

She said, "Money deposited into a checking account from our side of the fence can just as easily be sucked out when the time comes."

"But the Regional Administrator … you're going to have to brief him, won't you?"

Tanya said, "Don't worry about that, Henry. Just keep on driving."

She touched the thick manila folder next to her, thinking about how those collection of papers and photographs were going to be the key for her doing her part to avenge Emily. That had been all she had craved during that warm September morning more than a decade ago when the towers fell and her best friend died. When she had changed her career from the New Jersey State Police to the new agency of Homeland Security. The FBI, CIA, the armed services … they all did good work, but she wanted to be here, in the good old homeland, ensuring that the people who had allowed 9/11 to happen wouldn't have another chance to repeat their mistakes.

As for the Regional Administrator … to hell with briefing him about anything. When the time came, she could claim the news about the missing shipping container and its magic cargo had come in via a tip line, and that would be that. In the excitement of the arrests, news coverage, and death and destruction for those smuggling the container, other questions could be overlooked. When this thing broke over the next several days, it'd be the biggest domestic deal since those four airliners went awry more than a decade ago.

As for Zach Morrow, well, once before he had sacrificed himself for his nation. Perhaps he would have to do it again.

Tanya didn't feel guilty. She thought again of Emily, being in the second tower, fire and smoke behind her, leaning out of a shattered window on her office floor, looking down upon the streets of Manhattan below her, the back of her neck and hands getting scorched, smoke burning her lungs, people behind her shoving and screaming and trying desperately to get air to breathe, betrayed and abandoned by those who were elected and paid to protect her and the other thousands...

There was a loud burst of noise as a logging truck roared by, also heading south. Long, shorn tree trunks bound by chains were secured on a trailer. The passing of the truck made the Crown Victoria quiver from the truck's tailwind.

"Damn," she said, shaken out of her memories. "I sure don't like trees."

Daily Threat Assessment Task Force Teleconference Call
April 14th

Homeland Security representative: "… and I think we've reached the end of our call today. Anybody else?"

CIA representative: "Sounds fine by me."

State Department representative: "Ditto here."

FBI representative: "Hold on, I want to go back to the matter of the Mextel shipping container. It seems like—"

Homeland Security: "I don't think we really have time to get into that again. Let's just consider that matter closed."

FBI: "Closed?"

Homeland Security: "Closed. Let's just say the system worked."

[[[Cross talk]]]

FBI: "… last time somebody made an idiotic comment like that was when that Al-Qaeda moron tried to take down an airliner over Christmas with an underwear bomb. It's a miracle we didn't have an airliner break up and have bodies scattered around downtown Detroit. Despite being that close to disaster, your idiot boss said the system worked. That was bullshit then and remains bullshit now."

[[[Cross talk]]]

Homeland Security: "Tom, you know what the lesson of that day was?"

FBI: "I can hardly wait. Go ahead."

Homeland Security: "My so-called idiot boss still has her job. Thus endeth the lesson. Meeting adjourned."

SIX

In Laval, Quebec, about thirty minutes northwest of Montreal, Francois Ouellette, president of the Iron Steeds Motorcycle Club, sat behind his desk at the club headquarters and twirled a pencil in his fingers. Across from him was Michael Grondin, his deputy and second-in-command, and Michael's face looked pale. Francois knew why. Spinning a pencil in his fingers was never a good sign for whoever was sitting across from him.

"Before I go on, Michael, I want to make sure I have all the facts straight, before I make a decision, okay?"

Michael nodded. He was nearing fifty, was heavy around the waist, and had a thick thatch of black beard that started at his cheekbones and went down to mid-chest. He was balding up front and on top, and wore the rest of his hair in a long ponytail. Francois thought he looked like an idiot with the front of his head shiny bald like that, but kept his mouth shut and let others make the point. One of those others was a new kid that had been accepted into the club last month. During one rowdy drunken night at a campground deep in the Laurentian Mountains, he had playfully tugged at Michael's ponytail and said it looked like a horse's tail, attached to a horse's ass.

Michael went at the kid for a couple of hours with his bare fists, tire iron, and a propane torch, until the kid was crying for his mamma and begging for a quick end, which Michael eventually provided with an ice pick through his right eardrum.

So Michael was tough, but he was scared of Francois, which was pleasing indeed. Francois hadn't become president of the Iron Steeds because of his cooking skills. Pencil still twirling about, he said, "Andre and Pierre, we haven't heard from them since last night. Calls to their cellphones go unanswered. A call to that roadhouse … the Flight Deck. Whoever answers the phone there denies Andre and Pierre ever showed up. The guy they were to meet, that Duncan Crowley. Finally got a hold of that prick, and he's so smooth and apologetic, said he was still waiting for them to show up."

Michael nodded. "You got it right so far, boss."

The floor beneath his feet vibrated from heavy bass. The club's headquarters was here, on the second floor of the Slinky Pussy Gentlemen's Club, which had the advantage of screwing up nearly every surveillance system known to man due to the constant heavy music and loud conversation. His office was heavily insulated, with nice wood paneling, the motto of the club done in stitch work—"*A La Vie A La Mort*"—and framed prints of Winslow Homer. Francois didn't know why he liked the nineteenth-century American painter who did ocean landscapes. He just did, and he proved that point a few years back, at the tail end of the Biker Wars, when a rep from the L.A. branch of the Hells Angels came by to make the peace and made the mistake of laughing at the old prints.

Francois had tossed the guy through the nearest window, where he ended up in the club's rear parking lot with a broken arm and leg, and from there, negotiations for the peace came to a quick and productive end.

He said, "You've made the necessary calls. Provincial police, RCMP, Border Patrol, Vermont State Police, and New Hampshire State Police. About all we know for certain is that they went through the border crossing in Derby Line, Vermont, yesterday. Right?"

"Yes, boss."

Francois let the pencil drop to the top of his clean desk. "Hospitals, ambulance services, medical centers?"

"All blank, boss."

Francois took a big sigh. Damn, he'd have to tell Andre's mother what had happened, and he could just imagine the screaming and wailing he'd have to put up with. Andre wasn't too bright but he was his nephew, and his sister did love the poor bugger.

"All right," he said. "Andre's a little hotheaded but he'd never fly out on his own. Pierre would take a bullet to his balls before leaving Andre behind. So I think we both know what the hell happened."

Michael's face, if possible, grew more pale. Francois said, "That shipping container must be worth an awful fucking lot for this guy in New Hampshire to not let us in on the action. I mean, a real fucking lot, especially with him taking out two of our boys."

Michael said, "Manny, the provincial police guy who tipped us off on the container, he said the place was a fucking circus when it arrived. Snoopers around and surveillance teams, and when the container disappeared, everyone involved went ape shit. Word on the streets, there's an in-house reward to law enforcement, a million bucks to whoever finds it."

"A million dollars," Francois said dreamily. "For a reward. That tells you how valuable the damn thing is. Your Manny fellow, he still can't tell you what's inside of it?"

Michael shook his head. "No. Just that it's valuable, somehow it's attached to that Crowley character in New Hampshire, and that's it."

Francois picked up the pencil, twirled it one more time. "Okay. This is how it's gonna be. I want a zap squad sent down there. All right? Guys who know how to take orders. I want this Crowley and his family greased, but before they wrap it up, they're gonna have this Crowley guy tell 'em where and how that shipping container's arriving. Got it? Then before they whack him, I want his balls cut off, dangling in his face, and the guys to tell 'em that this was a cheery fuck you from Francois Ouellette and the Iron Steeds."

"How many guys do you want?"

"It's a zap squad, so two should be enough. They can slide in and out of the small town where that shithead lives without any problem. More guys than that, they can get in the way, get noticed. You remember that, Michael, or do I have to write a memo?"

Michael got up from the chair, his face red, like he didn't care for being put down like that. "I got it, boss."

"Good. But make sure you send the right guys. Smart enough to do the job, but not too smart and valuable so that if they get caught or get blown away, we take another hit to the organization. Losing Andre and Pierre … that's gonna hurt."

"Then maybe we shouldn't go at it again," Michael quietly offered. "Just ignore the whole damn thing. Sounds like it could be a wild goose chase, not worth the effort."

Francois was taken aback by Michael's words. "Did you just say that? Say we should ignore it? 'Cause I don't believe an Iron Steeds member just suggested to me that we should roll over and give it up."

"No," he replied. "I'm just saying, we should think this through, after losing two guys, that—"

"Michael, I want more advice from you, I'll fucking ask for it. Okay?"

His voice sullen, Michael said, "Understood, boss," and went out the door.

Francois rubbed at the back of his head, wondering how he would approach Andre's mother, when there was a soft knock on the door. It opened up and his talent manager, Brenda Aube, came in. She had on tight blue shorts that looked like they were painted on and a halter top that barely held in her impressive and natural rack. Her black hair hung down nice and long and she strolled over and said, "Talent review for the new girls, if you're interested."

"Always interested," he said. "What do you have for me?"

She whistled and a young girl came in, shy-looking, wearing a plaid skirt, white knee socks, and a light yellow turtleneck sweater. She had on black-rimmed glasses and her blond hair was done back in a ponytail. Brenda patted her on her head and left the room, closing the door behind her.

Francois crooked a finger and she came over. He pushed himself away from his desk. "What's your name, sweet one?"

"Megs," she said, her voice barely audible above the thumping from the music just below them.

"Closer, if you please."

She came over and he looked her up and down, and thought Brenda really needed a raise. He motioned with his right hand and without a word, she sank to her knees. One of the knee socks fell and he spotted a light bruise on the other knee.

Francois stroked her fine blond hair. "Where do you come from, sweetie?"

"Aumond. A small town. Hundreds of klicks away."

"Are you a runaway?" He felt her head nod yes against his touch. He said, "Do your parents know where you are?"

"No, they don't."

He lowered his hand, lifted up her chin so he could look at those eyes and the smooth complexion. "Megs, darling, do tell me, how old are you?"

"I'm … I'm eighteen," she said bravely.

"Megs …"

"Seventeen."

He gently pinched her lower lip.

"I'm … I'm just fifteen," she whispered.

Francois smiled and unzipped his pants as he pushed her head down. "Oh, yeah, that's what I love to hear."

SEVEN

AT THE TROIS RIVIERES truck stop on Route 112 in southern Quebec, outside of Sherbrooke, Brewster Flagg got off a Trailways bus, small leather bag in hand, shivering with cold as he stood in the paved parking area. Row upon row of idling tractor-trailer trucks stood still, diesel exhaust burbling up in the air. He had been at plenty of similar stops back in Georgia, Alabama, and Texas during the day, but damn, it was so freakin' cold up here. He started trudging towards the nearest row of trucks. He was hungry and needed to use a bathroom, but first above all, he had to find the right truck. It had been a long journey from Georgia to Indiana to Detroit, and then from Detroit to Windsor in Ontario, riding one dirty and smelly bus after another. The long hours on the road, dozing in the uncomfortable seats, finally coming to this place that fed the truckers and fueled the trucks that kept this socialist economy bumbling along.

Brewster couldn't help it. He yawned. A very long series of days, only made worthwhile because he knew in the deepest part of his heart that he was on a vital mission. For the past few years, ever since that Kenyan got into the White House and Brewster had lost his trucking job in Texas—thanks to NAFTA and letting those wet-back truckers come in and steal bread from his mouth and the mouths of so many others—he had fought the socialists and traitors that had taken his country away. At first he had joined the Tea Party and had gone to rallies and had heckled the occasional thick Congressman who had the stones to appear at an open house, but what had that accomplished? True answer: not a hell of a lot. Sure, the Republicans had done better in defeating Democrats, but as he later found out talking with some of his Tea Party buds, they had merely exchanged one group of paid-off clowns with another group of paid-off clowns. And both sets of clowns were under the thumbs of those who had money, who had connections, who thought everything except D.C. and L.A. was flyover country. If you were in D.C. or L.A. or New York, you got the bailouts and the aid. If you were anywhere else, well, you got screwed, day after day, week after week.

So he had decided to go the direct action route, and had gone dark for a while, popping up here and there to rob a couple of banks, fire some rounds into the windows of abortion clinics, and firebomb three Congressional home district offices across the South. It had felt good, actually doing shit instead of talking about it, but after a border protection tour in Arizona ended up a bloody mess, he had gotten drummed out of his local Tea Party chapter.

Pussies.

Brewster stopped. Almost out of breath. There it was—a light green Peterbilt tractor-trailer truck, with a half-sized shipping container that had been freshly repainted. Brewster went to the near rear tire, lifted his hand up on the tread, felt a set of keys there, pulled them down. He juggled them for a moment in his hand. Enjoyed the sensation. It had been a long time since had driven a truck, back when he worked for his cousin Troy Flagg at Long Line Trucking, outside of Irving. Then the place went under and unemployment ran out, and he had been at loose ends ever since, until …

Until that unexpected phone call a couple of weeks ago from Troy, wanting to know if he'd be up for a little driving. A little driving that might be dangerous. A little driving that might end up doing a world of good.

At first he had been reluctant, until Troy had told him where he was calling from: Waco, Texas. He had gone there as a pilgrimage to where nearly a hundred folks had been incinerated by the government, the government that was supposedly there to protect them. And Troy had reminded Brewster what date was coming up: April 19th, a day with a lot of meaning among the right people.

He opened the cab door, pulled himself in, and tossed his leather bag to one side. Within a few moments, the Peterbilt diesel engine roared into life. Brewster was no longer hungry, tired, or thirsty. He didn't even have to take a piss. He thought of April 19th, the day the first shots were fired at Concord and Lexington. The same day that the Branch Davidian compound was destroyed in Waco. The same day that the federal building in Oklahoma City was bombed.

April 19th was just a few days away, and what was in that trailer back there would overwhelm the memories of those previous dates.

"McVeigh was a fag," he muttered, as he maneuvered out of the parking lot.

EIGHT

AT THE BREAKFAST NOOK restaurant in Crowdin, an even smaller town north of Turner, Duncan Crowley sat in a rear booth with his brother, waiting for his meal. The place was half full, and Duncan took a sip of his orange juice. Cameron had on a plain dungaree jacket and his ponytail was freshly washed and pulled back.

Cameron said, "Clean-up went well. Went in there after Dickie and his nephew left, place was tight, was damn virginal."

"Glad to hear it," Duncan said. "Just so you know, I got a call about an hour ago from Francois Ouellette, wondering where his nephew was. I played innocent and charming, and he wished me well, and that was it."

Cameron raised an eyebrow. "Sounds good."

"Hell it does," Duncan said. "He should have been screaming at me, should have been threatening to kneecap me, but he was cordial and smooth. That means he's already decided to come at us with everything he's got."

"Christ," Cameron said. "What are you thinking?"

"I'm thinking I'm hungry, that's what," Duncan said.

A couple of minutes later, a young waitress with flowers tattooed on her wrists dropped off their order: coffee and a blueberry muffin for Cameron, and three pancakes and six sausage links for Duncan. His brother widened his eyes. "You better hope Karen doesn't find out what you're hoovering there, bro."

"I won't tell if you don't," he said, eagerly digging in.

———

When their second cups of coffee arrived, Duncan said, "What's the schedule for today?"

Cameron said, "We've got a meet with Chuckie Pelletier, and then you have a quick lunch with Karen. Then I want to check the set-up at that development I was telling you about, and later, a post office stop, pick up a new lens for my Meade. Not that I don't trust Lucy Lubrano when it comes to delivering my mail, but sometimes she can't reach high enough to get to the mailbox, drops it on the driveway."

"Sounds good," Duncan said. "I also might want to do a bit of wandering."

Cameron grinned. "Already figured it in. Anything else?"

Duncan said, "Later tonight, I want to pay an unannounced visit to Gus Spooner. You know the kid?"

His brother said, "Gas jockey over in Barnard, at your Route 3 convenience store. Not too bright but gets the job done. What's going on?"

"Ever get into trouble you know of?"

Cameron said, "Stupid kid got banned from the town dump in Turner."

"Banned? Really? What did he do, mix in recyclables with the regular trash?"

Cameron smiled wider. "Get this. He got banned 'cause of what he was doing at the dump store. You know the place. People drop off furniture, old TVs, clothes, books, dishes. Even though they call it a store, it's all free."

Duncan said, "I remember reading something in the *Turner Transcript* last year. Bit of a scandal. People were hanging around the town dump all day, picking off the best stuff, and then selling it from their houses a week or two later, at a yard sale. Is that what he was up to?"

"Some scandal. This is better. Seems like Gus Spooner liked hanging around the dump store. Most folks—instead of the yard-sale pickers—they either drop off stuff or poke around after tossing out their weekly trash. But Gus hung out there, hour after hour, day after day, and then some of the moms got creeped out. You see, the moms, they got a sort of unofficial trading club going on. Moms bring in clothes their kids can't wear, and they trade with other moms. Good way to get used clothing from families you know."

Duncan said, "Got a feeling where this is going."

"Yeah, to pervland, that's where this is going. Gus liked to do his part to recycle clothing as well, but he was picking out panties. And not grandma's cotton panties. Used little girl panties, the kind with flowers on 'em and pictures of Hello Kitty. So even though taking discarded little girl panties ain't against the law, near as I know, he was politely told by Chief Reynolds to stay the fuck away from the town dump." Cameron took a sip from his coffee cup. "So, what's the deal, then? Gus bugging somebody you know? He stealing fresh panties or something?"

"No," Duncan said. "I got word he's branching out. Seems there was a mistaken delivery of some cold medicine to our Route 3 store, and instead of returning it, ol' Gus has decided to use his home ec skills to cook up a bunch of crystal meth."

Cameron wasn't smiling any more. "You know where the stupid shit has set up shop?"

"Yeah," Duncan said. "Hunting camp up on Town Road Twelve."

"What time?"

"Tonight, after dinner. Seems to make sense."

Cameron said, "How did you find out?"

"Got told, that's all," he said.

Cameron wiped his hands on a brown paper napkin, then took out a fresh napkin and repeated the cleaning. "So, the person dropping a dime on Gus Spooner, the same person who told you about the shipping container from Mextel Lines? The same container I know shit about, including what's in it, and when it's coming across?"

Their waitress wandered by, put the check on the table. The bill was fourteen dollars and twelve cents. Duncan took out his wallet, removed a twenty, dropped it on the bill.

"Cameron," he said, stepping out from the booth. "I've had such high hopes for the day. Don't start, all right?"

Cameron said, "Whatever you say, bro. Whatever you say."

———

They were in Cameron's Honda Pilot, heading up Route 115, and then taking a right onto Post Road. The road was bumpy and cracked. Melting mounds of snow mixed in with dirt were on either side of the country lane. An old stone wall from a long-ago farm was on the left for a couple of miles, before the trees cleared away. Duncan sensed his brother's anger but kept his own thoughts to himself. There were plenty of other things to think through.

"Here we go," Cameron said, as they turned right onto a dirt driveway. Up ahead was an old farmhouse, at least a hundred years old, with a wide front porch and narrow clapboards. Two dogs, a German Shepherd and a yellow Labrador Retriever, came out, barking at them. The driveway ended in a wide bare spot. A light red Toyota pickup truck and a blue Ford Explorer with taped-up plastic covering the rear window were parked under a pine tree. A two-story barn was attached to the house by a low building whose shingles were nearly gone, and another newer barn was about a hundred yards away. Parts of the muddy and grassy yard were fenced in, with three horses and two cows slowly moving about.

The door to the house opened up and a large man ambled out, wearing dungaree overalls, muddy boots, and a fleece coat, unzipped. He came closer, with a thick moustache and a two-day old growth of beard. He was wearing a Paris Farmer's Union cap, and from inside his overalls, he took out a pistol with a long barrel.

"Cameron."

"Yeah."

"Looks like Chuckie Pelletier is coming at us with a pistol."

"You see that, too, hunh?"

"Heck of a reception."

His brother snorted, opened the door. "Don't worry about Chuckie, bro. I got it covered."

Cameron joined his brother and Chuckie Pelletier grinned, popped the magazine from the base of the pistol, checked it, and popped it back in. Duncan saw it was a Ruger semiautomatic .22. Chuckie said, "Hey, guys, glad to see you. Came just in time for a bit o' housekeeping. Come this way, if you don't mind."

Duncan slipped his hands into his coat as they walked around the farmhouse and to the rear of the yard. A smaller fenced-in area was there, being watched over by two young girls, both with long brown hair, pale faces, and hands pushed hard into soiled red down jackets. Being observed was a huge pig, snuffling around. A ways beyond, in a dry part of a pasture, an older man dressed in green work chinos and work boots sat on a green John Deere tractor, engine idling, a bucket loader up forward.

Chuckie said, "Rear barn is up there, do what you gotta do. Hold on, this won't take but a sec."

The large man went up to the fence, patted both girls on the shoulders. The younger one looked like she had been crying, but her older sister was fascinated at what was going on. She passed over something to her father. Chuckie took the Ruger pistol out, worked the action, and with his other hand, held out a little bag of grain over the fence line. He made a *cluck cluck* sound and the large pig snuffled over. Chuckie held up the little bag. The pig raised her head and Chuckie fired a shot into her forehead, making Duncan flinch. A sharp squeal and the pig collapsed on its side.

The John Deere tractor roared into action and rolled over. The two girls opened a gate into the fenced-in area. From the tractor's bucket the girls retrieved lengths of chain and wrapped them around the rear legs of the dead pig. With a whine the bucket loader came up, the pig swinging free.

Chuckie said, "That there's m'dad. He's gonna help the girls butcher poor old Pearl."

Duncan said, "Your younger girl doesn't look very happy."

"Can't rightly blame her, now, 'cause she grew Pearl as a project in 4-H. Got right attached to Pearl, hates to see her turn into bacon and chops."

Cameron said, "She looks like she's gotten over it."

Chuckie put the Ruger on safe and put it back into his overalls. "Yeah, well, when I told her I was gonna take the meat to Randy's

Butcher Shop in town and that she'd get twenty dollars for her share, she brightened right up."

The tractor moved a few yards, positioned the dangling body of Pearl over a large galvanized tub, and Chuckie's dad got off the John Deere tractor, went to a toolbox.

"Only one right way to butcher and clean a pig, and m'dad knows it, in and out," Chuckie said, thumbs under his overall straps. "Not like my neighbors, up over the ridge. The Thorntons."

"What did they do?" Duncan asked.

Chuckie's dad took a long knife from the toolbox, walked up to the head of the pig. The two girls held the dangling body still as he slit the pig's throat and blood gushed out. His son said, "Idiots were too lazy to gut and clean the usual way, so they cut open their pig in the back of their pickup truck. Least the damn thing had a plastic liner. Anyway, they went down to South Turner—they have a car wash— and they thought it'd make sense to clean out the guts and such by going through the car wash with the pig in the back."

Cameron laughed. "Fuck you say."

"Seriously, no, that's what they did. What a Christly mess, blood and guts and pig fat everywhere in the joint. Man . . . ."

Duncan said, "I'll never look at bacon the same way again. Say, if you don't mind, we'd like to take a look at the far barn."

"Guys, you pay rent there, that barn is yours."

"Want to come up with us?"

Chuckie looked over, smiling. "Duncan, that's a fine invite, but I'm gonna decline. You want to know why? Ever since you wild Injuns have started rentin' my barn, I've kept me and my family on this side of the fence. Don't know what you're doing in there; I can guess what you're doing in there, but it ain't my business. So don't take offense, but if I don't go up there with you, then I can always say to you and anyone else, I've never been in or near that barn. Is that all right, then?"

Duncan reached up, gently squeezed the man's left shoulder. "Nice and clear. Not a problem at all. We won't be long."

Chuckie shrugged. "Take as much time as you like."

———

Up at the barn, Cameron led his brother to a side door that had a metal doorknob with a numeric keypad. Cameron punched in the numbers and opened the door. He followed Cameron in, past a canvas wall blocking the way. Cameron closed the door and pushed the canvas away.

"Keeps the inside from being looked at, in case someone's peering in from the tree line," Cameron explained.

Duncan looked in, liked what he saw. Row upon row of metal troughs with leafy green vegetation growing up, reaching towards overhead lamps. A complicated system of irrigation hoses and drains snaked in and around the troughs.

"Nicely done," Duncan said. "How soon before harvest?"

"About another month. A couple of weeks later for drying and preparing. Then we'll start up all over again."

"Good, good," Duncan said, fingering a leaf from the nearest plant. "You trust Chuckie?"

"Near as I trust anybody. But he gave me a great bit of advice, before we started."

"What's that?"

"Chuckie knows his way around electricity, lighting, and wiring. When we set up the Gro-Lux lamps to boost the growth cycle, he said PSNH might be suspicious to see a spike in electrical usage, so he worked a way out of bypassing the central meter. A bit clunky, but it works."

"Thought Chuckie said he didn't know what was in the barn."

"He doesn't," Cameron said. "All he knows is that we needed extra juice. We could be running aquariums in there for all he knows, though I'm sure he has his guesses."

Duncan took in a deep breath, enjoying the intoxicating and thick smell of green things growing under a roof. But that was the only intoxication he allowed himself. Never, ever, under any circumstances, did he ever sample the merchandise.

"Good, glad to know it," Duncan said.

"Maybe so, but we're still vulnerable."

"How's that?"

Cameron said, "DEA or State Police ever get interested in picking things up a pace, they might send helicopters overhead at night, check thermal readings. The power use might not raise eyebrows, but if a helicopter hovers overhead with a thermal imaging device and finds this place glowing like Chernobyl, it won't end well."

"I guess setting up surface-to-air missiles would be an overreaction."

"Yeah, it would, but we could do two things, both expensive. First is to install shielding up under the roof, block the bulk of the thermal heat going up here. Second thing is what I'm going to show you after lunch."

"Something to look forward to," Duncan said. "All right, looks great, looks like Chuckie is happy, but for Christ's sake, he offers you something, refuse, okay?"

"What's that?"

Duncan couldn't help himself. He felt queasy. "If he wants to give me ham or bacon from poor Pearl, politely turn him down. Couldn't stand the thought of eating something I saw walking around just a few minutes ago."

NINE

IN HER SIXTH-FLOOR OFFICE in the Thomas P. O'Neill Jr. Federal Building in downtown Boston, Tanya Gibbs was getting ready for tomorrow's staff meeting when there was a hesitant knock on the door. She looked up and Walter Dresden was gingerly stepping in. He was overweight, with thick blond hair that looked ridiculous on his plain face. He apparently thought he was in the military, for every day he wore a uniform: black shoes, black trousers, white shirt, and narrow black necktie. On the rare casual Fridays, Walter would go wild with a narrow dark blue necktie.

"Ah, Tanya, ah, if I can just bother you for a moment," he stammered.

She went back to her paperwork, trying to keep calm and friendly. "What can I do for you, Walter?"

He stepped from one foot to another, like a grade-school student looking for permission to use the boys' room. "It's like this, ah, I made a mistake when I put you on that raw intelligence distribution list, especially, ah, about that matter in Quebec. The, er, missing shipping container. I was just hoping that, well, I hope that—"

Tanya quickly worked through the number of responses that she had available to her, feeling the first stirrings of her temper. She tried to squash it.

She lifted her head, smiled. "Walter, I appreciate that. I know you made a mistake. You're one overworked public service employee, just like everybody else in this building. You spend so many unappreciated hours doing what you can to protect America and its people. We both know that some of these raw intelligence reports, if they were to be made public, like the Quebec matter, would cause panic and disorders. That we don't need."

Walter still shifted his considerable weight, leg to leg.

She went on. "So as far as I'm concerned, the matter is closed. Don't worry about it."

She smiled, lowered her head again, hoping the knucklehead would get the message.

But he pressed on. "But, ah, if I may, Tanya, I feel a duty to pass this along to the Regional Administrator, as a matter of procedure, you know, I mean, based on your past experiences and job history, you must know that—"

Ah, yes, job history. She wasn't much for being on the street but she loved being behind the scenes, doing paperwork, working intelligence, compiling statistics, going into the New Jersey State Police after a couple of years on the street and being a comfortable, quiet drone in the background at headquarters in West Trenton.

Until 9/11. Until she saw the buildings fall during that longest of all long days. Until she had found out about the last desperate hours of her dearest friend, having to join at least a hundred others who leapt to their deaths from the doomed buildings, falling and falling and falling, seconds dragging by, knowing only pain and obliteration was waiting for you.

So she had gone into Homeland Security, an agency with an amorphous name, tentacles in everything from Secret Service to Coast Guard to border security and lots of openings and opportunities for someone like her. Someone with skin—or blood—in the game. Someone who wanted to make it right.

Her hands grew warm. "Walter."

"I mean, this was a mistake on my part, and I feel—"

"Walter, do me the favor of listening to what I have to say."

He did just that. She leaned over her desk and lowered her voice. "If you say one word about this matter to Gordie, that means I'll get dragged into what was a serious mistake on your part. In fact, Gordie may investigate and reprimand me for not officially reporting this when I had a chance."

"Tanya, I'm just saying—"

She kept on rolling, hating what she had to say next, knowing she had no other choice. This pudgy man was not going to get in her way. "That happens, I swear to God I will make it my personal mission in life to destroy you. Your career here will be finished. With a termination from Federal employment, that black mark against you—in this endless recession—means the best job you'll get will be scooping ice cream in Revere Beach. But I'll only let you have that job if I'm in a good mood, because if I'm not, I'll have your records hacked to show your future employers that you're a suspected pedophile. Now. You've angered me by threatening to go to Gordie. So I've changed my mind about this matter being settled. I know you have your chubby little fingers in a lot of information streams in the Region. Correct?"

"Ah, yes, that's true but—"

"So Walter, if you want to keep your position, and not be identified as a pedophile—you can't believe how easy it is to make an accusation like that stick—I want to know everything and anything you learn about the Quebec shipping container. I don't care if it's something as small or as stupid as somebody seeing it orbiting Venus. You will inform me instantly, or I swear to God, I'll hammer you. Don't think that I don't have other sources here in this building to know if you're holding out on me. Have I made myself clear, Walter? Do you have any questions? Do we need to discuss this any further?"

He shook his head so violently it was amazing that his blond hair didn't fly apart. He backed out of the office, bumped into a potted plant, and then scurried down the hallway.

Tanya sighed, looked out the window at all the nice tall and sleek buildings of downtown Boston, feeling nauseous at how she had treated poor Walter Dresden. This wasn't how her parents raised her, this wasn't how she usually conducted business. But there was a threat out there, a serious threat, even if she was the only one to see it, and she wasn't going to let that threat go unnoticed.

That's what happened more than ten years ago. There were hints, arrests, even reports of Arab men attending flight schools, and rumors of terrorist plots involving hijacked aircraft ... and what happened?

Nothing. Until that beautiful Tuesday morning in September.

Now it looked like it was going to happen again. The raw intelligence came in about a mysterious half-sized shipping container in Quebec, one that got the interest of a lot of law enforcement authorities, and now ...

Ignored. Just a mistake. A false alarm. Nothing to worry your pretty little head over.

She glanced over at the little bookcase in the corner of her office, noted the framed photo of her dear Emily, taken at her office at Colby Consulting in the World Trade Center. Now there was no Colby Consulting, no World Trade Center, and no Emily. All burnt, shattered, destroyed, reduced to their base atoms and molecules. Next to her was a framed photo of a woman with glasses and a mane of blond highlighted hair, wearing a US Customs uniform. Diana Dean, who helped foil the Millennium Plot to blow up the Los Angeles airport on the night of December 31, 1999. Dean had been working at the Port Angeles Customs station in Washington State, checking out the last ferry in from British Columbia. One of the drivers—later revealed to be an Algerian terrorist named Ahmed Ressam—was smuggling bomb-making materials in the trunk of his car.

And why had Customs Agent Dean given this man extra scrutiny? Had a threat warning been issued? Were rumors of a bombing plot passed around? Had Ressam been wearing an "I Heart al-Qaeda" T-shirt?

No. Agent Dean thought the driver had been acting "hinky." So she acted on her gut, on her hunch.

Emily and Agent Dean. Her daily overseers, back over there on the bookshelf.

Tanya took a deep breath, tried to ease the knot in her gut, looked away from the bookcase. In one corner of her office were a sledgehammer and a canvas bag that held a two-hundred-foot rope ladder. If this building were ever hit, she'd go through that supposedly unbreakable window with the sledgehammer and use the rope ladder to get out.

That was for her. And what she was doing now, with the help of that brooding and clear-eyed Coastie up north, was to make sure nobody else would have to worry about being trapped in a burning and collapsing building.

"Not going to happen again, Emily," she murmured. "Not if I can help it."

TEN

FOR THE REST OF the morning, Duncan directed his brother up and around a number of rural roads, again making sure they weren't being followed. Twice he had Cameron stop at one of the convenience stores he owned: one on Route 16 and the other on Route 115. The one on Route 16 looked fine and the Indian family that ran the place for him was smiling with pleasure at having him stop by. About the only thing he didn't like was the Indian food they were prepping—no offense, but he didn't really like the smells—but Cameron told him out in the parking lot that the locals really liked the Indian family and their food, making it one of his most profitable stores.

Outside the store, he had an unexpected encounter: an older man who stepped out of a green Subaru Forester parked at the gas pumps and said, "Duncan? Got a minute?"

Duncan tried to keep a friendly look on his face. It was Hubert Conan, his wife's uncle and newspaper stringer, who wanted to do a story about the Crowley business. He had on brown shoes, tan slacks, and a white shirt with snappy blue bow tie. A white fringe around his bald head made him look like an elder medieval monk. But his eyes were filmy and bloodshot, and his hands trembled.

"How's it going, Uncle Hubert?" he asked.

Hubert smiled. "Just fine, just fine. Listen, I was wondering if you were still thinking about me doing a feature story about you and your companies. I mean, you're the only real thriving businessman up in this part of the state. I think it'd be a great feature story."

"Tell you what, Uncle Hubert," Duncan said, reaching for the Pilot's door handle. "I'm still thinking about it. I'll let Karen know, soon as I can."

Hubert nodded, looked like he was going to say something, and then trundled into the store, shoulders slumped.

Inside the Honda Cameron laughed. "Thinking about it my ass."

"Family," Duncan said. "It's just family."

———

At the Route 115 store, Duncan went into the men's room, found the concrete floor slimy and old shit caked on the toilet bowl. Jaw clenched, he didn't say a word, just went back to the store, grabbed a pail and started scrubbing out the men's room. The store manager, a thin woman with large bug-eyes, was practically crying with apologies as she saw Duncan clean the bathroom.

When he was done, he said, "You're Elaine Doolittle, right?"

"Yes, Mr. Crowley."

He passed over the bucket. "Being a manager has its duties and responsibilities. Cleaning up other people's crap isn't fun, but it has to be done. Even I'm not afraid to get my hands dirty when I have to. Have I made myself clear?"

She just nodded, took the bucket, and tried running back into the store, water slopping over the edge of the bucket.

Back in the Honda Pilot, Cameron quietly said, "Do you want her fired?"

"What's her story?"

"Single mom of two boys."

"Think she's overworked, or lazy?"

"I'd guess overworked," Cameron said.

"Then leave her be," Duncan said, fastening his seatbelt. "But I want you to check the place a week from today. If it's clean, fine. If not, get rid of her."

"All right, then."

They drove for a few minutes. Duncan said, "Another thing. On this import-export matter coming up in the next few days, I'm concerned about our manpower. Especially if our Quebecois friends decide to come back for a more enthusiastic visit. How are you set?"

Cameron said, "Push comes to shove, bro, I think I can only rely on one or two members of the club. The rest are good for providing security or getting one-up in a bar brawl, but something like this ... I just don't know. Luke Munce did some time in the National Guard, he'd be good, but the rest would be a stretch."

He sped up the Pilot as they passed a logging truck heading to a mill down south. When Cameron re-entered the lane he gave a quick glance to his younger brother. "Of course, if I knew what was coming across, I could plan better."

"You'll find out soon enough."

"When?"

"Soon enough. So let's get back to personnel. Any suggestions?"

"Story in the *Union Leader* last week said the Washington County sheriff's department is cutting back on OT for the deputies. I suppose we could think about hiring a couple of the more desperate ones."

Duncan looked out on the road, passing yet another single family home or trailer, with an ATV or snowmobile in the front yard that was for sale. Lots of yard sales went on in this part of the county, for those who had no jobs or whose welfare benefits had run out. "That just might work."

"Bro, I was joking."

"Good on you," Duncan said. "I'm not."

————

Lunch was in a tiny strip mall in Turner where Karen Crowley had a hair salon, and a small office in the rear that handled the bookkeeping for his legitimate businesses. The other stores in the mall included a Citizens Bank branch, Turner Subs & Pizza, and an Ace Hardware store. Cameron went off to run some personal errands—"lucky for you, you have a wife to do the shopping and pick up prescriptions"— and Duncan walked into Karen's Cut & Curl.

His income stream was such that she didn't have to work, but she had made it clear, early on, that she wasn't going to be a stay-at-home wife. "Loved one," she had whispered into his ear one night, "I plan to be your kept woman for the rest of my wenchy life, but I'm going to be a kept woman who works and contributes to the household."

So after a couple of years of long drives to a UNH satellite campus about an hour south, she got her associate's degree in accounting and the skills to keep the books and do payroll. Since most of his businesses operated on a cash-only basis, her salon and the other interests allowed him a convenient way to launder funds.

Three other women worked with Karen, and he gave them all a cheery wave as he strolled in. Karen had on a white miniskirt, black pumps, and a tight black sweater. She took off her black salon coat and led him into the back office, where lunch waited: a steak and cheese sub for him, a large steak, cheese and mushroom sub for her, both delivered from Turner Subs & Pizza. Like about ninety percent of Italian pizza joints in the state, it was run by a Greek family, a mystery Duncan had never bothered to solve.

He sat down across from Karen and munched on his sub, drinking a Coke—he had tried Diet Coke once and instantly spat it out, thinking the foul stuff tasted like cold battery acid—and said, "So you get a large sub and I get a small one?"

She gently dabbed at a piece of cheese at one corner of her lip. "Part of your diet, love bug."

"You know I'm not overweight."

"Oh yes, your studly body is definitely not overweight, but your bad cholesterol is so high I'm surprised I don't hear your arteries clog at night. So eat up and be thankful I'm not giving you salad again."

The office was small, with no windows, the desk, two chairs, two filing cabinets, and a computer. "Okay, I'm thankful."

When they finished with lunch, she spent a few minutes going over spreadsheets for his convenience stores, his restaurant, and the gun shop, checking the cash flows and expenses. As she talked numbers she leaned over him. He enjoyed her scent and the gentle touch of her long red hair tickling his cheek.

"So there you go, hon," she said. "We're either on track or doing just a bit better than projections for this quarter, but there's bad news on the horizon."

"State going to vote in an income tax? Or sales tax?"

She rubbed the back of his neck as she tidied up the spreadsheets with her free hand. "Hon, the day that happens, mobs will burn down the capitol building in Concord, and there'll be a race on to see who could hang the most state reps. No, what's coming is going to be bad enough. Our Blue Cross and Blue Shield premiums are going up later this year."

"Damn," he said. "How much?"

"Our broker says sixteen, maybe eighteen percent."

"Double damn."

"Yes," she said, walking over to the filing cabinet in the office, bending over to put the spreadsheets away, exposing a lot of tanned, firmed legs. "But at least we're not in Massachusetts. You hear what happened down there? Blue Cross and Blue Shield of Massachusetts shit-canned their executive director after a couple of years of suckitude, and they gave him a firm handshake and fired his ass. Oh, by the way, they also sent him off with an eleven-million-dollar golden parachute."

"You've got to be kidding."

"Honey, after all these years, you're surprised? You know the Golden Rule: Them that has the gold, makes the rules. So insurance company premiums are going up all around the region, and some insurance guy who didn't do his job gets an eleven-million-dollar payout. God bless America."

She was still puttering around the open filing cabinet when he stood behind her. He put a hand on the small of her back and she said, "What's on your schedule for the rest of the day?"

"Little more work with Cameron. Then he and I have to go out later tonight. Business."

"Oh," she said, closing the file drawer, locking it up. "Just remember I'm off with the kids to my mom's tonight. Be back around nine. So you'll be a bachelor for at least a couple of hours. Lucky you."

He smiled at her. "Lucky me." Duncan touched her lips with his finger, then stepped back, locked the door leading out to the salon.

Karen rolled her eyes. "Sweetie, I've got Mrs. Blakely coming in for a trim and color in ten minutes."

He went to her, kissed her gently, then more forcefully, breathing in and tasting her, his right hand up under her short skirt. "If you're late, then you have my permission to comp her."

She kissed him back, softly sighed, "Hon, I don't need your permission for a damn thing."

His hand went up her smooth thighs, touching the lace of her thong underwear, gently pulled it away, as she moaned. His fingers probed and moved, and he was thrilled as always, to find her warm and wet and inviting for him.

She bit his ear, started to undo his belt. "You bad, bad boy," she whispered.

"Baddest boy you know," he whispered back, bringing up his fingers to taste her sweetness.

———

About forty-five minutes later and twenty miles northeast of Turner, his brother Cameron drove him down an unmarked dirt road until they came to a chain-link fence, posted with several No Trespassing signs. Cameron got out, unlocked the gate, and then came back to the Honda, drove a few yards, and went out again to lock the gate behind them.

The dirt road went on for a number of yards before turning into pavement. The paved road went up a slight incline, passing a faded wooden sign on three posts that announced Turner Overlook Estates with a phone number for a local Realtor office. Trees cleared away, revealing loam, dirt, and concrete foundations, as well as stakes with flapping orange flags. The foundations then blurred into half-built homes, and then two homes that were nearly complete. But those two homes weren't shingled and didn't have clapboards, only torn Tyvek coverings on the plywood walls. The road ended in a cul-de-sac and Cameron turned the Honda Pilot around and switched off the engine.

"Here we are," Cameron said. "Let's take a look."

Duncan joined him outside as they looked at the planned homes, which looked to total sixteen. Four were bare foundations, ten were half-built, with framework and plywood stanchions, and the nearest two were the most completed.

"Looks interesting," Duncan said. "Tell me what you've got."

Cameron said, "Got the idea from you, if you can believe it."

"I used to believe in Santa Claus and balanced federal budgets, so I guess I can do that."

Cameron laughed. "You know when we were up at Lake Palmer a couple of months ago, looking at those distressed vacation residences that had been set up for hunting and fishing? Including some Euro trash and Mexican millionaire or two? Couple of ex-congressmen? We even talked to a couple of 'em. Couldn't agree on a price, but I liked the remoteness of the properties, and how well they were built."

Duncan kept quiet. He remembered that trip very, very well, but for other reasons. Cameron pointed to the construction near them. "This development was designed as vacation homes for the rich and upcoming in Portland, Boston, and Burlington. But when crunch time came a couple of years back, the rich and upcoming become poor and struggling. The demand for vacation homes three or four hours away equaled the demand for men's ball waxing. There you go. Long story short, this place is owned by a Manhattan banking consortium that's doing its best to get rid of what they call toxic assets. Did some snooping around, bro, and this place is going to stay like this for two, three, maybe even four years."

"Sounds even better," Duncan said, feeling a warm affection for his tough-looking biker brother, whose rugged exterior hid an imaginative and inquisitive mind. He looked at the windswept hill, the tall pines, and along the far tree line, a red-tailed fox trotted along, pink tongue hanging out.

"So this is what I'm thinking," Cameron went on. "What we got going on with Chuckie and a couple of other farmers in the county is fine for now, but it's dangerous stuff. We've been lucky so far, but all it's gonna take is one pissed-off farmer's wife, or a teenage boy who's heard a rumor and is looking for a quick hit, or a curious State Police trooper who wants to do something spectacular for a promotion."

Cameron gestured to the homes. "Here we've got ten full foundations, enclosed and protected. With a little creative work, we could transfer our gardening activities here. Out of sight, out of mind, for at least a couple of years. Hell, with some judicious negotiation on your part, bro, you could probably buy the place for a tenth of what it was originally worth."

Duncan said, "Sounds attractive. But won't it take some work, getting the power set up here? Don't see any utility poles."

"You won't see any," his brother said. "This was going to be a high-class place for high-class people with high-class tastes. Can't have any unsightly utility poles, now, can we. So all the utilities are underground. With some creative work—maybe from Chuckie—we could tap into the nearest PSNH line without much problem."

Duncan looked around, saw the wind flapping the Tyvek covering on a couple of the near walls, the rotting plywood, the rebar still protruding out of the concrete. It gave him a chilled feeling, thinking about how many of these abandoned projects were scattered across the country, from wooded areas like this to the flat desert plains of Arizona to the outskirts of once powerful Detroit. How the hell did his America get to this place?

Off in the distance there was a dull roar that increased in volume as seconds passed. He and Cameron turned and Duncan said, "The west. Sounds like it's coming from the west."

A blur by the tree line and Duncan instinctively ducked as a dark green Air Force C-130 four-engine plane roared overhead, barely a hundred feet in altitude. The four propellers were a spinning blur as the aircraft rocketed over them and then disappeared beyond the far tree line.

"Christ," Cameron whispered.

Duncan said, "Training flight, I bet."

"What are they training for? Identifying trees and brush?"

"No, heard it from a guy who's in the Air Force reserves. Those aircraft are connected to Special Forces. They train to fly real low, hug the terrain. Supposedly this part of the state looks a lot like chunks of Afghanistan."

The sound finally went away. Cameron said, "Nice to see priorities are still getting funded. So, what do you think of my little proposal?"

Duncan smiled. "Damn it, Cameron, that's some fine planning, some fine thinking. Make it happen, all right?" He could tell his older brother was pleased with the praise. Duncan added, "Of course, it breaks my heart, thinking about those high-class people who won't be living here, who got stuck with the bills."

Cameron started back to the Pilot. "Don't know much about high-class people, but I know a lot of locals—plumbers, electricians, contractors—who got stuck when this development fell apart. They never got paid, and some of them are working as cashiers or clerks at Wal-Mart or Home Depot now, instead of owning their own businesses."

From where he stood, Duncan had a great view of the downside of the far slope, showing wooded areas, lakes, the scattered few buildings of Turner, and the near peaks of the northern White Mountains.

"What a darn beautiful country," Duncan said.

Cameron called out, "Yeah, but what a fucked-up nation."

———

Nearly an hour later, Cameron parked the Honda Pilot outside of the small one-story brick building that was the Turner Post Office. Turner's Main Street was just a couple hundred yards away from Karen's Cut & Curl, and Duncan smiled, thinking of his filling lunch and dessert. A good break in the day.

He folded his arms and looked across the street. A two-story brick office building, with a law firm taking up the entire second floor. Johnson & Carleton. Years ago, before he and Cameron were born, it was Crowley & Carleton. The ground floor of the building had a temp office agency, a satellite office from the New Hampshire Department of Health and Human Services, the Jade Dragon—a Chinese food restaurant—and a copy and print shop.

Years ago, as well, the whole block belonged to their parents. His leg throbbed, just below his right knee, where a titanium rod kept things in place. Some folks' injuries hurt in the morning, others gave notice when bad weather was approaching, and his leg always ached whenever he was across the street from where his family had once owned nearly half of downtown Turner.

The driver's-side door opened up and Cameron came in, smiling. A small USPS box was in his hand and Duncan said, "Everything in shape?"

"Super," Cameron said. "It's a new lens for my Meade telescope. The focal length and the—"

Duncan laughed, held up his hand. "For Christ's sake, Cameron, I don't understand all those details. Just tell me, what's it going to do for you?"

Cameron weighed the USPS box in his hand. "Some clear night, I'll come over and show you and the kids. Set it up with my Meade and its motor drive, with this lens, it'll look like you're flying over the mountains of the moon. Real good stuff, bro. Not as good as a video game, but it has the advantage of being real."

"Sounds like fun," Duncan said, looking again across the street. He recalled playing in the conference rooms up on the second floor, in his dad's law office, trying to climb the tall book cases with leather-bound law books. Doodling on long yellow pads with pens marked with the firm's name. The secretaries secretly passing over candy. The memories stirred something inside of him. His leg ached some more.

Cameron caught his eye. "Checking out the old family estate."

"Can't help it."

"I understand," Cameron said. He started up the Pilot. Duncan swiveled his head, saw there was no traffic coming.

The Honda stayed in park.

Cameron said, "Not a week goes by when I drive by there, bro, that I don't remember what happened."

"It was almost twenty years ago, Cameron. Forget it."

"Can't forget it, and you know it. I should have met with that son-of-bitch Caleb Carleton instead of you. You were too young. He could push you around, get drunk and mean, and deny he did anything screwy with Mom and Dad's wills. I should have been there. We had plans."

Duncan said, "Cam, just drop it, all right? Almost twenty years."

Cameron kept quiet. The Honda's engine was still idling. Duncan remembered the plans. He was going to go to UNH on a baseball scholarship and get something squared away after graduation.

Either make it up that steep ladder to the pros, or get a good career going with his business degree. With money coming in after getting out of school, it'd be Cameron's turn to go to college next, to study what always fascinated him: the night sky.

That plan was shot to pieces the night Mom and Dad died in a plane crash in Colorado. But other opportunities, as morbid as they were, presented themselves with their inheritance. But Dad's law partner, Caleb Carleton, said everything had been left to him and the firm. He and Cameron agreed one day to confront him, to demand what was theirs, but Cameron never showed up, and Duncan got into Carleton's Cadillac to continue the discussion, after the proverbial three-martini lunch.

Duncan put a finger on the box with the telescope lens. "My fault, too, Cameron. Let you down big time. I shouldn't have let Carleton drive off drunk with me next to him. When he wrapped the Cadillac around that maple tree and flew through the windshield … well, if I hadn't been with him, my leg would have been fine, and UNH would have still wanted me."

"Life does go places, now, don't it," Cameron said.

"It does, and there's still places it can go," Duncan said, raising an old topic. "I've said it a dozen times, if I've said it once. We're in a place where you could easily go back to school, get that degree, study astronomy and—"

"Duncan."

"Yeah?"

His biker brother sighed. "When I was maybe ten or eleven, there was a special-edition model being released, of the Saturn V rocket, complete with command and lunar module. Cost a bundle. At the time, I wanted it so bad for my birthday. But Mom said we couldn't afford it, so I didn't get it. Didn't get it that year, or the next. You know what? I could go on eBay and get it whenever I want. I got the money, for Christ's sake. But I won't do it. Fucking time has passed me by. So don't mention school again, all right?"

"Got it," Duncan said, looking away from his older brother.

Cameron shifted the Honda into drive and they went out onto Main Street.

ELEVEN

ZACH MORROW SLOWED DOWN as Route 115 wound around Gibson's Hill, offering a fine view of Turner, where he had spent the first eighteen years of his life. He pulled to the side, put the truck in park, looked off to the left. The town was as small as he recalled, two church spires rising up into the sky, the small brick and wood buildings clustered by the Bellamy River. Back inside of him were a collection of memories, a mix of good and bad, and he didn't feel like wasting his time dicking with them, deciding which ones to ponder over.

He shifted again and went out to Route 115, drove about a hundred yards more, when he stopped again. To the right was a metal sign in the shape of the state of New Hampshire, and in a Gothic script were the words: THE MONTGOMERY MORROW MEMORIAL HIGHWAY. The sign looked in pretty good shape. The last time he had seen a sign like this was nearly twenty years ago, the night before he left for Cape May in New Jersey for Coast Guard basic training. He had taken his dad's Lincoln—maybe it was thievery, maybe not—and had driven up here for a hard look at the sign, before pounding the Lincoln's accelerator and running the sign down.

Zach smiled at the memory. Damn road agent had done a pretty good job of installing the sign, and the first run-in had just knocked it over a bit. It had taken about five good tries before the sign was flattened, and along the way, he had dinged up the front bumper, fender, and the Lincoln's undercarriage pretty well. He had returned the Lincoln to the house, left the keys in the ignition, and hitchhiked his way south to Berlin, where he caught a Greyhound bus that eventually brought him to New Jersey.

Zach resumed the drive into town. This time, the sign would remain unmolested.

Besides, he was driving his own vehicle.

———

Zach spent about thirty minutes tooling around town, seeing only two new buildings, and a lot of the old buildings that were either empty or had been renewed into something else. Rexall Drugstore into a Family Dollar Store. Shawmut Bank into Citizens Bank. Turner Books & More into an empty storefront.

But a few places remained the same. One such place was the regional high school. School was in session and he drove by, noting that the damn building still looked like it did years ago. Near the front entrance was a handicapped spot, but when he had gone to school, that space was reserved for Duncan and his brother Cameron. Both rode Harleys once they had turned sixteen, and both called the nearest lot their own. Nobody dared take their space, even on days when they missed school. Cameron was a year older but due to a bout of illness early on in grammar school, he had lost a school season and attended the same classes as Duncan.

The school was two-story brick and stone, arched walkway out front, lots of exposed metal and stone, looking like its architect had mistakenly thought the 1970s was going to be the height of design and culture. "Death before disco," Zach muttered as he drove back into town, stopping at the town hall, a place that had remained quite the same for the past two hundred years.

He parked in front the small white building that looked like a church that had been plopped onto a tiny green lawn without its steeple. The steps were wooden and wide, and as he went through the tall, dark brown doors, he was struck by the scent of old papers and cardboard and ink. It was a familiar scent and he was surprised at how comforting it was.

Inside the floorboards creaked and he walked past a cork bulletin board with thumb-tacked flyers announcing a Ham & Bean Supper at the American Legion, new hours at the town dump, the hours of the registrar of the checklist, and a lost dog named Scooter. Ahead was a waist-high counter with a square wooden sign hanging announcing TOWN CLERK, and he was pleased at his luck. It was Nicole Martin, the town clerk when he had left Turner, and town clerk still.

She was heavyset, brunette, wearing a floral sweater with cat's eye glasses on a neck chain around her neck, sitting on a high padded stool. She smiled as he approached. "Well I'll be dipped in … it's Zachary Morrow, am I right?"

"That's right, Nicole," he said, stepping up, putting his hands on the polished wood counter. "You still embezzling funds from the taxpayers?"

"Hah," she said. "I should be so smart. Been a damn long time since I've seen your shadow around this place. How have you been?"

Lacking the time for a lengthy explanation, he said, "I'm doing all right."

She pursed her heavily lipsticked lips. "Sorry to hear about your dad."

"It is what it is," he said.

"Bah," she said, moving her padded stool closer to the counter. "Always hated that phrase. 'It is what it is.' When your dad is stuck in a rest home, his mind gone, feel free to tell me that it sucks."

He tapped his fingers on the counter. "Nicole, it is what it is."

She took that all right and said, "So, what can I do for this travelin' boy? Moving back to Turner? Want to register your car? Sign up to vote?"

He said, "I'm looking for someone I went to high school with. Duncan Crowley. Wondering where I might find him."

She nodded. "Sure. Our state's star baseball pitcher until he got in the car that day with one very nasty drunk Caleb Carleton. He lives in a nice little place up on Old Mill Road—you can tell it's his place 'cause it don't have no bathtubs or chickens in the front yard. But you won't find him there."

Zach smiled. "Are we playing twenty questions, Nicole, or are you going to show me some mercy?"

"Here's your mercy for the day. He owns the Flight Deck Bar & Grill, up near the Crowdin town line. Most days he's there about now, either having an early dinner or a late lunch. Go up there, you just might find him. Mind if I ask why you're looking him up?"

Zach turned from the counter. "Don't mind at all if you ask, Nicole."

As he walked to the door, she called out to him. "That's a good one, Zach. Didn't know if you knew this, but he's married now, with two kids. Ended up with Karen Delaney. You were sweet on her for a while, weren't you?"

Something warm and smooth seemed to roll around in his chest as he went out the door.

He knew what she had said but he went up Old Mill Road anyway, just for a quick look-see. The road was typical small-town New Hampshire: bumpy paved one lane, no yellow line down the center, drainage ditches on each side, old stone walls and new wire fencing strung along. There were a handful of small farms, two mobile homes with white picket fences bordering them, and as the road rose up, a dark-stained two-story home with a wraparound farmer's porch and an attached two-car garage. The driveway was empty. He was tempted to turn around in the driveway but decided that would be a dumb move.

Zach drove up about a half-mile, found a place to change direction in an abandoned family cemetery, and then slowly went back down the road, the house now on the right. Something sweet and sad ached within him as he saw the house, imagined Karen living in there, loving and cooking and laughing and raising her two children, being with Duncan.

Did she ever think about him? he wondered. Think about those few sweet moments, back in those days of supposed innocence in high school? When the two of them had shared the oldest story in the book, the late-spring romance filled with passion and fumbled kisses and one's very first physical joining with another? Lord knows he still thought about her, during so many long nights when he had been out there, in supposed harm's way, serving his country.

That was then. This was now.

He sped up and went down the hill.

Zach spent a few minutes in his parked truck, looking over the Flight Deck Bar & Grill. Originally it had been George Tasker's place—George having served aboard the *USS Enterprise* for a number of years—and since his death, it had changed hands a few times. At first it had started out as George's house, with a number of additions having been built on, and the joint looked like it hadn't changed much since Zach had left town. The lot was about half full, with a mix of motorcycles, pickup trucks, and some SUVs. The most popular color among the four-wheeled vehicles seemed to be rust or primer.

He went to one of his duffel bags, unzipped it. Inside was a number of weapons, from something that looked to be a ballpoint pen but which extended into a razor-sharp thin blade when properly pressed, all the way up to his collection of pistols, revolvers, a cut-down Mossberg 12-gauge pump-action shotgun and—just to wrap it up and show a bit of thanks to one's Israeli allies—a 9mm Uzi submachine gun. Semiautomatic, of course. Didn't want to be too blatant in dancing around gun control laws.

Zach pondered his little collection and then zippered it shut. He rummaged around in the other bag and pulled out his gifted cellphone from Tanya Gibbs, pressed the speakerphone button. There was an odd click as it found a dial tone, and after two rings, it was briskly answered.

"Gibbs."

"Tanya, this is your very special agent, Zach Morrow, double-ought nought. I'm ready to meet up with Duncan Crowley, find out what malfeasance he's up to. See if I can join in the fun."

Tanya was quiet for a moment, and she said in disbelief, "I told you to go in quiet and subtle, take your time. I only met with you yesterday!"

"Don't you worry about it, ma'am. I know what I'm doing. But I certainly can't guarantee it's going to be quiet or subtle. By the by, mind telling me what's in that shipping container?"

"Yes, I do mind. Very much."

"Is it a dirty bomb? VX gas? What is it?"

"Even with this encrypted line, I'm not telling you."

"My, you're certainly not being helpful today."

"Listen, Chief Morrow—"

"You also told me to call in once a day, or that our agreement is finished. You'll consider this a phone call, won't you?"

"Yes, but you can't—"

"Then I've completed my end of the bargain," Zach said. "Until tomorrow, ma'am."

He switched the phone off, thought about that slim pretty woman, down there in Boston. How she had come into his life and had given him a mission, as crazy as it was. As tiny and as attractive as she was, Zach thought she was the most dangerous woman he had ever met.

For she was a true believer.

Zach looked to his own disposable cellphone. Wondered if it was time to make that other call again.

Later, he thought, as he stepped out of the truck, unarmed, and went up to the Flight Deck.

———

He took a booth at the rear, checked the place out. Pool tables, three hi-def televisions hanging from the ceilings, no jukebox running but mixed sounds from the TVs, showing baseball, baseball, and a NASCAR race. On the walls were framed posters and photographs of Navy aircraft and warships. Despite the warning sign outside, four guys inside were wearing dungaree vests with the colors of the Washington County Motorcycle Club, which had been founded by the Crowley brothers. The four bikers stared at Zach as he came in, evaluating, checking him out, and when he just brushed by without a word or a glance, they went back to their pool game.

The waitress was a smiling teenager with short blond hair, and he ordered a basic cheeseburger with fries, cooked medium rare, with a Budweiser draft. As he waited for his meal, he looked around some more, and there, in the far corner, was Duncan Crowley. He was by himself, reading a newspaper—from this distance, it looked like the *Wall Street Journal*—and was picking at a salad. Duncan had aged well, with hair short and shoulders bulky. As he sipped his Budweiser, Zach kept on glancing at Duncan. He looked like a quiet guy, minding his own business, maybe an accountant or something. Definitely not some north woods criminal genius waiting to smuggle something over the border that got Homeland Security all up in arms.

The cheeseburger arrived and he was pleasantly surprised: it was a good size, juicy, hand-made, and one of the best he had ever eaten. He took his time eating and gauged the mood of the place. When he had snuck in here as a teenager and got his first beers years back, the place had seemed livelier. No hi-def TVs dangling, but loud music from the jukebox, people laughing, dancing. Oh, it wasn't paradise, but there was a sense of expectations, of possibilities, of getting out of school and finding a job at the mills or lumberyards or quarries. Working with your hands, making an adequate living, enough to own a piece of land, build a house, start a family.

Now? All of the big businesses in the county where someone with drive and strength could start a living were gone. What remained was small shops, welfare, food pantries, and living on the edge, where one bad snowstorm or one unpaid bill would mean disaster. In the pub there was an undercurrent of tension, as everyone seemed to stare at their drinks when the conversation dribbled off, wondering where it had all gone wrong. Decisions made in D.C., wars in the Middle East, trade agreements in Zurich, paper being passed from one financial institution to another in Manhattan ... all reverberated down to here, in this dingy pub, where people felt like the stars and planets were aligned against them, and they were probably right.

He finished his cheeseburger and fries, delicately wiped his fingers and lips. Now it was time to get to work.

———

Zach paid his bill, left a twenty-percent tip, and then ordered a pitcher of beer. He slowly worked his way through the pitcher, pouring it into his mug, and when he was sure he wasn't being watched, he'd open up a space between the wall and the seat cushion, finding a gap in the wood, and dumping most of it down there.

An hour passed with another pitcher, and then he got up and went to the bathroom at the rear. He was tempted to stop by the grill and thank the chef—a tall, scrawny man with a thin goatee and tattoos up and down both arms—but that would break his concentration. Zach worked his way back to his booth, stumbled, and bumped into one of the bikers just as he was making a shot.

The pool cue struck the cue ball off center, making it fly off the dingy green felt, clattering to the sawdust-covered floor. The biker, a guy in his thirties, whirled and said, "You stupid fuck, what the hell are you doing?"

Zach swayed. "Tryin' to get back to my place, asshole."

The biker took his pool cue, bumped the end into Zach's stomach. "Who you calling an asshole?"

Zach moved closer. "You feelin' okay?"

"Hunh?"

"I said, you feelin' okay? Tummy all right? Bathroom habits doin' fine?"

The man's three buddies laughed. He turned to them and laughed as well, and again poked the pool cue into Zach's stomach. "Jesus, how drunk are you, asshole? Why do you care how I'm feelin'?"

Zach said, "'Cause I'm about to check out your colon with your pool cue."

He moved snap quick, grabbed the pool cue from the guy's hands, flipped it up under the biker's chin. He grunted and fell back as Zach whacked him once, twice, and he fell back over more, going to the floor with an *oomph!* as he hit his back.

His three buddies moved in quick to back him up, but in the slow-motion focus of being in a fight, Zach knew their disadvantages: they were surprised, they hadn't trained to work as a group, and in coming at Zach all at once, they were crowding each other out, restricting their own movements.

While it only took seconds, it seemed to Zach that he was taking his time, going after one, the other, and then the third. The first got the cue across his nose, smashing it, causing him to howl. The second got the butt end of the cue thrust hard against his breastbone in three repeated motions, making him wheeze and bellow. The third was working a hand under his colors, coming out with a revolver—standard Smith & Wesson .38, it looked like—but with the now-bloody end of the pool cue. Zach smashed it from his hand. He yelled in pain, the revolver flew off into a corner as he grabbed his injured hand, and in a whirling motion Zach rapped the man against his kneecaps, collapsing him to the floor.

Zach wrapped things up quickly by nailing every one of the four bikers with the butt end of the pool cue to their foreheads, and he kicked the first one in the gut, causing him to bend over.

"Hey, remember I told you I was going to check out your colon with a pool cue?"

The guy moaned in reply. Zach nailed him in the balls with one more shot.

"Sorry," he said. "I lied."

Zach stood up, breathing hard, the pool cue slippery in his hands, and found himself looking into the working end of a double-barreled shotgun, the barrels cut down, just barely above legal. It was being carried by the cook, who slowly shook his head.

"Man, you sure move fast, but you can't move fast forever," the cook said. "So you better haul ass out of here 'fore the rest of the Washington County boys roll in."

Breathing hard, Zach said, "Damn, I thought I was just getting started."

The cook motioned with the shotgun. "Out. Now."

He looked over the cook's shoulder and caught Duncan's eye, gazing over the newspaper. Duncan's eyes seemed to seize Zach's look and he called out, "Bob?"

"Sir?" the cook called back, not moving, keeping the shotgun trained on Zach.

"It's all right," Duncan said. "Send him back here, will you?"

Another motion of the shotgun. "You heard the man. Go on back there. But leave the pool cue behind."

Zach found a napkin, wiped the pool cue clean, put it down on the pool table, and gingerly walked by the four fallen bikers as he made his way over to Duncan Crowley.

———

Duncan motioned him to sit, which he did, moving the chair around so that his back wasn't exposed. The four bikers got up slowly, muttering curses, looking over at him. He didn't flinch from their angry looks. One of them went to the corner of the pub, where he knelt down and picked up his revolver. Time seemed to slow down again, as Zach watched the hand, quickly wondered what the biker would do. But out of the corner of his right eye, Zach saw Duncan raise a hand, and that was that. The revolver went back under the T-shirt and vest, pool cues were picked up, and Zach was aware that people were talking and that his hands hurt.

Duncan looked at him quizzically. "I know you, don't I?"

"You should," Zach said. "In PE class I once beat your ass three times in a row in wrestling, back in high school."

Duncan smiled with enthusiasm. "I'll be darned. Zach ... Morrow? Right? Zach Morrow." He held out his hand and Zach gave him a hefty shake. Duncan said, "What have you been up to, besides taking on members of the local motorcycle enthusiasts?"

Zach said, "Right now, it looks like they're enthused to either shoot me or knife me when I go out in the parking lot."

Duncan said, "Oh, don't worry about that. It's all taken care of."

"Really? I'm impressed."

"Don't have to be," Duncan said, putting his *Wall Street Journal* aside. "Sometimes it's good for those fellows to get kicked down a notch. Otherwise, they get too arrogant, feel like they walk on water and own the joint. Since I own the joint, they play by my rules. Or they'll have to drive a half hour from here to find another place conducive to their drinking, pool playing, and hell-raising."

"You own the joint?" Zach asked. "Seem to remember you could throw the baseball a pretty fair distance back in the day, that you got a scholarship to UNH. How did that work out for you?"

Duncan gave a wry smile, extended his right leg, where he rapped the lower shin with his fist. "Bit of titanium stuck in there to keep things together. I was in a car accident just before I left for college, banged up my leg pretty badly. Even pitchers need two good legs to run on. So good-bye scholarship, good-bye college, back to Turner to find another path."

"Hope it wasn't too bad an accident."

"The guy driving went through the windshield, splattered his head against a two-hundred-year-old stone wall."

"Sorry to hear about that."

"Don't be," Duncan said. "He deserved it." He raised a hand, and the same waitress as before quickly came by. "Drink?"

"Sure," Zach said. "That'd be fine."

"Carol, whatever he's drinking, and just an ice water for me."

The drinks came to the table in under a minute, and after they both took a healthy swallow of their respective beverages, Duncan said, "What about you, Zach? What have you been doing since high school?"

"Joined the service, did some time, and now I'm on my own."

"Army? Marines?"

"Coast Guard," Zach said, wondering what kind of sneering remark was going to be tossed back at him, and was pleasantly surprised at what happened next.

Duncan looked impressed. "Really? Did you put in twenty years?"

"Close enough."

"What did you do? SAR?"

Zach shook his head. "No, not Search and Rescue. Obscure little unit, assisting in port and river security."

"Retired?"

"Out, but not on my own accord. Was forced out."

Duncan eyed him for a moment. "If you don't mind me asking, what happened?"

He took another sip from his Budweiser. "Kind of complicated, kind of classified. Let's just say I went on a mission with a clear and distinct set of orders, and along the way, exceeded my orders."

"Hell of a thing," Duncan said. "Any regrets?"

"Let's see, got a dishonorable discharge, loss of pension and benefits."

"Didn't answer the question."

"It'll do for now."

Duncan gingerly took another sip of water. Zach found it hard to wrap his mind around what Tanya Gibbs had told him about Duncan, about his illegal activities, about mobsters from Providence and Boston disappearing on this high school hero's watch, a mild looking guy who read the *Wall Street Journal* and ate a salad.

But Zach was also one for recognizing facts when they were slapped right in front of him. Like those four beaten and pissed-off bikers, who were now glumly playing pool instead of coming over here and trying to take him apart like a turkey on Thanksgiving Day. No, those large, hairy guys stood back with one hand motion on Duncan's behalf. That meant power, respect, and some serious mojo on Duncan's part.

Duncan said, "So what brings you back up to Turner?"

"When the government boned me, I decided to take a break, evaluate my options. But time and poor construction doesn't wait on options. I had a place down in Purmort. Came home yesterday to find the damn place burning down." He gestured to the front door. "Out in your parking lot is my truck with two duffel bags, containing my worldly possessions. I thought I'd come back to my home turf, poke around, see if I could do better."

"Where are you staying?"

"Don't know," Zach truthfully said. "I was thinking of the Golden Bough Motel, out on the Crowdin road."

Duncan shook his head. "Not your day for fires. Place burned down five, six years ago."

"The Blue Harbor then, is that still open?"

"Yes, but you shouldn't go there," Duncan said. "Pretty dirty place, some of the rooms rent by the hour, if you know what I mean. Hold on." He took a pen, scribbled something down on a paper napkin, slid it over to him. "There. Rogers' Bed and Breakfast. About the best place in the area. I'm sure they'll treat you right."

He took the napkin, folded it, put it in his pocket. "Sounds pricey."

"Mention my name, they'll take care of you," Duncan said.

"Appreciate that."

Zach finished off his beer and was planning on how to diplomatically remove himself from the table, when Duncan stared out across the room and the problem was solved for him. The door had opened to the pub and a bearded, long-haired man dressed in dungarees, gray turtleneck and the colors of the Washington County Motorcycle Club ambled in. Cameron Crowley, the older brother. Looks were exchanged and Duncan said, "Zach, it was fun to catch up but if you excuse me, I need to see my older brother for a second."

He quickly took the hint. Zach got up and after a quick shake, said, "Sorry for the blow-up earlier. Sometimes my temper gets the best of me."

"No worries."

"Thanks for the beer. You sure I can't pay for it?'

Duncan waved a hand. "On the house, to a fellow grad of good ol' Turner Regional High School. And I seem to recall that you kicked my butt in wrestling only twice, not three times."

Zach said, "If you say so, Duncan. See you around, all right?"

Duncan picked up his newspaper. "Absolutely. See you around."

Zach walked out of the pub, feeling the four sets of eyes watching him, and he wondered about Duncan and his hold on these guys as he went out into the parking lot. Without a weapon on him, he felt uneasy, and the back of his neck and hands tingled as he strolled across the dirt lot. But no one followed him, no one called out threats, no one ambushed him as he made his way back to his truck.

Which meant that Duncan was very secure, and very strong.

Something he couldn't afford to forget over the next several days, as he worked to take Duncan down.

Fellow grad or not, the man was his ticket to make everything right, and Zach intended to punch that ticket hard indeed.

TWELVE

TANYA GIBBS WAS HOME at her East Boston condo, resting and remembering. She was sitting on an outdoor deck, a checked red wool blanket around her legs, looking out at the lights of Boston and the parking lot beneath her. When she had first gone through this renovated mill building after being transferred to Boston, the realtor had tried to steer her to a unit that had a view of the harbor and Logan Airport.

The thought of looking out of her windows every morning and evening, seeing the place where American Airlines Flight 11 and United Flight 175 had left that fateful Tuesday morning... she had almost run out of the room in a panic. So instead of the harbor and airport view, she got a stirring view of a parking lot and the city of Boston.

Which was fine. She sipped from a hot cup of cider and crossed her legs underneath the blanket, thought she could see the lights of Simmons College. Untrue, of course, but the thought comforted her. That's where she had met Emily Harrison, who had been from Manhattan and had, as she had said, been exiled to an all-women's college in Boston by her alpha personality father. Unlike her roommate, Tanya had come from a small town in New Jersey, had been shy, and

117

hadn't liked big cities that much. But a laughing and confident Emily had taken her under her arm, brought her to nightspots throughout Boston, helped her navigate the tangled mess that was the MBTA, and had also taught her the fine art of passing over fake phone numbers to goofy male suitors.

After graduation, the friendship had continued, Tanya becoming a police officer in her own hometown, then entering the State Police and getting to Trenton, working as a sergeant for the New Jersey State Police Intelligence Services Section. For her part Emily started making oodles of money at Colby Consulting, the company that had been started by her father. Although Tanya had started off as a street cop, she found she enjoyed being behind the scenes, collecting bits of information on gangs or Mafia families, passing along intelligence reports upstairs to be evaluated and used by other State Police units.

She and Emily met for lunch every month or so in Manhattan, Emily sometimes taking her to the Windows of the World restaurant in the South Tower for a good long meal, and while Tanya was a good girl and never had a drink, Emily would stretch out a Long Island iced tea. Their next lunch, in fact, had been scheduled for the second Tuesday that September morning.

Then, like reliving a vivid clip of a horror movie, Tanya Gibbs recalls that Tuesday morning at her office in Trenton. She had just grabbed a second cup of coffee and was heading back to her cubicle to look over a statistical report for her section commander when she heard some voices coming from a nearby conference room. She walked in and joined a huddle of men and a couple of women, grouped around a television set in one corner, squatting on a high metal stand. Her first thought at seeing the footage was that her State Police co-workers were watching a thriller movie, something with Bruce Willis or Arnold Schwarzenegger. Smoke and flames were licking up and out of one of the World Trade Center towers. Damn good special effects, she thought, thinking maybe a couple of the guys in the room had worked a security detail when the movie was made, and that they were watching a sneak preview.

One of the women, an admin aide from across the floor, suddenly bolted out, tears in her eyes, "Oh Christ, I hope John was late to work this morning. Oh Christ."

Tanya's hands were empty. She didn't remember dropping the coffee cup. She went up to a State Police captain she knew, a gruff Irishman named Callaghan. "What's going on?"

He didn't turn away from the television screen. Tanya noted with a cold stillness in her heart that the news crawl on the bottom of the screen said, LIVE COVERAGE OF WORLD TRADE CENTER DISASTER.

Callaghan said, "Looks like a private plane crashed into the North Tower. That's what we're hearing."

Tanya thought, South Tower. Emily's in the South Tower. She'll be okay. She's in the South Tower.

From one of the men near the television: "Must be the dumbest pilot in the world. Visibility is perfect."

"Maybe the son-of-a-bitch had a heart attack. Like that lame Charlton Heston movie, sequel to *Airport*. Guy in a private plane had a heart attack, crashed into a 747."

"Bullshit," another voice said. "Looks fucking deliberate."

"What about that B-25 bomber, crashed into the Empire State Building back in 1945?" somebody demanded. "That was an accident."

Callaghan was chewing on his lower lip. "Sure it was. In the middle of a fucking fog bank."

Tanya was now at her desk. She didn't know how she had gotten there. She picked up her office phone, was going to dial Emily's number, and—

119

Drew a blank. She couldn't remember Emily's number. Damn it! It was like one of those horrible dreams when you have to call the police, and you can't find the phone, then you find the phone, and it won't work, and when it does work, 911 goes to a busy signal and—

She threw a desk drawer open, fumbled through pencils, paper clips, pay receipt stubs, and candy bar wrappers, until she found one of Emily's business cards. She picked it up and then put it on her desk. Her hand was shaking. She dialed the number, and when she got Colby Consulting, she punched in Emily's three-digit extension.

It rang.

It rang.

It rang some more.

Tanya was about to hang up and try Emily's cellphone when it was picked up. "Colby Consulting, Harrison," a familiar, breathless voice answered.

Tanya sunk against her chair, almost burst into tears. "Emily! Sweet Christ, girl, what are you doing there? Get out!"

Emily said, "Hey, it's okay. Something happened over at the next tower. Looks like a plane crashed into it. We're fine, but I think we're going to have to reschedule lunch, Tanya."

"I don't care how fine you are, get your ass out of there!"

Emily chuckled. "Stop talking about my big ass. Besides, word's just come over the PA system. Something about Building One being in a state of emergency, but we're fine and to stay at work. Guess they don't want us to get run over by fire trucks or something. So the boss just led us all back to our desks."

Tanya raised her voice. "Emily, leave! Stop talking, just leave!"

From over the phone, she heard distant yells, screams, and Emily said, "Hold on, looks like—"

The phone went dead. She heard shouts and gasps from the conference room. She ran back, pushing aside the other men and women, and up on the screen, she saw a blossom of flame and smoke erupt out of the South Tower.

"Saw it," Callaghan whispered. "Fucking saw it live. It was a goddamn airliner, it was. No fucking private planes. Fucking hijacked airliners. We're under attack."

Phones were harshly ringing, strained voices were rising from the other cubicles, a few shouts from guys racing down the corridor. Tanya went back to her desk. Dialed and re-dialed the Colby Consulting number. No answer. Just rang and rang and rang. Same with Emily's cellphone. Went straight to voicemail. Tanya took a deep breath, and then another. "Emily, it's Tanya. You get out of there now. You hear me, girl? Get the hell out of there now!"

Through the next confusing hour, she kept on dialing and re-dialing Emily's cellphone, as her own phone rang with information requests, reports on latest terrorist threats, and even one sobbing man, mistakenly connected with Tanya, looking for his wife, who worked for the Port Authority. Their building went into lockdown, sirens echoed from the parking lot, and word was spread that the State Police were setting up a Forward Command Post at Liberty Park in Jersey City.

She was trying to prepare for an emergency 10 a.m. status meeting when her cellphone rang. She glanced down at the phone and froze when she saw the incoming number: it was Emily's.

By now the office area was so noisy that she got on her knees, underneath her desk, pressing the phone against her ear. "Emily? Is that you? Emily?"

A burst of static. "… help us …"

"Emily? What is it? Where are you?"

She pushed the cellphone against her right ear, pressed her left hand hard against the other one, hoping to block out the noise from the office area. "Tanya? We're on floor one-oh-four ... ten or eleven of us ... help ..."

"Emily, can you get to a stairway? Or to the roof?"

Two men were standing next to her cubicle, loudly arguing over how best to get off-duty State Troopers recalled and where they should go. Tanya wanted to stand up and scream at them to *shut the fuck up!* But she was afraid of missing what her friend was going to say next.

Coughing, choking. Static. "... somebody broke one of the windows with a chair ... we can't breathe ... Tanya, help us, God, help us ..."

She was clenching the cellphone so hard she thought the plastic case would break. "I'll make sure you get rescued, hon. I won't let you down."

"....so fucking hot, Tanya ... smoke so thick ... helicopter ... can you get a helicopter to rescue us ... oh God, Tanya, I'm so scared ..."

She started crawling out from underneath her desk. "I'll do it, Emily. I'll do it. Hang in there, Emily, you stay there and I'll get you saved."

"... so fucking hot ... God, the fire, the fire!"

The cellphone cut off.

Tanya got up on her desk, started flipping through her Rolodex, frantically looking through the card, until she got to the one marking the Aviation Unit.

The line was busy.

Damn it to fucking hell!

She tried again.

Still busy.

Tanya pulled out a State Police directory, started working through the listings, dialing number after number, and—

"Ramsay, Aviation."

She nearly fainted at her desk. "This is Sergeant Tanya Gibbs, Intelligence Services Section. I need to get a helicopter up to the World Trade Center, South Tower. There are civilians trapped on floor one-oh-four."

"Shit, Sarge, what the fuck do you think we can do?"

"Who the hell is this?"

"Don Ramsay. I'm a goddamn mechanic and everything's already up in the air."

"I don't care. Get word to somebody." Her voice started rising and she couldn't help herself. "We've got people trapped on floor one-oh-four."

"What the hell do you expect them to do? Drop a rope or something? There's no way we could get a chopper close enough!"

"I don't fucking care!" Tanya dimly realized that people in the office were looking her way. "Get a hold of somebody up there or I'll get your ass fired!"

There was a muffled gasp and groans on the other side of the offices, and Tanya said, "Do you fucking hear me? Do you? I want a helicopter sent to the South Tower, floor one-oh-four, or—"

Somebody reached past her, pushed down the handset. The phone was disconnected. She whirled and Callaghan was there, his face pale. He gently took the phone from Tanya's hand and put it down. She said, "What the hell do you think you're doing?"

Callaghan didn't say a word. He just took her elbow and brought her to the conference room, where the television was still on. The room was filled with State Police officers, men and women both, and all were silent, staring at the television. One of the World Trade Center towers was still burning furiously. But something was wrong. Something was wrong. Where the other tower stood, there was only a thick plume of smoke and debris.

Callaghan said, "Tanya, I'm sorry. There's no more South Tower."

Ah, yes. No more tower, and a while later, no more World Trade Center. Then just over a year later, when she told her section chief that she was leaving her career at the New Jersey State Police to join a new organization called Homeland Security, he said, "Just one question, Sergeant. What do you think you can do there?"

Without hesitation, Tanya said, "I lost my best friend on 9/11. Straight up, I want revenge."

Her section chief pursed his thin lips. "That's a big order. A lot of other people are doing what you want to do. Special Forces, CIA, NSA, the entire armed forces of the United States. What makes you think you can do any better?"

She shook her head. "You don't understand. I don't want revenge against terrorists. I want revenge against the bureaucrats, the intelligence officers, the politicians, and everybody else who ignored the signs before 9/11. The ones who were too PC, too afraid to make waves, too fat and lazy. I want to make sure I'm there to make a stink when we get word another attack might be coming. Next month, next year, or next decade, you know we'll get hit again."

Her boss smiled, nodded. "Sounds good to me, Tanya. Sorry to lose you but good luck and raise hell."

Tanya sighed, sipped at her now cold cup of cider, looking at the bright and peaceful lights of Boston. Lots of long years in Homeland Security, slowly climbing the ladder, biding her time, up until a few weeks ago, when word accidentally came to her of a suspicious trailer bearing deadly cargo. A trailer that had disappeared.

Now her time had come. Now it was time to raise hell.

THIRTEEN

In the rear parking lot of the Slinky Pussy Gentleman's Club, Michael Grondin, second in command of the Iron Steeds Motorcycle Club, leaned into the open passenger's-side window of the GM Savana cargo van to brief the two men one more time. Louis Fontaine, the one closest to Michael, nodded at all the right places while he hoped his dopey partner and driver, Jean-Paul, didn't say or do anything to piss off Michael.

"So remember," Michael said to Louis. "Nothing fancy, nothing too clever. Okay? You find Duncan Crowley, you tune him up, you get the information we need about the cargo container and where it's going. Once you get what we need, waste him. But for God's sake, don't you fucking waste him until you're certain you got what we need. Otherwise I'll have to explain to Francois why you two screwed up. He's gonna want to know what I did to make sure it didn't happen again, and I'll show him both your heads in a shopping bag. Separated from your fucking necks, you understand."

Louis said, "Absolutely, I understand, Michael."

"Glad to hear it. Jean-Paul, you understand?"

Jean-Paul was in his early twenties, with thick, wavy black hair and a moustache that looked like it had been started only a few days ago. Louis couldn't understand how he was a member of the club. He had to have pull with somebody, either the old timers or guys higher up who had influence, otherwise Louis thought Jean-Paul would be challenging his skills by polishing the chrome work on the club's bikes. But no, here he was, the designated driver for their little mission south to upstate New Hampshire.

Jean-Paul said, "Oh, yeah, Michael, I've got it covered. No problem."

Michael grunted. "If I had a goddamn loonie for every time one of you characters said no problem, I could afford to go to Orlando three times a year, instead of two. Jean-Paul, you got the directions and descriptions?"

From the center console, Jean-Paul pulled out a BlackBerry. "All here, Michael. I promise, we won't get lost."

Michael said, "Just make sure you don't. Remember, no dicking around, no unnecessary stops. Francois is counting on you both. Get the job done and you'll be happy with the rewards you'll get. Now, any questions?"

Louis kept his goddamn mouth shut, and was hoping his companion would do the same. Over the years of riding with the Iron Steeds, he had done stuff from guarding crystal meth labs or escorting Oxycontin deliveries, to breaking a guy's leg or arm when he got behind in weekly payments, and occasionally providing rough justice and discipline to the younger members when required.

But this? This was the first time he was being sent out on a zap mission, and although the objectives were clear, and their firearms—Chinese-made SKS 7.62mm assault rifles with cut-down barrels and folding parachute stocks—were carefully hidden away in the van, Louis was so nervous that it felt like his bladder was about to burst. First, he had never gone in cold-blooded on a zap mission, and second, sure, the rewards would be great—like choosing any one of the girls in the club to have for a month—but the price for fucking up was too serious to think about.

So no questions to Monsieur Grondin, he thought. Let's just get the hell on our way.

But no, no luck for him tonight, for Jean-Paul grinned once more. "I see this Duncan guy has a wife, two kids. What's the thought about collateral damage?" There was now a dreamy tone to Jean-Paul's voice that creeped out Louis.

Michael said, "Waste 'em all, Francois doesn't care, but by God, you'd better have that container information squared away before you do that."

"I see, I see, I get that," Jean-Paul said, "but if there's an opportunity to … play around some, before the family gets zapped, will that be all right?"

Even that caused Michael to grimace. He slapped one hand on the open window frame and said, "Get going, you two jerks. You've got a long drive ahead of you. But push to get to the border as soon as you can. Francois wants this wrapped up as soon as possible, so no wasting time, no dilly-dallying, don't get lost. All right?"

Michael stepped back and Jean-Paul switched on the engine, and in just a handful of moments, they were in traffic, heading south. Louis kept his mouth shut for a bit and then he couldn't stand it.

"Look, back there, what the hell did you mean about playing around with the family? Were you serious?"

"'Course I was serious. Why the hell not? If they're going to get greased, what difference does it make if we play around some with them before we get it done?"

Louis folded his arms. "Speak for yourself, Jean-Paul. I'm not interested. Christ, who are you interested in? The wife? The kids?"

Again, that creepy dreamy state of Jean-Paul's voice. "If the opportunity is there, why limit yourself?"

With disgust in his voice, Louis said, "Christ, I'm glad there wasn't a family dog listed there in our briefing."

Jean-Paul said, "What do you have against dogs?"

"Shut up and drive."

FOURTEEN

As they drove to their last project of the day, Duncan said to Cameron, "Sometime tomorrow, I need for you to get some information. You saw the guy I was talking to, before you left the bar?"

"The guy who fucked over Bobby, Jimmy, Luke, and his brother Larry?"

Duncan came to a complete halt at a stop sign, looked to the left and the right, and then resumed driving after slowly turning right. They were in his maroon Chevy Colorado pickup, and their tools for the evening were on the spare seat in the rear.

"That's him," Duncan said. It was just after eight p.m. He said, "His name is Zach Morrow. You and I went to high school with him."

Cameron stroked his beard. "Zach Morrow ... seem to recall a guy named Zach waxing your ass during three or four wrestling matches, our senior year, in phys ed class. Thought he looked familiar."

"Stop exaggerating, Cam. It was only twice, and I should know. It was my ass he was slamming around on the wrestling mats. So, what I want from you is a background check, as good as your sources can quickly provide."

From inside his dungaree vest, Cameron took out a soiled and creased pocket-sized notebook. With pen in hand, he said, "Go."

"Zach Morrow. Resident of our fair town until graduation. Then joined the US Coast Guard. From what he told me, he was assigned to specialized unit dealing with security. Obviously well-trained, considering what he did to your four boy-o's."

Cameron scribbled some more. "Anything else?"

"Yeah. He says he was dishonorably discharged, but was vague on what happened. So see what you can find out. And second … he said he's looking for a job around here, ever since his home caught fire, down in Purmort."

"House burning down, that'll be the easiest to check. But why the background check? What you figuring?"

Up ahead a light green Volvo with Vermont license plates and bearing a bumper sticker that said VISUALIZE WORLD PEACE was ambling along, well below the forty-mile-an-hour speed limit. Duncan slowed down and noted the double-yellow line. No passing.

"What I'm figuring is two things. You're a smart brother, Cameron. See if you can't guess one of them."

Cameron closed up his notebook, returned it to his vest. "What you said earlier today. About getting more personnel. You must be thinking about Zach."

"Why not?" Duncan said. "He's from around here, he's got experience. You should have seen how he dealt with our four buds before you arrived. He didn't hesitate for a second. He went at them like a starving tiger racing through a vegan convention. No mercy, no doubt, just raw skills, like he couldn't wait to kick the crap out of them. But he was cool about it, you know? When he came over a couple of minutes later to talk to me, *click*, it was like he changed the damn channel. He focused on our conversation, wasn't boastful or full of himself. Very impressive."

His brother stuck his hands in his vest. "The other thing. I think I know what that is, too."

"Go on." The Volvo up ahead was still traveling along at its own sweet speed, which was still ten miles below the posted speed limit.

"You said earlier that you thought you were being watched. Nothing specific, nothing to do with our barbarian friends to the north, but still being watched, just the same. Right? Funny thing, a day later, who pops out of nowhere but a guy we went to high school with. Who's got some skills in the black arts. Who shows up at the Flight Deck pub, which you own. Hell of a coincidence."

"Yeah, you're right."

"So what are you thinking?"

Duncan peered ahead, looking for the double-yellow line to break into a passing zone, but no such luck. "I'm thinking you do your due diligence on our friend Zach. If he comes back with no issues, no problems, well, maybe we'll see if he'd like to join our employ."

"If I come back with anything hinky?"

"Still room at Walker Quarry?"

"Christ, yes. Understand he's driving a shit-ass pickup truck?"

"Yeah."

"Piece of cake. Truck gets dumped somewhere else, he can end up in the quarry. Bing, bang, boom, done."

"Sounds good."

The Volvo's brake lights flickered once, twice, and then the car resumed its slow speed as the narrow road curved its way past forests and farmland. Duncan tapped his fingers on the steering wheel. It was getting late. He said to his brother, "So what are you thinking, bro?"

Cameron gestured to the Volvo. "I'm visualizing a fucking rocket launcher, that's what I'm thinking."

———

Eventually the Volvo got on Route 117, making its way west back to the People's Republic of Vermont before the occupants would be forced to buy a handgun or tax-free booze or something. Duncan got his truck back up to the speed limit, but never ever over the limit, especially when engaged in a bit of night work. He was proud of Cameron and his intelligence sources. It was amazing what he got his fingers into, but it made sense, once you thought about it. The Washington County Motorcycle Club's members included guys and gals from all types of work and backgrounds, and they had friends, or friends of friends, all who could offer some bits of info if the money was right.

They made their way onto Town Road 12, a dirt lane that rose high up in the hills. Duncan checked the last three digits of his odometer—six-one-two—and pulled over after advancing only about five or so yards, far enough so they couldn't be seen from the paved road they had just left.

Duncan said, "You sure Gus Spooner's here tonight?"

"Yeah. Made a phone call to his girlfriend. Made myself sound all mysterious and shit, about delivering chemicals and test tubes and Bunsen burners. She gave him up after about one minute. She'd go far in the CIA, don't you think?"

"Maybe. You know, I'm in a pretty good frame of mind tonight. Let's do the psycho brother set, and if you want, you can be the bad psycho."

"I was bad psycho last time."

"Yeah, but I thought you'd like being bad psycho."

"Most times, but shit, I'd like to mix it up some, all right?'

Duncan said, "Hey, like I said. I'm in a pretty good frame of mind. I'll be bad psycho." Cameron smirked and Duncan said, "What's so darn funny?"

"Some would say that wouldn't be much of a stretch."

"That's hilarious," Duncan said. He switched on the overhead light and reached behind the driver's seat for the gear. "Before we wrap up tonight, I want their names and addresses—the people who told you it wouldn't be a stretch for me to be bad psycho."

Cameron stared at him. "Bro, are you serious?"

It was Duncan's turn to laugh. "Heck, no, Cam. I was just getting into character."

———

He resumed driving with the truck lights off, being able to see through the night with the aid of a Yukon Night Vision 1x24 Monocular device—available on Amazon for just $319.97—situated on his head. His brother had an identical device, and they both kept eye on the road and the dashboard. The night was illuminated with a ghostly green-gray glow, but it allowed them to drive up the road without giving away their presence. Oh, whoever was in the nearby cabins would *hear* them approach, but wouldn't *see* them approach. Most people involved in something illegal panic when they see something; sound was just sound.

Duncan focused on the road, once seeing a raccoon waddle across, and then Cameron called out, "You're at six-seventeen on the odometer, bro."

"Thanks." He pulled over as best as he could, looked out the window, saw a wooden sign to the left nailed to a birch tree that said WILLIAMS. He and Cameron opened the doors—the overhead light having earlier been switched off—and both got dressed in rural battle-rattle gear: bulletproof Kevlar vests, utility belts with knives, pepper spray, and plastic flex cuffs, and holstered to their sides as well were their choice of semiauto pistols. Duncan went with 9mm

Beretta Model 92, while his brother made do with a 9mm Glock 17. Slung over their chests were matching H&K MP5 semiautomatic 9mm rifles, with banana-shaped magazines. Both also carried small black hard plastic carrying cases in their right hands.

Night-vision gear still on their heads, they slowly walked up the dirt and gravel driveway. Birds cried out in the darkness, and there was the constant buzz of insects. They both stayed quiet, walking up to the target house. Their boots crunched on the road, as if they were walking on peanut shells. On either side were trees, low brush, and saplings.

Duncan whispered, "Home in view."

"Christ, tell me something I don't know," Cameron whispered back. "Can't you smell the damn thing?"

The breeze shifted and Duncan noted it, sharp and stinking, the lip-curling stench of sulfur, and pretty much the best sign that someone up ahead was cooking meth. Before them was a chalet-style one-story house, triangular in shape, supported by round concrete columns. As promised, the front porch was sagging and about ready to collapse on the front dirt lawn. Pulled up to the chalet were a Volkswagen Golf and a two-door Toyota Tacoma pickup truck.

Cameron silently went to both vehicles and with quick work of his folding Hunter knife, took care of eight tires. There was a hissing of air as the vehicles settled to the ground.

Duncan knelt down, opened his black case, removing an Optix 2000 high-powered Xenon spotlight, which sent out enough candlepower to signal the space station by Morse code. Cameron had the same spotlight model, and both of them removed their night-vision goggles. Cameron went to the rear of the chalet as Duncan went up to the front porch, quickly aiming the switched-on light through the floor-to-ceiling windows. The sudden flash of light put everything in sharp focus, the rotting wood, the dirty windows, the shapes moving suddenly from within.

Duncan went through the front door and Cameron broke through the rear, spotlight in his hands, and both of them shouted, "Down, down, down! Hands on your head, hands on your head, hands on your head!"

Inside the stench of the sulfur was even stronger. Duncan took in the crowded first floor of the chalet. Three guys on the floor, hands folded on the back of their heads, stoves and beakers and boxes of chemicals. He and his brother quickly flex-cuffed all three of the young men, dragging them outside as they yelled and shouted and squirmed. Duncan ignored the protests and struggles as he and Cameron got them out of the chalet and onto the dirt. Duncan went to the guys and gave each a quick kick to the ribs, and pressed the working end of the H&K MP5 submachine gun to the base of their necks.

"Stay still, keep your mouth shut, or you die here, right now," Duncan growled, trying to put movie-style menace into his voice.

He looked around the area. Besides the VW and the pickup truck, looking sad with their flat tires, there was a picnic table, a couple of lawn chairs, and a woodpile. In a jumble at the bottom of the woodpile were a collection of tools, including ice picks, saws, shovels, and hammers.

Cameron knelt down, grabbed each guy by the back of his hair, pulled up his head. When he got to the third guy, he said, "Gus, old boy, so sad to see you here."

Duncan got the other two guys to their feet as Cameron pushed Gus back against the pickup truck. All three were in their mid-twenties, wearing baggy pants, sweatshirts, sneakers, with bad skin and poor facial hair. The two guys on the left stood quiet, legs trembling, as Duncan made a public motion of unslinging his semiautomatic rifle and working the action, making a very satisfying *snick-snack* sound.

All Hollywood bullshit, of course—nobody with any brains ever went into a hot zone like this without all weapons fully chambered, which is why their pistols were—but he and his brother were playing roles tonight.

Again, keeping his voice low, Duncan said, "Why waste the time? Let's hose these three assholes and get on our way."

He lowered the H&K and the two guys to the left started crying, begging, sniffling, but Gus seemed to be keeping his cool. Not bad for a panty-sniffer.

Cameron said, "Hey, bro, let's be cool, all right? I'm sure these two guys were just along for the ride, am I right? They don't deserve to get whacked."

One of the guys dropped to his knees, begging some more, but Duncan tuned out the pleas. He was still looking at Gus Spooner, who looked defiant, standing up against the disabled pickup truck in front of the busted-in chalet.

Duncan said, "You mean, they didn't know the rules of the road? I find that hard to believe. They look ... well, I was going to say they looked pretty bright, but no, they look as dumb as a bag of hammers. Still, even as stupid as they are, I can't believe they didn't know the rules about crystal meth in this county."

Cameron strolled over to his younger brother. "Maybe so, but hey, shouldn't we show them mercy? I mean, if they were stupid, they shouldn't be punished. Much."

Duncan shook his head. "Cripes, I don't know ..."

The one kneeling on the ground yelled out, "Rules? We didn't know anything about any rules? Please ... tell us ... we didn't fucking know!"

Duncan cackled. "Okay. Here's the rules. We're the Crowley brothers. We don't care if you steal from the town, or steal from your mom, or steal from the food pantry. We also don't care if you deal in grass or sell booze to teenage girls or boys or anything like that. But crystal meth … nobody here sells it, deals it, or even thinks of cooking it around here."

Gus spat on the ground. "Why?"

The guy who wasn't kneeling, who had a wisp of a goatee, said in a strangled voice, "Gus, are you so fucking stupid? Leave it alone!"

Gus looked at his friends. "Fuck, no. This is private property, up in the woods. Why should you give a shit what we're doing here?"

Cameron said, "It's enough for us to say no, dipshit."

Duncan went up to Gus, put the H&K barrel against his stomach. "Let me tell you, then, Gus, what the deal is, just to expand on what my brother said. You may find this odd, but we and the law enforcement community agree on one thing: crystal meth is pure poison. People using crystal meth get so wired and strung out that they'd sell their pre-teen daughters to whoredom for another hit, or shoot up a village store to get to the cash register. When law enforcement finds out about people making and dealing crystal meth, they come down like the wrath of God upon anyone and everyone who's dealing with it. My brother and I, we want local law enforcement to worry about speeding tickets and game laws. Not meth. 'Cause if they spread a big enough net to look for meth, they may take a good look at us in the process. Have I made myself clear?"

Gus's two friends betrayed him like the Italians did to the Nazis in 1944, nodded and said yes, no problem, we didn't know about the rules, we'll never do this again, you can count on us.

But Gus was proving to be a hard case. Cameron said, "Gus, care to say anything?"

"You got me this one night, I'll give you that," he said sourly. "But you can make tons of money with just a little effort and cold medicine. So maybe I'll start up again. Why the fuck not? Who elected you kings of the county?"

Cameron said, "Maybe we'll light off the chemicals in that dump, burn it to the ground. Local fire department will see what's left in there and let the State Police in on your little secret."

"Fuck," Gus said, "go ahead. My dad, he hasn't been up here in years, it's a piece of shit. He keeps on saying he'll come up and renovate the place, winterize it, so we can have nice family memories one of these days. So burn it. Hell, I'll even help you. Nobody will be able to connect this to me, unless you rat me out. And I hear the Crowley brothers aren't rats."

Duncan laughed. "Bro, Mr. Spooner is proving to be one tough little son-of-a-gun, isn't he?"

Cameron said, "Surely is."

He put the H&K against the side of Gus's head. "Why not splatter what passes for brains here against the truck and call it a night?"

Gus winced. "You got two witnesses, that's why."

"Not if I pull the trigger a few more times."

More shouts, demands, yells from the other two men. With defiance, Gus said, "You can't do this to me. My dad is chief selectmen in Crowdin. If we get killed or get disappeared, he'll have the State Police come in and investigate. They dig deep enough, your names will come up. So I'm protected."

"Gee, I guess you are protected from being murdered," Duncan said. "You're one lucky, lucky boy." Duncan started laughing, harder and harder, and Gus's two former friends sidled away, like they wanted to be far away from whatever was going to happen next.

Duncan suddenly stopped laughing. "Cam, my dear brother, will you do me the distinct honor and favor of freeing Mr. Spooner from his bonds?"

Cameron stepped forward, snapped open his folding knife, and spun Gus around. With one quick flash of his hand, the plastic flex cuffs were cut free. Gus rubbed at his wrists and Duncan went up to him, hammered the stock end of the H&K against his crotch. Gus howled and fell to his knees.

Duncan went over to the woodpile, rummaged around in the tools, found what he could use. He slung the H&K over his shoulder, grabbed Gus's hair, dragged him kicking and wrestling over to the picnic table. He struggled and tried to fight back, but Duncan kept his grip firm on the young man's greasy hair.

At the picnic table, he made sure Gus was sitting up, his back against the near bench. Duncan said, "Which hand do you use to jerk off?"

"What? Hunh? The fuck you asking me?"

Duncan pulled the hair tighter. "Listen carefully. The hand you use to jerk off, spank the monkey, choke the chicken. When you take your sweet chubby girlfriend out for a wild night of McDonald's cheeseburgers followed by a rental DVD of the latest Adam Sandler opus, and all you get out of it is some deep kissing and boobie fondling, what do you do when you're left high and dry? Which hand do you use, Gus?"

"My ... my right ... I'm right handed."

Duncan did it all quickly, so Gus wouldn't resist, so his two friends would be even more impressed on how their night of amateur pharmaceutical development was turning out. He flattened out Gus's left hand, put a long nail on the top of the hand, and with one hard and swift motion, pounded the nail through his hand with a small hammer.

Gus screamed and screamed, his voice as high-pitched as a girl. Duncan stepped away. Of the other two guys, one was leaning back against the VW, like he was afraid he was going to faint, and the other was bent over at his waist, vomiting into the dirt. Gus's screams started to fade away, as he panted and gulped and panted, his other hand gingerly touching its wounded companion.

Duncan knelt down, grabbed Gus by the chin. "Maybe you're right. Maybe you are protected from being killed in this county. But that's one get-out-of-stupidity-free card that can only be used for that one thing—sudden death—which leaves lots of possibilities. Like being a live model for the local production of *Jesus Christ Superstar*. Am I now getting through to you, Gus? Am I? Hell, I even was nice to you, letting you keep your right hand in one piece."

Gus was sobbing, nodding, writhing against Duncan's touch. Duncan said, "Now, just so we're clear on what you've agreed to do, you're going to leave meth making to any place else in the world that's not Washington County. Right?"

Another nod. Duncan said, "Tsk, tsk, Gus. I may not require a notarized statement, but I do require some words. So give me the words. You've got two feet and one more hand available."

"Please … please don't hurt me anymore … I promise … no more meth making … nothing …"

Duncan turned his head to the cabin. "That's delightful. So I'm going to ask one more favor. All right?"

More nods, more snorting sobs. "Yes … anything you want … anything …"

"You and your buds. Clean that cabin out. It's an insult to your dad, an insult to the woods. Be careful, too, that stuff inside there can burn from just a spark. Miracle it hasn't blown you up already."

Duncan got up, motioned to the two supposed friends. "You guys gonna help Gus here clean out that cabin?"

"Yes, sir."

"You bet."

"Will either of you ever do anything to do with crystal meth in this county, ever again?"

Both violently shook their heads no, like they were life-sized bobble dolls, Item Number 1412 from the Rural Nitwit Supply Catalogue.

"I'm also sure the thought of going to the police or anyone else tonight is out of the question. Like that ad for Las Vegas says, What happens on Town Road Twelve stays on Town Road Twelve. Correct, gentlemen?"

Another series of vigorous head shakes. "Fantastic," Duncan said. "Hope we meet again under better circumstances, but I shan't hold my breath. Cameron?"

"Yes?"

"It appears our work here tonight is done, wouldn't you say?"

Cameron slung his H&K MP5 over his shoulder. "I'd say so."

Duncan started back down the driveway. Gus called out, "Please … oh God, please … my hand … will you help me with my hand?"

He looked to Gus's alleged friends. "Guys? Feel like helping a brother over there?"

Neither one of them moved. Duncan said, "All right, but just this once …"

He found the discarded hammer, picked it up, and using the claw end, yanked the nail out.

Gus screamed again.

———

Back at the truck Duncan slowly stripped off the gear, suddenly tired, sweaty, and thirsty. Both doors were open and the switched-on dome light now illuminated the interior. His brother got done ahead of him and Duncan asked, "What do you think?"

"Wanna be more specific? Can't read your fucking mind, you know."

Duncan said, "About Gus and his pals. What do you think? Are they going to play nice and leave crystal meth to the professionals?"

Cameron opened up the glove box, took out a little cleaning cloth, tore it open, and rubbed it on his hands and face. "Those two buddies of his, sure, I can see them running out and never playing again. But Gus ... I think I was wrong about him. He may work pumping gas and be a panty-sniffer, but tonight, he had brass ones. Didn't back down until you stuck his hand like that. Plus, you humiliated him in front of his friends. Could be trouble later."

"What kind of trouble? Leave us off his dad's Christmas card list?"

"How the fuck should I know? All I know is that you insulted him, wounded him, and he might do some payback down the road."

Duncan stopped in the middle of taking off his vest. "Mind telling me what's got your panties in the proverbial bunch?"

Cameron said, "Bro, there's psycho, and there's real psycho. I didn't know if you were playing tonight, or if it was real. Either way, it was some scary shit."

"Was supposed to be scary," Duncan said. "It doesn't matter if you or those three up there are wondering if it was real or not. What matters is if I do."

He shrugged off the vest, winced. Cameron said, "You hurtin'?"

"My shoulders are aching some," he said, putting his gear behind the driver's seat, covering everything with a plaid blanket. "Nights like this, I think I'm getting too old for this nonsense. You, too, my friend." Duncan got into the truck, turned the key, powered her right up and let the lights suddenly flash up the dirt road.

His brother got in, slammed the door. "Tell me that's what this whole delivery thing is all about. One big score to settle things so we don't have to be out hassling three morons who only have the skills not to blow themselves up while cooking meth."

"That's part of it, and before you ask, I swear, Cameron, all will be made clear at the right time. Trust me."

Cameron said, "I trust you, Duncan. I just want to make sure you're gonna do things worthy of it."

———

They backed out down the road, and then drove back to Turner. The interior of the truck smelled of sweat, exertion, and sourness. Duncan knew where the sourness was coming from, and it was from the older man sitting next to him. Poor Cameron. In their long brotherhood, they had gotten along most of the time, with Cameron settling early into the role of the hardier if not as business-orientated older brother. Sure, there had been disagreements over the years, but nothing serious, nothing like this current score that was digging at Cameron, like battery acid slowly corroding away a vital connection. Duncan knew what was being corroded; it was their lifelong reliance on each other, and Duncan felt bad about what he had done.

The road curved to the right as they traveled through the night. Trees hugged both sides of the road, with turnoffs here and there, marking night roads that led up into the dark hills. No other traffic was visible. He remembered when they were younger, driving like this during that summer when he had gotten that baseball scholarship to UNH, before the car accident. Warm night and the windows down and a strange oddity in the atmosphere, so they could pick up hard rock stations from Cleveland and Cincinnati as they rolled, mile upon mile, down the night roads. Vows and promises and plans being exchanged, being discussed. Duncan would be the first to school, with an education that would set him up—or if the ghosts of Babe Ruth and Lou Gehrig approved, a pro career in the majors.

All along, he would be planning for Cameron to take up the rear, going to school as well, explore that love of astronomy.

That had been something back then, when everything seemed possible, and with a suddenness that surprised him, he now decided to spill it all to his older brother. The chances of it all going bad, all going south, wasn't worth the chilly silence next to him. That innocent summer back then, when everything had been new and bright, well, things abruptly lurched and changed for the worse. Mom and Dad dying, their wills screwed up, and that late-afternoon drive with Dad's law partner, Duncan determining to make it all right. The accident. The injury. Everything crumbling. Cameron going away to state prison for a stretch for beating up a guy who had been abusing his wife, said wife being Cameron's girlfriend at the time … but they had hung in there, the two of them, making a life for themselves in Turner.

He took a deep breath. Enough. Time to come clean.

"Cameron?"

No reply.

"Cameron?" he said louder. "Look, I need—"

His brother said, "You need to look in your rearview mirror, like now."

Duncan glanced up.

Blue strobe lights from a police cruiser, right behind them.

FIFTEEN

IN A SECOND-FLOOR GUEST room at the Rogers' Bed and Breakfast, Zach Morrow stretched out on his bed, history book by John Keegan in his hands, thinking he should have put a couple of bath towels on the fine Amish quilt before lying down. It had been a long time since he had been in such a luxurious room. The attached bathroom was about as big as the living room back at his destroyed double-wide, and the bed was soft, huge, and comfortable. In a polished wooden hutch at the foot of the bed, a hi-def television was deftly hidden away. Overall, the room smelled pleasant, of cut flowers or a woman's freshly washed hair.

He crossed his feet, thought some. This room was a world away from the sawdust-covered floor of the Flight Deck Bar & Grill. When he had parked his pickup truck at the rear of the bed and breakfast—a restored Victorian-style home with lots of turrets and fancy gingerbread trim—he felt out of place next to the BWMs, Audis, and Volvos. But the woman with black-rimmed glasses and a cheerful smile checking him in had been sweet and kind. She became even more sweet and kind when he had mentioned Duncan Crowley's name, which earned him a ten-percent room discount.

He breathed in the scent of the room. What now? He felt he had done well, meeting with Duncan, making an impression, and having Duncan look him over. No doubt the lovely Tanya Gibbs thought he was moving too fast, but so what? It wasn't her butt on the line up here in the northern reaches of Washington County. It was him. By God, he'd get the job done, no matter what.

Zach swung off the bed, went to one of the duffel bags, took out the disposable cellphone he had used earlier. One more call and it'd be time to dump it. He had a few more hidden away. He dialed a number and waited and waited, until an older man answered, the same man as before.

"Yes?" the man asked.

"It's me, Zach," he said, repeating the practiced words, knowing the coded message that was being sent south. "Really, can't you help me out?"

"I'm afraid I can't."

"Please," Zach said. "You know what happened to me wasn't fair, wasn't fair at all."

The older man said, "Please don't call me again," and then hung up.

He put the phone down, and returned to the bed. His stomach grumbled. He hadn't had dinner yet. But still he waited.

Duncan Crowley knew he was here, knew he needed a job, and sitting still was the best thing for him to do.

SIXTEEN

DUNCAN SLOWED DOWN HIS Chevy Colorado pickup, switched on the turn indicator, the police cruiser staying right on his tail. He lowered the window. The night air was cool. Cameron said, his voice tight, "Whatever happens tonight, bro, I'm not going back to prison. Not ever. So you keep that in mind."

Duncan said, "Be cool, Cam. All right? Maybe I have a burnt-out taillight. Or the rear license plate fell off. No need to get wound up."

"Easy the fuck for you to say," Cameron replied. "All these years you've skated along, while I'm the one with the record."

Duncan put the Chevy in park, noted Cameron shifting his position, as his right hand lowered to his belt. "Stop moving around so much, Cam. You're giving the cop back there an excuse to get suspicious. Why do that?"

Cameron said, "Suspicious? We've got enough firepower back here to take on half the police forces in the state. You don't think that's a problem? I'll tell you what happened, bro, is that little fuck Gus Spooner dimed us out the moment he got some Oxycontin into him and got his hand bandaged up. You remember that joke you said about his dad leaving us off his Christmas card list. Does that sound funny now?"

"Look at your mirror," Duncan said. "Is the cop back there a local or a statie?"

Cameron said, "All I see is headlights, blue lights, and trouble. I see lots of trouble."

Duncan looked to his side view mirror, saw the cruiser door open up, a figure come out. "Cameron, there's not going to be a shoot-out, understand? You know how it works: traffic stop is made, call is made to Dispatch to do a records check. So if you start blasting and I drive us the hell out of here, the word on us will be out in minutes."

"So the fuck what," Cameron said, his Glock semiautomatic pistol in his hand, his hand now lowering to his side. "Those minutes, I'll be free and clear, won't I."

"Leaving me high and dry?"

"Be a change for you, wouldn't it," Cameron said.

He was going to say something sharp in reply but the interior of his Chevy truck cab was lit up from a flashlight. "Evening, folks," a woman's voice came out. "Would like to see your driver's license and registration, please."

"Absolutely," Duncan said. "My license is in my wallet, my registration is in the glove box. I'm getting them both now."

He leaned across, hoping his jacket didn't ride up enough to reveal his own firepower strapped to his side, and he popped open the glove box. Luckily he was anal when it came to keeping records like this at close hand: the registration was right on top, in a clear plastic sleeve, and wasn't buried under a pile of napkins, store coupons, and ketchup containers.

Duncan hunched up, removed his wallet, took out his license. Both were passed over to the cop. Cameron sat still, staring straight ahead.

The flashlight came down, the license and registration were both examined, and then returned. "So you're Duncan Crowley, of Turner. Correct?"

"That's right, ma'am."

"Understand you own a number of businesses in this county."

Duncan said, "That's also right, ma'am."

The flashlight was lowered and the woman cop said, "Thought as much. I'm Melanie Pope, the new chief in Crowdin. I was heading home after dropping off some late paperwork at the district court. This is unusual and all, pulling you over as part of a traffic stop, but I was wondering if I could ask you something."

"Ask away," Duncan said.

"Thing is, as the new chief in town, I want to make a good impression. We have Old Home Week coming up in three months, and I'm supposed to meet with the celebration committee in two days. Any chance I could ask you and your company to make a charitable donation?"

Duncan tried not to burst out laughing. "Just so I'm clear, you made a traffic stop to ask me that question?"

"That's right," she said, not embarrassed at all. "I suppose I could have called or sent a letter, but I like the direct approach."

Cameron still stared straight ahead. Duncan said, "Tell you what, call my wife Karen tomorrow. She runs a hair salon in Turner, called Karen's Cut and Curl. You tell her that you talked to me, she'll look at the books, and figure out what we can donate. That sound fair to you, Chief?"

"More than fair," she said. "I'll leave you two be, then, and see you later."

But before she stepped away, she flashed her light back into the truck's cab. "Who's your passenger tonight, Mr. Crowley?"

"My brother," he said.

"Not very talkative, is he," she said, keeping the flashlight trained on Cam's angry bearded face, with pockmarks and old scars. Duncan was afraid of what was going to happen to Cam: he had seen that same look before, back over the years, at the Flight Deck Bar & Grill, or at the motorcycle rallies in Laconia, or any other place, when Cameron felt like he had been pushed into a corner and was about to explode.

Duncan quickly said, "You're absolutely right, he's not very talkative at all. You see, my brother sometimes isn't all there. He's slow, forgetful, and quick to get angry. Some doctors say he's slightly retarded. But we've learned over the years how to take care of him. We find a nice quiet drive out in the country before bedtime usually means a good night's sleep, without him wetting the bed."

"Oh," the chief said. "Sorry to bother you then. Good night."

"A good night to you as well," Duncan said, and after putting the registration back into the glove box, he sat still, waited until the Crowdin police chief safely got back to her cruiser, she not knowing just how close she had come to the finality of death tonight. All it would have taken would have been a quick glance behind the seat to see the miniature armory and protective clothing. A few sharp questions on her part and he doubted he could have held Cameron back from blasting away at her.

The cruiser pulled away and Duncan flexed his fingers on the steering wheel. That had been so damn close, so very damn close …

"You know this new chief?" Cameron asked.

Duncan carefully said, "Not really. What do you know?"

"Some hard charger, supposedly ex-military cop. Decided to move up north, get away from it all."

"Good for her."

"Still … retarded?" Cameron demanded. "Is that what you called me, retarded?"

Duncan started up the Chevy, went out onto the road. "It worked, didn't it? Don't you think you'd rather be called retarded, instead of getting into a bloody shoot-out with a cop?"

Cameron raised up his Glock, put it on his lap. "Don't be so fucking sure," he said.

Duncan stayed quiet. After about a mile, Cameron said, "Hey, weren't you going to say something back there, before we got pulled over?"

"Forget it," Duncan said.

SEVENTEEN

So now they were in New Hampshire, and Louis Fontaine was getting more and more pissed with Jean-Paul Mailloux, who had been driving ever since they had left the Slinky Pussy Gentlemen's Club. They had stopped for gas, take-out food, and piss breaks, and not once had Jean-Paul given up the driving. Louis needed something to take his attention away from the little shit's humming along with the radio, or the way he picked his teeth and nose, or the way he drifted from lane to lane like he was falling asleep.

At least they had gotten through Customs in Vermont with no problem—even with the Chinese semiautomatics hidden away in the rear of the van—and along the way, Louis learned why Jean-Paul was in the Iron Steeds. It seemed the punk's aunt was Brenda Aube, the go-to gal for Francois Ouellette's dancers at the club.

Somewhere in the darkness of an empty stretch of road, Louis said, "So Brenda, she's really your aunt?"

Jean-Paul laughed. "Yeah, she is, if you can believe it. She's one wild and twisted gal. Wouldn't believe the stories I could tell you."

Louis grunted and Jean-Paul said, "When I was younger, my mom, she was in the hospital for a hip replacement, and I had to stay with Brenda for a few days. Mom didn't want me raising hell at home, so I was with Aunt Brenda and she caught me one night, smoking her cigarettes. Really pissed her off. Wanna guess how she punished me?"

Louis put his elbow on the doorframe, rested his head on his hand. "No, not really."

"She dragged me to the Slinky Pussy one morning. You know, the joint's only closed from eight a.m. to ten a.m., so that's when she brought me. Francois, he'd have the place running 24/7, but they need at least a couple of hours every day to give it a cleaning. Wash the dishes, mop the floors, and clean the leather couches in the private dancing rooms out back. Don't need to tell you what gets spilled back there, eh?"

Louis closed his eyes, wished this night, this trip, this everything was over. It was rugged enough to volunteer for a zap trip like this, but to be assigned with this clown ... He kept his mouth shut, hoping Jean-Paul would take the hint, but the idiot didn't.

"So there I was, and Aunt Brenda, she thought she'd punish me by putting me back in the dressing rooms, gather up all the soiled clothes from the dancers for the laundry pick up. Can you believe that? Horny teenage boy, dumped in the dressing room? Man, I got the laundry bagged up but when I was through, sweet Jesus, my crotch was so sore from—"

"Jean-Paul, for Christ's sake, just shut up, okay?"

"Hey, it's just a story, and—"

Louis turned to him. "Look. We've got serious business ahead in an hour or so. So let's stay focused, all right? No more stories about your aunt or strippers' panties. Let's talk about what we do once we get to Turner."

The headlights of the van cut through the darkness and the narrow, twisting night road. They went through a marshy area, and about twenty meters off to the right, two moose were plodding through the mud.

Jean-Paul sounded cross. "All right. What do we do when we get to Turner?"

"You've been driving and yapping ever since we left Laval. You tell me what you think, then."

He shrugged. "I dunno. We find him at that restaurant, or his house, drag him into a dark corner, work him over, get the info we need ... zap 'em. If we get his wife and kids ... zap 'em after playtime. If you don't want to play, fine, give me time and—"

"Oh, for Christ's sake, bundling those strippers' clothes must have melted your mind. We have to be sure before we go in. Do some recon. Make sure he's either at the restaurant or at home, maybe we grab his wife or kids beforehand. Shit, we have to have sort of goddamn plan, now, don't we?"

Jean-Paul said, "You've done this before?"

"I've gone plenty of other things. You?"

"Shit, man, you're thinking too much. This'll be slick as shit, just you see."

"Never been accused of thinking too much. Jesus," Louis said. "Look, here's something to think about, okay?"

The van drifted across a single yellow line, and Jean-Paul cursed and tugged the steering wheel back. Louis said, "Couple of years back, me and a guy named Phillie Tours, we went over to Buffalo to pick up a cousin of his who had a couple of run-ins with the Buffalo cops. His cousin Bobby was a dopey shit, but he had a chance to come back up north with us and keep his nose relatively clean. So that was the job. Straight pick-up. Kid was expecting us, best we figured, he even had his bag packed. Problem was, we were supposed to get him at 63 Clinton Street, and instead, goddamn Internet direction program sent us to fucking 63 Clinton Avenue, on the other fucking side of town."

Jean-Paul said, "Sorry to say, Louis, you're boring the shit out of me."

"Oh, it gets better, so keep your yap shut and ears open, okay? So it's late at night, me and Phillie, we were picking up his cousin, so we had our colors on. No big deal, hunh? So we go up to the house, we knock on the door and expect cousin Bobby to come out, all happy and shit, and what happens? Later we find out it's a goddamn house full of Colombians, they think we're there to rob them and shit. Instead of the door opening up, one of the Colombians, he goes to the picture window and lets loose with a fucking shotgun with double-ought buckshot. Damn near takes off Phillie's arm, sprinkles me with a couple of pellets, and we go down on the porch. Shit, we don't know what the fuck is happening, so we grab our own pieces, return fire, pumping rounds into the front windows. So there's a goddamn firefight breaking out, we don't know who's shooting and don't particularly care, and then something inside the house catches fire."

Louis took a breath. "We tumble our asses off the porch, reload, and we take up position behind a stone wall. By now I'm pissed and bleeding, Phillie's convinced somebody's whacked his cousin, and he's practically spurting blood into my goddamn face, so we're not in the mood to show any goddamn mercy. The house is real lit up, flames coming out of the windows, and Colombians are bailing out of the front door, and me and Phillie, we're wasting the little fuckers as they come out. A couple of 'em stay behind, try to put up a fight, but by then, the flames are licking at their brown asses, and they come out too, and we nail 'em. So the whole front lawn's full of shot or burning Colombians, and me and Phillie decide it's time to get the fuck out, screw cousin Bobby, but then, it gets seriously weird."

Jean-Paul said, "Hate to admit it, but I'm not bored any more."

"Won't be long," Louis said. "So we get up and try to get to our van, and we can't move. The whole fucking neighborhood is out there, and me and Phillie, that's it, we think we're dead. Looks like we're the only white guys in the whole fucking block and all these people are out there, watching the house burn, seeing us bleeding and with pistols in our hand, and maybe we got three or four rounds left between us. Like Custer's Last goddamn Stand, we know we're dead. And then … a fucking party starts up!"

Jean-Paul glanced at him. "A what?"

"A goddamn party! There's booze and cigars and pot, and one Chink guy, he's a registered nurse or something, he bandages us both up, and between getting drinks put into our hands and hot Asian chicks rubbing up against us, we find out the Colombians have been the shitheads of the neighborhood. Raising hell, loud noises, dumping trash in other people's yards, threatening to kill anyone who's pissing them off. Complaints to whatever's left of the Buffalo police doesn't help, so they see us come along, see us open fire and waste the little fucks, the neighborhood thinks we're goddamn heroes! Like the cavalry, riding to the rescue, but not Custer's cavalry, no, we're the ones that got the job done. Shit, it took us forever to get out of there, but we had to, because eventually the Fire Department showed up and once they saw all those fucked-over Colombians, the police came, too. So we hauled ass."

"I guess," Jean-Paul said. "Did you finally pick up the cousin?"

In spite of the long drive and the general stupidity of his companion, Louis laughed. "Yeah, we did. We were a couple of hours late, we went to the right fucking address, knock on the door. Cousin Bobby, he answers the door, first thing he says is, 'Why the hell are you so goddamn late?' I broke his fucking nose, I did."

Jean-Paul said, "You broke it? Not Phillie?"

156

Louis shook his head. "Nah, his arm hurt too much, so he had me do it. There you go. So Jean-Paul, that was the job. About as slick as shit as you can make it, and it got screwed up so bad, it was unbelievable. We were lucky we didn't end up dead in the street. So when we're heading like this, into strange turf, to find a guy who probably whacked Pierre and Andre, and we're supposed to go to him, guns up, get info from him, and then zap him? Shit, I don't care what you think, Jean-Paul. It ain't slick as shit, it just ain't. So don't make believe it is."

Jean-Paul finally shut up, and Louis just looked out the windshield.

There was so much darkness ahead of them, past these woods.

EIGHTEEN

When he got home, Duncan Crowley gave his wife a kiss and a firm pat on the butt, and went to say good-night to their kids. He went to the left down the hallway, knocked softly on Amy's door, and walked in. The room was cluttered with toys, dolls, pillows, and a couple of low bookshelves, and there was a sudden movement from underneath the blankets. He tried not to smile. He went up to the blankets and gently removed them, found his eight-year-old girl looking up at him, long blond hair on the pillow, a kid's book in one hand, a pink Barbie doll official flashlight in the other.

"Amy, you know the rules," he said, taking the flashlight and book away. "No more reading after nine p.m."

She smiled, knowing it was the way to get into her daddy's heart. "I know, but I just wanted to do one more chapter, and then one more chapter, and then ... well, I didn't know what time it was."

He put the book and flashlight on her nightstand, kissed the top of her head. "Rules are rules. You know that."

Amy snuggled under the blankets. "Are you gonna tell mom?"

"Are you going to remember the nine p.m. rule?"

Another heart-breaking smile from his eight-year-old. He was instantly and insanely jealous of that unknown young boy out there who was going to eventually take her away from him and Karen. "Yes, Daddy, I'll remember."

He kissed her cheek this time. "Good girl. Sleep well, okay?"

"Night, daddy."

———

Back to the hallway, another soft knock. He went in and their ten-year-old son was in bed, watching a game between the Red Sox and the Seattle Mariners. The volume on the television set was low and Lewis said, "Hey, Dad. Sox are up, three to one."

"Glad to hear it," he said.

His boy was no longer of the age when he allowed kisses or hugs from his father, so Duncan made do with a hard rub of the top of his head. Unlike his sister, Lewis's hair was a dark brown, like his own. He was in bed, sitting up, a copy of *Sports Illustrated* on the blanket next to him. If his sister's room was Hannah Montana and Justin Beiber, Lewis's bedroom was Big Papi and Jon Lester.

There was a small desk next to the bed with a matching chair, and Duncan took the chair, reversed it, and sat down as he watched the inning close out with his son. When the side was retired, he got up and checked the time. "Television's off at ten," Duncan said. "Got it?"

"But what if the Sox are losing?" Lewis asked.

"Then you'll get up tomorrow and check the box score, and you'll feel good because you didn't waste time watching them lose."

"And if they're winning?"

"Then you won't miss anything, because they were winning when you went to sleep. Good try, Lewis. Ten o'clock and the television is off."

He got to the door before Lewis got to him. "Dad, I was talking to Coach Ronson today, after practice. He said you were the best pitcher he had ever seen in his years of coaching."

His hand on the doorknob, Duncan said, "That's awfully nice of him to say. But remember where he's coming from. Not many kids up in these parts are interested in baseball. So I think he was just being polite."

Lewis said, "Maybe so, dad, but he said it was a sin when you got in your car accident and hurt your leg, so you couldn't get that scholarship and try out for the minors. Dad … do you ever wonder what it would have been like if you had made it in the big leagues?"

Duncan turned and hating himself for it, easily lied to his boy. "Never, Lewis. Not ever. Now get back to the game, and make sure the TV's off by ten."

———

His sleep that night was restless, with periods of wakefulness, hearing Karen's soft breathing and the occasional creaking noise from the house, punctuated by light dozing where he had dreams of being chased and of having needed weapons in his hands crumble away like they were made of soft clay.

Duncan suddenly woke up. A light was flashing in his eyes. There was a soft pinging noise. His blood seemed to ice right up and seize his heart. On the nightstand next to the bed, next to the tiny clock radio with red numerals, was a little black box that was connected to the perimeter alarm system for the house. Duncan had motion-detection sensors set up about the yard, extending a couple of hundred feet in each direction. They weren't fancy, but they were designed to alert him whenever body masses of a certain weight were approaching the house.

Like now.

There was no alarms screeching or bells ringing. Nope, just the tiny black box next to him that made a soft pinging noise every thirty seconds, in addition to a little flash of light aimed at his side of the bed. Dear Karen could sleep through an earthquake, but in his years of work experience, he had learned to be a light sleeper.

Ping. Flash. Ping. Flash.

Duncan reached out, touched the top of the black box. The noise and the light stopped, but his work was about to begin.

———

He quickly swung out of bed, reached between the mattress and box spring, where a .357 stainless-steel Ruger revolver rested. Weapon in hand, he got dressed in the dark and slipped out of the bedroom. He closed the door behind him and went down the hallway, ensuring the doors to the kids' rooms were closed as well.

In the kitchen, next to the gas stove and the stainless-steel refrigerator—which Karen had initially loved but now despised because the smooth surface showed every fingerprint and smudge—was small black-and-white television set. The screen on the set was divided into four quadrants, showing the front of the house and the driveway, the side yards, and the rear yard, which fell away to a wood line. The image showing the driveway was reasonably clear, because of a streetlight up the way, but the other views were pretty shadowy.

Damn.

Duncan slipped the Ruger into the waistband, went through the darkened kitchen and through a side door, into the garage, where his Chevy truck and Karen's Toyota RAV4 rested, near his and her Harley Davidsons covered in cloths. The only light in the garage came from two nightlights, and that was enough. In a minute or two he went into a locked storage box underneath a tool bench, and emerged with a Kevlar vest, a set of night-vision goggles, and a Remington 12-gauge shotgun with an extended magazine. A semiautomatic rifle, like the H&K MP5 he and Cameron had borne earlier, would have more fire-power, but at nighttime, the explosive burst and sound of a Remington shotgun was much more impressive.

Duncan went to the back door of the garage, crouched down, and opened it slightly. He spent a few minutes like that, scanning the rear yard with the aid of the night-vision gear, revealing the night in a ghostly shade of gray-green. Nothing. A swing set, picnic table, and small above-ground swimming pool for the kids. To his left the rear deck with grill and table and chairs. No assassins in sight.

He slipped out, making sure the door was shut behind him. Staying low, he moved across the lawn and took a spot near the swimming pool, .357 Ruger firm in his waistband, shotgun in hand. Back and forth, back and forth. Nothing. There was the sound of night birds, insects, and far away, coming from the state highway, some brave or foolish soul who was out riding a motorcycle in this frigid night air.

But nothing here, in the yard of the Crowley residence.

He didn't like it. Didn't like it all. Something had tripped the damn alarm system.

From the swimming pool, there was a low, decorative hedge work, where he scurried next. It was cold and he wished had grabbed a coat before getting all gung ho out here. Too late now. He knelt in the dew-wet grass, again scanned the property. The alarm system was good but had one weak spot: it didn't tell you where in the yard the trespasser was coming through, only that he was out there, some-where. Sure, he could have spent the money for a larger upgrade, a more complicated system, but hell, it was always something on the famed "to do" list.

An owl hooted out there, the noise deep, bone chilling.

Another scan.

Nothing.

He went to the other end of the hedgework, chest pounding, mouth suddenly dry. Gunplay had never bothered him much but he was hating every second of this. His family was in that house behind him, safe and warm and asleep. They were depending on him for safety, for protection, for so very much. Any other normal father in this valley wouldn't be out here if he feared for his family's safety. No, that normal father would call the cops and let them take care of it. But Duncan wasn't under any illusions.

At this time of night, the sole chief and patrolman for the town of Turner were in bed. Any 911 call would go to a central state dispatch, and from there, to the State Police, and from there, to whichever lonely State Police cruiser was roaming around this empty part of the state. Which meant that if there was real trouble out here, chances were that the cops and others would arrive in time to take crime scene pictures and liver temperatures of the deceased.

But not here, and not tonight.

Something moving, down by the tree line. Duncan flattened himself out on the wet grass, cursed himself for not upgrading the alarm system, and for not upgrading his night-vision gear. There were better night-vision sets out there that had telescopic capabili-ties, but they were pricey.

Idiot, he thought. If he could mortgage the house right now to have that kind of gear in front of his face, he'd do it. As it was, all he could see was a shape out there, moving slowly. Couldn't zoom in to see who it was or what he was carrying.

Took a breath. Shotgun firm against his shoulder. Waited, running possibilities through his mind. If it was a kid or something, just a warning shout out to the yard that he was trespassing and needed to get the hell out of here would do. If it was a man, same message. If it was a man approaching his house, armed, then he'd wait until he was close enough to hear him breathing and with one pull of the trigger, he'd take the son-of-bitch out at the knees.

A noise from the approaching figure.

What the heck?

The figure seemed to drop, like he was coming to the house on his hands and knees, lumbering along, looking like a ....

Like a damn black bear.

Duncan let out a breath, relaxed against the cold and wet grass. A black bear. That's all. The surveillance system was supposed to be sensitive enough to tell the difference between a person or a deer or a black bear stumbling along, but obviously, it needed to be tuned up.

Still. Good to know.

He rolled over on his back and an armed figure was looking down at him.

NINETEEN

IN HIS LUXURIOUS BEDROOM at Rogers' Bed and Breakfast, Zach Morrow is wide awake, and remembering.

Remembering his last mission in the employ of the Federal government. A hot, humid night, about five miles away from a small container ship that was heading up the west African coast, traveling to Lisbon. The ship had halted off the coast of Sierra Leone, supposedly to make temporary repairs to a faulty boiler. During that time, he had slipped off the stern of the boat in a specially designed Zodiac craft with muffled, high-speed engines and a low gunwale, allowing it to move stealthily among the boat traffic coming out of the Sierra Leone River. Years before, this type of mission would have been tasked to a Navy SEAL unit, but now the SEALs were busy in the deserts of Iraq and the high mountains of Afghanistan. So it had gone down the food chain to the US Coast Guard and Chief Petty Officer Zach Morrow, who had gone in from the Atlantic to the capitol city of Freeport, and up the river.

He had plenty of experiences with rivers, traveling up and down slow-moving, turgid streams, or navigating fast-moving rapids and whirlpools and eddies. Iraq, Iran, Pakistan ... so many countries, so many rivers. Dropping off and picking up. Delivering weapons, supplies, gold ingots. Most river work was done at night, all missions a success, if you could call that, year after year. He was getting tired of doing work that didn't seem to add much to the equation.

And what was that? Damned if he knew. Once he thought the equation was doing good, but after all the shooting and misery and betrayals, he now thought the equation was just getting out alive.

This particular trip was timed down to the ounce and the second, going up the river in another edition of Sierra Leone's ongoing civil war, Zach being assigned to slide in and slide out, retrieving a two-man Agency surveillance group that had gotten its extraction process screwed up. Practically lying down in the boat before its controls, carefully navigating his way up the river—seeing tracers firing off in the distance, the thump of explosions, and the glow of villages burning—Zach only had one proverbial bump along the road, where the river narrowed and a powerboat overloaded with fighters from one of the local militia groups nearly ran him down. The militia boat swerved around and came back for a closer inspection. Flashlights from the craft lit up the river and Zach couldn't risk being halted, discovered, or slowed down. Maneuvering close to the powerboat with his thumb controls—with the militiamen hanging over the sides of their boat, holding AK-47s or flashlights—Zach slid up next to them and tossed in a delayed time-fused MK-45 combination fragmentation and incendiary grenade.

The subsequent explosion and fire were pretty impressive, and Zach was sure that any observers on the riverbank would probably think the damn thing hit a mine or was struck by an errant RPG round.

Checking his timepiece, Zach was pleased to see he was a minute ahead of schedule. Checking the GPS coordinates and the timepiece again, he slipped on a monocular viewing device, started scanning the right-hand riverbank, with sandbars, low brush, and cypress trees. Something flashed, flashed again, and then began flashing in a regular pattern. An infrared strobe light, keyed to the same frequency as his viewing device. Anybody else out there on the river or on the opposite riverbank wouldn't see a damn thing, and Zach definitely wasn't anybody else.

Slowing the engine, he slew the craft to starboard, aiming right for the strobe light. In a few seconds, the wide prow of his Zodiac bumped and ground against the sand. He clambered out, stretched, and a man approached him from the shadows.

"Charlie Golf?" the man asked.

"The same," he said. "Ready?"

"Christ, we've been ready for days."

From the brush, another man emerged. From his vision gear he could see they were tall, wide, and tough-looking, wearing jungle gear, heavy boots, and weapons strapped to their waists. They dragged out bulging duffel bags and hard-plastic equipment containers. Working quickly, they put their gear in the stern of the Zodiac, tied them down, checking to make sure they were secured.

The second guy said, "Shit, just one of you?"

"One riot, one ranger," Zach said. "One covert river op, just me."

"Sounds fucked."

Zach said, "Anything bigger would bring attention. You're about sixty seconds away from heading home. You want to wait for a Carnival cruise ship or something?"

The first guy said, "Gary, shut up, will you? Christ, let's get the fuck out of here, I don't care if we're riding on surfboards if it means—"

A soft male voice. "Sir? Sir? Can you help? Please?"

The two Agency guys whirled as one, pistols out, gripped in a two-handed combat stance. Zach was just as quick, pulling down his cut-down M4 7.62mm rifle from a quick-release strap on his back.

A man appeared from the darkness, wearing a suit and necktie, holding the hand of a woman next to him, a child at either side. A family, out for a nighttime river walk in the middle of a civil war where some civilians were having their hands chopped off for fun. For Christ's sake.

Gary said, "Folks, just back away, all right? We don't want to hurt you. Just go away."

"Please, can you help? My name is John Ernest Benjamin, and—"

"Pal, I don't fucking care if you're Oprah's uncle, move along," Gary said, holstering his weapon.

The other Agency guy said, "Lighten up, Gary."

Gary said, "You lighten up, Paul. We're wasting time, and I'm not in the mood to play diplomat; I want to play going home."

Zach looked at John Ernest Benjamin and recalled his briefing on the container ship, before heading out tonight. "You're J.E. Benjamin, of the Peace and Liberation Party, correct? The presidential candidate?"

The man smiled, nodded. His wife was quietly weeping. The children were wide-eyed, frightened. In the distance was the hard stammering of automatic gunfire, the glow of villages burning, screams of the tortured and dying.

"Yes, yes, yes, I am," he said. "Please, if I may. I received assurances from your embassy, a Mr. Koch, who said to me, many times, that if there were troubles, then my family and I, we would be taken care of. We were told to go to the Milamba Airstrip to be evacuated. Alas, no one arrived. Rebels came instead, burned the buildings, killed many. My children, they saw these two men here driving away. Knew they were Americans. We followed, the best we could. Please."

Gary said, "Sad story, but not our problem. Let's screw."

Zach said, "This man and his family received a promise from the Embassy."

The other Agency man holstered his weapon as well, turned to Zach. "Bud, there ain't no embassy there. The Marines evacuated everyone two days ago. Gary's right, let's get out of Dodge."

Zach stood in the river water, looking at the calm and dignified man, his wife, his two children. His hand was still entwined with his wife's. Zach thought about all the other missions he had done, none of them particularly sticking out in his mind. Something sour seemed to grow in his mouth. "We can take them."

"The fuck we can," Gary said. "Look at your boat. There's no room."

Zach said, "We dump your gear, there's plenty of room."

Gary laughed, started sloshing through the water to the Zodiac. "What are you, the goddamn tour director? Your job, pal, is to get us the hell out of here with our gear. No passengers allowed. So do your fucking job, all right?"

The woman's shoulders were trembling from her weeping. J.E. Benjamin started whispering in her ear. Paul came through the water, said, "Bud, I know how you're feeling, but it's not our problem, not our job. Sorry to say, it's collateral damage. It happens during wartime. Unavoidable. We've got to get out of here, and—"

Zach raised up his M4. "You and your friend there, dump your gear. Now."

Movement from the both of them.

Zach said, "Gary, Paul, your hands where I can see them. I swear to God, your hands move, I'll cut you down where you are."

Gary swore and his companion said, his voice soothing, "Bud, we can't do that. This stuff is black ops gear, top of line surveillance, satellite linkage ... we just can't dump it in the goddamn river. In case you haven't noticed, the whole place out there is blowing up. We got all sorts of nutcases roaming around out there, including al-Qaeda cells, and Chinese and Russian operatives. Our stuff is worth more than gold. We can't just dump it here, have some moke pick it up and sell it."

Zach said, "Then it should sink pretty fast, hunh?"

"Bud—"

"We made a promise to this man and his family."

Gary said, voice low, "The hell we did. Some embassy flunky made the promise. Not us."

"No," Zach persisted. "The United States made him a promise. I'm going to make sure it's kept."

He moved to the stern of the boat, keeping his M4 up, hand going out, Paul saying, "You're way the fuck above your pay grade bud … I'm warning you … this will goddamn sink you."

"I'm Coast Guard," Zach said. "We don't sink."

He grabbed the first case, Gary's hand moved, and he moved quicker, firing a shot, Gary spinning around, "You fuck! You fuck! You fuck!"

Paul said, "Did you just pop him? Did you?"

Zach said, "No wonder you're a field operative, you've got a stunning grasp of the fucking obvious. Now. Drop your weapon, do the same with your friend's. I'm gonna be busy here for a second."

He grabbed the hard-plastic cases, hauled them off the Zodiac. It was hard going, but he looped a tie-down strap through the carrying handles. Taking another grenade, he set the timer for five minutes, then set the whole floating collection down the river. He pointed the M4 to the two Agency men. "We're shoving off with this man's family. If you'd like, take a moment to bandage Gary's arm."

Gary's voice was constricted. "You stupid fuck. You stupid Coastie fuck. Your career is dead, dead, dead, and when we're out of here, I'm gonna pay you back."

Zach said, "Bold talk for a man depending on me to get you both out of here."

Bright orange tracer fire stitched the night sky. There were more distant screams. Zach said, "We all move quietly and quickly, we can be safe. But don't get any funky ideas about dumping me over the side as we head down river. It takes about six weeks to get qualified to operate that Zodiac, and about six months to be really good at it. And I'm the best, fellows; that's why I'm here."

An explosion shattered the river downstream as the Agency's cases were blown up. Gary and Paul cursed some more and climbed into the Zodiac. Zach went to J. E. Benjamin and his family, and held out his hand, bringing them to the boat.

"Welcome aboard," he said.

TWENTY

THE WET GRASS SOAKED through the back of Duncan's shirt as he grabbed his Remington to bring it up as a sweet and familiar voice quietly said, "Honey, what have I always told you about playing without me?"

It felt like the elephant foot that had been crushing his chest had just been lifted up. He took one deep breath and another. "Babe, there's nothing more arousing than seeing a hot woman with a hot weapon."

Karen came closer, squatted down next to him. She had on knee-high black Wellington boots, a short black lace nightgown that reached mid-thigh, and a Kevlar vest and was carrying a Colt Model 1911 .45 semiautomatic pistol.

"Having a helpless man at your feet isn't too bad, either," she said. "How are you doing?"

"Cold, wet, tired. What got you out here?"

"Had to get up for a drink. Saw you were gone. Saw your Ruger was gone. What's going on?"

"Black bear sniffing around out back."

"You let him live?"

"Not in season." Duncan rolled over, got up. Karen stood up as well. He kissed her and rubbed her head. "Thanks for backing me up."

She touched his back, his butt, his legs. "Jesus, honey, you're sopping wet. How about we go back in, I draw you a hot bath?"

"Why not just a change of clothes?"

Karen took her free arm and slipped it into his. "Don't tell me the magic's over, honey, that you'd turn down a hot bath from your sweet baboo."

"The fact you're still in bed with me every morning convinces me of magic. Let's go in before Lewis and Amy come out with a baseball bat and a Barbie flamethrower."

———

Fifteen minutes later he was in the bathtub, hot water and suds around him, holding a glass of Jameson's and water. Karen was next to him, wearing her black lace nightie, slowly washing his shoulders and back with a soft washcloth. He let the heat burn out the ache in his bones, felt the soothing sensation of Karen's hands on him.

They were quiet for a while, and he took a long sip of his drink. Karen nuzzled his neck, kissed his ear, her hair tickling his bare shoulder. "You jumpy?"

"Yeah."

"More than usual?"

"Oh, yes," he said. "Just got word, the shipment schedule's been moved up. Won't be next week. More like in two days."

"A problem, then?"

"Yeah," he said. "People, resources … not everything's in place. Then there's Cameron … I've been leading him on way too long."

"You had to do what was right, hon," she said softly. "Don't fret about it."

"Lately, that's all I've been doing, fretting. He's stood by me for years. Now, I'm cutting him out."

She squeezed the washcloth out, wiped his shoulders. "Not true. He abandoned you once."

"Years ago."

"But it's that one time, when he was out banging Mrs. Hampton, that got you—"

"Karen, you don't need to repeat it. I already know that story."

"So why are you cutting him out? Mmm? Want to remind me?"

He rattled the ice cubes in his glass. "Because it's so very dangerous. If it goes south, which is a good possibility, there'll be lots of trouble, lots of Fed interest ... bullets flying hither and yon, and a good chance that I wouldn't just be arrested, Karen. If the Feds were pissed enough and creative enough, I could be declared an enemy combatant, get myself Gitmoed."

She kissed his near shoulder. "Truth is, you wouldn't look good in orange."

"Truth is, you look good in a potato sack."

Another kiss to the shoulder. "Stop changing the subject. So you're cutting Cameron out to protect him, or to make sure he wouldn't screw it up by opposing it?"

"Bit of both," he admitted.

"If it does go through ..."

"Then I can stop fretting. In the meantime ... I made a mistake."

She put the washcloth down. "Now, or earlier?"

"Earlier, some. I wasn't thinking straight. Being out there in the cold, I knew I had made a mistake. Karen, we've had some agreements, you and I, over the years. Stone cold agreements with no fighting, no discussion, no seeking wiggle room."

"Duncan …"

"Karen, 'alas, Babylon,'" he said quietly.

Karen opened her mouth as if to argue, then sat down on the bathmat next to the tub. She sighed, her face flush. "You said it, love. Alas, Babylon. When?"

"Tomorrow. The kids go to school but not home. You choose the place. Don't tell me. Just make it happen. You, too, all right? Pack a bag and go to work like nothing's going on, but don't come home. Let me know later where you are."

Duncan looked at those stern green eyes of hers, trying to gauge what she was thinking. Only twice before had he done this, using as a phrase the title of a 1960s post-apocalyptic novel they had both read in high school, written by Pat Frank. In that book, an Air Force intelligence officer warned his brother of an impending nuclear war by saying "alas, Babylon." No such war was coming to Turner, but conflict certainly was. Earlier he had uttered the words when he had heard of tough men coming up here from Boston and the second time from Providence.

Damn, he should have done it earlier. That bear out there … it could have easily been a two-legged predator, not one on four legs.

Karen leaned over, her freckled cleavage impressive and enticing. She kissed his lips. "No argument from me, sweetie. We'll be gone after breakfast tomorrow."

"Thanks."

She suddenly took the wet washcloth, gently slapped it across his cheek, leaned in, and whispered. "This shipment … if it works as you say, then we'll be safe, won't we? No more alarm systems, no more weapons in easy reach, no more 'alas Babylon.'"

"That's right. If it works."

She tugged his ear, hard. "Then make it work."

Later Duncan Crowley is in his bed, next to his loving and well-armed wife, wide awake, and remembering.

Two months after graduating from high school, he sat in the reception area of his father's law firm, Crowley & Carleton, waiting for Caleb Carleton to come out and continue their discussion. The room was familiar but it was oh so strange to be sitting here like any other client or visitor, instead of being the son of one of the two senior partners. Earlier this was just a place to pass through before going to Dad's nearby office, but that office was now empty. Everything in there that belonged to Dad had been boxed up and delivered to their home, in plain white cardboard boxes. No notes of sympathy, nothing personal at all from Caleb or the other lawyers and staff. Just stuff in bubble wrap, from coffee cups to framed prints of the family.

He rubbed his hands together, looked up at the clock. His brother Cameron was still late. This was supposed to be a meeting with the three of them, to get things straight, ever since last month when Mom and Dad had gone out for a quick vacation trip to Colorado, where their commuter plane had iced up at night, flipped over, and dove into the side of a mountain. Besides everything that had gone on—from dealing with funeral arrangements and sympathy cards and flowers to going to bed every night with that cold hard feeling inside of you, that this is it, you are an orphan, with your big brother as your family and that is *it*—there were disturbing things as well.

The biggest was that Caleb Carleton had kept on dragging his feet and postponing meetings and not returning phone calls when it came to discuss Mom and Dad's will and the trust fund that had been set up for both sons. Finally Duncan had come into the office last week, had not left until he had made a firm appointment for a meeting with him and Cameron, and here he was, alone.

Earlier he and Mr. Carleton had gone to lunch at Rosie's Restaurant in town—he had a cheeseburger and coke, while Carleton had steak tips and three martinis—and over the meal, Carleton had danced around the missing paperwork, the missing funds. "Later, later," he had said. "We'll get this all settled later when we get back to the office. Promise. Now, tell me more about that scholarship. I also heard stories that some scouts from the Yankees and the Orioles have been checking you out." So that's how the lunch went, Duncan eating as fast as he could to get the darn thing over with, Carleton nursing each of his three drinks.

Duncan looked around the reception area to the law offices, feeling out of sorts, out of place. This had been a fun place to visit when Dad had been here, a place where he could play and steal pencils and hide among the book cases full of law books, but now … the only thing left were the memories. It wasn't his anymore, like their house, filled with ghosts and shadows and possessions of his dead parents.

The door to Carleton's office flew open and he came out. He was portly, wearing black shoes, gray slacks, a white dress shirt with French cuffs, red suspenders, and red bow tie that was sagging under his fleshy neck. His gray hair was thick and combed back, and he waved at Mrs. Turin, the head secretary, as he came over to Duncan.

"Duncan, Duncan," he said. "Just got an important phone call from the county courthouse. I have to make a filing there right now, or an important case of mine will be tossed out. I'm sure you know the importance of timely filings. I'm afraid we'll have to finish this another day."

Duncan stood up and was going to say, *all right, I understand,* but something bitter seemed to bite in his mouth as he noted the reception room and the empty office that had belonged to his dad.

"No," Duncan said. "I'll come along with you, Mr. Carleton, and we can talk about it in the car."

Carleton's face was scarlet and it looked like he was going to say something sharp. Maybe it was the presence of Mrs. Turin or something else, but he snorted, returned to his office, and came out with his matching gray suit coat and a soft leather briefcase. Duncan fell into step with him and they went out the rear entrance, down to a small parking lot. The lawyer said, "Really, Duncan, I don't know how long I'll be at the courthouse."

"That's all right. I don't mind waiting."

Inside the Cadillac, it took three tries before he could get the key into the ignition, and by the time they got out on Main Street, the interior of the car stunk of sweat and booze. Duncan realized with a sharp taste of fear that the three martinis hadn't been the first drinks of the day for his father's law partner. The guy was drunk out of his skull, and the car moved across the center line twice as they head out of town.

Duncan said, "If I may, Mr. Carleton, I—"

"You know, kid, the law can really be a pain in the ass," he said, the words starting to slur. "You start off, nice and eager, ready to defend the defenseless, help the helpless, and what do you end up doing? End up defending one group of assholes from another group of assholes."

"I see, but—"

He slapped the steering wheel for emphasis. "Every goddamn day. And the bills! Christ, you have to meet payroll, you got utilities, you got dues, you gotta bring in expert witnesses and shit like that to get things done, and when you bill out, what do you get? Thanks for keeping my idiot daughter out of jail? Thanks for getting me that settlement check from PSNH? Thanks for making sure my son-of-a-bitch husband gets to pay child support? Hell, no. They bitch over your bills, they bitch over your filings, for God's sake, they bitch over everything…"

The car sped up. Duncan made sure his seatbelt was secure and tightened. Carleton sneezed and closed his eyes and wiped his nose with his wrist.

"Mr. Carleton, I really don't understand the delay in getting the paperwork filed with probate," Duncan said nervously, as the Cadillac roared down the road, twenty miles over the speed limit. "I mean, it seems like—"

With one hand draped over the steering wheel, Mr. Carleton suddenly pointed at Duncan with the other. "Jesus fucking Christ, what's the urgency, hunh? You're a young kid, in such a goddamn hurry. What's the problem?"

Duncan swallowed. He had never seen Mr. Carleton—who had been over at their house so many times for dinners and Sunday football games and cookouts—be so angry, so wound up.

"There's no problem, I'm sure," Duncan said, staring out at the trees and stone walls rushing by. "Cameron and I, we want to ensure that—"

"Cameron!" Mr. Carleton snorted. "What a loser he is … he's going to be trouble, just you see … in fact, I heard he got rousted off Bailey Hill last month, claimed he was using a telescope to look at the stars or some damn nonsense. Hah. Chief Harnsworth was sure he was using it to spy on a girls' slumber party down the street."

The Cadillac roared through a curve in the road, tires squealing, Duncan grabbing onto the door handle. Duncan said desperately, "Cameron's not a loser. He's smart. So what if he wears his hair long and—"

"If he's not such a loser, why isn't he here with you, eh? Why?"

"I'm sure there's a good reason," Duncan said. "I just know."

"And you!" Mr. Carleton said, again turning away from the road to chastise him. "You have a bright future ahead of you! A pitching arm that can bring you to the majors! A scholarship! You and your loser brother, you're worried about a goddamn will … a goddamn trust … The truth. Damn, you've been badgering me all this time and I wanted to spare you the hurt, you poor kid. The truth is, sonny, your dad had everything, and I mean every last goddamn penny tied up in the business, and there's nothing left for you and your brother! Not a damn thing!"

Duncan couldn't believe what he had just heard. More tires squealing, and he turned to the lawyer and said, "That's a lie! That's a damn lie! My dad would never have done that!"

A hand flew out, catching Duncan on the chin. He fell back as the man's voice roared again, "You ungrateful little snot, I should —

Duncan closed his eyes. Another curve was coming up. The Cadillac flew off the road, there was scraping and bumping as the undercarriage ground its quick way over saplings and rocks and boulders, and a sudden crackling crash and a burst of pain, and that was it.

That was it.

Daily Threat Assessment Task Force Teleconference Call
April 15th

FBI representative: "… going back over my notes, I'm still concerned by the situation concerning the Mextel trailer reported missing five days ago. We even received a Threat Level Alpha message from our Canadian friends. Custom stations from Maine to Michigan were put on high alert. Even the Osprey drone surveillance system along the northern border was brought in for real-time intel gathering and evaluation. Now you're telling us the alert's been cancelled?"

Homeland Security representative: "Not cancelled. Just reevaluated."

FBI: "What the hell is the difference?"

Homeland Security: "A lot of wasted effort and overtime, that's the difference. We got better intelligence. That's all you need to know for now."

Department of State representative: "What do the Canadians think about this?"

Unidentified: "Who cares what the Canadians think."

[[General laughter]]

FBI: "… serious for a moment. I don't like the idea of a trailer going missing that results in a Threat Level Alpha status, even if it is from the Canadians, and then the alert is cancelled. A lot of nasty stuff can be hidden in a truck trailer. I just want it on the record that

I'm not satisfied with the response I'm getting from Homeland Security."

Homeland Security: "Duly noted. Now, Tom, are you emphasizing this because you want to protect your butt if that trailer shows up?"

FBI: [[Expletive deleted]] If it drives into an underground parking facility at the Capitol Building, packed to the roof with ammonium nitrate, then I want to make sure that at some point, the FBI raised a concern."

State Department: "Can we move on to the next agenda item, please?"

CIA representative: "Agreed. I have a lunch date I can't afford to miss."

TWENTY-ONE

When the morning status meeting for the Region One administrators of the Department of Homeland Security concluded, Tanya Gibbs called out softly, "Gordon, if I may, could I see you afterwards?"

Gordon Simpson, the Region One administrator, nodded from the head of the polished conference room table. "That'd be fine, Tanya. In fact, I need to talk to you about a couple of matters."

"That would be nice, thank you," she said, although she spared a glance at Walter Dresden, trying to see by his looks whether that character had confessed all to Gordie. But Walter looked cool and calm as he picked up his BlackBerry and legal pad, and strolled out with the other administrators and officers of Region One. The door was closed and she was alone with her boss.

Gordon Simpson was a tired old man who had some sort of illness that no one knew anything about, but which caused him to spend many an afternoon at Mass General. His dark pin-striped suits were baggy about him, and his face sagged, like a frog whose muscles and tendons were failing at their work. He stared at her from across the table, his wrinkled and freckled hands on the table.

"Tanya," he said.

"Gordon," she said.

He raised up a hand, looked at his yellow fingernails. "You've been quite active these past few weeks. Conducting after-hours meetings, traveling to New Hampshire, Maine, Vermont. It's quite an impressive output, Tanya, save for one thing. You haven't filed any progress reports, any after-meeting memos ... it puts me in a very awkward position."

She gave him her best smile. "My intent is not to put you in an awkward position, Gordon. Or any other position. My apologies."

Gordon sighed and looked at his fingernails again. Tanya looked over his shoulder, through the sixth floor window, out towards the Boston skyline. Near as Tanya could figure, Gordon had been drifting along from one government job to another, from the US Navy Reserves to Department of Defense to a single term as a Congressman in New Hampshire—where he had lost re-election, in a state where incumbents were practically guaranteed a job for life, now that was an accomplishment!—and after some lobbyist work, here he was, head of Region One, after some favors were called in and strings were pulled, no doubt. No counterterrorism background, no immigration experience, just a gray bureaucrat who had bobbed along the currents of political decisions and events.

Just like the type of gray bureaucrats prior to a certain September day who thought they were doing a good job protecting the country, protecting Tanya's best friend Emily and thousands of others.

He said, "You need to keep me in the loop for what you're doing, Tanya. It would make my job that much easier. Especially since we're having a GAO audit coming due here next week. How would it look if they discovered I was letting you operate without proper supervision?"

Tanya moved her legal pad over three inches. "I see. Gordon, those are all valid observations. I appreciate you bringing them to me. In fact, to show you my level of cooperation, I'm planning to have an unannounced drill with members of the New Hampshire State Police in a few days, along with other local law enforcement agencies."

"Unannounced? Why? And what kind of drill?"

"Unannounced so they don't get ready for whatever I'm throwing at them," she said. "The drill will be a rapid-response to a border incident occurring at their northernmost county up there, Washington County. A cross-border incursion from Canada."

"What kind of cross-border incursion?"

Wouldn't you love to know, she thought. She said, "Not sure as of yet. Might be something as simple as a group of Middle Eastern illegals coming over via a stolen van."

Gordon pursed his thin lips. "You'll show me the drill protocol? Give me a heads-up on participants? And a thorough debriefing afterwards?"

No, no, and no, she thought, thinking of her dead Emily. What was deceit to protect the other Emilys out there? "Of course, Gordon. Of course."

He winced for a second, like something inside of him was burning and hacking its way through his digestive system. He belched, didn't apologize, and said calmly, "I know what you think of me, Tanya. You don't think I'm up for the job. You think all I care about are budgets, forms, protocols."

She took a breath. "I think we have a vital role here in this Region, as a gateway from northeastern Canada, to protect the people here and elsewhere."

"You don't think I'm doing my job?"

"With all due respect, Gordon, I think there's a lot more we can be doing. Including you."

"You may use the words *with all due respect,* but I'm not hearing it in your voice."

Tanya said, "Then I'm afraid I can't help you, Gordon."

He stared at her and said, "I see. Because I'm slow, I'm old, because I don't know my way around computers, Blackbirds—"

"BlackBerrys," she corrected, instantly regretting having done that. Damn it, she thought, no need to irritate him further.

But she was wrong. He didn't seem irritated at all. He just blinked at her, like that damn frog again, like she was nothing more than an insect to be observed. Or eaten.

"Thank you," he said. "BlackBerrys. So I don't know much about current technology, all the satellites and zoom-bang stuff, but I know people, Tanya. I know what makes them tick, I know what makes them want to work twelve hours a day, or be sent away overseas for six months away from home, or work in obscure and dangerous parts of the world that will never get them a headline or a medal, but only a cold grave."

Tanya said, "I appreciate that Gordon. But it seems we spend most of our time here coordinating with New England state bureaucrats, seeing if we can get them surplus radiation monitors, and doing play drills in Boston Harbor or at the nuclear plants, instead of doing real work. No offense, I don't see many people here working twelve hours a day, or worrying about being shipped overseas. We both know the most dangerous place to be in this building is in front of the elevator banks at 5:01 p.m."

"We do the work assigned to us."

"True, but I also think we need to focus on the second word in our department. Security."

Gordon said carefully, "Tanya, we're part of a larger organization, and we have to follow the proper directives from the Secretary. Procedures and protocols must be followed, even if you personally disagree on the direction she has given us. Or if some of your coworkers take offense. Or if your uncle, Senator Warren Gibbs, has other ideas of how we should operate."

"My uncle has nothing to do with me, or Region One, or how I operate. And I haven't spoken to him in many, many months."

Another slow blink of the frog eyes. "Perhaps, Tanya, but it's no secret that your uncle, if elected, proposes some drastic changes in the way Homeland Security operates. Changes that many of us oppose, including those in Congress. To make the agency more of an offensive organization, more of a paramilitary force, to—"

"To make it do what it was designed to do," she said, feeling the heat rise in her face and hands. "To protect the innocents."

"Like your college roommate? Lord knows, you do seem fixated on her. Tell me, were you ... particularly close in college? Is that it?"

She took another deep breath. "That's a cheap shot."

"A true shot?

Tanya said, "Gordon. Please. I'm just here to do my job the best I can, and if it makes you happy and feel less awkward for me to file the proper paperwork and memos—instead of working to protect the people of this region and the nation—then fine, Gordon, that's what I'll do. That way, you'll be happy, the GAO will be happy, and the American people definitely won't be happy if we're so focused on following procedures that we let something bad happen on our watch."

Gordon said, "Whatever you say. You may go, Tanya."

"Good," she said, standing up. "I was about to leave anyway."

———

In her office, Tanya made a phone call to Concord, New Hampshire, to the Department of the Safety, which was in charge of the State

Police. She was eventually connected to a Major Carl Kenyon, whom she had met years ago at a police convention in Trenton.

"Carl? It's Tanya Gibbs, remember me?"

An intake of breath. "Tanya ... it's been a very long time. How have you been? Still in New Jersey?"

She swiveled in her chair. "Doing fine, Carl. I'm now with Homeland Security, in Region One in Boston. Involved in a variety of matters, most of them classified. Tell me, they treating you all right in Concord?"

"Can't complain, much," he said. "But, if you don't mind, I'm kinda pressed for time and—"

"Now, Carl, speaking of time, I was hoping you could make time for me. Say, tomorrow afternoon."

"About what?"

"We're planning an unannounced drill up in Washington County in the next few days. Responding to a cross-border incursion. We'd like your assistance in setting up this drill with other agencies in the area."

The State Police major laughed. "That's a good one, Tanya. You know it takes months of planning to set something like that up. Hah. No, seriously, when do you want to this. This summer? This fall?"

She swiveled the chair back and forth, hating what she was doing, knowing it had to be done. "How does Friday, Saturday, or Sunday night sound?"

"Tanya, this is goddamn impossible."

"Tell you what, Carl. Why don't you set up a time for tomorrow afternoon. We'll get together, go over the plans for this drill. Then we'll have a nice dinner and retire to a local bar. We'll have a reunion of sorts. You remember that night in Trenton, don't you? At the Hyatt? When I ended up in the wrong hotel room, with a duplicate of your room key? You haven't forgotten that, have you?"

She heard not a word, just heavy breathing on the other end of the phone. She went on. "I popped in, catching up on my voicemails with my BlackBerry, and my, it sure was some damn surprise. I remember it was like yesterday. You in bed with another police officer, from Alaska, I believe. This office was straddling you, riding you ... and that officer was looking right at me. Straight on so I could see his face quite clearly, and his moustache."

"Tanya ..." His voice sounded strangled.

"So I left the room and about a half hour later, you met up with me at the lobby's bar. You told me you were involved in an upcoming classified Northeast Regional FEMA training session that could really bump my career, and we made a deal, didn't we. I mean, we were both adults, we both wanted something ... so you got me that training slot. I promised not to reveal to your sweet, chubby, plain vanilla wife what I saw in that hotel room. After all, it's not like she's from Cambridge or Brookline and would be open-minded about such a thing. As you told me, she's from a small town in western New Hampshire, and your nickname for her is Dr. Livingstone, because all she knows is missionary."

No reply. His breathing continued.

"I also remember one more thing. After we made our agreement, you looked relieved. You said that if I ever needed anything else from you, to call. So here I am. Calling."

He coughed. She said, "So let's have a reunion, you and I. It's been a number of years. We'll meet in Manchester, we'll go over my unannounced training requirements, and then I'll reaffirm my commitment to keep your secret."

His voice was shaky. "That sounds ... well, that sounds all right, then."

"Good," she cheerfully said. "You're still married, right? To chubby, vanilla Miriam? Should I call to clear this with her?"

"No," Carl said, his voice strangled. "You don't have to. I'll take care of it all. The meeting, the liaison with other agencies, and dinner. I'll set you up a room at the Center of New Hampshire in Manchester."

"Carl, that sounds delightful. I'm looking forward to it. What time do you want to see me?"

"Let's do four p.m. tomorrow."

Tanya said, "It's a date," hanging up the phone.

Then she looked out the window to the buildings of Boston. Her stomach clenched and rolled, and she barely made it to her office wastebasket before throwing up.

TWENTY-TWO

AFTER A RESTLESS NIGHT, Zach Morrow got up, showered—spending a few minutes trying to decide which tiny bottle of shampoo and conditioner to use, deciding to go with one that didn't have twelve syllables in its name—and went downstairs to breakfast. He was hungry and was tempted to go see if the Bel Aire diner in Crowdin was still open, but the cooking smells kept him back.

He sat at a wide chestnut table with other overnight guests, including two older men who talked quietly between themselves and who were impeccably dressed in pressed chinos and turtleneck sweaters, an older man and woman who sniped at each other throughout breakfast—"I told you I wanted tea, not coffee!" "Then speak up, woman." "Turn up your damn hearing aid, then"—and a young couple from Maine who were apparently on their honeymoon. They ate and looked at each other and then broke out in giggles, like they were secretly recalling their overnight fun.

The waitress was a cute girl with short blond hair and six or eight earrings in each ear, and after going through a short list of the different vegan, locally grown, and granola-type breakfast cereals, Zach smiled sweetly at her and gave her a five-dollar bill.

"Honey, if you can get me three scrambled eggs with cheese, six pieces of bacon or sausage, white toast, and a jar of coffee, I'll double this later."

She deftly pocketed the five-dollar bill, winked at him, and went out to the kitchen.

———

When he finished breakfast, he gave the waitress a ten-dollar bill. As he was going up the carpeted stairs to his room, wondering what he was going to do for the day, the manager of the bed and breakfast— a woman named Stephanie Martin, who was cheerful, had short blond hair and black-rimmed glasses—called out after him.

"Mr. Morrow? A moment?"

He went over to the B&B's office, a cubbyhole with a small desk, filing cabinet, and chair, which Stephanie was occupying. "Mr. Crowley called while you were having breakfast. He was hoping you would join him in an hour." She passed over a slip of paper. "That's his cellphone number. He said he would pick you up, if that's agreeable. If not, he said you could call him."

Zach folded the paper, slipped it into his pants pocket. "Sounds agreeable all around."

"By the by, are you enjoying your stay? Is your room fine? And how was breakfast?"

"Stay is enjoyable, room is great, and breakfast was filling."

She turned back to her desk. "So glad to hear it."

Then he thought for a moment. "Excuse me, but I was wondering. Do you have a computer I could borrow? Just for a moment?"

Stephanie said, "I don't see why not. Need to check your e-mail?"

"Need to do something, that's for sure."

———

Duncan Crowley walked along an overgrown logging road with his brother Cameron. The air was crisp and cold, and the way was wet and covered with last year's fall leaves. Sometimes he liked coming out here to have sensitive conversations, just to jazz things up. Keeping a pattern meant opening yourself to being watched or listened to by anyone interested in your activities. He didn't like keeping patterns.

Cameron said, "This is what I know about Zach, the guy who waxed your ass in phys ed."

"You sure like harping on that," Duncan said.

"Gives me pleasure, why the hell not." He produced his small notebook, went to the last page. "Born and raised here in Turner, went to our regional high school. Nothing out of the ordinary there. But his dad was Monty Morrow. Remember? The executive councilor for this district. Former Turner selectman."

Hands in his coat pocket, Duncan kicked at a rusting piece of equipment on the ground. Decades ago, this whole area was logged and re-logged, with lots of forest fires and erosion along stream banks. "Yeah, I remember now. Seemed to have his fingers in everything political, from road agent elections to congressional races."

"Yeah, well, he had his fingers and his dick in a lot of other things as well. You'd think the guy's last name was Kennedy, the amount of tomcatting he did."

Duncan said, "Funny, don't remember hearing that when we were kids. Go on."

"So I found out that, after he graduated, Zach had a job lined up, working down at the State House in Concord for some legislative research committee. Guess dear old dad wanted to start grooming him, maybe set him up to do his own political career, follow the family business. Never happened. Zach left Turner and joined the Coast Guard. Near as I could learn, him coming back the other day was the first time he'd been back to Turner since he joined the Coasties."

"Zach told me he was dishonorably discharged. True?"

"Quite true. Just under a year ago. Funny thing, my guys say his record is just bare bones. All they found out is that he was involved with something to do with port and river security. There's hints of other things—deployments overseas to Africa, the Middle East—but just dates, no details of anything he did. Then his dishonorable discharge, supposedly for disobeying direct orders on a deployment. No details of the deployment in question. That's it."

"His house burn down in Purmort, like he said?"

Cameron laughed. "Like I said, easiest thing to check out. Yeah. Double-wide he lived in burned right down to the concrete mat. Fire department got there in time to save the concrete. Cause under investigation."

"Glad to hear that. What did Stephanie at the bed and breakfast say?"

"Quiet guy. Went into his room. Lights out about eleven p.m. Didn't use the house phone, but he did make a cellphone call about thirty minutes before going to sleep. Oh, and this morning, when he had breakfast, he didn't like any of the offerings, so he paid off the waitress to get something off the menu."

Duncan walked a few more yards, sniffed the air, tried to imagine a time when men and machines roared through here, cutting down trees, raising up sparks, digging in the dirt. Funny what time did, to even something that now looked like wilderness.

"What's your gut say, Cameron?"

His brother exhaled. "He's got the skill set, that's for sure. He's also hungry. When you get dumped like that with bad paper, it affects everything. These troubled times, companies aren't going hire somebody like Zach Morrow. Too much baggage. Plus, you don't get your pension, don't get medical coverage. Then you have his house burning down ... Yeah, I could see him coming back up here, back home, maybe start out new."

Duncan said, "Good round-up. But your gut, Cameron. I know you trust it, and I trust it, too. What's it saying?"

Cameron turned around, started going back down the overgrown road. Duncan stayed in step with him. "Too much of a coincidence. You got the shipment coming in, you're talking about needing extra skilled hands, and boom, here he is. With a perfect record. Maybe too perfect."

They walked along for a minute or two, and as they came to Duncan's Chevy Colorado, he said, "My gut sort of sounds the same. Last night ... a bear was sniffing in our yard. Got me up, I got out with weapon in hand, waiting ... and last night, I told Karen to take the kids and bail out of town for a couple of days. Besides the bikers ... I still think we're being looked at. That's one hell of a coincidence."

"So what to do with Zach?"

Duncan shoved his hands farther into his coat pockets. "I'm going to meet him in about thirty minutes. I'm thinking of taking him up to the butcher shop, near our gun store. Maybe have a serious one-on-one discussion."

"Want some help?"

"No, I think I'll be good. But thanks anyway. I'm not going to get too physical. Maybe just put the fear of God into him. If he passes, fine. If not, well, there's always the quarry."

Cameron nodded. "Yeah, there's always the quarry."

About mid-morning, Louis Fontaine was recalling his marching orders, about going on this zap mission, and he was about five minutes away from dumping the mission and zapping the stupid shit next to him. Last night they had gotten into Turner, and all he wanted to do was to conduct a little pre-op surveillance, just a bit of intelligence work, and that went down in a disaster like the goddamn Hindenburg. Near midnight last night Jean-Paul had held up his BlackBerry and giggled, and said, "Shit, Louis, I'm sorry, but my handheld is dead."

"What the fuck you mean, it's dead?" Louis had asked.

Another set of giggles. "Guess I forgot to charge it up."

"So charge it up already," he had said.

"Guess I forgot the charger, too."

Oh, fuck me, he had thought. The directions, the photos, all the stuff that they had gotten back up at the clubhouse, gone. They had nothing on paper. So Jean-Paul had driven around Turner, looking to ask someone for directions to either the Flight Deck Bar & Grill, or to Duncan Crowley's house, but at that hour of the night, the place looked like it was inhabited by the living dead. The businesses were all dark and only a few homes had lights on.

Jean-Paul had wanted to rent a hotel room for the night, but Louis had quickly shot that down. "Christ, how stupid can you be? We zap this fucker and his family, and you want some motel owner to tell the cops about two guys from Quebec who spent the night before?"

So they had parked the van down a deserted road, spent a lousy night on the upholstered floor—with one blanket to fight over during the long smelly hours—and now they were randomly driving around.

"We could go to the town hall, look up his tax records. Or voting records. Or something."

Louis felt like hitting his hand against his head, over and over again, just to get this droning voice out of his skull. "Jean-Paul, we got to a public official, what do you think will happen after the Crowley family disappears? Hunh? Why not send up a fucking flare while you're at it?"

Jean-Paul said, "Well, what do you want to do? Jesus Christ, all you're doing is bitching and moaning. I'm not hearing any constructive suggestions."

"Here's a goddamn constructive suggestion," Louis said. "Next time, you stay the fuck home in Quebec, I'll go by myself. With paper intelligence, not a goddamn smartphone without a goddamn charger. Then maybe the goddamn thing will be slick as shit."

———

Tom Leighton was working his shift at the Irving service station in southern Turner when he saw a familiar-looking Volkswagen Golf pull into the lot. The inside was empty so he could give Gus Spooner his full attention when he came in, but Christ, Gus looked like shit, and there was a bandage on his left hand.

"Sweet Christ, what the hell happened to you?" Tom asked. Gus looked behind the counter, to see if anybody else was around. When he saw Tom was by himself, he held up the injured hand.

"Ran into the fucking Crowley brothers," he said crossly. "Look what they did to me."

The bandage was big and lumpy looking and covered the whole hand. "Shit, pal, what did they do?"

"Goddamn Duncan Crowley, he was pissed at something I was doing. He and his shit-ass brother ambushed me, beat me up some, and then put a fucking nail through my hand, nailed it to the seat of a picnic table."

Tom felt light-headed, hearing and seeing what had happened to his friend. "Holy sweet Jesus. What did you do to tick him off?"

Gus went to the coffee stand, filled up a cup with his right hand, and came back to the counter. "What did it matter to him, hunh? Christ, all I was doing, with Barry and Freddo, was trying to cook up some meth. What's the problem with that? I mean, it wasn't like I was doing it in his yard or something. But the goddamn freak and his brother, look what they did."

Tom whistled. "Must have hurt like hell."

Gus said, "Wouldn't give the fuckers the satisfaction. Kept my mouth shut and took it like a man, that's what I did. Goddamn Crowley brothers ... you've had some run-ins with them, haven't you?"

Tom remembered the other night, being inches away from falling into the quarry, all because his uncle was doing kiss-ass with the Crowley brothers and wouldn't go against them. His own uncle, threatening to kill him!

"Yeah," Tom said. "I have ... and didn't like it. Who would? Goddamn Crowleys."

———

Jean-Paul slowed the van down, said, "Look. There's a gas station. We go in, buy a cup of coffee, grab a cruller, say we're making a delivery to Duncan Crowley, ask for directions. All these small towns, the people know each other. Hell, they fucking marry each other's cousins and shit."

Louis was hungry, exhausted, and tired of trying to put some sense into this fool. "I don't know …"

"Shit, what else can we do, hunh? Call Michael Grondin, tell him we don't have the directions and information?"

"Your fault."

"Yeah, but he'll say we're a team. And we both fucked up."

Louis put a hand to his forehead. "Fine. Pull up to the gas station. Maybe we'll luck out."

———

Tom looked up as the two guys from a parked dark blue van strolled in, and for no reason whatsoever, he felt uneasy. They had a bearing about them, like they knew their way around with fists or weapons. Both had on jeans, dark gray fleece coats, and the one on the left had a thin moustache, while the other had a full beard. They went up to the coffee counter and talked French among themselves while Gus stood by, sipping from his own coffee.

When they came over to pay, the beefier of the two, the one with the beard, said, "Hey, was wondering if you could help us out."

"Will give it a try," Tom said.

"Looking for a fella, lives here in town. Name of Duncan Crowley. We're s'pose to drop something off for him. You know where he lives, eh?"

Tom knew exactly where Duncan Crowley lived, but these guys … their eyes were kinda dead. He also didn't like the way they were anxiously looking at him, like if he didn't give them the proper reply, they'd knock the shit out of him.

So he didn't know what to say, but Gus spoke up. "Duncan Crowley? Sure, I know where he lives. You guys want the address? Directions?"

The other guy, the one with the scraggly moustache said, his French accent heavier, "That would be fine, sir, thank you."

———

Louis walked out of the Irving service station, a cup of coffee in one hand, a glazed doughnut in the other, feeling a bit better than when they had gotten to Turner. Jean-Paul gently nudged him.

"See? See? We got just what we needed … and that kid, he looked pretty skanky. Not the kind of kid who'll go to the cops. Am I right?"

Louis said, "Let's just eat up and get over there, okay?"

Jean-Paul said, "Oh, this is going to be great."

———

Tom stared at his friend Gus, who was smirking, watching the two guys get into a van with Quebec license plates—"Je Me Souviens" the license plate said, and his uncle Dickie once told him that was French for "I Am A Souvenir"—and Tom said, "Are you fucking stone cold dumb? You just gave those two guys directions to Duncan Crowley's house? What the hell were you thinking?"

Gus picked up his coffee cup with his good hand. "I'm thinking those two guys are going to tune up Duncan Crowley. If you and me are lucky, he'll get a taste of the shit he and his dick brother have been shoveling out over the years."

Tom's guts churned, looking at the bandage on Gus's hand. "You nutcase, look at what he did to your fucking hand for cooking meth.

What do you think he's gonna do to you if he finds out that you gave directions to those two guys?"

His friend took a self-satisfied sip from his coffee. "Don't be such a pussy. What do you think, those guys are going to Duncan's place and the first thing they're gonna say is how they got there? Christ, relax already."

Tom said, "No offense, but I'm going to start relaxing the second you head out."

———

Zach Morrow was waiting outside of Rogers' Bed & Breakfast when Duncan Crowley pulled up in his maroon Chevy pickup truck. Zach got in, shook the offered hand, and settled back in the comfortable seat. He had on jeans, a Coast Guard Academy sweatshirt, a jean jacket, and underneath the sweatshirt, in a small leather holster against his right hip, was his .32 semiautomatic Browning pistol.

"They treat you all right there?" Duncan asked.

"Did just fine," he said.

"Glad to hear it. Hey, want to take a ride, talk old times?"

Zach buckled his seatbelt. "Sure. Why not?"

———

Jean-Paul called out, excitement in his voice, "There it is, there it is!"

Louis wanted to tell him to shut up, but yeah, there it was, just like the kid with the bandaged hand had said. Dark-stained house on Old Mill Road, on the left side, and shit, luck was with them.

He said, "Don't slow down, just keep on driving. But look there. The guy said Duncan drove a truck, his wife drove a Toyota. Look what's there in the driveway."

"Yeah, a goddamn Toyota. How far we going?"

"Far enough to turn around, or find a place to park."

The road rose up and after a couple of minutes, there was an old cemetery on the left with narrow lanes leading into it.

"There," Louis said. "Take a drive down there, see if we can hide the van."

Jean-Paul backed into the cemetery, slowly going back, until the lane disappeared in a low grove of bushes and pines. Louis's heart was thumping, his hands warm and tingly. He got out and Jean-Paul met him at the taillights. Jean-Paul opened the rear door, and with a few movements of his hands under the bumper, unsnapped a release bolt. The floor was now loose, and Louis lifted it up, exposing a small, padded interior housing the two Chinese-made SKS semiautomatic rifles.

He picked one up, handed it to Jean-Paul. He took his own, checked the magazine, worked the action.

"All right, close it up," he said. "Leave the keys in the ignition."

"What, suppose somebody comes by, steals it?"

Louis said, "Look the hell around. Who the hell's gonna steal this? The Prince of Fucking Darkness? No, leave the keys in the ignition. We need to leave in a hurry, I don't want you telling me you can't find the keys, or the keys were left behind."

"Shit, okay, then."

In a few minutes, they were moving down through the woods, heading to the house.

Duncan took in Zach Morrow as he drove up to the butcher shop. Zach was his age, of course, but he was wider in the shoulders and there was something in his eyes, like he was constantly looking, observing, evaluating. His brown hair was thin, shot through with gray, and was cut short. There were fine wrinkles about his eyes, like he had spent a lot of time outside, squinting in the sun.

Duncan said, "So what are you hoping to find out here?"

"Crap, I don't know," Zach said. "A long shot, I know, but I didn't have any other place to go. My bad paper from the Coast Guard means most employers won't even look at me, and with my place burning down ... it was like God was giving me a swift kick in the butt to go someplace else. So to Turner I came. Hell, even if it means somebody who knew my dad takes pity on me ... shit, bills need to get paid, pity or no pity."

Duncan said, "Things are tight all around, bud. If you want, I could poke around, ask a few questions."

Zach looked over, eyes filled with gratitude. "Really? Not shitting me, are you?"

"Not a bit."

"Man, I'd owe you big time if anything came from that. Christ, ever since I got kicked out, it's like I can't get a break. Like everything's stacked up against you. If I was a goddamn Wall Street banker or Detroit carmaker or a union, you'd bet there'd be money and government aid for the asking. But put nearly twenty years in the service of the nation, screw up once, and then it's fuck you very much."

Duncan took the turn on Gilman Road, leading up the gun store and the butcher shop. This time of the year, the gun shop was only open on weekends, until the weather got warmer and the flatlanders started rolling in.

"Yeah, that's tough all right," Duncan said. "Seems to be a lot of that going around. You know the golden rule, hunh? Those who have the gold, make the rules."

"Quite true."

"So. Mind telling me what you did that got you dishonorably discharged?"

Zach looked out the window. "Someday, maybe. But not today."

———

Louis led the way, holding the SKS close to his side. Thing was, people driving around really didn't expect to see men out and about carrying semiautomatic assault rifles, so the best way to move around was to keep it lowered and parallel to your body. That way, there was nothing sticking out to get anyone's attention.

Jean-Paul said, "What do we do when we get there? Polite or blitz?"

Louis said, "She's a housewife. Probably home alone, maybe with a kid or two. Forget polite. We'll go straight for blitz."

Jean-Paul smiled. "That sounds great. And remember ... I don't want to lose any chance for playtime."

Louis said, "How the hell can I forget something like that?"

———

Zach felt something cool waft up against his skin as Duncan pulled into a dirt lot. In front was a log building for what was called Washington County Weapons & Surplus. Near the building was a shed that had a sign announcing SEASONAL DEER BUTCHERING: BEST PRICES GUARANTEED. There were no other cars in the lot. The woods were nearby and in the distance, the peaks of the White Mountains.

Duncan switched off the engine. "Couple of my businesses. I've been lucky since my accident back then. Got a bit of an insurance pay-out, bought a little gas station and convenience store, worked my ass off, got married, and Karen, she started a hairdressing salon. Boy and girl later, bunch of other businesses as well, we're holding our own. In better shape than a lot of poor families in this county."

"Good on you," Zach said, easing his breathing, keeping his eyes on Duncan's hands. The man's voice was calm and soothing, but Zach remembered the story of the mob-types who came up here and never returned. So if those hands moved suddenly, he'd bail out on this side of the truck, grab his Browning, keep the truck between them. If things went to the shits, okay, at least he was on top of things. If he overreacted, well, he could blame it on PTSD or not having been breastfed or something like that.

Duncan said, "Like what you said earlier, about being boned even when other people were getting taken care of. A hell of a thing, isn't it? Don't have to tell you, people up here, they're poor but proud. They're not looking for a hand-out, but just a fair goddamn chance. Like the paper mill down in Berlin. Hundreds of blue-collar jobs at good wages, that place was about to be closed 'cause the Canadian firm that owned the place was shipping everything back home. So these Iranian brothers came up here, made all these promises to the right people, got Federal funding, and they took the place over."

Zach nodded at all the right places, kept sight on the man's hands. Maybe he was being paranoid, but he remembered a training session once, with an ex-Aussie SAS guy, who said not to worry, paranoia was just another definition of heightened awareness.

Duncan went on. "People started getting suspicious, you know, when they started selling off some of the assets, especially when the

Iranians kept on promising the proceeds were going to be used to update the equipment. Then one Monday morning, the place is padlocked, the boilers are dead, and the Iranians have skipped town, living on some island in Caribbean."

"Remember reading about that," Zach said. "Thought the word was, they couldn't be extradited because of some treaty or something."

Duncan tapped the steering wheel. "Official story, of course. But we ignorant mountain folk—just like you, Zach—some of us think up here that the government doesn't want to bring those brothers to justice because of all the embarrassing info they might reveal about how and where they got their Federal funding. Payoffs to certain Congressmen and committee members. That sort of thing."

"Like Whitey Bulger," Zach said.

"The South Boston gangster?"

"Yeah," Zach said. "Mean son-of-bitch, ran drugs and other shit down in Boston, responsible for killing lots of people. Government could never prove anything to put him away. Reason being, of course, that he was a confidential informant for the FBI's Boston office. Once that little fiasco blew up, he went on the lam and the FBI—shocked that their CI was a serial killer—put him on the Top Ten fugitive list. Took 'em nearly sixteen years to find him and lots of people think—me included—that the FBI didn't want to find him, because of all the juicy details he had hidden away about the corrupt FBI office in Boston and the nonsense they were up to."

"Hell of a world," Duncan said. "That's why ever since I could, I haven't relied on anybody else to take care of my family and friends, except for me."

Duncan's left hand went off the steering wheel and down to his side. Zach started to move.

TWENTY-THREE

Louis and Jean-Paul cut through the woods and through a neighbor's backyard, and then into Duncan Crowley's yard, SKS rifles at their sides. There was a kids' swimming pool in the rear, some hedges, and a swing set. On the rear deck was a barbecue gas grill and a picnic table. The two of them went around the garage, past the Toyota RAV4, and to the front door.

Unlimbering his SKS, Louis said, "This is how it's going to run. We get her to the door and blast our way through. I'll take the lead."

"Why the fuck should you take the lead?" Jean-Paul said.

"Idiot like you, you forget your battery charger, you think I'm going to let you take lead?"

"Hey, that's—"

"Shut up. Stand to the side, so she can't see you."

At least Jean-Paul did that. He moved to the left, near a small juniper bush, and Louis turned so his body was blocking the view of his SKS. He rang the doorbell, waited, and then rang the doorbell again.

His heart was thumping but he was taking long, deep breaths, getting into the zone. The SKS felt so damn good in his strong hand.

From inside, a shadow approached, jelling into the figure of a woman. She opened the door slightly, smiled as he opened the glass storm door. She was a good-looking piece of flesh, big smile, shoulder-length red hair, just a bit of make-up, nice rack in a white buttoned-lace blouse, tight jeans.

"Mrs. Crowley?" Louis asked.

"Yes?" she said. "What can I do for you?"

Still smiling he pounced, lowering his shoulder so he punched right through the open door. She fell back, stumbled, her face startled, screaming, and the door swung open so hard it hit the wall. He raised up the SKS, pointed it at her, and said, "Sit the fuck down! Sit the fuck down now!"

Jean-Paul was right behind him and keeping the rifle up, pointing it at her impressive chest.

Louis said, "Jean-Paul! Close and lock the door."

"Got it."

Louis heard the door shut behind him, looked down at the woman, splayed out on her butt, holding herself up by her manicured hands on the floor of her fine and clean kitchen. He liked the way she looked, down beneath him. Took a breath. "Is anybody else here?"

She shook her head, bit her trembling lower lip. "No."

"You sure? I send my pal around, he's not going to find your husband, or kids, or anything else, right? 'Cause if he does, we'll hurt you, sweetie, we'll hurt you good."

Another shake of the head. Her voice quivered. "I'm here alone. I was getting ready to go to work."

Jean-Paul was standing nearby, rifle at the ready. Louis said to him, "To the living room. Tell me if it's clear or not."

Jean-Paul went to the living room, adjacent to the kitchen, where the attractive Mrs. Crowley was sitting on her ass. "Clear, Louis."

"Good." He motioned with the rifle. "This is how it's going to work. You're gonna slide back across the floor to the living room, up on the couch. You're not going to stand up. You're not going to crawl. You're not going to scream. You're gonna go right up to the couch."

The woman did as she was told, Louis moving in time with her, scanning around, taking in the living room, the view from the rear deck sliding glass doors, seeing two couches, two comfortable-looking easy chairs, a big-ass television on one wall, a couple of bookcases, some potted plants, and kids' toys on the floor.

Her face scarlet, breathing hard, Mrs. Crowley got up on the couch. Jean-Paul stood next to her, the SKS just a couple of feet away.

"What do you want?" she said.

Louis smiled. "You'll find out. First, I'm the one asking questions. What's your first name, hon?"

She paused, swallowed. "Karen."

Louis nodded. "Karen, your husband has been a true prick. We need to talk to him. So we'll start with that."

"He's not here."

"Guess we know that, Karen. So where is he?"

She shook her head. "I don't know. We own a few businesses. He likes to go around, visit them, see how they're doing."

"Like your pot farms? Or the places you store your booze and cigarettes from smuggling?"

Karen said defiantly, "Wherever he is, he's not here."

"When's he due back?"

"Probably dinner time. Just after six. Unless he calls to say he's running late."

Louis said, "Yeah, running late. Running late 'cause he's whacked a couple of our friends. Why the hell do you think we're here? To make a flower delivery? We're here 'cause your hubby's got a lot of blood on his hands."

Again, defiance in her voice, Karen said, "I don't know anything about that."

"Good for you. Look, we can't wait all fucking day for him. So you're gonna call him, have him come over."

She said, "For what reason?

Louis said, "Shit, I don't know. You said you were heading out to work. Call him up, tell him you got a car problem. Flat tire."

"It's a new car," she said, looking to him and Jean-Paul.

"Don't give a shit," Louis said. "You can tell him a fucking volcano erupted in the backyard, sweetie, we're going to need him over here, like now."

"What for?" she said.

"What for?" he repeated, stepping closer. "Remember what I said earlier, about asking questions? Not your place to ask questions."

She crossed her arms, he saw her hands were shaking. "I get him over here, I'm no fool, you're going to hurt him. Or worse."

Jean-Paul stepped in, pushing the barrel end of the SKS into her right tit. "Tell you what, sweetie, you don't get him over here, I'll shoot your right boobie off, and then we'll try again."

Louis admired Jean-Paul's creativity, but he was disgusted to see that Jean-Paul was tent poling in the crotch of his jeans.

Tears started pooling in her eyes. She clasped her arms tighter. "All right," she whispered. "There's a portable phone on the counter."

She got up from the couch, and Louis said, "Park your ass down. Jean-Paul, go behind me. See if there's a portable phone there. If so, bring it back."

Jean-Paul moved past him and then returned with the phone. He waited, and Louis nodded to him. "Okay, give it to her." She took the phone.

Louis said, "Jean-Paul, stand in front of her. Honey, I'm going to take a seat here, next to you." Louis took the seat, put the SKS on safe—just in case she went nutty and tried to grab it—and said to her, "I'm going to be right here, you're going to put that phone up to your ear, then you're going to make that phone call. I'm going to be listening in so I know you're not calling the local Officer Friendly or sheriff's department. You call your hubbie, say the car won't start, can he please come over here and help you out. If everything's fine, we'll just sit still and wait for him to show up."

He shifted his weight on the couch, got closer to her, smelled her perfume. It was nice. He said, "But if you try to say anything more than that, if your voice isn't your usual cheerful tone, if you try to pass along a code word or phrase that raises questions, then I'm going to wait here with you. But my friend Jean-Paul over there"—and Jean-Paul offered a creepy smile—"he'll depart. He'll go to the school where your kids are, and he'll pull a fucking Columbine on them. Don't think he won't. Have I made myself clear?"

She was crying silently, face red, tears running down her cheeks, and Louis smelled ammonia, looked down, and saw the fine Mrs. Crowley had peed herself in her tight jeans. "Just … just give me a second to compose myself … all right? Just a second."

Louis looked at his watch. "I'll give you thirty, honey. Then you'll make the goddamn call."

———

Duncan opened the truck door and noted Zach jerking in surprise, like he thought Duncan was going to come up with a pistol and blast at him in the truck. This guy was good, no doubt about it, and as he stepped outside, he was trying to go through the options. He had thought maybe he'd just take the guy into the deer butcher shop, get him secured, start talking to him straight.

But how to get him secured?

Get him into the butcher shop first, then worry about the interrogation process later.

But damn, the guy was good.

"Come on," he said to Zach. "I'll show you around the remotest part of the Crowley business empire."

———

Zach almost went to his piece when Duncan's hand went down, but the guy was only opening up the truck door. Zach did the same and joined him outside, and they started walking to the gun shop across the gravel and dirt lot. Duncan said, "A bit out of the way, but the tourists and flatlanders, they love coming up in the summer and fall seasons, see us rustic rubes with all our guns."

"That they do."

"You hunt?"

"Used to, back in school. Lost my taste for it once I got into service. Plus I was busy going to other places."

Duncan gestured to the deer butcher shop. "You ought to come inside with me over here. There are some great trophy racks in there."

Zach looked to the tiny concrete and wooden building with no windows, one door.

He knew he would put a couple of .32 rounds into Duncan's chest before getting within ten yards of going into that place.

———

Duncan saw Zach hesitate, instantly knew it wasn't going to work. This guy in front of him wasn't going to go easy into the butcher shop, no matter if he told him that the place was holding a host of hot nymphos from Brazil. He had his 9mm Smith & Wesson in the truck under the front seat and was carrying a backup piece in a waist holster—a .380 Bersa—and he'd have to move quick, to get the drop on him, and not in a way he wanted to do it—

His cellphone rang.

———

Louis sat close to Karen, enjoying her scent, the touch of her leg against his, and seeing how Jean-Paul's idea of having some playtime was pretty attractive. Not the kids—fuck that shit—but man, he wouldn't mind tearing off a piece of her before they got everything all wrapped up.

The phone rang once and he could hear the guy's voice nice and clear. "Karen? What's up?"

She said, "Oh, Duncan, you wouldn't believe it. I don't know what's wrong but the damn RAV won't start up. And I'm late for work. Any chance you could come pick me up?"

Duncan sighed. "You sure? None of the girls from the shop can help you out?"

"I tried but they're wicked backed up. Come on, honey, you know I'll make it worth your while."

Jean-Paul grinned nastily, and even Louis felt a stirring in his groin. He abruptly felt jealous of the man who got spend time with this woman here, in this handsome house. Louis's own quarters were a cheap rented condo unit where he could hear kids screaming and loud televisions through the thin walls, where his own kitchen was filled with greasy pizza boxes and empty Molson bottles. And the women ... sure, he had tasted the talent at the Slippery Pussy, but shit, they were pros, either with lots of tats, bad teeth, or faded track marks on their arms and thighs. Not like this classy piece of ass sitting next to him.

A slight burst of static followed by a chuckle. "Yeah, I know you always make it worth my while. I'm at the gun shop. I'll be there in about ten minutes. Bye."

The soon-to-be-late Duncan Crowley hung up the phone, and Karen handed the portable over to Louis. He took it—the receiver warm from being held in her hand—and she said, "There. I did it."

Louis got up. "Glad to hear it."

There was a noise, as Karen loudly exhaled. "All right, I did that for you, and I want to know one thing."

"I said no questions, sweetie."

Karen said, "Not really a question. Just looking for confirmation. You're Louis"—pointing to him—"and you're Jean-Paul, am I right?"

Louis said, "Yeah, you're right. So what?"

Even though her face was flushed, jeans stained, and tears were in her eyes, her voice suddenly grew strong. "Because, you damn fools, once my husband kills you both, I want to tell him who you were."

TWENTY-FOUR

DUNCAN SNAPPED HIS CELLPHONE shut, made a production of putting it a little leather case on his belt. "Need to go rescue my princess of a wife. Car won't start and she needs to get to work. Care to go for a ride?"

Zach seemed to relax. "If it's not a bother, I don't see why not."

Duncan nodded, started back to his truck. "Great. Maybe we'll catch an early lunch or something."

Zach kept quiet as Duncan got in, started the truck up, and circled around the dirt lot and back down the paved road. He was disappointed he hadn't been able to slide Zach into the butcher shop for a bit of creative Q&A, but the day was still young. Once he got Karen squared away, then maybe he'd take Zach over to the Flight Deck. The restaurant had a deep, quiet basement that just might work. If the questioning didn't work out for his former classmate, well, Zach could stay in the basement for a while. And if things did work in Zach's favor, then the both of them could have an early drink while discussing employment possibilities.

Options. Duncan was always in favor of them.

Zach kept quiet as Duncan drove up Old Mill Road, heading to the Crowley household. He was embarrassed at feeling like he was back in high school again, since he was going to see Karen for the first time in nearly twenty years. What an unexpected pleasure. He was sure his buds from the Guard would be laughing their nutsacks off if they knew what he was feeling. Zach had gone and done many things in the service of his country, and had bedded a fair number of women—including one extraordinary evening in Marseilles with two female Air France attendants—but *bedded* was the key word. He had never had a real, long-time relationship with a woman, and despite what he knew of Duncan and his criminal history, he still envied the man.

His relationship with the young Karen Delaney had been a spring fling of cuddles, kisses, exploration, and mutual vows of love and eternity—until he had gone off to work that summer as a counselor at a camp on Conway Lake. When he had come back, Karen had found someone to keep her company over those few months: Duncan Crowley, star baseball player, a pitching phenom in the Granite State even in his junior year.

Duncan said, "Old homestead is up ahead."

"You got kids?"

"Two," he said. "Lewis and Amy. Lewis is a sports nut like his dad, and Amy is a strong-headed handful, just like her mom."

For the second time in two days, Zach noted the fine house, not a McMansion or anything overwhelming, but a solid, pleasant house, a great place to have a family and raise kids.

While also running a county-wide criminal enterprise.

Duncan turned into the wide driveway, parking to the right of the disabled red Toyota RAV4. He left the truck's engine running and said, "Be back in a sec. Hey, you dated Karen a few times back in school, right?"

Zach tried not to smile. "I sure did."

Duncan got out. "I'm sure she'll be glad to see you, catch up on old times."

"That'd be great," Zach said, and he meant it.

———

From his vantage point, kneeling behind the couch where Karen Crowley sat, Louis had a brief glimpse of a pickup truck with an extended cab pulling into the driveway, and then his view was blocked by the Toyota. Jean-Paul was standing near the large television set, hidden from sight by anyone coming through the front door, SKS held at the ready.

Karen's voice wavered. "Can . . . can I go to the kitchen? Meet him as he comes in?"

Louis laughed. "What? So you can make a break for it? Not hardly, hon. Nope, you're going to stay right here until your dear hubbie comes through that door. Tell me now, is he right-handed or left-handed?"

"Why do you care?"

He poked the back of her neck with the business end of the Chinese semiautomatic rifle. "Again with the goddamn questions. Just answer mine. Right or left?"

"Right-handed, you bastard. He's right-handed."

"Glad to know. You let him in and get the door shut, and don't say a goddamn thing before then, or Jean-Paul ducks out the rear door and goes to the local school."

A shape appeared at the door.

Duncan was thinking about Zach, back there in the truck, also thinking about getting the RAV4 fixed, so he was pretty darn occupied when he opened the storm door and main door, going into the kitchen. Karen was sitting on the couch, eyes red-rimmed, hands in her lap, not saying a word. He instantly knew he was walking into disaster.

His hand flipped back to his waist holster, knowing with a black hardness he was too late, as a man rose up behind the couch, holding an assault rifle. He was bulky, with a shaved head and a beard, and said quietly, "That hand keeps moving, your wife's brains are going to be splattered over this fine couch."

Duncan froze, staring at the man, who stared back with the firm and confident gaze of a man who had it all in control. He said, "All right, hand's coming back."

"Put them up, then, high up in the fucking air."

The man stepped around the couch, keeping the rifle's barrel pointed at Karen's sweet head. Duncan stared and stared at the man, burning his appearance into his mind. His eyes flickered around the kitchen, looking for a knife, a cleaver, a hammer, anything that could be used.

He said, "Keeping your right hand up in the air, reach around with your left hand, with two fingers—two fucking fingers only—take out your piece, drop it on the floor."

Duncan said, "Guy, I'll do anything and everything you want. Just let my wife go."

The other man grinned. "Nice try, but it's not going to happen. I'm going to need some answers from you. This sweet piece in front of me will ensure my questions are answered. But let's start with getting that weapon away."

He took a deep breath, and then another. He couldn't bear to look at his wife. Keeping his right hand up, he slowly lowered his left hand, turned so everything was visible to the gunman. With his two fingers, he pulled the .380 out and dropped it to the floor. The metal hitting the tile was quite loud.

"Kick it over here."

Duncan gave it a swift kick. It slid across the shiny tile floor and spun as it hit the living room rug. "Iron Steeds?" he asked.

"Good guess, genius."

Duncan tried again. "Let my wife go, lock her in a closet or something, but let her be. Your beef is with me. Not her."

With a one hand, the gunman ran his fingers through Karen's hair. Duncan clenched his teeth, feeling his blood heat and rage sprint through him, seeing his woman, his wife, the mother of his children, being violated.

"Not your choice, pal. You had a chance to reach a nice little agreement when two of my buds came here the other day. But no, you decided to be a stupid fucker. So this is what happens to stupid fuckers. Come on, step forward, hands on the back of your head, fingers laced together."

Duncan slowly went by the kitchen counter, to the living room, evaluating, looking, noting the coffee table in front of him with a large stoneware vase, thinking that may be of use, but as he went deeper into the room, he saw the second gunman.

"Get your hands off my wife," he said, looking back at the first man.

The man grinned, suddenly tugged Karen's hair, making her yelp. "What are you going to do about it?"

Never in his life had he ever felt so trapped, so helpless, so useless.

———

Zach waited, engine rumbling, sitting still in Duncan's truck. His super secret cellphone was back at his room at the bed and breakfast, so at some point today he'd have to tell Tanya of his progress, or lack thereof. He still had a problem gauging what was going on with Duncan's pleasant face and inviting approach. At one point, he was practically promising to find Zach a job up here in the perpetually economically depressed North Country, and in almost the same breath, up on the deserted side of a hill, he was inviting him to come into a small concrete shed used for butchering deer.

He folded his arms. What the hell was taking Duncan so long?

———

Louis loved it, loved it, loved it. Everything was coming together and he couldn't believe how this was going down. Maybe Jean-Paul was right. Maybe this going to be slick as shit after all.

"All right, pal, you've gone far enough. Stand still. Jean-Paul, cover him."

Jean-Paul stepped closer, SKS right up to his shoulder, looking straight down the open iron sights.

Duncan stayed still. Louis gestured with his SKS. "Slowly take your left hand down, undo your belt and pants, let 'em fall."

The man stood still. Not moving. Staring at Louis with pure blood-fed hate. Louis didn't care. In fact, he enjoyed the feeling. The guy was staring at him with such hatred as well as weakness at being in this position. It was a great combination.

Louis said, "Our previous guys probably dicked around with you and didn't show you the proper respect. Not respect like kissing your ass, but respect when you go into somebody's yard and meet their fucking pit bull. We're not going to make that mistake. You're smart, you're armed, you move fast. So drop trou, bro, or I'm going to take this shirt"—grabbing the collar of Karen's blouse—"and rip it off your wife."

Eyes filled with fury, the left hand slowly went down and started working at the belt.

———

Duncan tried to take it as slow as possible, knowing time was the only ally he had in this room. He had two guys in front of him— both armed with semiautomatic weapons, both pointed in his direction—and all he had were his bare hands. There was the heavy vase before him, and behind him, about a yard or so away on the floor, was the piece he'd had to drop.

He lowered his left hand, started to slowly undo his belt, fumbling his belt on purpose, feeling sick at heart for what was happening to him and Karen. He always knew that the life he had chosen, the life he had led, meant a good chance of a violent end somewhere along the way. But he had always hoped that his end would not involve Karen.

His temples throbbing hard, his mouth tasteless, he did as he was told.

———

Zach checked his watch again. This was stupid. This was taking too damn long.

He opened the door and got out, moved forward, walking in front of the pickup truck and the Toyota RAV4. To see Karen Delaney—all right, Karen Crowley—would be a pleasant distraction from what was going on.

At the front door, he reached for the doorknob and then quickly dropped down and moved back.

There was a man inside there, pointing a weapon at Duncan Crowley.

Zach took a breath, grabbed his .32 Browning, took a pause. All right. Time for another look.

He raised his head up, grabbed another quick peek. Through the kitchen and to the living room, Duncan's back was to him, hands held up. A woman, no doubt Karen, was sitting on the couch, facing towards the kitchen. A guy was on the right, pointing a rifle at Duncan.

What to do?

Run up the street, find a phone, call 911? And how long before a cop arrived? He knew Turner and its surroundings. One cop on duty, maybe two. They'd have to call backup from the other towns, from the county sheriff's department, and the State Police. SWAT? Hell, they'd have to call in the State Police SWAT unit, which would take hours to get here, no doubt about it.

It didn't look like Duncan or Karen had hours. Or even minutes.

He reached up to the doorknob, hesitated. Going through like this ... opening the door would bring that gunman looking straight at him, with Duncan in the crossfire, hell, with Karen just a few feet away.

It was like a switch deep inside of him had been closed, for the first time in a long time.

Zach was now back in the world he knew best.

He let his hand drop.

———

Louis whistled. "Tightie whities? A guy like you, I'd thought you'd be wearing something naughty black, or bright red. Got such a foxy wife, I'm disappointed in what I'm seeing."

Duncan said, "I'm sure you are disappointed. It's probably neater and bigger than what you see in the bathroom mirror every morning."

Jean-Paul giggled, pissing Louis off. He said, "I want some answers. You dick around, you give me any grief, then this pretty lady will be hurting. The more you fuck with me, the more the lady hurts."

Louis waited. Jean-Paul looked confused. Duncan just stared and Louis sensed Karen was trembling.

"Well?" Louis demanded.

"Well, what?" Duncan asked. "You said I'm to answer your questions. Fine. But you haven't asked any questions, genius."

Jean-Paul giggled again. Louis quickly turned and said, "Shut the fuck up, will you."

————

Duncan kept avoiding Karen's gaze. He had to stay focused on these two characters. Seeing Karen staring at him, pleading and begging with those eyes, would throw him off-kilter. The older one with the beard and bald head seemed to be in charge. But his younger pal— the one called Jean-Paul—was definitely getting under the man's skin. He felt a faint flicker of optimism. They weren't a crew used to working together, which meant if a challenge were to erupt, they wouldn't work as a team.

The older one said, "The shipment. When's it coming in?"

Duncan tried to look puzzled. "What shipment is that?"

"The one my boss wants to know about. The one that Andre and Pierre came to talk to you about. That fucking shipment."

Duncan shrugged. "Man, I ship a lot of stuff back and forth across the border. High-grade marijuana. Beer and liquor without the proper tax stamps. Same with cigarettes. Which shipment are you interested in?"

He liked the look of confusion on the big man's face. He seemed distracted, hesitant.

Then his companion Jean-Paul stepped in.

"Louis, what the hell are you doing, letting this asshole jerk with you?" The younger one came over, slapped Karen right on the side of her face.

Duncan moved, Louis pointed his weapon right at him, and a shadow moved across his eyes.

———

Zach moved in a crouched run, going around the two-car garage, to the side yard and then the rear yard. Swingset, kid's pool, some low shrubbery. Rear deck with grill and outdoor furniture. He kicked off his shoes, climbed up the side of the deck, everything slowing down, everything sharp-focused, seeing splinters on the deck, spilled barbecue sauce on the side of the grill, the smear of kid's handprints on the sliding glass doors leading into the living room.

His Browning up in a two-handed combat stance and damn it all to hell, a complication. A second gunman inside! He hesitated. Now what? With one gunman, there was a chance, an opportunity.

His mind raced along, even though everything else seemed so damn clear and slow. Angles, options, placement of targets. Karen's head visible above the couch, Duncan there, pants around his ankles, bald-headed gunman to his rear, second gunman coming into view, second gunman now moving, going to the couch.

Slapping Karen.

Automatic rifle lowered at his side.

Time!

———

Louis was startled at the sudden slap, pissed once more at Jean-Paul stepping into it, and he turned and—

Explosions.

Glass shattering.

Louis turned, gunfire roaring all around him, Jean-Paul shouting, falling to the ground. A guy had blown through the rear deck sliding glass door, pistol in hand, the glass shattering, plowing through.

Louis whirled about, brought his SKS up, aimed at the man, ready to splatter his guts across this clean light blue carpet, and—

The trigger wouldn't move.

The trigger wouldn't move.

Fuck, he hadn't taken it off safe!

Something hammered at the back of his head. Gray and black swam over him.

———

Duncan saw Zach sprint in front of the rear sliding glass door, so he dropped to the carpeting, grabbed Karen's ankles, tugged her off the couch. She yelped and fell and he jumped on top of her as gunfire erupted, glass smashed, Zach burst in. The younger guy cried out and the older guy moved back, moved back, bringing up his rifle, and …

Nothing happened!

Duncan saw his chance, grabbed the heavy stoneware vase, bounced it off the back of the big man's head.

———

Zach felt glass cut at his face and hands as he blasted his way through the freshly shot sliding glass door, the younger gunman falling to his knees, dropping his rifle. Duncan was out of view, Karen was now off the couch, and the first gunman brought up his rifle and Zach thought, fuck, it'd be so fine to have a vest on, but the guy couldn't get a shot off. Zach brought his Browning up and then Duncan moved whip-fast, holding an ugly piece of pottery in his hand, smacking it against the guy's bullet-shaped head.

Zach got off another shot but missed, and then he turned to the first gunman, on his knees, gurgling, trying to get to his weapon. Zach kicked his face, looked over, saw the bigger guy was up and running to the door, rifle in one hand.

Duncan shouted, "Zach! Get him! Go get him!"

The guy threw the door open, disappeared.

Zach gave chase.

———

Outside, his lungs burning, head bleeding and aching, Louis started running through the yard, heading to the cemetery where the van was packed, feeling sorry for poor Jean-Paul—the guy had definitely taken one or two rounds, but that fucking ship had sailed.

As he ran, the same ridiculous phrase kept on running through his head: *slick as shit, slick as shit, slick as shit.*

He turned and saw the squat man who had burst into the living room had made it around the corner of the house, was running right after him.

Louis raised up the SKS, flipped the safety off, yelled out, "Eat this, motherfucker!"

Fired off round after round after round, as the guy plastered himself to the ground.

———

Zach saw the guy running, saw him stop and whirl around, rifle raising up in his hands, shots raining out, no real aiming, no discipline, just ripping off a magazine. There was a slight grassy enfilade to the right. He flattened himself out, letting the rounds whip over his head.

———

Duncan stood up, yanked his pants up, Karen sitting against the couch, crying, sobbing. He retrieved his .380 Bersa, grabbed the rifle—recognized it now as a Chinese-made SKS semiautomatic—placed it in safe, tossed it onto the couch. The younger guy was on his side, moaning, holding his right shoulder. Blood seeped through his fingers. He was crying.

Duncan kicked at the hand, causing him to scream. He stepped on his good shoulder, pushing him down to the ground. He pointed his pistol right at the kid.

He tried to catch his breath. This was the man who had broken into his house, had threatened his wife, had *hit* his wife.

"Answer me now," Duncan said. "Are you two the only ones here?"

"Fuck ... oh fuck ... it hurts so much ..."

Duncan moved his foot, pressed it against the fresh bullet wound. A sharp and loud scream burst out. He removed his foot.

"Answer me," he said, voice even and determined. "Are you two the only ones here? Are there any more shooters out there?"

Jean-Paul moaned, cried, and Duncan winced as a gunshot rang out.

———

Louis kept running, the rifle feeling fucking heavy, the tree line coming real close, real close now, get to the tree line, pound a few more shots at that guy chasing him, and then he'd have it made. Thank God he had told Jean-Paul to leave the keys in the van's ignition! Get in the van, turn on the engine, and get the hell out of this small town with that crazed freak back there who had beaten the Iron Steeds once again.

Slick as shit, slick as shit, slick as shit ...

———

Zach got up, saw the guy had made pretty good distance. There were lots of thoughts racing back there in his mind—not your fight, way out of your jurisdiction, call the cops, let them handle it, you can't screw up your original mission—and the guy was still running at a good clip.

A pistol shot at this distance was complicated.

A maple sapling was nearby. He ran over in his stocking-covered feet, found a branch at the right height and angle. Took the .32 Browning, put both hands around it again in the combat stance, braced his forearms against the branch, aimed over the open sights, worked the angle, the speed, where he wanted the bullets to land. He aimed at a space below the man's buttocks, fired off three quick rounds, each round working up the man's spine.

The gunman arched his back, yelled, fell.

———

Louis was about to turn when the weight of the universe seemed to hammer at his back.

———

Duncan turned, shocked. Karen was there, her Colt .45 semiautomatic in her slim and pretty hands. Smoke wafted out from the barrel. He looked back at the younger man. His eyes were open, his mouth was still, and there was a bloody hole in the center of his chest.

Karen said, "I think I might have overreacted, hon."

Duncan gently took the pistol from her hand, gave her a long hug. "Not a problem, Karen. Not a problem."

———

Pistol still in his hand, Zach took his time going up the slight hill, his socks damp from the grass and soil. The man he had shot was crumpled on the ground, legs and arms splayed out. Zach was focused now on the man, making sure there was no movement, no action. The rifle was about a yard away from his right hand. Zach moved closer, picked up the weapon, and tossed it away.

The man looked dead. Three rounds had gone into his back in a nice tight group. Not bad. He circled him twice and then went to the rifle, popped out the magazine, tossed it down the hill, worked the action to expel the live round, then threw it up the hill. He looked at the man again. His skin was losing its color, turning the shade of chalk. Zach quickly checked for a pulse on the side of the man's cool neck, pleased and not surprised to find nothing.

He stood up, looked around the neighborhood. A couple of isolated trailers down the road, that cemetery up the hill. Gunfire in a rural northern New Hampshire neighborhood? It would take 105mm mortar rounds impacting in the near fields before someone would be concerned enough to call the cops.

Zach looked at the dead man one more time. "Thanks, pal, whoever the hell you are," he said.

TWENTY-FIVE

KAREN SAT ON THE couch, Duncan's arm around her, his other hand holding his .380 Bersa. She cried and told him what had happened, cried some more, and apologized over and over again for letting them break in, for not using the dish towel warning system, and Duncan murmured and said "it's all right, it's all right," all the while wishing his lovely and deadly bride had waited a couple of minutes before wasting that Iron Steeds biker. A few more minutes and Duncan would have found out if there was a backup crew out there, or just how much Francis Ouellette knew about the upcoming shipment, and other bits of useful information.

But damn it, no information was going to come from the rapidly cooling corpse over there. Which was a pity.

Karen said, "Duncan?"

He kissed the side of her head. "Yes, love. Talk to me."

"You're not mad that I shot him, are you? I knew you were trying to ask him questions ... but he poked his rifle in my chest. He terrified me. He slapped me. I had to ... had to shoot him."

231

Duncan kissed her again, harder. It didn't matter any more, what he or hadn't learned.

"You did all right, hon. You did just fine."

———

Zach approached the house and reached into Duncan's truck, switched off the ignition. No use wasting gas or giving an idling engine wear and tear. He put his .32 Browning back into his holster and slowly approached the front door, hands held out in front of him.

"Duncan!" he called out. "It's me, Zach! I'm coming in. Okay? I'm coming in!"

In his training he had heard so many disastrous tales of friendly fire—especially that poor son-of-a-bitch football star Tillman, giving up millions of dollars to get zapped in the 'stan by his own troops—and he didn't want to add to that depressing list. He stood still at the door, called out again, "Duncan! It's Zach! I'm coming in!"

From inside the house, Duncan yelled back, "Got you, Zach! Come on in!"

He slowly opened the door, kept hands out and open, and went through the kitchen and into the living room. The second gunman was on his back on the living room floor, apparently dead, for his chest wasn't moving, and neither was anything else. A frightened Karen Crowley was sitting next to her angry husband.

Duncan got up. "How did it go?"

Zach said, "He's down. About halfway up that side hill, going to the tree line. I didn't see anybody else out there."

"We heard the gunfire. You okay?"

"Bit winded but that's to be expected. Used to swimming more than running. My feet are cold and wet, which isn't a problem. That,

I'm used to. Plus I got some scratches, coming through your patio door."

Duncan said, "Zach ... Karen and I, we owe you more than you know. Look, we'll talk about all of this later, but there's lot to be done. Can you keep view of the rear deck? I've got a call to make."

Zach popped the magazine out of his pistol, inserted a fresh one he kept in the side holster, worked the action. "You can count on it."

"Glad to hear it."

Karen spoke up, eyes wide with amazement. "Zach Morrow ... I thought that was you. What in the hell are you doing here?"

He smiled at her. "Doing good, it appears."

———

Duncan went to the kitchen, locked the door leading outside, took a breath, grabbed his cellphone. He dialed a number from memory and it rang and rang and rang. He looked to his wife on the couch and to Zach, standing nearby, pistol in hand. A close-run darn thing. And to think he and his brother were suspicious of Zach!

The phone was finally answered. "Cameron here."

Duncan said, "You know who this is. We've had a fire."

Cameron quickly said, "Contained?"

"At the moment. I need back-up soonest, including a clean-up crew. I'm also going to need you to get Amy and Lewis out of school, get them someplace safe. I'll have Karen call the principal's office, get it all straightened out. Also, get some support staff to get fixings for a barbecue. It's gonna be a long night."

"Got it," Cameron said. "On my way."

The tightness in Duncan's chest eased some when Cameron hung up. Things were in motion. He went back out to the living

room, looked to the dead guy on the floor. He thought about drap-
ing a sheet or a blanket over the body, but the hell with that. Any
sheet or blanket would have to be thrown away, and he wasn't going
to waste Crowley belongings on someone who had broken in, had
threatened and assaulted his wife.

To Karen he said, "Cameron and the boys will be here soonest.
Zach and I have got things under control. What can we do for you?"

She rubbed her cheek where she had been slapped. "I need to
make sure Lewis and Amy are protected."

"Done," Duncan said. "Cameron is on his way to the school now,
he'll find a safe place to put them up for a while. If you can call the
principal, Mr. What's-his-name—"

"Mr. What's-his-name is Mr. Horatio Spenser, if you ever decide
to go to a school meeting, Duncan Crowley," she said, her voice sharp.

"Duly noted," Duncan said, secretly pleased at seeing her displea-
sure. That was the Karen he knew and loved, not the weepy, scared
woman who had been here earlier. "What else can we do for you?"

She got off the couch, headed down the hallway to the bedrooms.
"I intend to call the school from the bedroom, strip, take a shower
for about a week, and then get dressed. I'll depend on you strong
brave men to keep me safe."

He went after her, gently took her arm, kissed her and kissed her.
"You kept yourself safe. That was a wonderful accomplishment.
Kept your cool and did fine."

She said, "I feel pretty good now, but I think I deserve a collapse
later."

"You will. Now go get your clothes off, take a shower, and stay
away from any windows."

That got him another kiss as she walked away.

———

Zach kept watch over the rear deck and yard while Duncan watched the front of the house, pacing around like a wounded lion, eager to get back into the hunt. Zach was stunned at how quickly things started to happen. Within a few minutes there was the roar of motorcycles as two bikers rolled into the driveway and got off. They weren't wearing colors—both had jeans but one wore the jacket of a local heating and cooling repair company, while the other had on a pharmacist's smock—but they came in as Duncan took control.

"Barry, you and Fred go outside, take some cover, but keep view of the yard," Duncan said. "Two shooters are down; one here and one outside. I don't know if there are any others out there."

Zach was impressed with their response. They didn't ask any questions, they didn't stare at the body on the floor or the shot-out sliding glass door. Both men brought semiautomatic pistols out from side holsters and went back outside as a dark green Honda Pilot suddenly braked to a stop outside on the street.

Cameron Crowley barreled through the front door, carrying an H&K MP5 submachine gun under his long tan farmer's jacket. He ignored Zach and went straight to his brother.

"You okay?"

"Fine."

"Karen?"

"She's shook up, got manhandled some, but she's in the shower now. She was a warrior queen, Cam, did well."

Cameron relaxed, slung the H&K over his shoulder. He stared at Zach. "I know you," he said.

Zach stepped forward, held out his hand. "Zach Morrow. Fellow graduate of Turner Regional High School."

The handshake was firm and to the point. "Glad to see you, bud. Also glad to see you were here."

Duncan said, "You and me both, Cam. You and me both. Zach was here with me, stayed outside when I came inside. He could have run away or called the cops, but he put his ass on the line. Shot his way through the rear sliding glass door like Bruce Willis on steroids. Got this guy on the ground, nailed the second shooter outside, even though he was packing a semiautomatic rifle. Look, what we're going to need is—"

Cameron held up a hand. "Bro, what you're going to do now is nothing. I got it under control. Your kids are out of school, safe. They're up at Paul Gagnon's place, and you know him, even the Staties are afraid to mess with him even though he's in a wheelchair. The kids will be fine."

Zach saw Duncan release a breath of air. His older brother kept talking. "You should check on Karen, get a change of clothes, a big stiff drink. But nothing else. Take some time, both of you come out into the living room and then we'll figure things out. But go."

Duncan hesitated, grinned. "All right. I don't usually like taking orders from my big brother, but this time, I'll make an exception."

———

Down the hallway, Duncan knocked on the door to the bathroom. The shower inside was running. "Karen?" he called through the door. "It's Duncan. I'm opening the door."

He stepped into the warm steaminess of the bathroom. To the left was the combination tub and shower, in front of him was a his and her vanity, the toilet off to the right. On the very edge of the vanity, closest to the shower, was his Ruger .357 revolver, the one he kept between the mattress and box spring. A shadow was moving behind the curtain, and Karen stuck her head out. Her red hair was plastered against her head, and her eyes were swollen. He was certain she had been bawling in the shower.

He said, "Amy and Lewis are safe. They're with Paul Gagnon for the duration. Cameron and his boys have shown up. Everything's going to be taken care of."

She nodded, bit her lip. "Could use some help in here, washing my back."

Duncan paused. What he really wanted to do was to get back to the living room, start overseeing the clean-up and talk more to Cameron, again give his thanks to Zach. That's what he wanted to do, what should be done, but one look at Karen's troubled face convinced him otherwise. He stripped off his own clothes, conscious they were soaked through from his sweat, and Karen stepped back as he got into the shower.

Karen allowed him a moment under the flowing water, and he wet his head and chest and back, and stepped back. He soaped up his hands and a washcloth and started working on Karen's sleek back. She moaned in pleasure and leaned forward, holding herself up by putting her hands against the near wall.

He rubbed and washed, rubbed and washed, and she said, "Do my hair?"

"Sure."

He rinsed his hands and then put a glop or two of a combination shampoo/conditioner, and worked that into her thick, wet mane. She sighed again and the water splashed around and he stepped closer, as Karen sighed once more.

Duncan said, "I'm sorry I failed you, sweetie. Deeply sorry."

She shook her head against his washing hands. "No apologies necessary. If anything, I should apologize to you. I was too trusting when I opened the door. I should have been more suspicious, especially since you said 'alas Babylon' last night. I didn't even bother to check the surveillance television. If I did, I might have seen they were carrying weapons. They got the drop on me, they got the drop on you. I'm so sorry."

He recalled the shame, the embarrassment, the sheer humiliation of standing in his own living room, unarmed, hands up, pants around his ankles, as his wife was mauled and manhandled.

"That's just an excuse," he finally said. "I should have gotten you three out of the house earlier. I should have insisted you carry a piece at all times, instead of relying on one being within reach. If it wasn't for Zach..."

She turned and put her forearms across his shoulders, face to face. Water ran down in rivulets across her full, freckled breasts, the pink nipples stiff and erect. She kissed him. "Zach Morrow... why in the world is he here?"

He put his hands on her slim hips. Even with two kids, she was in great shape. A bit heavier than her wedding day, but it all went to making her curvier and rounder, like a ripe sweet peach. "He was in the Coast Guard, got kicked out for disobeying orders, something like that. Was living in Purmort until the other day, when his double-wide burned to the ground. Came back to Turner to see what's what. Looking for a job."

She nuzzled his throat. "You're going to help him, aren't you."

"You know it."

She raised up her head, let the hot water race through her hair and down her face. She lowered her head and said, "This can't happen again."

"I know."

"That shipment... when's it coming in?"

"Day after tomorrow."

"If it goes well?"

"Then I'm done, out, free. No more living on the edge, or over the edge, for you, me, and the kids. Especially the kids."

That earned him another kiss. "Good. Make it happen. And honey?"

"Yes?"

"Tell Cameron, as soon as you can."

"I'm meaning to but—"

She brought a hand to the back of his head, cupped it, her fingers tracing patterns through his wet hair. "He deserves to know. See how quickly he rode to the rescue when you made that call? That's your older brother. Do the right thing, Duncan. Tell him."

He touched her nose with his finger. "All right, wench. I'll tell him."

"Good," she said, stepping closer, her sweet curvy breasts pushing into his chest. "Now, this is going to sound kinky and strange, love bug, but after all that happened ... the violence, the shooting, the rescue ... your wench is so goddamn horny."

Duncan felt himself stir at her words. He kissed her deeply, tasting her, devouring her, and broke away. "For real?"

She nodded, reached down, fondled him. "Christ, yes."

"We'll have to be quiet."

"So what," she said, pressing into him again. "Besides, I love your tightie whities."

———

Zach sat on a stool inside the kitchen, looked over the granite counter, watched and listened as Cameron and the members of the Washington County Motorcycle Club swung into action. Once the perimeter was secured, a pickup truck with a cab on its rear backed its way on the front lawn. A rubberized body bag was brought into the living room—Zach wondered what kind of motorcycle club had ready access to body bags—and the younger of the two shooters was bagged up and brought out. He was shortly joined by his older companion, and the pickup truck drove off.

Cameron said, "Couple of our guys went up the hill where the second shooter was running to, found a van with Quebec plates parked in the cemetery up there. That's being taken to a garage, get examined. See if we can find something out."

By then other members showed up, and a couple of guys worked to replace the shot-out sliding glass window, while other guys worked to steam-clean the carpeting. Some women arrived as well, bringing the essentials for a barbecue. Cameron just kept an eye on everything, pointing things out, commenting, encouraging, as his folks did their job. Cameron eventually came over and sat down on a stool across from him.

"Mind telling me how this went down?" Cameron asked.

Zach said, "I met up with your brother this morning. We were driving around, talking, and he brought me up to the gunshop he owns up on Gilman Road, with the butchering shop next door. He wanted to show me around, and then his cellphone rang. It was Karen. Said her car wouldn't start, could he come pick her up. We both ended up here."

"Unh-hunh," Cameron said. "Then what?"

"Pulled into the driveway, Duncan kept the truck running, said he'd be back in a minute or two. I waited and waited, and nobody came back. I went to check in on him and before I strolled through the front door, saw Duncan with his hands up, saw Karen on the couch, and a guy standing between them, holding an assault rifle."

Cameron said, "Good planning, not rushing through the front door."

"Couldn't see how I could have gotten away with it. Plus, there was a second guy with a rifle, not in view. He could have sprayed me by the time I got to the kitchen. So I rolled out to the backyard, got up on the deck, and saw the second gunman. Things got complicated as I was running through the options, and then the second guy came over and slapped Karen."

"That's when you stopped thinking, hunh?"

Zach nodded. "Fired a couple of times, nailed him and got the glass door shattered, good combination, got into the living room. Lucky I just got a couple of scrapes. Duncan dropped, got Karen off the couch, the bigger of the two tried to fire but either his SKS jammed or he had on it safe. He was working to clear it when your brother whacked him on the back of his head. He broke free, got out the front door. I followed, gunfight ensued, and that was that."

"Good shooting on your part," Cameron said.

"Mind telling me who these guys were?"

"Bikers from a club just outside of Montreal. Called the Iron Steeds. They control a lot of the crystal meth, weed, heroin, and prostitute traffic in Quebec."

"They're far from home," Zach said.

Cameron ignored the observation and said, "One of my crew, he said that the guy up on the hill had three entry wounds in his back. So you shot him in the back?"

Zach said, "If he had been facing the front, I would've shot him in the front. If he had been sideways, I would have shot him sideways. Figured it made no matter which way he was facing."

"Damn straight," Cameron said.

———

Duncan left the bathroom to his wife, humming a tune, towel wrapped around her, drying her hair and getting her make-up ready.

There was just one moment, before he left, when she pointed to her clothes on the bathroom floor and said, "No offense, handsome, but those clothes are to be burned. I won't wear them again."

"Got it," Duncan said, and he went down the hallway, the kitchen and living room nearly filled with people. He was greeted like a dad coming home after a dangerous stay at the local hospital, and men slapped him on the back and shook his hand, while the women gave him hugs and kisses. A fan was blowing air over a wet spot in the rug where it had been cleaned, and two women were busy washing the new sliding glass door for the rear deck. In the kitchen, one of the younger male members of the Washington County Motorcycle Club was spackling a hole in the wall from one of the bullets that had flown through this room not more than an hour ago.

He took it all in, feeling warm satisfaction that he was alive, with a woman and children who loved him and depended on him, and that he had friends and supporters throughout the county who would come here in nearly an instant to help. Outside on the deck, some women were working around the smoking barbecue grill, and coolers had been set up. From a portable boom box, Garth Brooks was singing about friends in low places. A good cover, for if anyone were curious as to the sudden appearance of motorcycles and trucks at the Crowley residence, the barbecue would answer any questions.

He grabbed a Molson Golden Ale, waved at Zach, and cornered his brother. Cameron had a cheery look on him, which was understandable: he had come through in a big way to make it all right.

"Cam, a moment?" Duncan asked.

"You got it, bro."

They went out to the deck and went to the far corner, both of them leaning across the railing, looking out to the yard and the descending sun. With nothing said or noted, still, everyone else on the deck clustered on the other side, to give the two brothers space and time to talk.

Duncan took a long, cold swallow of the Molson. It tasted great. He said, "What do you got?"

"We got two guys from the Iron Steeds, armed with Chinese-made SKS assault rifles," Cameron said. "One dead in your living room, with two apparent .32-caliber gunshot wounds to his right shoulder, and what looks to be a .45 through the center of his chest. Zach was using a .32 Browning…the .45?"

"Karen."

"Well, shit, good on her."

"Keep that to yourself for now," Duncan said. "Don't think she's in the mood to talk about it. Go on."

"Yeah. Second shooter found up on the slope of the hill over there. Nice tight grouping of .32 shots to his back. That Zach…never knew he was that talented back in high school, except, of course, that time he—"

"I know, I know, the time he whipped my ass in phys ed. Got it."

Cameron laughed. "I love reminding you of that. So yeah, nice grouping in the back. Think of that—from what you told me, he ran out with no shoes, going after a guy carrying semiautomatic rifle, only using a pistol. Usually the guy with the bigger gun wins in a fight like this."

"No, not really," Duncan said. "Usually the guy with the bigger balls wins…and Zach had brass ones."

"Thinking about hiring him?"

"Oh yes, without a doubt. I mean, sure, we both had concerns, but I can't see somebody doing undercover work for the cops gunning down two Quebec bikers and then hanging around the house, staying for a barbecue and drinks. Cam, he's a guy we can use."

"You say so," Cameron said. "So to go on … I had a few guys doing a search farther up the hill, went through the Nute family cemetery. Dell Turner found a GMC van with Quebec license plates backed in, keys in the ignition. Searched it, found a dead BlackBerry, bunch of trash from McDonald's and such, and a nice little hidey hole in the back where we're sure they smuggled the Chink rifles in. We powered up the BlackBerry but it's locked out with a code."

The bottle was sweating moisture in Duncan's hands. "That Francois Ouellette sure moves fast. You guessed it right."

"Not something to be happy about. When they had you and Karen in the house, what were they after?"

"What do you think? The shipment coming through their territory to our territory. In two day's time, which I just found out. They wanted the details."

"Gee, imagine that," Cameron said, sarcasm in his voice, "somebody wanting details."

Duncan sourly recalled what Karen said, and something made him hesitate. Later, he promised himself, later.

His brother added, "So here's what I'm thinking. We got two days before we have to stand ready for the deal you set up. To get up to Canada and back would take a half day, at most, if we go in quick and get lucky."

Duncan said, "What are you talking about, Cam?"

He turned to his younger brother, said in amazement, "I'm talking about going up to Montreal and ringing Francois Ouellette's bell, that's what. The fucker went right after your family. We should head up north, go to that tittie bar he has that serves as a clubhouse, and blast it to the North Pole, put his head on a pike, and come back home in time to catch the Red Sox game."

Duncan rubbed at the beer bottle's label. "Your words are warming me right up, Cam, but no."

"No?" Cameron asked, stunned. "No? Couple of days ago you went Dark Ages on two guys who made a threat or two against your family. Today two guys come in, molest your wife, threaten you, make threats against your kids … and you're going to leave it be?"

Duncan said, "Need to stay focused, Cam. The shipment. Can't afford to let that slip up. I hope you understand."

"Yeah, sure, whatever you say," Cameron said, turning away, and that was it.

Duncan reached over, grabbed his brother's elbow. "Okay. Details. You want details?"

Cameron seemed to struggle between pride and wanting to know what was going on, but the struggle didn't last long. "Yeah, I want the details. This shipment. What's in it? How much are you getting paid? What makes it so goddamn important?"

Duncan said carefully, "I don't know what's coming in. I'm not getting paid a cent. But you and me, we've been promised a million dollars."

Cameron seemed taken aback. "A million … bro, what the hell's coming across?"

"Like I said, I don't know. All I know is that it's in a half-sized shipping container, originally from the St. Lawrence Seaway. It has to come across with total secrecy and security."

Cameron repeated. "One million dollars … can't you guess what's in it?"

Duncan said, "Don't want to."

In the yard there was some laughter, shouts. The party seemed to be really kicking in. "Okay," Cameron said. "You don't know what's in it. But who's behind it? Who set it up?"

Duncan sighed. "I'll tell you, but the decision is done. All right? Not in the mood for debate, discussion, dissent, or any other words starting with the letter 'd.'"

"All right, fair enough. Who came to you, and when?"

Duncan said, "Remember a few months ago, when we were up at Lake Palmer? Looking at those expensive fishing and hunting camps for those Europeans and Middle Eastern characters, Mexican millionaires, even a couple of ex-congressmen? The ones that were still a ways from being completed?"

"Yeah. I remember."

"Okay. You had to go to the bathroom or something, and one of the Texan guys who owned a chunk of the development chatted me up. Talked about the history of smuggling from Canada to New Hampshire, back during Prohibition. Wanted to know if stuff still got smuggled across the border ... and by the time you came back from the bathroom, we had struck a deal."

Cameron said slowly, "Some Texan you don't know is paying you one million dollars to smuggle a shipping container across the border, into the States?"

"Yeah."

"So why didn't you tell me earlier?"

"Because I didn't want you raising a fuss about this deal. I know it's not our usual business but man, the money ... we could do a lot with that money, Cam."

"Anything could be in there, bro. Terrorists. WMDs or something like that. Biowarfare. Weapons. Drugs. Guns. Bombs. Shit, Duncan, what kind of deal is this?"

He finished his Molson. "A one-million-dollar deal, that's what. Something we could use to help out our family, help out a lot of other families out there that are being ignored and forgotten."

"Duncan ..."

"Sorry," he said. "That's all for tonight."

TWENTY-SIX

EIGHTY KILOMETERS NORTH OF the New Hampshire border, Brewster Flagg pulled the Peterbilt tractor-trailer into the parking lot of a stripper bar named the Golden Raspberry. It was off Route 257, east of Charlottsville, Quebec, and the lot was filled with other trucks similar to his. He let the engine idle, looking at the bright neon lights outside of the one-story wooden building. Brewster was cold. He was always cold, ever since coming to this damn frozen shithole.

He rubbed his hands, looked through the dirty windshield. There was a craving inside of him, one that had been growing stronger every mile—or friggin' kilometer, all right then—as he got closer to his goal. He had tried to resist, tried to fight, but here he was, about to give into temptation.

Brewster sighed, switched the engine off. He was a true Christian patriot, but he also knew he wasn't perfect. Even the truest and purest of patriots were not perfect. Some of them he had admired over the years had succumbed to these very same temptations, and they were much tougher men than he. So perhaps it would be all right, after all, when it would all be done.

He stepped down from the cab, walked across the lot, hands in his thin coat, shoulders hunched up against the cold wind. For the love of God would he ever be warm, ever again? Earlier as he driven into the lot, the door to the bar had looked dark, foreboding, with its black glass. But as he got closer, it looked inviting, whispering to him that beyond the dark door, delights and temptation and pleasures awaited.

He opened the door. Smoke and lights and music assaulted him, made him stop for a moment. Still time to turn back, to do what was right ... but when he saw the sluts dancing up on the stage, he had to go in. A scrawny, bearded man with a sheepskin vest, tattoos on his arm, sitting on a bar stool, blocked his way in with a beefy arm. "Ten bucks, pal," he murmured.

Brewster pushed a hand into his pants, pulled out the unfamiliar and colorful bills, paid the cover charge, and then went in. He felt free, almost exhilarated, after crossing the threshhold into this den of sinful pleasures. Other times, when he was in Houston or Omaha, he would always be looking over his shoulder, to see if any other members of the Tea Party were partaking as well. But here he relaxed, knowing no one in this place knew him or knew where he had come from.

He took a red-cushioned seat up front, where he could see the sluts more closely, and sweet Jesus, he was happy to have a round table in front of him to hide the swelling in his crotch. After a couple of minutes, a waitress strutted over, wearing high heels, fishnet stockings, a tiny black skirt that barely covered her crotch, and a low-cut white halter top that was see-through. Dangling from her swollen navel was a piece of jewelry.

He ordered a Jack Daniels, straight, with a water chaser, and went back to watching the sluts dancing before him. There were two of them, both blond, and one had huge bouncing boobs, while the other one had firmer tits with thick nipples. They danced about the stage, swirled and rotated on poles, and twice they embraced and kissed, almost making him pop his load without even touching himself. They had on white high heel shoes and slowly stripped off their clothes, until they were down to transparent G-strings.

Twice during their dancing, each of them came to him on the stage, on hands and knees, where they belonged. He slipped the colorful funny-looking money in their G-strings, his fingers touching their sweaty, naughty flesh.

Oh, sweet God!

Then the music changed, to some of that nigger music that was so popular. The dancers changed out as the naked blondes strutted off, to hoots and whistles. A thicker-set woman with red and blue hair came up, and he lost interest in her moves. He drank two more Jack Daniels—the harsh whisky burning delightfully down his gullet—and a soft touch on his shoulder made him jump.

"May I sit with you, friend?" the woman asked, the blond dancer with the big natural tits. She had on a pink see-through robe, and all she wore underneath was the G-string from earlier. He couldn't help staring at those incredible breasts. He had seen spectacular women before in Houston and Austin and San Antonio, but those women had been sculpted, polished, with fake boobs, lips, and butts. This slut, at least, was all natural, all real. He motioned her to a nearby chair.

"My name is Candy," she said. "What's yours?"

"Brewster," he stammered. "That's my name."

She put a hand on his thigh. "Brewster, you were a true gentleman tonight. I appreciate that. You're so different from all the other customers here."

His throat was constricted, but he smiled and nodded at her. She leaned over him, her robe falling open, and she spoke in his left ear. "Would you like a private dance, Brewster? Just you and me?"

He managed to find his voice. "That'd be great."

She put her long fingernailed hand on his shoulder, gently kissed his cheek. "Oh, honey, that would be wonderful. But the managers who run this joint, they demand payment up front. One hundred dollars, with a tip if you think I've done a good job. Is that fair?"

"Yes, quite fair," Brewster said. He pulled a wad of bills from his pocket, slid out five twenty-dollar bills—they had the picture of that wrinkled English bitch queen—and passed them over to her. She smiled, folded the bills, and slid them into her G-string.

Candy stood up, grabbed his hand, and in a slight daze of excitement and lust, he walked with her, hand in hand, as she took him to the rear of the club. There were three doors, all marked PRIVATE. She unlocked the near door, led him into a small room. It had a thick cushioned chair, pillows, rugs, and a shelf with a music system. She switched on the music, started dancing. He stared, mouth watering as she writhed and danced in front of him. She tossed her robe off, and then her G-string. She straddled him, humping him, her sweat and scent overwhelming.

"Oh, a shy one, eh?" she whispered. "Don't be shy. Touch me, Brewster, wherever you want. I don't mind."

Hands warm, he reached up, grabbed one breast, and then the other. She winced and said, "Oooh, not so hard, lover, not so hard." She raised herself up, and he suckled on one thick salty nipple, and then the other. It seemed like the room was slowly spinning, as he felt drunker than at any time in his life.

"Mmmm, that feels good," she murmured. She took his right hand, brought it up a smooth thigh, to her pubic hair, as he gently probed and fingered her. His head throbbed, feeling her warm slickness. He gasped and arched his back as she worked on his crotch. She unzipped his pants, worked her hand past his underwear, and then touched his cock ...

Oh, Jesus, too fucking soon!

Candy stroked his cock, once, twice, and he groaned as he sprayed over her probing hand. "Oh, oh, oh!" he gasped, and the dancing slowed and she murmured, and she had a cloth in her hand, which she used to wipe him. Then she put him away, like a little child who had soiled himself.

Candy smiled. "Oh, that's all right, honey. If you'd like, for another hundred, you can stay for a while. Perhaps you'll be ready for another round, after you rest up."

Now he felt dirty, filthy, used. The room—which earlier looked exotic and sexy—now looked tired and worn. The woman, who had seemed so curvy and alluring, was older than he had thought. In the room's light, he saw the wrinkles and scars on her skin. He pushed her off his lap, spat in her face. "Go to hell, cunt."

He redid his pants, got up, and went out the door. Head down, he moved quickly past the chairs and tables, not looking at the sluts dancing on the stage, no interest at all in staying here. He went outside and the cold air was hurtful, reminding him he had strayed from his true Christian path.

Brewster made it back to his truck, then suddenly knelt on the ground, the soil cold against his knees. He stayed there, the soil and gravel cutting into his knees, praying for forgiveness.

He slowly stood up, retrieved his keys, and climbed up in the Peterbilt cab. A couple of bikers, dressed in leather pants and jackets, looked at him, laughing, carrying cardboard coffee cups in their hands. Brewster got in and started the truck, the rumbling of the diesel engine almost comforting. He looked in the side mirror, at the shipping container that was back there. It was dull green, though once upon a time he knew, it had been bright yellow, with MEXTEL LINES painted in red and blue.

According to his cousin, what was in this shipping container would make the destruction those ragheads did more than a decade ago seem like child's play. Brewster was sure he knew what was going to happen on that blessed April 19th. What was back there would do its damage, enough damage so that internment camps would be set up, illegals would be deported, shitheads impeached and removed from office, and real hope and change would finally come.

He shifted the truck into first and went back out on the highway, heading to his destiny.

TWENTY-SEVEN

Zach Morrow was working on an ice-cold Coca Cola, talking to a bleached blond woman in tight jeans and with a low-cut yellow top showing off an impressive amount of cleavage, said cleavage covered with tattoos of roses and unicorns. Her name was Tiffany and she was describing how she had bagged her first moose last year. The living room was filled with partiers, people talking and eating barbecue, but there were no loud voices, the music wasn't cranked up to make the framed photos shake, and the trash was carefully deposited in plastic cans set up around the living room and kitchen. It was a party, but it was also a party where employees or those in some sort of debt to Duncan Crowley were in attendance, having fun but being careful not to step over any boundaries.

The tattooed woman went on. "Joey, my boyfriend then, we went up to Aaron's Swamp, that's where the moose love to tromp through and feed on the plants. I got there and I had to make the shot, 'cause I was the winner of the state lottery that gives you license to shoot a moose. But Joey brought along his .308 bolt action, weighed a fucking ton. I tried to pick it up and even with the scope, it was hard to make the shot, wavering all around. Joey had a good thought—pretty damn rare, I know—so he pulled out earplugs he uses at the sawmill, sticks them in to protect his hearing. I hold the rifle, balance it on his shoulder, moose was still there, chewing, and bang, one shot and I dropped him. But what a Christly job to drag him out and get him butchered. Goddamn thing weighed almost a ton."

Zach politely nodded. "Sounds like you did good."

Tiffany smiled, shrugged. "Truth is, it's not much of a challenge. Poor dumb bastard just stands there, staring at you. Still, you get a goodly amount of meat." She stepped closer, smiled wider. "Funny thing is, Joey and I have split up, but I'm still eating that poor dumb moose. I love meat. Tell me, do you like meat?"

Zach was thinking of an appropriate answer, when there was a touch at his elbow. Duncan said, "Tiffany, sweetie, mind if I take this fine man away before you corrupt him?"

She curtsied, lifted up her Coors in salute. "Corrupt? *Moi?* See you later, fellas."

Duncan said, "Let's go for a walk, all right?"

Zach nodded and they went out to the deck, down a set of steps, and out to the lawn. "Nice party," he said.

"Yeah, but what a hell of a reason to hold a party." Duncan stopped and stood there, looking back at the house with the lights and the partiers and the flickering barbecue. "All thanks to you."

Zach said, "I was happy to do it. But I was scared shitless through it all."

"I doubt that, but I'll say this, too: I owe you big. I'll always be in your debt, no matter what I do for you."

"It's all right, Duncan."

He stood there with Duncan for some long seconds in silence, and then he said, "You're a smart fellow, so no insults on my part,

Zach. I'm sure you figured out I do more than just run a restaurant, gun shop, and some gas stations. Am I right?"

"When you got two guys with Chinese rifles in your house, doesn't seem like they're complaining about the high price of gas," Zach said.

"That's for damn sure," Duncan said. "So because I owe you, I'll tell you the real deal."

Zach had an idea of where this was going, but he kept his mouth shut. Like he had learned so many times in government service, not talking or volunteering information often equaled keeping your head on your shoulders and your career alive.

"So here it is," Duncan went on. "I have other interests—criminal interests, most would say. I grow and sell weed. I also loan money to folks who can't go to banks, who don't have the right credit scores. I also smuggle cigarettes up to Canada, and I smuggle booze into New Hampshire. Sometimes vice versa depending on what the market will bear."

Zach kept with his silence, wanting to see where this was going.

Duncan said, "Any questions?"

"Seems to keep you busy," Zach said.

"It does," Duncan admitted. "But I'll tell you straight out, way I see it, I'm providing a service to the people around here. Smokes and booze cheaper than they can get from local shops and the state liquor store. Weed for those who like it. I don't use it myself, but heck it was legal in the States until the 1930s. Even Bing Crosby and JFK were known to take a toke or two. And it's being legalized other places now, too."

"Sounds fair enough," Zach said.

In the gathering twilight, Duncan eyed him. "You're not being sarcastic, are you?"

Zach said, "Hell no. Remember, I'm a homeless guy who got screwed over by the Feds, without a pension, without health insurance. If you want to make a living smuggling and growing pot, that's fine by me." A moment passed. Zach said, "The two bikers who came to your house. They pissed about something you're doing?"

"Smart question," Duncan said. "The bikers are from a big club up in Quebec called the Iron Steeds. They didn't mind much that I did a little cross-border work. But they found out I was involved in something worth a lot of money. They wanted a piece of the action. I refused. They upped the negotiations, I refused again. This was their latest attempt."

Zach said, "Holy Christ, what do you think they'll use next time? Smart bombs?"

Duncan laughed. "That'd be a heck of an escalation, wouldn't it. But we'll get back at them when the time is right."

"I can't believe you're just going to sit back and relax."

Duncan's voice grew sharper. "Might be some loose ends to tidy up, right around some people's throats, but that'll be for later. Right how, though, I have a question: You want a job? You want to come work for me?"

Zach said, "That's two questions, if you're keeping score, and the answer is yes, and yes again. But here's my own question: I don't want to sound ungrateful, but what kind of job? Working at your restaurant? One of your convenience stores? Helping mule a couple of bales of marijuana?"

Duncan said, "Way I keep count, that's four questions, not one. But here's your answer: I need someone I can trust, someone handy with a weapon, someone who'll watch my back if trouble comes stomping through."

Zach pretended to think that over for a moment. "Security, then?"

"Yeah."

"Something to do with what those bikers were after?"

"Maybe," Duncan said. "Probably. How does a thousand bucks a week sound?"

It didn't take much for Zach to put enthusiasm into his voice. "Holy shit, Duncan, that sounds pretty goddamn good."

"Fine," he said. "To show you my appreciation, I'll consider you on the clock from the minute you came on my deck weapon in hand."

"That's pretty generous," Zach said.

"Maybe so, but it's deserving. Also, don't say no, but I'm going to make arrangements for you to get out of Rogers' Bed and Breakfast tonight. We'll have your truck and your belongings brought here, you can spend the night at my house. I insist."

"Hard to say no to something like that," Zach said. "So what's on the agenda for tomorrow, then?"

"Nothing as dramatic as today," Duncan said. "But I will give you a tour of my other interests, and we'll start talking about what to be ready for. Cameron will be in on this, too."

Cameron then strolled by, hauling a tripod and a shoulder carrying case, followed by a couple of younger female attendees. He headed away from the partiers and the house, and Zach said, "What the hell does he have there, a rocket launcher?"

Duncan laughed. "No, that's his hobby. Cameron is an amateur astronomer, and he's good. I mean, he's really good. Some people claim to be stargazers, but Cameron, not only does he know the constellations, he can name the stars in each constellation. He can look up and point at a star, and say, no, that's the planet Jupiter. Or Saturn. Or Mars. He could have gone far ... if things had worked out differently."

"Sounds like he's pretty serious for being an amateur."

Duncan said, "I can tell you how serious he is, if you'd like."

Zach shrugged. "I guess I'm now your employee, so sure, tell me."

"Cameron's got a pretty little spread on the other side of Turner, up on a hilltop. Nice three-sixty view of the night sky. Even built a little shed to house a nice big-ass telescope, with motor drive, heater, the whole works. Well, couple of years back, this hedge fund trader from Manhattan decided to build a summer place down the hill from Cameron's. Not really a problem, we don't mind people moving in, so long as they know the rules and are polite. So what happened is, once the place was built, the guy had floodlights on all night long. Real stupid, I mean, what did he think, starving wolves were going to besiege him there or something?"

"Does sound stupid," Zach said.

"Right. Cameron, he tried to reason with the guy. Told him that the floodlights were washing out the night sky, that it really wasn't doing anything in terms of safety or protection or whatnot. In fact, all it did was waste electricity and ruin a good one-fourth of the sky for stargazing. Cameron told the guy that if he had shades put over his floodlights, they could still do their job without ruining it for everyone else. Cameron even invited the guy to come up to the house for a friendly beer and some stargazing, to show him how his floodlights were ruining it for Cameron and his telescope. But the hedge fund guy was having none of it. Said it was his property, he could do what he wanted, and that some long-haired biker wasn't going to tell him what to do."

"Sure is surprising that a guy in hedge fund work has such lousy negotiation skills," Zach said.

"Yeah, I agree. So near as I can figure, Cameron tried three different times, very politely and neighborly, to resolve the issue of those darn floodlights."

"What happened the fourth time around?"

Duncan shrugged. "Never was a fourth time. One weekend when the hedge fund guy wasn't visiting, the place burned down. By the time the Turner volunteer fire department worked their way up the dirt access road, it was just smoking timbers in a cellar hole. Local fire inspector said it was an act of God."

Zach said, "That's what I call a serious amateur."

———

Back at the house, the party went on for about another half hour, during which time Zach's truck and belongings were brought to the Crowley residence. He had a charming minute or two alone in the kitchen with Karen Crowley. She kissed him on the lips near the refrigerator and said, "I owe you so much, Zach. My word ... nearly twenty years, and look at you ... and when you come back for a visit, you make it one to remember."

"Didn't plan it that way, but I'm glad it worked out."

She kissed him again, murmured, "Thank you so very much" and went back to the crowd.

Cameron came in, carrying his telescope and tripod, and when he had brought the equipment out to his Honda Pilot and came back into the house, he stood in the kitchen and simply said, "Time."

The word "time" was repeated and passed on, and the barbecue was extinguished, the trash was picked up, any left over food was put on plates and covered in foil, and people started streaming out. Motorcycles and car and truck engines were started up, and then someone grabbed his hand in the kitchen. Tiffany, the bosomy tattooed lady and moose hunter, pressed a napkin with a phone number scrawled on it into Zach's hand.

"Call me," she said. "Still have some moose burgers or sausage if you're interested."

"I'll keep that in mind," Zach said.

Soon enough, the place was empty, save for him, Duncan, and a yawning Karen Crowley. Duncan said, "Hon, off to bed. If Zach doesn't mind, I'll set him up in Lewis's room."

Duncan led him down a hallway to a bedroom that obviously belonged to his son, with Red Sox posters on the wall and the usual debris of a young boy. Fresh sheets were put on the bed, and Duncan said, "Small bathroom through that door. He shares it with his sister, Amy, but they're with friends tonight. So no worries, okay? Just have a good night's sleep, and we'll have breakfast in the morning." Duncan shook his hand. "Me and Karen, we're going to be sleeping deep and well tonight, all thanks to you. You saved our lives, Zach. That we'll never forget."

Zach said, "Go on, before you make me choke up."

When the door closed behind Duncan, Zach sat down on the boy's bed, looked at his two black duffel bags on the floor. Never forget, he thought. He was sure Duncan would never forget this evening.

He was also sure Duncan would never forgive Zach for what was going to happen two nights from now.

———

After showering and brushing his teeth, Zach got dressed in a pair of shorts and put his .32 Browning on the nightstand next to the digital clock and the latest issue of *Sports Illustrated*. Next he went to his duffel bag, pulled out the super-duper spy cellphone Tanya Gibbs had given him. He pressed the speakerphone button, which went to speed dial, and surprise of surprises, it went to voice mail. Tanya's soft, almost childish, voice, said, "You know who this is. Leave a message."

To Zach it seemed like Tanya was still in high school, looking for her newest BFF to leave a message, and he decided to do what he could. "Tanya, it's Zach Morrow. I'm now in the employ of the Duncan Crowley criminal enterprise. You should also know that a Quebec biker gang wants to steal the shipment, which should be arriving in two days. When I find out the exact time and location, I'll let you know."

There. He hung up, and then dug around in the duffel bag until he found a new disposable cellphone. He dialed a number from memory, waited for the man to answer as before, and he said, "You know who this is. You know it's not fair, what happened to me. My next calls won't be so polite. I deserve better. Can't you help me?"

The older man said, "Stop calling me, damn it," and hung up.

Zach sighed. Can't keep a man from trying. He switched off that phone and slipped into a strange bed that belonged to the son of a man Zach was soon going to betray.

It seemed that thought should have kept him up, but he went to sleep almost instantly.

———

A noise and Zach sat straight up in bed, feeling out of sorts, out of place. Just where in hell was he? Then he heard it from next door. Whispered giggles. The squeak of a bed. Duncan Crowley in bed with the young girl he had been in love with so many years ago, when he had been privileged to play with that sweet, sweet body for a short several weeks.

Now she was with someone else, and maybe there was a hint of jealousy. A touch of melancholy, of what might have been.

Most of all, there was the thought of being in his old hometown, alone in bed. Had he ever thought it would come to this? He shifted and rolled over, and there was silence from the room next door. He found himself recalling with surprise the voice and shape of the young and attractive Tanya Gibbs.

TWENTY-EIGHT

On Highway 412 outside of Montvert, Quebec, Sergeant Albert Lavalley of the Sûreté du Québec watched a tractor-trailer roar past him, heading west, and he swiveled his head to catch a glimpse as it sped by. The truck was a traditional Peterbilt diesel, but its load was a light green half-sized trailer. Unusual to see half-sized trailers on this highway, and he recalled an intelligence bulletin that had been issued a few days ago, at district headquarters. It said a half-sized trailer with a Mextel Lines logo painted on the side had gone missing from a terminal at the St. Lawrence Seaway, and that it should be immediately stopped and detained if found.

Then, oddly enough, the bulletin had been recalled two days later. Albert had never seen that happen before, but unofficial word had come down from the district commander to forget the whole thing.

Sure. Forget the whole thing. Except it looked like the whole thing had just sped by.

He checked the dashboard clock. Twenty minutes and he'd be off shift, so maybe he should let the truck go by.

Maybe.

When he had been a child, Albert had been adopted by Quebecois missionaries, working outside of Port-au-Prince in Haiti. Growing up here in Canada—a hockey puck in a snowfield, some of his friends had joked—he knew how lucky he was, to be in this safe and secure province, so far away from the armed militias and grinding poverty of his homeland, where starving families actually ate cooked dirt patties. He eventually had gotten used to the snow, cold, and ice hockey, knowing he was safe, knowing he would never again go hungry. So it was his drive and joy of life that got him here, a respected sergeant in the Provincial Police, married to another Haitian girl with a child on the way.

A drive that kept him up on the job, doing his duty, even with less than twenty minutes to go. So what if the bulletin had been recalled. Something odd must be going on with that truck.

He made a U-turn in his police-issued Charger, switched on the blue lights hidden in the radiator grille, and sped up the highway, chasing after the mysterious truck.

———

Brewster Flagg glanced at the sideview mirrors, whispered, "Fuck," as a police cruiser came up behind him, lights flashing from its radiator. Only two days to go and he had to be pulled over like this, out in the middle of nowhere. There was no way he could outrun the cruiser, so he switched on the truck's directionals, downshifted, and eased the truck to the right. All around them was flat farmland; not a house or another car in sight.

That was a good thing.

———

Albert pulled the cruiser up to the rear of the truck, parking out far enough in the lane to give him protection from any passing traffic when he went to check on the driver. He reached for the Motorola radio microphone, picked it up, and got a burst of static in reply. He tried again to let Dispatch know he was making a traffic stop, but he couldn't tell if he had gotten through or not. *Merde.* The radio had been malfunctioning for most of his shift; now it looked like it had finally crapped out.

He put the microphone back in the holder, grabbed his cover, and opened the door. Quick license, registration, and cargo check, and he'd use his cellphone to contact Dispatch to see if anything else should be done. Then if all went well, he'd be home in time for dinner. And tomorrow, ah, tomorrow, Gracie had her appointment for her first ultrasound. Maybe they would find out if she was carrying a son or a daughter. Wouldn't it be something if they could leave the OB-GYN's office knowing that.

Hat firmly on head, he strolled up to the Peterbilt cab.

———

Brewster looked down from his seat, couldn't believe what he saw. Up here in the frozen north, far away from any city at all, and what was coming at him? A darkie in a police uniform! Amazing!

He undid the door, opened it up, and turned so he could see the cop coming at him. He thought of Troy, good ol' Troy, who had warned him, weeks ago: *Whatever you do, cousin, don't get stopped by the cops, and if you do get stopped, don't let anybody see in the back! No matter what!*

The darkie cop stopped, looked up at him, hand on his holster, other hand holding a metal-clad notebook.

"*Bonjour, monsieur. Permis et enregistrement, s'il vous plait?*" he asked in a squeaky voice.

Brewster said, "Sorry officer, I don't speak French."

"Ah," the cop said. "American?"

Better fucking believe it, he thought. Aloud he said, "Yes, sir, that I am."

"Very good," he said. "May I see your license and registration, if you please? Then I'd like to take a look inside your trailer."

Brewster smiled. "Of course."

He turned in his seat, went to his leather carrying case.

———

Albert stepped back as the driver went to get his paperwork, and in the afternoon sun, he noticed something about the half-trailer. He could make out letters underneath the paint job. MEXTEL. He touched the side of the trailer. The paint was still sticky.

He turned back to the driver, saw him step down from the truck.

In his hand he was carrying a pistol.

Albert slammed his hand down to his holster.

———

Brewster brought up his Colt .45 Model 1911 semiautomatic pistol, pulled the hammer back, and fired off a round. The *boom!* was ear-splittingly loud and the darkie fell like a sack of potatoes. Not known among many of the PC fag-types out there was that this pistol was designed to knock down crazy Muslim darkies out in the Philippines back in the late 1890s, and it sure did its job back then.

Just like now. The darkie cop was flat on his back. Brewster walked up to him and—

The darkie rolled over and quickly scrambled under the trailer! The fucker!

Brewster knelt down, peered under the trailer, and—

A gunshot blew him back.

———

Albert saw the flash of light, heard the *boom* of the shot, felt a hammer blow to his chest as a bullet struck his protective vest. He fell flat on his back, banged his skull on the pavement, and, moving quick, he rolled and crawled underneath the trailer.

Baise! He scrabbled at his holster, grabbed his Glock 9mm, and when the driver knelt down to look at him, he popped off a round.

The guy fell back. Albert kept on crawling.

———

Brewster got up, his ears ringing. Fucking darkie managed to get off a shot, and nearly took off his right ear. He rolled over, saw movement, and fired three more times under the trailer.

———

Albert screamed as something tore at his foot. *Rien!* He moved up, held himself up by his elbows, looked over under the trailer, saw...

Nothing.

———

Brewster trotted around the front of the truck, the diesel engine still idling, and he saw the cop on his belly, one of his feet a bloody mess, and he aimed at the darkie's head and pulled the trigger again.

———

Albert jerked as another hammer blow slammed into his neck and shoulder. His arms lost strength. He was on his back. His mouth was full of fluid and he spat it out, his chin wet, and he closed his eyes. Thought of Gracie. Thought of his unborn child. Thought of sweet mamma and poppa, a white couple who had rescued him from a bad life, and—

Somebody was near him. He coughed and choked and spoke up.

———

Breathing hard, hand shaking, Brewster got over the darkie, saw his last shot had torn into his shoulder where it met his neck, and blood was drooling down his chin. The cop gurgled and looked up and started talking.

"*Monsieur,*" he whispered. "*Laissez-moi seul. Laissez-moi vivre. Je vais être un père. S'il vous plaît.*"

Brewster put the muzzle end of the Colt .45 against the darkie's forehead.

"Sorry, don't speak the lingo."

He pulled the trigger.

Fuck, he thought, as he got up. He'd have to wash his hands before he started up again and got out of here, and fast.

TWENTY-NINE

Tom Leighton was working his shift at the Irving service station when Gus Spooner came in, face white, his left hand still bandaged. "Did you hear what the fuck happened?"

Tom was rubbing the counter with a wet cloth. "No, what's going on?"

Gus looked around to make sure they were alone. "I don't know the details, man, but some heavy shit went down at the Crowley house yesterday. Some gunplay, and later on, you know that van with the Quebec license plates that was here earlier? Well, it got drove off and there weren't no Canadians driving it. Your uncle Dickie was driving it."

Tom felt like he was going to shit his drawers. He took off his Irving jacket and tossed it in the corner. "That's it, I'm quitting, I'm outta here."

"What the hell are you doing?"

"Shit, don't you see? All it'd take is somebody telling Duncan or Cameron that those Canadian guys were here yesterday, and man, it'll take about one second for them to put it together. I'm getting the hell out of here."

"Out of Turner?"

"Hell no," Tom said, pushing past Gus. "I'm getting out of the state. Hell, maybe even New England. What do you think's gonna happen to me or you when Duncan finds out those guys got directions from here? Remember when they bought some coffee and doughnuts, I gave them a receipt? Suppose that receipt is found in the van, hunh?"

Desperation was now in Gus's voice. "Shit, I didn't think about that. Look, please, can I come with you? Hunh? Just take me by my trailer so I can get some things."

Tom hesitated, and then said, "Fine, shit, whatever."

Outside they got into Tom's Chevrolet T10 pickup truck, and he sped quickly to Turner Farms, a mobile-home park outside of town. As he drove he kept his head moving about, looking for a maroon Chevrolet Colorado or a dark green Honda Pilot, the Crowleys' vehicles. He still felt like shitting himself. Tom pulled up to Gus's mobile home and Gus scrambled out and said gratefully, "Tom, I'll be right back. Thanks, bud."

"Sure," he said. He waited until Gus got into the light blue trailer and then he shifted his truck into reverse, roared out of the tiny driveway, and got the hell out of the park. He glanced up in his rearview mirror, saw Gus burst out of his trailer, run after him, waving and yelling.

To hell with it, Tom thought. Every man for himself when it came to going against the Crowleys.

He wondered if California would be far enough.

———

Prior to her early-afternoon drive to New Hampshire, Tanya Gibbs was in her office in the Federal building in Boston, when there was a hesitant *tap-tap* on the door, like some deranged woodpecker looking to find insects in a telephone pole instead of a tree trunk. Walter Dresden, once again exploring the outer limits of men's fashion by staying with black shoes, black trousers, white shirt, and black necktie.

"Walter, I'd like to say it's a pleasure to see you, but I'd be lying," she said impatiently. "I need to leave here in three minutes. What is it?"

"Ah, that matter involving the ... er, missing shipping container in Quebec. It seems there's been a development ... not earth-shattering, but a bit of information. It appears that there's been a brief intelligence interception ... no further data available ... that the container will be crossing the United States border sometime tomorrow."

She no longer cared that she had to leave in three minutes. "Really? How reliable is this information?"

"Fairly reliable," he said, voice apologetic. "Came from the domestic Canadian Signals Intelligence Services ... alas, they were unable to pinpoint the crossing point. It could be Maine, New Hampshire, Vermont, or er, New York ..."

Not very likely she thought. Not with Duncan Crowley's name attached to that container. Only one place to come over, and that was New Hampshire, Duncan's home turf. For place and time, she was relying on her rogue Coastie to pull through.

"And there's no change in status? No raising of the Alert level or putting the Customs stations on standby?"

"No, nothing like that at all."

"Walter, thank you very much." She got up and gathered her soft leather carrying bag. "Feel free to go to the building cafeteria, buy yourself a cookie, and charge it to my expense account."

In her government-issued Crown Victoria, she was heading out of the city with Henry Wolfe, her driver and bodyguard. Another lovely perk of the job was not having to navigate or worry about the paved meandering cow paths that were Boston roads. Sitting in the back like this, she let Henry worry about the stressed maniacs out there who thought green lights meant go like hell, red lights meant go even faster, and that yellow lights were for wimps. She, on the other hand, could review paperwork, strategize, and think things through. Street gangs could be outside her Crown Vic, tossing Molotov cocktails at each other, and with Henry at the wheel, she could give a crap what was going on outside.

When they finally made I-93, heading north to New Hampshire, she said, "What news of our independent contractor?"

"Our tracking devices show that not only has he been in the Turner area, we've also been able to narrow down a resident location," Henry said, not referring to any notes or cheat sheets, talking clearly. "The home of Duncan Crowley. He's been at that location for at least eight hours, according to the latest data dump. Plus you got a voicemail message from him last night. It appears the shipment will be arriving sometime tomorrow."

"Really?" she asked, thrilled. "He said it was tomorrow?"

"Actually, when he made the call, he said it would be arriving in two days. Hence, tomorrow."

I'll be damned, she thought. Walter's information from about ten minutes ago had just been confirmed. Two sources, then, that it was going to happen. She felt her heart race at the anticipation of what was going to happen next. Oh Emily, she thought, I'm going to do it this time. Going to do what others failed to do more than a decade ago.

"Did he say anything else?"

"He indicated that, quote, he was now in the employ of the Duncan Crowley criminal organization, and that he would contact you sometime today, unquote."

"Wonderful."

"But there's one other thing. He also said that a Quebec biker gang was also interested in the shipment."

"Canadian bikers? Gee, I'm really worried." She laughed. "Henry, you work and work, and gamble and gamble, and sometimes, both the work and the gamble pay off. Damn. All right, when we get up to Manchester, drop me off at the Radisson at the Center of New Hampshire. You'll be released for the rest of the day. Pick me up tomorrow at nine a.m. Any questions?"

Henry said, his head staring straight ahead, "Anything you need from me tonight, ma'am?"

She said, "Have as much fun as one can have in Manchester, Henry."

Tanya looked out the window, smiling, arms crossed. Henry glanced up at the rearview mirror. "You seem quite pleased, ma'am."

"I am," she said. "You know your history?"

"Some."

"The Pashtuns of Afghanistan have a saying that's been picked up by everybody from the British to the Sicilians, that revenge is a dish best eaten cold."

Henry said, "Who are you getting revenge on, ma'am? The ones behind the trailer coming in?"

"No," she said, thinking again of the burning twin towers. "The ones letting it come through."

———

Tanya was working on her third glass of wine, looking at her date sitting across from her at J.D. Tavern's restaurant at the Center of New Hampshire, a large Radisson hotel in the middle of the state's largest city. He was Carl Kenyon, a major in the New Hampshire State Police. On this night, he looked afraid of her, a feeling that should have been pleasing, but which instead she found depressing. She was sure that in most ways, the good major did a fine job for the State Police and its citizens, but tonight, she was going to use a weakness of his to get what she wanted.

Other times, other places, she would go through channels to get what was needed, but this wasn't other times or places. Something bad was coming across the border, and she was going to use the man across from her to make sure it was stopped. A distant part of her was sickened and ashamed for what she was about to do, but it had to be done. There was no other way. That distant part … at night it would come out in full fury, sometimes making for some long, sleepless nights, internal discussions about the ends justifying the means … and at some point, just before the sun came up, she would finally fall asleep.

Tanya said, "Carl, it seems this unannounced drill is starting earlier than I thought. It's going to be happening sometime tomorrow night. Place confidential, but I'm sure I'll be able to give you specific information later. Let's just say it's going to be in the northern reaches of Washington County."

Carl was about ten years her senior, with close-cropped gray hair, a large pock-marked nose, and wide shoulders. He wasn't dressed in standard uniform of the N.H. State Police—green uniform blouse, Sam Browne belt, and striped trousers with the unusual color of military pink—but was in a dark blue blazer, blue striped shirt, and red necktie.

"Tanya, that's ... you know that's impossible. A drill like this takes weeks to set up."

She nodded. "Which is why it's going to be unannounced. You take weeks of preparation, then it isn't a readiness drill. It's a predetermined three-act play where everyone knows their lines and their positions. This way, its much more realistic, much more useful for all concerned."

He frowned. "What's the drill scenario?"

"Unauthorized shipping container coming in from Quebec to New Hampshire, being smuggled across the border. Your folks will take primary; anyone else you can scrape together will serve as security and backup."

"Tanya ..."

She put her wine glass down. "Carl, really, I need your full cooperation. Please don't force me into doing something I don't want to do."

"I'm sorry. I can't do it. It's impossible."

Tanya sighed, opened up the purse at her side, took out her Black-Berry. She toggled a few switches and passed over the BlackBerry to Carl. He took one glance at the tiny screen and his face drained of color, such that it was nearly the shade of the tablecloth. He tossed the phone back at her. "Shut that fucking thing off and put it away."

She refused to look at the picture that was on display. Bad enough she had carried it all these years, just in the unlikely event that she would need to use this angry man sitting across from her, but it was like some cursed jewel that was in her possession, that she could never get rid of.

Carl leaned over the table. "You fucking promised me, back in Virginia, that you'd never say a word to my wife about ... about that night. So where the hell did you get that photo?"

Tanya suddenly felt queasy again and had to take a deep breath. Even the thought of avenging her dead friend wasn't helping. She finally pulled herself together and said, "I know you remember that night, Carl. I had my BlackBerry up to my ear, checking messages. When I got into your hotel room by accident … I saw what was going on the bed. It was nearly automatic, just in case something untoward happened. So I took that photo of you and the other officer. A bit blurry but both of your faces are quite clear."

The color roared back into Carl's face. "You fucking bitch, you promised—"

"I did promise," Tanya said. "I promised that I wouldn't tell your wife a word. Which I plan to keep. But I didn't make any guarantees about not releasing that photo to the colonel who runs the State Police. Or the governor. Or a newspaper reporter or two."

It looked like he was struggling not to leap over the table and strangle her. She pressed on. "So please don't put me in a box, Carl. Be a good boy and cooperate. Or—if I may be excused for using such rough language—people of prominence you know in this state will soon be looking at a photo of you with your dick up another man's ass."

Now her stomach was really queasy, and Tanya put her hands on her lap so Carl couldn't see how they were shaking. Carl's hands, however, were clenched on top of the table, the knuckles nearly glowing white.

"You fucking bitch," he repeated in a rough whisper. "You'll get your drill. But that's it."

She nodded, hoping the relief flooding through her wasn't showing. Tanya said, "Fair enough, Carl. And to show there are no hard feelings, when the drill is over, we'll get together and I'll show you my BlackBerry as I delete that photo. Heck, even if you'd like, I'll even give you my device, so you know the photo will disappear."

Carl took a hefty swallow from his water glass. "How do I know there's not other copies floating around, on a thumb drive or a DVD?"

Tanya smiled, again feeling sorry for the blustery major sitting across from her. "I guess you'll just have to trust me."

Carl snorted. "They'll be making snowmen in hell before I ever trust you."

Tanya picked up the check. "Truth be told, I don't blame you."

———

At the Slinky Pussy Gentlemen's Club in Laval, Quebec, Francois Ouellette got up from his desk as his deputy and second-in-command, Michael Grondin, came in, dressed in jeans, a Montreal Canadians hockey team sweatshirt, and as always, wearing that ridiculous ponytail.

"Are we all set?" Francois asked calmly.

"Yeah, boss, we are. He's in the basement back quarter. Bruised a bit, but he'll be all right."

"His name again?"

"Manny Beaudoin. An intelligence officer and liaison with the Sûreté du Québec. We've exchanged favors over the past year. He's the one that gave us the original information on the shipping container and Duncan Crowley."

Francois stepped around his desk. "Then let's see what additional information the good officer can provide us."

———

Through a back stairwell in the club that was only used by him and Michael, he went down two flights, to the basement. There, the two of them walked across a cement floor packed high with cases of beer and hard liquor, along with some hot electronics that were in the midst of being transported across Quebec and into Ontario, and a couple of pallets filled with cardboard boxes of stolen cold medicine, to be eventually cooked into crystal meth. In the far corner of the basement was a steel door with a combination lock, which Michael spun open. A heavy *click*, and the door opened up. Michael pressed ahead and Francois followed, smiling in satisfaction at what he was seeing as the door closed behind them.

In the center of the room was a comfortable wooden chair bolted to the floor, and seated in the chair was a man in an ill-fitting gray suit. He was balding, with a silly-looking comb-over on his head, and his skin was pasty white. His eyes were wide with fear, which made sense, since his ankles and wrists were handcuffed to the chair. There were two other chairs in the room, and a flatscreen television hanging from the near wall. Francois and Michael took the empty chairs.

The man licked his lips. "This is outrageous. I demand you let me go, right now, or there'll be hell to pay. Do you know who I am?"

Francois sighed, picked up a remote television controller from the arm of his chair. "Certainly, Monsieur Beaudoin. We know who you were. We also know that you're an intelligence officer and liaison with the Sûreté du Québec. Alas, we also know that you're a bit of a pervert."

Francois turned, aimed the remote up to the television screen, pressed the Play button. The screen flickered into life and it showed a bedroom, with a naked Manny Beaudoin and two giggling girls joining him on the bed.

Manny let a whispered "shit" escape from his lips.

Francois said, "From what I understand, a few days ago, you were at home, by yourself, when you got a visit by two young ladies who said they were on a petition drive to stop oil sand expansion in Alberta. I see one thing led to another. Why not? They're both very attractive young ladies. Unfortunately, Monsieur Beaudoin, you should have checked their identification before bedding them. Both of those ladies are quite underage."

Another whispered "shit" from the man in the chair. Francois went on. "What this is all about, Monsieur Beaudoin, is our desire to receive more information about that shipping container that has the entire province in an uproar. You see, my associate and I, we're very eager to locate this container."

Beaudoin said, "So's nearly every fucking cop in the province."

Francois said, "Eventually. So here's our problem. We've attempted in our own, primitive clumsy ways, to find this trailer. Unfortunately, four men we've sent to get information on this trailer have failed to return. Regrettable, but part of doing business. But those levels of business losses are unacceptable. So we need to know more about that trailer."

He tugged at chains holding his wrists and ankles to the chair. "I've already told you everything I know!"

Francois said, "Which is why we're all here. This is what you've told us. That the shipping trailer contains something quite valuable. That it was once stored at the St. Lawrence Seaway terminal. It's now missing. Duncan Crowley, a criminal from northern New Hampshire, is somehow connected to this trailer. True so far?"

An uncomfortable-looking Beaudoin nodded, looking up at the screen where he and two girls were going at it.

Francois said, "We need to know more. We need to know it right now."

"But I don't know anything more!"

Francois gestured with his right hand. "If we don't get additional reliable information, Monsieur Beaudoin, then my associate here will distribute this DVD to your superiors. You can imagine what will happen to you and your career once this recording is made public."

Francois toggled a switch on the remote and the volume increased. Beaudoin closed his eyes. "Turn it off, damn it, turn the fucking thing off!"

The sound went mute, but the DVD kept on playing. Beaudoin licked his lips and said, "The container … it's not the standard shipping container. It's about half-size, allowing one driver to maneuver it by himself."

"Very good," Francois said. "Do go on."

"It … its yellow, and has the logo of Mextel Lines painted on both sides. Red and blue. But … but they're pretty sure it's been repainted. So it's a half-sized shipping container with a fresh paint job. That's what everyone's looking for."

"What's in the trailer?"

"Swear to Jesus, I don't know. Only it's something very, very valuable."

Francois pursed his lips. "Is that it … really?"

A quick and eager nod of the head. "Really, that's all there is. Honest to Christ."

Francois got up, and Michael stood next to him. "Very good, Monsieur Beaudoin. We appreciate your cooperation."

He turned to leave with Michael, to go back out the door, and the man called out, "Hey! What about me? Aren't you going to let me go?"

Francois looked to Michael, who reached into a pocket, took out a small key, went over, and unlocked his wrists. He then dropped the key in the man's lap. "That we are, Monsieur Beaudoin. You're free to go. Feel free to take the DVD with you as well."

Francois and Michael left the basement. Francois said, "You burned another copy of the DVD, right?"

"Of course," Michael said.

"Nice investment."

———

Back in his office, Francois said, "Truck like that needs diesel, driver needs food, shit like that. Closer it gets to New Hampshire, the sparser the roads and towns. So this is what's going to happen. You get word out to everyone that belongs to the club, has ridden with the club, that has friends in the club, or that belongs on our fucking fruit-of-the-month list. Get out a description of that half-sized shipping container with a fresh paint job, heading to New Hampshire. Anyone finds it, they're to call it into us, and follow it, so we have the best information. Got it?"

"Got it, boss."

"Good," he said. "Then, goddamn it, we're not sending anyone else in except for you, me, and a couple of very hard men. This time, we'll do it right, grab that container, zap Crowley and his fucking boys, and find out what's so valuable that everyone with a police badge and government ID in Quebec has gone apeshit looking for it, posting a million-dollar reward."

Michael kept quiet. Francois didn't like the man's attitude. "Did I fart or something, Michael?"

His deputy said, "Just thinking, that's all. Wondering if this is still worth it. We might get a firefight down at the border. You know how freaky the Yanks can get about the border. We get in a scrape down there, might mean lots of attention."

"Michael," Francois said evenly, "you let me worry about that. All right? In the meantime, do what I've said. Every last item."

Michael nodded. "I'll get the word out, boss."

"Super," Francois said, sitting behind his desk. "But one more thing, Michael."

"Yes, boss?"

He picked up some papers. "Get that freaking ponytail cut off before we go, okay? Makes you look like a fag."

———

As dusk arrived in Turner, Zach was tired from spending the day with Duncan Crowley, who had insisted that Zach come along on a trip down memory lane, driving in and around Turner, checking out some of Duncan's businesses. The day had begun with breakfast in the big kitchen, with Karen insisting on cooking for the both of them. Anything you want, she had said, with a wink and a smile, anything at all.

So he had gone with French toast and bacon, fresh coffee and orange juice. Duncan had wanted the same thing, but Karen had frowned and given him a bowl of oatmeal. "He may look fit," she had said, "but his cholesterol level is so far off the chart they have to tape an extra one to it." Duncan had such a sorrowful look on his face, Zach had secretly passed him two slices of bacon under the table, like he was feeding the family dog.

The day had been a long drive of going in and around Turner, as Duncan pointed out the stores he owned, the gas stations, and the Flight Deck Bar & Grill. He also mentioned in passing other business interests: converted barns that grew marijuana under artificial light, and small warehouses at the end of dirt roads that held cases of whisky, beer, and cartons of cigarettes. Duncan had explained, "Smuggling has been going on around here since Colonial times. Nowadays, it depends on the tax stamps, the prices, and the exchange rate between the American dollar and the Canadian dollar. Sometimes it makes sense to smuggle booze and butts north, other times, it's the opposite."

Zach had said, "How the hell do you do this without cops paying attention?"

"What cops?" Duncan had said. "Most of the towns around here don't have a police force. Those that do, it's a one- or two-man force. The sheriff department serves arrest warrants and such for the county, and that's about it. The State Police patrols the main roads, responds to 911 calls when they can. If you're quiet, careful, and not too greedy, it's easy to pass under whatever radar's bouncing around out there."

Now they were back in Turner proper, and Duncan slowly drove by the regional high school. He said, "So there it is, our alma mater. Thought I'd go far away from there, with my pitching arm, but real life sort of plays roulette with your ass, don't it."

"True," Zach said.

"Mind telling me something?"

"No promises, but give it a shot."

Duncan said, "You waxed me a few times in wrestling, but never again. Why's that? Did I improve that much?"

Zach laughed and looked at the dreary building. "Truth? Duncan, after I beat you the third time, the phys ed coach took me aside and told me to cut the shit. Even then, you were getting attention as somebody destined for the majors. He didn't want me to hurt you, nail your arm. I told him to go screw, and then he went to my dad, and he convinced me otherwise, with the end of his leather belt."

Duncan said, "Jeez. Sorry about that, Zach."

"Not your fault. Our fathers … they set the tone, don't they. Your dad was a lawyer, wasn't he?"

"Yeah. Darn good lawyer, but poor judge of character. After he and my mom died, and after his corrupt partner got killed in that car crash, what passes for a legal community up here came together and tidied things up. Left me and my brother holding an empty bag. Your dad ... quite the politician, right?"

Zach sighed. "Politics was his first and last love, with time left over for chasing strange. My mom put up with it as best as she could, but she had other issues. Bouts of depression, rage. She might have done better with some psychiatric help, but hell, you know how it is. Nearest medical facility for something like that was a fifty-mile drive, and trying to keep that secret in a small town like this ... Never happen."

Duncan said, "So here we are. You and me. Now that I've shown you my deep and dark secrets, how about revealing one of yours?"

Zach froze, wondering what Duncan was getting at, wondering if he could get to his .32 Browning in time, wondering if this whole drive around town had just been a goddamn ruse to relax him.

"Ask away," he said, keeping eyes straight and focused on Duncan's hands.

He smiled. "Your dishonorable discharge. What the hell was that all about? Getting drunk on duty? Beating up a superior officer? Saying something nasty about the First Lady?"

Zach said, "It was because I did what I was trained to do. Save lives."

"There's more to that, Zach. Go on, tell all."

So that's what he did.

———

Duncan pulled out of the school parking lot as Zach told the story of his travel into Sierra Leone. He found it hard to drive without swiveling his head constantly to look at Zach as his old classmate calmly talked about his last mission, going up a river by himself, in the middle of a civil war, gunfire and explosions echoing around him.

"Then I reached the rendezvous point, where two Agency guys were waiting to be picked up, along with all of their gear. I got there, loaded them up, and before we were going to shove off, four civilians came out of the brush. Dad, mom, and two kids. Dad had been a prominent politician and was hiding out because of the war. He said an official at the American embassy had promised him safe passage. That official had been evacuated, and safe passage never showed up."

"Sounds like a mess," Duncan said.

"You bet," Zach said. "I figured if we dumped the gear for the Agency fellows, we'd have enough room to take all four back with us. The Agency guys violently disagreed. I managed to convince them through my charming personality and force of arms to change their mind. They did. The gear was destroyed, the family and the two Agency guys and yours truly were successfully evacuated."

"What a story," Duncan said.

"War stories usually are. But this one had a messy ending. I had obviously disobeyed orders by not picking up the gear, and by taking four civilians out on a covert op. So that's why I got cashiered."

Duncan drove up Gosham Road, a narrow country lane with farmland all around them. In one pasture, sheep grazing, and in another, three horses ambling about. He said, "At least you got them out. Not much of a trade, I'm sure, but it must have felt good, saving those four."

Zach turned away, looked out the passenger's-side window. "You'd think. But not all good stories have happy endings. That ending was pretty messy, too. After a few months, when a truce was negotiated, the guy I rescued was invited to go back to Sierra Leone. Against most advice, he and his wife went back. His kids, at least, stayed behind with some relatives in London."

"What happened?"

Zach kept on looking out the window. "They were seized at the airport. He was forced to watch as his wife was beheaded. And then he was machine-gunned to death."

————

Zach kept quiet as Duncan maneuvered the truck up the road, and then the asphalt petered out and the road became well-packed dirt. Duncan said, "One more stop, and then we'll get home. See what my Karen has set for dinner."

"That sounds like fun," Zach said.

Duncan turned right at a mailbox marked COOPER and went down a dirt driveway. He pulled to a stop in front of an old farmhouse with a wide porch that had a new green metal roof. Nearby was a barn and two out buildings. Parked in the yard were a yellow school bus with TURNER COOPERATIVE SCHOOL DISTRICT stenciled on the side, a Volkswagen beetle, and a white Chevrolet Ram pickup truck with rust chewing along the side panels.

Duncan said, "This here is where Nat Cooper and his family live. I need him for the job tomorrow night and just want to get things straight with him. Shouldn't take more than a few minutes."

They both got out of the truck and an English Springer Spaniel came bounding out of the barn, a dirty green tennis ball in his mouth. "Hey, Tucker, how goes it," Duncan said, rubbing his head. Following the dog was a man in his late forties, wearing worn jeans, muddy work boots, and a gray hoodie sweatshirt over which he had a light blue down vest. His brown hair was thick but cut short, and his chin was receding. He was grinning as he approached Duncan, holding out his hand. He had a two-day growth of beard and one of his incisor teeth was missing, making a black splotch in his smile.

"I'll be damned, look who's come up all the way to see little ol' me," the man said as Duncan shook his hand.

Duncan turned and said, "Zach Morrow, this is Nat Cooper. All around good guy, truck driver, farmer and independent contractor. Nat, Zach Morrow. Ex-military guy and a new employee of mine. How's it going, Nat? How are the girls?"

Nat kept grinning, though Zach noticed that his lips were curled some about the right side of the mouth, like he was trying to hide his missing tooth. He said, "Kelly and Stacy, both doing well, both kicking ass on their softball teams. Looks like they're gonna have a good season."

"And Dora?"

"Dora's good," he said. "Still drivin', still threatenin' the kiddos when they raise hell on the bus. And your brood?"

"All fine," Duncan said, walking about and putting an arm around Nat. "Tell me, has Dora been baking lately? You know how Karen loves those apple pies of hers."

Nat grinned. "S'pose we could find one or two, if we dig enough in her kitchen."

Duncan said, "So, Nat, why aren't you answering your phone?"

He shrugged apologetically. "Our land line got service cut off two days ago for non-payment. Might just let it go for now because of the bills we owe on it. Dora's trying to get a cellphone set up, but that might be a few more days. 'Cause of our credit, we're gonna need somebody to co-sign it for us, and that'll probably be her dad, once he comes back from Maine."

Duncan lowered his arm, rubbed his hands together. "This is short notice and all, but might you be available for a job tomorrow night?"

His smile got wider. "Hell, yes, Duncan, I guess I would be."

"Don't you want to know it is?"

Nat said, "Hell, you've always been straight with me before, Duncan. I figured with a record like that, it'd be all right."

"Darn nice of you to say, Nat. What I need is your truck driving skills, take a load from up in the northern reaches, maybe go down to Concord or the Manchester airport, long-term parking area, depending."

"How long?"

"Not more than two days."

"You got yourself a deal, Duncan," Nat said.

"Don't you want to know the pay?"

Nat said, "The pay will be fair, that's all I need to know."

Duncan gently slapped him on the shoulder. "That's fine, Nat. I wish all of my negotiations went so easily. So tell me, is your Dora in the house?"

"That she is," Nat said. "Go ahead, go look her up."

"I'll do just that, see if I can't sweet talk an apple pie out of her. Meantime, why don't you show Zach your prized pets."

Duncan strolled away, went up the front porch, and into the house. Nat turned to Zach and said, "Come along, fella, let me show you what's what."

He followed Nat into the near barn, where there was a strong scent of hay and manure. Inside were three of the largest creatures Zach had ever seen: oxen, each in its own stall, each towering above and looking down at them with wide brown eyes. Nat said, "My prize oxen. Bring them out to all the fairs from spring to fall, in pulling contests."

Across from the stalls was a large piece of mounted plywood, and stuck on the plywood were scores of blue ribbons. Nat pointed to them proudly and said, "That's what we got last year. Can you believe it? Won almost every competition we entered, thanks to their hard work, and thanks to Duncan Crowley."

Zach said, "Why Duncan Crowley?"

Nat moved some straw around with his right boot. "Tell you the truth, what happened was a couple of years back, I was an independent trucker. Didn't make a lot but enough to get along. Then most of the companies around here, the ones that hired me out, they either got sold or bought out. My trucking contracts dried up, and when the cost of diesel kept on going up and up, had to declare bankruptcy. Things got real tight. You know how tight? Tight is when you go through the seat cushions, looking for coins back there, coins you can wrap up and bring to the bank so the electric don't get shut off."

"That's tight," Zach said, looking at the peaceful brown eyes of the three oxen, their nostrils gently moving in and out.

"Damn right," Nat said. "Things got so bad, I was planning to sell these three, even though they and their ancestors have been part of the family for decades. Cooper family has always been known for their prize oxen, since the early 1800s. Tough times, but Duncan Crowley, he heard about my troubles and came over to help. No damn welfare or bailout, I'll tell you, but money for work. He's a good man, he is. He truly is a good man."

Zach said, "That's what I hear."

———

Outside there was shout and Duncan emerged from the house, carrying a small paper package. A stout woman with long black hair and wearing tight jeans and a black sweatshirt followed him out, smiling. He turned and yelled out, "Thanks, sweetie, for the pie and the good wishes!"

Handshakes were exchanged all around on the front lawn, and Duncan said to Nat, "Come to my house tomorrow at five p.m. for a briefing for what happens later."

Nat said with a smile, "Dora give you permission to let me out tomorrow night, then?"

"Surely did," Duncan replied. "Said to make sure that your worthless carcass comes back in one piece."

Inside the truck cab, Duncan started up the engine and paused, his hands fussing with the brown package next to him, as Zach entered from the other side. Nat trudged back to the barn, followed by the English Springer Spaniel, dirty tennis ball still in his mouth.

Zach said, "Good people."

Duncan said, "They're all good people. Throughout this county, there are lots of good people. You hear about people falling through the cracks? People up here, they've been falling into canyons the past few years, and nobody gives a damn. The state and the Feds do what they can, but these years at least, war's been declared on the rural and poor."

Zach said, "You forget every four years."

Duncan laughed, put his truck into drive, and started going out the driveway. "Damn, you're right. Every four years, time of the New Hampshire primary, all those nice sounding, well dressed folks come trooping through promising help for industry, help for medical care, help for everything. They grab the people's votes and then head off to the next primary, and that's it. About the only place that makes out during the primary season is Channel Nine, the television studio. Gosh, the money they make from commercials. That's about it."

Back on Gosham Road, Zach said, "What's your other job, then, Duncan? Helping everybody you can?"

"I do what I can, Zach, do what I can ... but I know it won't last."

"Why's that?"

Duncan pondered that, and said, "My dad, he used to love watching old TV shows, programs he loved when he was a kid. Got them on VHS and made me and Cameron watch them. Some of the craziest stuff you ever saw, like *Welcome Back, Kotter* and *Three's Company* and older stuff, like *My Mother the Car*. Couldn't believe the crap he made us watch."

"Some people might call that child abuse," Zach said.

A laugh from Duncan. "Sure enough. Anyway, he also liked the old Ed Sullivan shows. Comics who were as dry as toast, funny animal acts, and one guy that always stuck in my mind. Can't remember his name none, but he was this guy who had these tall sticks, and on the sticks, he'd rotate these white plates. Know what I mean?"

"Sure," Zach said. "I remember that, too."

"Yeah. So this guy would put one plate up, and then another, and then another. And he'd be going back and forth, back and forth, trying to keep the plates moving so they wouldn't fall. My dad thought it was hilarious, watching this guy run back and forth, back and forth, 'cause eventually, the plates would start falling and breaking. Funny, hunh? But I asked my dad, why the heck didn't he just grab the plates and prevent them from falling. Dad said, that's not the point. The point of the act is to have those plates fall and break."

They came to the intersection of Gosham Road and Route 117. Duncan looked left and then looked right as he took a left out on the road. "That guy is me, Zach. I got lots of plates in the air, and I can't afford to let any one of them fall. All I need is for one curious cop, one ticked off weed smoker, or one guy who thinks I'm charging too much for smuggled smokes, and those plates will fall—and my butt will be in jail for a long, long time. Then, I won't be able to help anyone, including my family. Zach, that's intolerable. That's why the shipment tomorrow night matters. It's going to set me up so I can get out of my illegal stuff, be able to go straight for the first time in nearly twenty years, and still be in a position to help out where I can. Do you know what I mean, Zach? Do you?"

Chest tight with betrayal and with a haunted tone in his voice, Zach said, "By God, I do."

THIRTY

Tanya Gibbs was outside of the Center of New Hampshire when her government-issued cellphone rang. Her head throbbed with pain as she grabbed her phone out of her overnight bag. It had been a long night after her dinner meeting with Major Kenyon of the State Police. She had gone up to her room, switched on HBO, and worked through two more bottles of wine. She had switched off her cellphone, told the front desk not to put through any calls, and had watched two movies in a row, some childish pieces of crap with lots of explosions and fire-balls and special effects.

Unfortunately her room didn't carry Turner Classic Movies. She thought Ted Turner was a pompous blowhard who claimed to be an environmentalist while busily fencing off and using thousands of acres in Montana, but damn, the man knew how to run a cable chan-nel. She could spend hours surfing through TCM, watching movies that would still be classics centuries from now, while those hours of trash she suffered through last night would be forgotten in—

She punched the phone on and put it to her ear, wincing once more. "Gibbs."

"Madam, it is I, your special agent up in the north woods," Zach Morrow said. "How's it going for you?"

"It's going," she said, wishing she had brushed her teeth once more before checking out. "What do you have?"

"Two things," he replied. "Number one, the delivery is definitely on for tonight."

She forgot her head was hurting. Tanya said, "Do you have a time and location?"

"Not yet," he said.

"Contact me the moment you get that information," she said, trying not to let her voice tremble. Emily, she thought, oh Emily.

"Ah, that's where the second thing rears its ugly head. We need a face-to-face meeting today. As soon as you can."

Her excitement disappeared like a snowflake on a frying pan. "Impossible," she snapped. In the thin line of traffic on Elm Street, her Crown Victoria was nosing its way towards her, driven by the always reliable Henry Wolfe.

"Then make it possible," Zach said. "Make it possible, or I'm done, I'm through. And you won't get one more bit of information."

Anger racing through her at being so very close, her voice quavering, she said, "I'll break you, Morrow. The number of ways I can break you reaches to the infinite."

"Perhaps," he said. "But there's a clock ticking. Meaning this shipment is going to roll across the border in a number of hours. If you want to intercept it, you need me. Oh, you can break me into pieces at your convenience later on, but I don't care. I'm broke, no pension, no healthcare, no home. I have a black mark on my record that even rules out working at McDonald's in the future. So keep that in the back of your mind when you're thinking of all the possible ways of hurting me."

She closed her eyes. So damn close and to have this happen!

"I can give you ten minutes," she said, exhaling in frustration. "Where and when?"

"When is in approximately fifty minutes. The where is north on Interstate 89, a rest stop run by the state, right by Exit 40. Has a nice large parking area, with picnic tables among the trees, where you and I can have a productive, adult conversation. I'm sure you'll love it. Deal?"

She sighed, feeling her stomach roll and dip from last night's drinking and this unexpected phone call. "I'll be there."

Tanya snapped the phone closed, put it back in her overnight bag, and slowly walked to the Crown Vic. Henry helped her in and when he got up forward, she said, "Change of plans. I need for you to get on Interstate 89, heading north. There's a rest area you'll stop at, by Exit 40."

"Certainly, Miss Gibbs," he said, easing out into Elm Street, the main drag of downtown Manchester. "What's going on?"

"Our Coast Guardsman is apparently having second thoughts," she said, settling into her seat, hoping the drive north would be a smooth one, for her stomach was roiling indeed. "I need to go up there and reignite his enthusiasm for his mission."

"And what if that doesn't work?"

Tanya fastened her seatbelt. "To quote another broad with a lot on her plate, 'We are not interested in the possibilities of defeat. They do not exist.'"

"Who said that?" Henry asked.

"Queen Victoria of Great Britain."

"That was some broad."

She closed her eyes. "Tell me about it."

———

On a windswept knoll of land off I-89, where the state of New Hampshire had placed a rest area cunningly disguised as a white Cape Cod house, Zach Morrow waited in the large and nearly empty parking lot, leaning against the fender of his Ford F-150 pickup truck. Before him, a tree-covered valley swept out, with only the interstate and a few distant houses visible. Behind him, a hill sloped up, the trees thinning out and with picnic tables scattered about. A fair wind blew and he brooded as he looked to the ramp leading up to the rest stop from the interstate.

Last night, after the behind-the-scenes tour of Turner, he and Duncan Crowley had returned to his house, where Karen had made a roast pork dinner for them, Cameron, and the two children, Lewis and Amy—allowed to visit home for the night. Lewis was a high-wired bundle of energy, sprinting from the kitchen to the living room, up and down the hallway, wanting to show Zach his pitching stance, which, as he had proudly explained, "I learned from old VHS tapes they have at the high school, showing dad when he was kicking Manchester Central's ass." Amy was just as energetic, but she wanted to show him drawing after drawing of horses. At first, Zach had assumed he'd be seeing creations one step above stick figures, but the girl knew perspective and shading, and the horses were startling life-like. He looked around at the family and the home life and thought about all the places he had lived—BOQ barracks, temporary housing, rented apartments near military bases—but never, ever had he ever called one of those places home. Envy had come to him, envy of Duncan and what he had.

Later, with a new lens for his telescope, the bearded and long-haired biker Cameron took them to a dark part of the yard, where he gave a half-hour tour of the moon, including one splotch of gray and black that was the Sea of Tranquility, where Armstrong and Aldrin had landed nearly fifty years ago. Cameron had announced, "We'd have

296

Luna City there if it wasn't for the fucking politicians." Karen had shushed him, since the kids were around, but Duncan had laughed and they had all gone back in, and Zach had slept on the pull-out couch. This morning, after breakfast—and once again, he had slipped Duncan a couple of slices of bacon—Duncan said, "Hey, go out and take the day off, all right? See you back here for dinner."

So he stood and waited, and then saw the Crown Vic come up the ramp.

———

Driving his silver Audi, Francis Ouellette pulled into a dirt lot outside of a small private airport a few kilometers west of Laval, Quebec. Nearby was a dark blue Bell 429 helicopter, its main rotor blade slowly rotating. He got out and Michael Grondin approached from a dark green BMW, not smiling, his hair cut short. Damn, at least the good fellow was still following orders. Two other men got out of the BMW and stood by the trunk. They were members of the club—a short, squat guy named Johnny, and an older guy with a white beard named Phil—and were the hardest of the hard men they had.

Michael had a folded-over map in his hand, which he spread open on the hood of the Audi. Francois said, "What do you have?"

"A little luck for a change," Michael said. "About an hour after we put the word out, got a call from one of our affiliate clubs, southern part of the province. The Knight Stalkers. Think they could come up with an original name for once."

"Maybe they're originally from Newfoundland," Francois deadpanned.

Michael said, "Yeah, maybe. Anyway, night before last, two of their members was at a tittie bar in Charlottesville. Saw a tractor-trailer truck with a half-sized shipping container pull in and pull out after the driver got a private show."

"What made them call?" Francois asked.

"Trailer was the correct size, and it was freshly painted. The guys were positive they saw a company logo underneath the new paint job, but they can't remember the whole name. Just the first letter. An M."

"Christ, that's good stuff."

"Gets better. Seems the driver was some American Southern trash boy. Drank up a bit, got a private dance, but when he let loose, got all spooked and ran out, like he was ashamed or something. So that's a connection, eh? A shipping container that has all the badged types with their panties in the twist, and it's being driven by some Southern shithead. Sounds pretty damn important, explains the hefty reward."

Francois said, "What's the map for?"

Michael went on, still not smiling. "So this is where we're at. I put the word out to the Knight Stalkers with a description of the truck, and it's down here, on Route 257, about as close to the New Hampshire border as you can get. They've got a good mobile and stationary surveillance going on with their club members, but the damn funny thing is, the truck's going around in circles. Down one lane, zips over on a connecting road, and then back up again. Hour after hour."

Francois tapped the map. "The guy's waiting for the word to cross the border. He's biding his time."

Michael gestured to the Bell helicopter. "That's what we don't have a lot of: time. Drive will take too damn long, but we take the chopper over there, we can be down there in less than an hour."

"How did you set up the chopper?"

"Pilot's girlfriend is hooked on smack. We give the pilot a clean, steady supply, and he's our airborne taxi driver."

Francois looked at the two other men. "Johnny and Phil know what's up?"

Michael took the map off the Audi's hood. "They know enough. We need them for a truck hijacking worth a fuck-load of money. Anything else they need to know?"

"That'll do for now," Francois said. "Let's get a move on."

Keys in hand, he opened up the Audi's trunk, took out a dull gray duffel bag, and started walking towards the waiting helicopter. Johnny and Phil saw his movement, opened up the BMW's trunk, and took out their own gear.

Francois gently slapped Michael on his back. "A hell of a job, Michael, a hell of a job."

His second-in-command kept quiet. Francois added, "You look pretty damn good, now, since you got that haircut."

"Whatever," Michael said.

———

Tanya said to Henry, "Pull up there by the pickup truck. Keep the engine running. I'm hoping it won't take long."

Henry drove in by the pickup truck, and Tanya saw the Coastie guy standing there, leaning against the fender. He looked tired, a bit wired, but there was still a presence about his face and his eyes that struck her. There were only two other vehicles in the long empty parking lot, a Wal-Mart tractor-trailer truck, parked to one side, and a light yellow van with Wisconsin plates, the side door open, mom and dad up forward, arguing over a map, a young boy and girl racing around the van, shrieking and giggling.

"That might be your plan," Henry said. "He might have his own."

Tanya opened the rear door. "You know what they say: when it comes to plans, God's on the side of the heaviest artillery."

———

Zach unfolded his arms as Tanya approached. She had on a mid-length black dress coat, clear nylon stockings, and sensible flat black shoes. Her face was flushed and she looked queasy, like a teenage girl who had come home after sneaking into a local college frat party. Zach said, "My, looks like you had one hell of a night."

Tanya said, "Never mind what I look like. Let's get going, if you don't mind. I don't have much time."

Zach said, "A pleasant good morning to you, as well. Come over here, there's a picnic table we can use. But please, no naughty words. You'll note there are innocents around."

He turned and Tanya muttered something under her breath. About a half dozen strides past a cement sidewalk and a sign telling dog owners to clean up after their pets, there was a wide wooden picnic table. Zach sat down and Tanya gingerly sat across from him, like she was afraid the wood was made of balsa, and that she would crash to the ground.

Zach said, "The move is on for tonight. But I'm not going to tell you where and when unless you answer me something."

"Which is what, pray tell?"

"What's in the trailer?

She frowned as she crossed her legs. "Not your concern."

"The hell it isn't," he said. "I'm your point man on this little black op, and I deserve to know more."

"Nope."

"All right, tell me this. The shipment's coming to Duncan Crowley, who, among other things, runs the Washington County Motorcycle Club. Did you know that a motorcycle club from Quebec, the Iron Steeds, are after the same shipment? That they've threatened to kill Duncan and his family unless he gives up the shipping container?"

Tanya smiled. "Motorcycle gang from Quebec. What did they threaten to do? Beat them over the head with baguettes? Choke them with Camembert cheese?"

Zach's hands felt cold as he matched the steady look of the woman across from him. "No, they've threatened him twice. The second time, they sent down two bikers armed with submachine guns. They took Duncan and his wife hostage. They were threatening to rape and kill his wife if Duncan didn't roll over and give up information on the shipping container."

"What happened, then?"

"I happened," Zach said, hands feeling even colder. "I appeared on the scene, saw what was going on."

"Did you call the cops?"

"Tanya, certain times and places up there, there are no cops. So I did what I had to do. I shot and wounded the first biker. Chased the second biker out of the house. He turned and tried to shoot me. Missed. I returned fire. Didn't miss."

Tanya stared at him, eyes wide, face more pale. "Did you kill him, then?"

"Please," he said crossly. "I wasn't trained to wound my opponents."

"And the cops?"

"Don't know a damn thing," Zach said.

"What happened to the other guy, the biker you wounded?"

"I came back to the house, found he was dead."

"Christ," Tanya said. "Killed by Duncan?"

Zach shook his head. "Killed by Duncan's wife. Seemed she didn't take too kindly to be being assaulted, kidnapped, and threatened. So that's where I'm at, Tanya. I need to know what's in that goddamn trailer. I find out now from you, or I leave. You won't find that trailer without me."

Defiance in her voice, Tanya said, "Maybe we don't need you anymore."

Zach laughed. "Tanya, you ever been up in that part of the state? I know when you saw me in Purmort, you thought you were in the wilds of New Hampshire. You have no clue. Purmort, that's a goddamn Times Square compared to what's up in the northern woods. The roads peter out to dirt lanes, there's no towns, just isolated homes here and there, and some hunting cabins. There are forests, lakes, streams, swamps and the occasional logging road, snowmobile route, utility rights-of-way, and smuggling paths that have been used for centuries. Tanya, you could have the entire fucking 10th Mountain Division up there looking for the trailer tonight, and there's a damn good chance they won't find it."

Zach reached into his coat pocket, took out the cellphone and the tracking device that had been placed under his truck. "These both let you know where I am, in real time. So here's your new real time adjustment. When I leave here, the only way you'll know where I am and what's going on will be through my good graces."

He could tell she was struggling to keep it all under control. She said, "Please stop being obstinate, Zach. I need that information."

"I'm sure you do," Zach said. "But you don't have much leverage. What, you're going to threaten me with jail? Three hots and a cot? Sounds better than what I've got, and if you think I could become somebody's bitch in prison, think again."

Tanya took a breath, folded her hands across the picnic table. "I think I know what happened. You've gone back to your old town, met

302

up with old friends and acquaintances. They've welcomed you back as the prodigal son or something. Maybe a couple of beers, couple of meals, couple of laughs. You're looking at Duncan Crowley and his friends and his family, and you're thinking, hey, these are good people. Why should I narc them out to the Federal government? What's a little weed, a little booze, a couple of dead gangsters … Is that what you're thinking, Zach? Hunh? Losing the taste of battle?"

"Don't fret about what I'm tasting. So what's in the container? Smallpox? Nerve gas? Something worse?"

"Even getting your pension and benefits back, that's not enough now, is it," Tanya said. "You've got to believe you're doing right, even as you betray them. Tell you what, Zach. Admit that little point I just made, and I'll tell you what's in the shipping container."

Zach didn't like where this was going, but damn the woman, it was like she could read his freaking mind or something. But when push came to shove, damn it again, she was right. He had to know.

"All right," Zach said. "I need to know what's in that shipping container. Before I betray those folks up in Turner, I need to know why it's so important."

Tanya seemed to shrink some, like she was feeling the weight of the universe upon her. "According to the intelligence intercepts I saw, what's in that half-sized shipping container with MEXTEL LINES painted on the side is a WME."

He hated to admit it, but he was confused. "What the hell is a WME?"

"WME," she explained. "Weapon of Mass Effect."

"I thought they were called Weapons of Mass Destruction."

She shook her head. "That was then, this is now. Current administration thought *Weapons of Mass Destruction* was too scary, too spooky. So they changed the name. They're good at that, you know. Remember when we started bombing Libya? That wasn't war. That

303

was the kinetic application of military force. Like tax hikes are investment in children's future, nonsense like that. But whatever you want to call it—dirty bomb, nuclear device, weapons-grade anthrax, or any other bio weapon—it's in that shipping container and it's coming into the United States tonight, through the good graces of Duncan Crowley."

"I don't believe it."

"Hah," Tanya said. "Don't care if you believe it, you asked what's in the container. And I just told you: a WME being smuggled into the United States."

Zach cleared his throat. "I don't believe Duncan or anybody else associated with him would do such a damn thing."

"For the right amount of money, anyone will do anything. Look, you've been up there for a couple of days. Has Duncan Crowley talked about his politics, his views on government? Somehow I don't think he belongs to the American Socialist Party. Am I right?"

Zach said, "Most people up there have antigovernment views. How can you blame them? They've been lied to, dumped on, cheated on, by both political parties, by government leaders of all kinds. But Duncan Crowley is not the type to bring a weapon like that into the United States. I'm positive."

"Certainly," Tanya said. "People never thought Timothy McVeigh was the type either, right up to the time when he took down the Murrah Building in Oklahoma City."

She checked her watch. "Is there anything else, Zach? Truly? Look, against my own better judgment, I've told you what's in that shipping container. It's a weapon of some sort, designed to cause mass casualties against American civilians. Duncan Crowley is no doubt being paid a considerable amount of money to make sure it gets safely smuggled into the United States. I'm sure Duncan and his pals don't have fond thoughts about big government and big-city types. So what's it to them if several thousand government workers or urban residents get smoked in the next week or so?"

Zach couldn't look at her anymore. He looked to a van parked nearby, where a young boy and girl played, laughing and having the time of their lives. He stayed still.

Tanya slowly got up, tightened the belt around her coat. "So now you know. I have to leave. And what about you?"

The boy was about nine, the girl maybe about eight. They were so full of life, so full of love. He tried to imagine them being someplace like Fenway Park in Boston, or Independence Hall in Philadelphia, holding each other's hands, walking together, walking past a half trailer that had been parked, the trailer suddenly going up a split-second flare of light and heat matching the interior of the sun, turning them into carbon atoms. He also tried to think of Duncan Crowley helping bring that trailer across the northern border, through those very dark woods.

"Zach?"

"Tell me one more thing, and then you've got my agreement."

"Fair enough."

He recalled his last day at the bed and breakfast, using that nice woman's computer. "I did some research on you. What I could, because you've successfully kept your name out of the press. But I found a lot about your uncle. The senator from Ohio. Warren Gibbs. Probable future presidential candidate. You told me that first day that you were off the reservation. Are you doing this on his behalf?"

"Not for a moment."

"Really?"

She slowly sat back down. "I'm doing it on my friend Emily's behalf. And for three thousand other dead people, and their friends and family. To make sure nothing like that ever happens again."

The wind grew sharper. "Like that first day, I'll ask you again. Why just you? What do you see that everybody else in your office doesn't?"

Her face pale, her lips quivering, Tanya said, "What I see is a photo I saw a week or two after 9/11. Not many people know this, but there are plenty of videos and photos from that day that have never been made public. Too sensitive for the poor American people, I guess. But I saw one photo that's always been in my mind. A bloody lump of clothes on Ranson Street, beyond the rubble pile. Bare feet is about the only thing you can identify. But I was able to identify something else. A pink and blue silk scarf around the bloody torso. A scarf I gave to Emily a month earlier for her birthday. So that's what I see, Chief. That scarf … and thinking about how it fluttered in the air during those long, long seconds it took for her to fall to her death."

Zach sat so very still, unwilling to do or say anything else at the moment. Tanya used her right hand to wipe at one eye, and then the other, and she cleared her throat. "So do I have your agreement?"

He reached over, picked up the cellphone she had given to him. "Yes," he said, his voice hoarse. "Yes, you do."

She got up and walked away from the picnic table. He watched that slight and pretty figure get back into her government car and then ride away. He took a deep breath, let the air out. Zach put the assigned cellphone back into his coat pocket, took out his latest disposable phone. Once again he dialed a number from memory, and once again, an older man answered.

"You know who this is," Zach said, desperation in his voice. "You know I wasn't treated fairly. For the last time, can't you help me?"

"You know I can't," the older man said. "For Christ's sake, stop calling me."

"To hell with you, then," Zach said.

Back in her Crown Vic, Tanya Gibbs sat back, and fastened her seatbelt as Henry Wolfe backed the government vehicle out into the lot. She turned and saw the solitary and yet powerful figure of her Coastie there, ready to do what was right. She kept on looking at him until the trees got in the way, when Henry started heading north up on Interstate 89, looking for a quick place to make a U-turn and head south.

"How did it go?" he asked.

"Went just fine," she said.

"I take it defeat wasn't an option?"

She settled back in her seat, so very tired. "Not for a moment."

Daily Threat Assessment Task Force Teleconference Call
April 16th

Homeland Security representative: "Anything else, then?"

FBI representative: "Yeah. I know you don't want to hear this—"

Homeland Security: "I'm thrilled the FBI is ahead of the curve."

CIA representative: "A refreshing change."

[[Laughter]]

FBI: "But concerning that missing trailer. The one from Mextel Lines. Latest word we received from the Canadians was that it might have been sighted in Quebec. Now our liaison officer in Quebec City reports that one of their provincial officers was gunned down yesterday following a traffic stop."

State Department representative: "Go on."

FBI: "Thing is, the officer reported to Dispatch that he was pulling over a tractor-trailer unit while he was on routine patrol."

Homeland Security: "Did he indicate it belonged to Mextel Lines?"

FBI: "No."

Homeland Security: "No follow-up messages?"

FBI: "No, it looks like the patrol unit's radio failed."

CIA: "Any witnesses to the shooting?"

FBI: "No, but look—"

Homeland Security: "I'm sorry, what do you have, really? An unfortunate shooting connected to a traffic stop. But no witnesses, no indication that the Mextel Lines unit was involved."

FBI: [[[Obscenity deleted.]]]

Homeland Security: "A pleasant accusation coming from you, Tom, I'm certain. But if you'd like, I'll show you my birth certificate to indicate otherwise."

Unidentified: "Will it be the short-form or long-form certificate?"

[[[Laughter]]]

THIRTY-ONE

DINNER IN THE CROWLEY household that early evening was a splurge of lobsters from the nearest Hannaford supermarket—about an hour drive away—that Karen expertly boiled in large kettles. Amy and Lewis were not there, being safe and guarded at another friend's home in Turner, so it was just Karen and the Crowley brothers, along with Zach. He kept quiet through most of the meal as they cracked open the shells, dug out the sweet lobster meat, and dipped it into melted butter. After dishes had been cleared away and everyone had slices of apple pie, the doorbell rang like it was timed. In came Nat Cooper, the farmer who had the prize-winning oxen, and a slim biker named Luke Munce with short blond hair. Luke's face was puffy and Zach recognized him as one of the four pool players he had beaten the shit out of back at the Flight Deck Bar & Grill just two days before.

Zach wasn't too sure how to approach him, and he decided a direct effort might work. He met up with Luke in the kitchen and held his hand out. "No hard feelings?"

Luke grinned, shook Zach's hand. "The fuck there's no hard feelings. Me and my buds, we were having a nice game of pool when you went all berserk on us. If it weren't for Duncan, we would have nailed your ass later. But there's a job to be done, and Duncan and Cameron vouch for you, so that's how it's gonna be. Tonight I'll be at your side and if shit starts flying, I'll have your back, but I won't forget that night."

Zach said, "I won't forget either, and if the shit flies tonight, I'll have your back as well."

Luke nodded. "Guess that's the best it's gonna be."

Zach followed Duncan as they went downstairs to the basement. To the right was a play room with kid's toys, SpongeBob Squarepants throw pillows, and a weight system. To the left was a door with a combination lock. Duncan undid the lock, opened the door, switched on the lights, and in they went.

The room was small, with no chairs. It was not a place for sitting or relaxing. On a long wooden table were a collection of weapons—semiautomatic pistols, H&K Model MP5 submachine guns, a .308 Remington rifle, and two Remington .12-gauge shotguns—Kevlar vests, Maglites, and other military gear. A large-scale topographical map was tacked up on the near wall, showing the far northern reaches of Washington County and the southernmost section of the province of Quebec.

Duncan said, "Cam, we all clear?"

"Room was swept this morning, bro. Nothing bad's going on."

"All right, this is what we've got," he said as he went up to the topo map. "I've sent the necessary information via text to our driver up here in the wilds of southern Quebec. At ten p.m. tonight, we'll be meeting him here"—he tapped his finger on the map—"about fifty yards over the border, at location Q. Location Q is the 112-mile marker for a Hydro-Quebec right-of-way that's never been used.

Then Nat will meet up with the driver and take over the driving responsibilities. We'll be there to escort and make sure everything's copacetic for the first twenty or so miles. The plan is, we get back to civilized roadways and get on Interstate 93 south. We break away so it doesn't look like a goddamn convoy. Looks like the turnover spot will be the Manchester airport early the next morning. Drop the truck off at long-term parking, leave the keys on the front left tire. Nat, you can catch a Trailways bus back up north, and I'll make sure the original driver has enough funds to take him wherever he wants. Nat, you up to that?"

"Whatever you need, Duncan," he said.

Duncan lowered his hand. "There's a hunting camp here, at the intersection of this logging road and a fire road. I'll point it out as we pass it tonight. That will be our fallback and rendezvous point if things go to the shits, all right? Less than a half mile away from location Q. But I don't expect anything to go wrong. We've done lots of product movement up there over the years across that section of border. Only thing we've run into are the occasional lost black bear or horny moose."

Zach folded his arms as the briefing went on about weapons and options and how long the evening should last. Although he had never been here before, the room was a familiar place. A locked environment, the smell of gun oil, weapons on display, topo maps on the wall, and the nervous energy of a small group of men planning their excursion into the dark woods and along night roads. He had done it so many times in bunkers in Iraq, aboard ships in the Pacific, Atlantic, and Indian oceans, and at an airbase in Afghanistan. The only difference here tonight was geography, and, of course, the outcome. Zach knew what the outcome was going to be. Everyone here in the room would either be arrested or shot, the shipping container seized, with a lot of people in this county losing their protector and savior. A hell of a thing, to go out on an op like this, where the ending was already predetermined. If he had been back in the Guard, he would have stormed out of the briefing room in disgust.

Still … a weapon coming across the border? A dangerous weapon that could kill thousands? He still could not believe what he had earlier heard from Tanya Gibbs.

Duncan clapped his hands together. "All right, that's what we got, kids. Any questions?"

Zach thought, oh, what the hell, let's see what happens. "Yeah," he said. "The shipping container. What's in it?"

It was like he was at a Temperance Society meeting and had suddenly asked everyone for his or her favorite cocktail recipe. Save for Duncan, everyone's faces seemed to be set into granite. Duncan, though, was grinning.

"Really?" Duncan asked. "You want to know what's in the container? Is that it? Guys, does anybody else here want to know what's in it?"

Nobody said a word. Even in this small room in the basement of a home in New Hampshire, Zach felt as exposed as he had ever been.

Duncan shrugged. "Looks like you're outvoted."

"Didn't think this was a democracy," Zach went on. "Way I see it, I've already had a run-in with two armed fellas who were intent on doing grievous harm over what's in that container. I figure something causes that much animosity, I might want to know what's inside, so I can tell if it's worth running into a couple more better-armed fellas."

Duncan's voice, though quiet, was tinged with menace. Zach could see how such a quiet-looking guy could run such a show up here in these north woods. "You want out?" he slowly asked.

"Not looking to leave, not looking to go out," Zach said. "Just looking for information."

"Cam," Duncan said, turning to his brother. "I think Doctor von Braun has the answer Zach's looking for."

Cameron smiled, leaned back against the wooden table with the weapons. "Not my department," he said, and then he laughed.

Zach looked at Cameron and then his younger brother. "Sorry if I'm dense, guys, but I have no idea what that meant."

Cameron said, "Tom Lehrer, the folksinger, did a song about Wernher von Braun, the German rocket scientist who came over to the Americans after the war. He was pretty slippery when it came to his wartime guilt and what he did. Lehrer's song said something about the rockets went up, but where they went down wasn't his department, said Wernher von Braun."

Duncan added, "That's what I'm saying, Zach. It's not my department, not your department. All we care about is getting that trailer safe over the border from Canada. So right now, no fooling, no time: are you in or are you out?"

Zach didn't hesitate. "I'm in."

Duncan looked around at his rather small band of brothers and said, "Okay, we head out in about thirty minutes. Last chance for a piss break or to grab a drink of water. No booze, goes without saying. Cam, you want to hang back for a second?"

The other men went out and Nat, the last one, said, "Thanks for the kind words about the pie, I'll make sure to pass it on to Dora."

"You do that," Duncan said. When the door closed he said, "Well, Cam, what do you think of Zach? You concerned?"

His older brother shrugged. "Guy's ex-military. On the outs. He's agreed to work with you, and don't take offense, but you're not exactly the straightest guy around. So I'm not surprised he's asking questions, maybe getting cold feet."

Duncan scratched at his chin. "See what you mean. But still … sometimes I think there's something a bit off, like he's observing me from a distance, judging me. Like when he first came by the

Flight Deck. He did something odd there, something I'll tell you about later."

"What does Karen think?"

"She thinks he's fine, that he's on board. But then again, she's biased."

"Why's that?"

"He's the first guy she ever slept with, back in high school."

Cameron pondered that. "Think he's doing it again?"

Duncan headed to the door to go back upstairs. "Cam, I'm generous, but I'm not that damn generous."

———

Upstairs Zach saw Nat and Luke go into the living room, talking and joking like the neighbors and old friends they were. Both sat on the couch and got involved in a tale concerning the local road agent, an improperly installed drainage ditch, and how a farmer's pile of manure was washed out during a heavy rainstorm and ended up in the driveway of his neighbor. The neighbor was a recent refugee from the Socialist Republic of Massachusetts who had escaped up to Washington County to get back to nature. However, the recent refugee was complaining that half a foot of cow shit distributed on his driveway wasn't exactly the kind of natural encounter he had been hoping for.

Zach went into the kitchen, where Karen was washing up the last of the dinner dishes. Unbidden, Zach grabbed a dish towel and started drying. Since he didn't know where anything went, he carefully wiped each pot and dish dry, and then stacked them on the wide counter.

Karen smiled, revealing a dimple on one side of the cheek. "Thanks for volunteering," she said. "Most of Duncan's buds are okay, but I think they'd rather tear apart a motorcycle transmission than lend a hand in the kitchen."

Zach said, "Rather be in a kitchen than on a motorcycle, tell you the truth."

"Why's that?"

"Motorcycles are scary."

She chortled at that. "Seeing what you did the other day when Duncan and I were in trouble … and motorcycles scare you? You're a funny man, Zach Morrow."

He carefully polished a wineglass. "Don't mean to be funny. What happened yesterday, and other things I've been involved with, I've always felt like I'm in control. On a motorcycle, unless the road is empty, I'm not in control. An oil patch, a rough piece of pavement, a teenage girl driving and texting … *boom*, you're down on the ground, without a ton or so of metal wrapped around you to protect you."

Karen opened up a top cabinet, reached up to stack some wide light blue plates. From a corner of his eye, Zach saw the top of a red thong panty. He didn't avert his gaze. Karen closed the cabinet door. "True enough. I have a cousin, she works in the ER over at Dartmouth-Hitchcock, outside of Hanover. You know what they call motorcyclists who don't wear helmets?"

Zach finished off another wineglass. "Organ donors."

"Naughty boy, you heard that already."

He picked up a serving spoon. "I've been around some, Karen."

She gently nudged his hip with hers. "So you have, so you have. Ask you something?"

"Go right ahead."

"You're not married, and I gather you don't have anyone steady. Why's that?"

316

Good question, he thought, one he had asked himself before enough times. He said, "Not something I haven't thought of, I'll give you that. Best answer is that in my line of work, I moved around a lot. Didn't have time to settle down and look around for a life partner. Made some friends, had some relationships, but nothing permanent."

Karen started putting silverware away in a counter drawer. "You said that was the best answer. Was it a truthful answer? Or do you have a better one kicking around in that mind of yours?"

He looked to her, recalled again with stunning force the memories of their brief time together, the whispered vows, the new and raw passion, the sheer erotic vibrancy of being with a woman for the very first time. Karen looked back with a comfortable expectation, like she wasn't judging, that she would accept anything he would say.

Zach let out a breath. "Sometimes I think it's the way I was brought up. My dad ... he cheated on my mom. A lot. That was my role model for what a married man did. What he did to my mom was disgusting. I've often thought that's why I've stayed away from the whole long-term relationship question. Because of my dad."

Karen gazed at him for a moment, and then laughed and snapped a wet dish towel at his butt. "Hah. Blaming your dad. Sounds like an easy excuse. No offense."

Damn, he so enjoyed being in this kitchen with her. "No offense taken."

"Glad to hear it. Do me a favor?"

"Name it."

She surprised and thrilled him by dropping the dish towel on the counter, stepping forward, grabbing his ears forcefully with her strong hands, and kissing him firmly on the mouth. "You be safe tonight, Zach Morrow, and you take care of my husband. I'm trusting you. Do you understand?"

Hating himself for saying it, knowing the phone call he would have to make shortly, Zach said, "Understood, Karen."

———

After they were dropped off, the Bell 427 helicopter lifted off from the dairy farmer's field in southern Quebec—Francois Ouellette not knowing and not particularly caring what town they were in—with he, Michael, Johnny and Phil trooping across a spread of pasture, avoiding cow shit in the process, carrying their equipment bags. They went through an open gate by a dirt driveway next to a collapsing barn where a muddy light red Jeep Cherokee was parked. The two front doors of the Cherokee opened up and a man and a woman stepped out. The man was short, squat, and wide, wearing jeans, knee-high boots, and a dull yellow farmer's coat. He had a navy watch cap pulled over his head and his black goatee was streaked with gray. The woman was much younger, wearing tight jeans that had slits cut away in the thighs, and a white hoodie sweatshirt that couldn't hide her impressive chest. Her brown hair was long and wavy, and her eyes were brown as well, laughing, like she half hoped the fierce men approaching her would take her someplace fun for some serious partying.

The man walked up, extended a hand. "Guy LeBlanc, of the Knight Stalkers, glad to help."

"Francois Ouellette," he said, not bothering to explain who he was. That didn't need explanation. "What do you have?"

Guy said, "The truck you're looking for just stopped going in circles. He's refueling now and we got him in view, at the Pont du Louis truck stop. We're thinking he's prepping for his next stage. We're about ten, maybe fifteen minutes away."

"Sounds great."

Guy motioned to the Cherokee. "My wheels, at your disposal. Sherry here, she's gonna be your guide once you pick up the trail of that truck. Nobody else knows the woods, paths, and roads down there like my Sherry."

"Sherry your wife?" Francois asked, and Sherry put her hands in her hoodie pockets and laughed.

"Not damn likely," she said. "Guy is my uncle, aren't you, Guy."

Guy grinned like he was hiding something naughty, something special. "That I am, Sherry. I want you to take these gentlemen and take them wherever they need to go. They need food, drink, you pay it and I'll reimburse you, got it?"

Sherry smiled again. "Whatever you say, uncle."

Francois looked to his three men. "Okay, let's pile in." He looked up at the sky. "Would like to get a lead on this fucking truck before the sun sets."

Michael—still unsmiling—brushed past with his gear, followed by Johnny and Phil. Sherry went to the front of the Jeep Cherokee, opened the door and got in, and then started the engine. Francois shook Guy's hand again. "This works out, you and the Knight Stalkers, you'll get a cut of our meth traffic in this part of the province. Plus you'll all be comped for life at our club."

Guy nodded in satisfaction. "Does that include blow jobs for me and my guys?"

Francois picked up his equipment bag. "Don't push it."

———

In an underground staging area north of Concord, New Hampshire, where the governor of the state and his staff would retreat if the

319

Russians, Chinese, or Canadians ever decided to wreak havoc upon the Granite State, Tanya Gibbs sat in a small, stuffy conference room, with a frowning Major Carl Kenyon of the NH State Police sitting across from her. Carl didn't look very happy, and Tanya could hardly blame him. He had scratched together a team for this unannounced drill—a health physicist from the Department of Public Health, about a half dozen members of the somewhat-secret State Police Rapid Response Unit, and an equal number of deputy sheriffs from the Washington County Sheriff's Department, who seemed pathetically eager to prove themselves tonight—but so far, all they were doing was waiting.

And waiting.

Tanya wasn't about to tell them that she was waiting for a phone call from Zach Morrow, so they sat and talked and drank coffee as each minute oozed by. She sipped at the awful cup of coffee—New Hampshire being New Hampshire, they probably reused the same coffee grounds two or three times as a cost-saving measure—when her government issued cellphone started ringing.

Tanya picked it up. It didn't have any cutesy Top Forty hit music or Broadway musical or comedian's voice as a ringtone. It was a phone, damn it, so it had a real phone sound.

"Gibbs," she said.

"This is Zach Morrow," the tired voice announced. No jokes, no wisecracks about being a super dooper secret agent or anything like that. No, Zach sounded tired, defeated, and depressed, a trifecta victory that should have cheered her but instead made her feel glum. She felt like it was a hell of a thing to turn that cocky and confident Coast Guardsmen into someone so submissive.

"Go on," she said, drawing a yellow legal pad near her. "What do you have?"

Zach said, "The meet is on for ten p.m. tonight, in the northern part of Washington County, on a remote access road. All I know is that there's a Hydro-Quebec right-of-way extending through there, and they'll be meeting at mile marker 112. I'm sure you and whatever smart folks you have will figure it out."

She wrote quickly. "Besides yourself and Duncan Crowley, who else will be there?"

"A man with trucking experience to take over the driving once they cross the border, Duncan's brother Cameron, and a biker named Luke Munce. The last two, in addition to me, are providing security."

"I see," she said. "Are you and they armed?"

"Heavily."

"What are the rules of engagement?" Tanya asked, her writing hand firm but cold, as Carl hungrily looked at her, intrigued at what she was doing.

Zach breathed. "Rules of engagement, near as I can figure, is to safely escort that trailer through the border and shoot anyone who gets in the way."

"Anything else I should know?"

Zach said, "No. Gotta run, don't want to make the Crowley brothers suspicious."

"Very well, see you later tonight."

She put the phone down on the pad, took a deep and satisfying breath. This was about to get very interesting. "Carl," she said.

"Yes?"

"This is no longer an unannounced training exercise. I've just been informed that a shipping container carrying a possible Weapon of Mass Effect will be transiting the Canadian border at this point, up in Washington County." She scribbled out the directions Zach had provided to her, passed it over to the major, who quickly picked it up.

She went on. "Under Confidential Protocol Four of the Renewed Patriot Act, Amended, I am now taking control of your State Police unit, as well as the sheriff's deputies from Washington County, and the state health physicist. I now have complete command over your men, as well as those deputies. Our mission tonight will be to seize that trailer and arrest the driver, and anyone else that might be there. The information I have is that there will be about a half dozen heavily armed men in wait. You will have tactical control of your forces. But bottom line, I want that trailer seized at the border, and any opposing forces either arrested or neutralized."

Carl stared at the piece of paper in his hands, his knuckles pale. "You've got to be joking."

A flash of temper flared through her. "No, Carl, when I'm joking, I show off my tits. Do you see any nipples?"

He looked up, anger burning in his eyes. "I need to run this by my Colonel, I need to contact your Regional Administrator, I can't —"

Tanya looked at her watch. "We have just over two hours to get everybody up there in place to intercept a Weapon of Mass Effect, to save thousands of innocent lives. If you want to play safe and secure bureaucrat, so be it. It won't be my wide and hairy butt sitting at a future Congressional hearing, testifying on why he was instrumental in letting a deadly weapon pass through our border unmolested."

Carl kept on staring at her with hate in his eyes, and Tanya gave it right back to him. She thought of those days and nights as a safe college student in Boston, her best friend Emily at her side, both of them confidently planning their futures, their lives, in the certain knowledge that they would remain close friends for the rest of their lives.

That last part was true, but neither of them could have ever imagined that one of them would die in an act of war. Some things were just beyond imagining.

He folded the paper with the directions in half, then in quarters. "Very well," he said, his voice just above a whisper. "You've got me, you got my guys, the deputy sheriffs, even the Public Health character. But if this gets fucked up in any way whatsoever, it's going to be your ass in front of that Congressional hearing. Not mine."

Tanya gathered her belongings and stood up. "Works for me."

THIRTY-TWO

BREWSTER FLAGG SLOWLY DROVE the Peterbilt truck down the narrow and bumpy dirt road, parking lights on only, as he followed the texted directions. He should be at the turn-off in just about thirty minutes, if all went well, and it should. Except for that fuck-up with that darkie Quebec cop, it had been pretty smooth. He thought about his cousin Troy, how proud he'd be that Brewster had gotten so close to getting the job done. Just a little more time, and across the border he'd be, and then this truck with the special cargo would get to where it belonged.

DC, Manhattan, Chicago ... he really didn't give a shit. Just as long as it was taken off his hands and parked where it would do the most damage, the most impact. That's all that counted.

Up ahead a rabbit skittered across the dirt road. So many others out there didn't know what counted. He remembered a hot day in Arizona where he had been hiking in the lonely desert, just a few hundred yards away from the Mexican border. He had been with two other Tea Party members, guys named Chuck and Robbie. All three of them were wearing surplus Army gear, carrying rucksacks and holstered pistols. They had been patrolling and checking things out, doing the real border security work the fucking government wouldn't do, and Brewster had gotten tired of the whole thing. His skin was burnt, he was rationing his water as best as he could, and sand and pebbles kept on getting into his boots, so he had to stop every half hour or so to empty them out. A hell of a thing for a grown man to do; no job, welfare benefits cut off, and now, out where the National Guard should be, defending the border.

Then they came across two wetbacks sitting in a little shade underneath some overhanging rocks. Their shoes were dusty and torn, their clothes filthy, and their lips were swollen, cracked. Robbie could speak some of the lingo but Brewster knew what they wanted when they started whispering, "*agua, agua, agua,*" holding out their empty brown hands.

"Shit," Brewster had said. "I don't have any water to spare. Tell the fuckers to go back home."

Robbie said something to the two young men, and one started jabbering real quick, and Chuck said, "What the fuck is he saying, Robbie?"

"Usual shit, about how he and his buddy here, they just want some water, please, just a bit, their coyote should be here any sec, they got jobs lined up, please, they're gonna get jobs driving trucks from some—"

That had been that for Brewster. He pulled out his Colt .45, walked up to the first spic, nailed him in the chest, got the second one in the chest, too, as Robbie and Chuck just stood there, frozen in the heat.

Then it was quiet for a second, so quiet he could hear the other two guys breathing, and they started screaming at him, tugging at his arms, pushing him around, and he held up his pistol and said, "Back off, assholes! You heard what that shithead said! He and his buddy were gonna get driving jobs, jobs that belong to me and other real Americans."

"Fuck it, Brewster, you capped those two without even thinking," Robbie yelled, his face bright red.

"Screw you, I thought it through well enough! Way I see it, I just saved two guys from Arizona or New Mexico from getting fired 'cause these guys aren't gonna be there to steal their jobs. Besides, they were dying of thirst anyway. Were you gonna give up your water to those beaners? Were you?"

Robbie still looked pretty pissed, but Chuck stepped in and said, "Yeah, maybe Brewster's right. Maybe they were gonna croak anyway. Shit, let's head back, all right? Forget the whole thing happened."

A good plan, but about thirty minutes later, they came across another wetback, better dressed than the other guys, an AK-47 hanging off his back, and Robbie said, "Shit, he must be the coyote for those two back there," and when he started jabbering and unslinging his AK-47, Brewster didn't hesitate, and shot him down.

It was then a real long walk back to where Chuck's pickup truck was parked off a dirt access road, made even longer since neither Chuck nor Robbie said another word to Brewster. A week later, Brewster was out of the local Tea Party—"just consider yourself freakin' lucky we're not turning you into the sheriff" one of the leaders had said—and that had been that.

So now he peered ahead through the darkness, his Colt .45 right next to him, thinking of what he was doing, of his cousin Troy, knowing Troy would have approved of what he had done back there in the Arizona desert.

Desperate times called for desperate measures, and these times were about as desperate as one could imagine.

———

The five of them drove north in a dark brown Chevrolet Suburban, with a few detours and turnarounds to ensure they weren't being followed. Nat Cooper was driving, with Luke Munce next to him. There were a couple of folded-over maps resting next to Nat, but Duncan knew his driver didn't need any such assistance. Through years of snowmobiling, hunting, and driving on his ATV, Nat knew his way around this part of the county better than any man he knew. In the Suburban's middle seat, Duncan was on the left, his brother was on the right, and Zach was in the middle, keeping quiet. Luke was talking to his girlfriend on his cellphone up forward when he frowned and put the phone away.

"That's it, guys," he said. "We're officially in the dark zone."

Zach asked, "What's the dark zone?"

"No cellphone coverage, no Wi-Fi, even GPS has fits up here," Duncan said. "We are in terra incognita, beyond the pale. For outsiders who play here, it's not a good thing. Couple of times last winter, snowmobilers got lost on the trails and they were lucky to make it out alive. They thought all they had to do was dial 911 and the nice folks from Fish & Game would come and rescue them. But we're not going to get lost tonight, are we, Nat."

Nat laughed and turned the Suburban to the left, down yet another unmarked dirt road. "Unless I got dropped on my head last night and Dora forgot to tell me, nope, we're not going to get lost tonight."

A few more miles passed as a nearly full moon rose to the east. The road dipped and became muddy as they traversed a swamp, and in the bright moonlight, three moose were seen on the right, about a foot deep into the muddy water, gently chewing water plants. Luke said, "Lots of good meat out there."

Cameron said, "Yeah, but no place to put it."

Duncan spoke up. "That's enough talk about hunting out of season. You know how I don't like lawbreakers."

Even Zach joined in the laughter, and Nat slowed the Suburban down, lowered his window, took a flashlight and illuminated a birch tree trunk on the left, where an aluminum pie plate had been nailed. "That there's the access road to the Byron hunting camp, our rendezvous point if things go bad. So remember the pie plate."

Duncan said, "The plate come from Dora?"

"No, it didn't," Nat said.

Duncan reached over, gently tapped Nat on the shoulder. "Thought maybe somebody who ate one of Dora's pies was so happy that he nailed the pie plate in her honor."

Cameron snorted. "Christ, stop sucking up to him already. Hire her on as a pastry chef or something, will you?"

Nat resumed driving, took a left, a right, and then a long stretch where the road widened into a thin pasture. He pulled the Suburban over to the left and then made a three-point turn, so it was now facing the direction from which they came. Nat switched off the engine and announced, "Keys are in the ignition, fellas, if we need to leave in a hurry and I'm otherwise engaged."

Nobody said anything. Duncan listened to the peepers, and then the *hoot-hoot-hoot* of a night owl out on the hunt. In the dim light from the rising moon they waited, until Duncan said, "Gentlemen, now's the time when we start earning our pay. Let's get to it."

———

The young lady named Sherry was driving the Jeep Cherokee along the back roads, going nice and slow, peering ahead as she caught the taillights of the target truck in front of them. Francois sat up front with her, while Michael and the other two Iron Steeds members—Johnny and Phil—sat in the back, jammed in, shoulder to shoulder, cheek to cheek, firearm to firearm. Too bad if they didn't like it, because that's the way it was going to be, but Francois didn't worry about that; he was too busy admiring the young lady's driving skills. Even though night had fallen, she was driving on the narrow dirt road with no headlights or parking lights, just depending on the moonlight to guide the way.

Earlier she had said, "The guy up there, I don't know who he is or where he's from, but he doesn't know these roads. I do. So he's going slow, he's being cautious, and all I have to do is hang back and watch his taillights, make sure I don't do anything to draw his attention. I can follow him for dozens of klicks like this, because the deeper he goes in, the slower he goes."

Francois still couldn't believe she was getting away with it as the night went on. She saw a flare of taillights ahead and she said, "Damn, he's stopped. Hold on." She quickly braked and the Cherokee slid to a stop. They waited, the engine gently idling. Francois held his breath. From behind him Michael said, "Boss, why the fuck are we dicking around like this? Why don't we just drive up there now and take the fucking thing?"

He paused, and said, "For one thing, on this narrow a road, even one pissed off driver—if he's alone—can bottle us up and cause us some damage before we nail him. Another thing is, speaking of narrow, there's not much room to maneuver around."

Silence from the rear, and Michael spoke again. "No offense, boss, but that's bullshit. You want to see this truck cross over into New Hampshire so you can fuck over Duncan Crowley and tell him you're stealing his precious cargo before wasting him. That's the real reason, isn't it."

Francois said, "Maybe it is, and what's wrong with that? We sent four guys down to Duncan Crowley, including a nephew of mine, and none of them came back. Word gets out that the Iron Steeds would take such bullshit without doing something in return, Christ, not only would the Hells Angels come stomping back to raise hell in our territory, fucking motorcycle gangs from Uruguay would think we'd be easy to push around. So yeah, Michael, revenge is on the menu tonight. You got a problem with that?"

"Not at all, boss," Michael said, sarcasm edging his voice.

He was going to say something else to Michael, maybe tell him to try saying that again, with more sincerity in his voice, when Sherry spoke up. "Looks like he's moving again."

"Good," Francois said. "Don't lose him."

"I won't," she said, shifting the Cherokee into drive. "His tail-lights are nice and clear."

"Glad you're so confident."

"I am," she said, her voice inviting and sultry. "Tell you what, if I lose this truck tonight, you can give me a spanking."

Francois felt something warm and tingling stir in his groin. "Maybe I'll give you a spanking later, no matter what happens."

She laughed. "Promises, promises."

———

Zach stepped out into the cool night air, listening to peepers cry out in the woods. His eyes adjusted to the darkness and the moonlight, and he was able to find his way around pretty well. The back hatch of the Suburban was popped open—the rear dome light having been disabled—and gear and weapons were distributed to Nat, Luke, and Cameron. Small Maglite flashlights with red lenses were passed out as well, so their night vision would be protected. Zach slid on a Kevlar vest and snapped it shut, and with an apologetic voice, Duncan passed over a 9mm H&K Model MP5.

"When we got your gear over from the B&B, I saw that you had an Uzi," Duncan said. "Fine weapon, but for events like this, I like everyone to be issued the same thing. If bits of lead start whizzing around, it's good to know the guy next to you can pass over a full clip if you run out."

Zach said, "Works for me." He took two additional 20-round clips and said, "Duncan, if it weren't for that pitcher's arm of yours and your bum leg, you could have had one hell of an interesting career in the service of your country."

Duncan laughed. "You're joshing me, aren't you."

He slung the H&K over his shoulder. "No, I'm not. You've got good planning and tactical skills, you know your weapons. As they say, you could have had a heck of a military career, traveling to foreign lands, meeting exotic people … and killing them."

Nearby Cameron laughed at that, and Zach said, "At least, that's what I heard."

Nat and Luke helped each other get loaded up, and Zach stood apart, watching them. They were civilians but in their own way they were pros, and he had to admire them. Zach tried not to think of what darkness was waiting up here, so close to the Canadian border and to ruin. He tried to focus on getting his pension back, his medical coverage, and to have that dishonorable discharge made into something more honorable, but any thoughts of honor tonight were making him nauseous.

He was pleased when Duncan provided an interruption, when he glanced at his watch. "Still got plenty of time. What do you think, Cam?"

Cameron said, "Nat, Luke, and Zach can stay back here, provide perimeter security. Let's say you and me, we start walking up to the rendezvous point."

Duncan said, "All right, I guess we can do that. Zach, you okay with staying with the other two guys?"

Zach shifted the weight of the semiautomatic rifle on his back. "Like the man said, I was born ready."

Duncan said, "I don't know, the thought of you in diapers and carrying a pistol just freaks me out."

———

In the rear of a NH State Police cruiser, Tanya Gibbs kept her own counsel as the vehicle roared up Interstate 93, leading the way with its flashing blue lights on but with siren off. The road was so empty tonight that a siren wasn't needed, but *empty* was a relative term. Behind the speeding cruiser was a small convoy of other State Police SUVs, as well as several cruisers from the Washington County Sheriff's Department and her own government car, being operated by Henry Wolfe. Up forward a State Police sergeant was driving, while Carl worked the radio microphone and cellphone. As much as she thought he was a tortured soul—his wife must have the patience of a saint—she also had to admire his tactical and communications skills. Despite being tossed a near-impossible task, he was making it work.

He put the radio microphone down and swiveled to talk to her. "We need a staging area up there, near that Hyro-Quebec right-of-way, and it looks like we got it. A hunting camp is nearby, owned by the Byron family. Dispatch is trying to contact them but no one's answering the phone. My feeling is, we go to the camp, appropriate it, and then apologize later. Sound all right to you?"

"Sounds fine," Tanya said. "What's our ETA?"

"We're going to be off paved roads in about thirty minutes. Figure another half hour after that."

"Real wilderness, then."

Carl said, "You have no idea. In fact, just so you know, we're going to be losing all cellphone coverage in a few minutes, including texting and whatnot. No coverage this far north. So if you need to contact your witch doctor or financial adviser, now's the time to do it."

Tanya said, "Thanks for the suggestion." Which was funny, for she really did mean it. She took out her BlackBerry and texted a message to her boss, Region One Administrator Gordon Simpson:

HAVE RECEIVED RELIABLE INTELLIGENCE THAT AN AT-TEMPT IS NOW ENGAGED OVER THE NEXT FEW HOURS TO SMUGGLE A WME ACROSS THE CANADIAN/NEW HAMPSHIRE BORDER. PER CONFIDENTIAL PROTOCOL FOUR WITHIN RE-NEWED PATRIOT ACT, AMENDED, HAVE ASSUMED DIRECT CONTROL OF LOCAL POLICE FORCES TO INTERCEPT AND SEIZE SHIPMENT. WILL ADVISE LATER WITH ADDITIONAL INFORMATION, LOCATION, OUTCOME. GIBBS.

Once the message was completed, Tanya typed in Gordie's e-mail address, carefully leaving one letter out of the address line. That way, the message would never be delivered; it would bounce back to her own device. Whatever inquiry might take place later, she could rightfully claim that in the heat and excitement of the moment, she had misspelled Gordie's email address.

For you, Emily, for you, she thought.

As a follow-up to the text, she also dialed his direct number, and at this hour of the night—as expected—it went straight to voicemail. "Gordon, this is Tanya Gibbs," she said. "Just wanted to ensure you got my text regarding—" With that, she whistled and hissed into the phone, then clicked off the connection.

Carl watched her actions with mild amusement. "What the hell was that all about?"

"Just exercising due diligence," she said.

"Sounds like you're trying to confuse your boss."

"If you knew my boss," she said, "you'd know it wouldn't take much."

———

In the quiet of the night, and in the dim light from the red-lensed flashlights, Duncan walked with his brother north, only a few yards now from the Canadian border. They both had on their rural battle-rattle gear, with H&Ks hanging off their backs, and amid the cool breeze and night sounds, Duncan felt at peace, even though he was prepared for the night to descend into chaos and gunfire. But this wasn't the first time he had been put in such a position, and being here again was comforting. It was like everything for the past twenty years had been leading up to this last moment, the last big deal of his oddball criminal career.

He said, "Cameron, I want to apologize for keeping you out of the loop for so long."

His brother said, "Hell of a time to be bringing that up."

"It's been on my mind."

"That's something, I guess."

They strolled along on the narrow but well-built road in the darkness, the red beams from their flashlights illuminating the way. Years ago Hydro-Quebec, the enormous electric utility for that province, had planned a new series of transmission lines to come through this part of northern New England. This area of land had been purchased as a right-of-way for the eventual construction, and roads had been built to handle the trucks and other heavy equipment from Quebec to New Hampshire. But lawsuits, environmental pressures, and a collapsing economy had derailed the project, leaving behind some well-maintained roads that Duncan had discreetly used over the years.

Duncan tried again. "It wasn't that I didn't trust you, Cam. I trusted you too much. But this deal … it had potentials. If anything, I was afraid that you'd ask too many questions, try to talk me out of it, and that you'd succeed."

"Hah," Cameron said. "Have I ever succeeded in talking you out of anything?"

"There was Susan Sheldon back in high school."

"I knew she had a plan to get knocked up by any boy bright enough to get her out of Turner," Cameron said. "I was presenting you with facts, not trying to convince you to do anything else."

Something ahead clattered through the woods at their approach. A coyote, fox, or the ever-elusive Eastern mountain lion.

Duncan said, "All right, leaving that aside, I've got something else to spring on you."

"Go for it."

Ahead of them was a cleared area, maybe ten feet wide, that stretched off to the left and right as far as one could see.

"This is the last one, Cam. The last score."

Cameron turned to him, pointing the MagLite on the ground. "Meaning what?"

"Meaning that once we get that truck safely over the border and to where it belongs, I'm done with the life. The criminal life, the illegal life, the life on the edge. I've been at it too long. I've stretched out my luck as much as I can, and it's not fair anymore to Karen, the kids, or you. When I told you earlier that this was going to set us up, I meant more than just having a fatter bank account. I meant I intend to be done."

Cameron stayed quiet for a moment or three. "That's a hell of a spring you just sprung there, bro."

"I know it."

"So what about us, then?"

Duncan said, "This is what I've been thinking. I get out of the life, and if you want to keep it up, go for it. Just don't ask me for advice, or counsel, or to be involved in any way. I want out, Cam. If you want out as well ... then I can make it worth your while."

Cameron said, "Damn it, that's one hell of a thing to be dumping on me, time like this. Couldn't it have waited?"

"This container that's coming across, that's the key, Cameron. The key to my new life, and your new life, if you want it. That's why I'm dumping this on you tonight. C'mon, you know we've been very, very lucky these years. By keeping a low profile, we've kept our heads attached to our shoulders. The time to quit is now, while we're ahead."

Again, Cameron seemed to ponder Duncan's words, and he said, "Can't say it's not an attractive proposition, though I would miss the life, that's for sure. It's nice to be top dog. But it'd also be nice not to put in the hours, have to look over your shoulder all the time. Thing is, I've been thinking about taking some time off. Was wondering when I could tell you. Guess now works."

"How much time?" Duncan asked.

"Six months, maybe a year."

Duncan was shocked. "Really? What for?"

"Saw an advertisement in *Sky & Telescope* magazine. Unpaid internships with the SETI Institute are opening up, and I'm sure I could get in."

"The what institute?"

"SETI. Search for Extraterrestrial Intelligence. Out in California. Doing real science, with other guys and gals who have the same interest in space and astronomy. It ... it'd be something great, being with people like that, day after day, night after night."

Duncan said, "This is the night for surprises for the both of us, hunh? Go for it, Cameron. It'll be the perfect time for it."

"Maybe so, but you're forgetting one thing. The Iron Steeds. After the container gets through and payment gets made, you could take out a full-page ad in the *Montreal Gazette*, saying you and me are going on the straight and narrow. That still won't make a difference to the Iron Steeds. They'll want their pound of flesh. Or kilogram of flesh, however they figure it up there."

"Maybe we could pay them off, set up a truce."

Cameron gave a sharp, bitter laugh. "Bro, get real. They sent four of their guys down here, and none of them are ever going back. I don't think the Iron Steeds will step aside for some money, jugs of maple syrup and a card of apology."

"Like the man says, I'll make him an offer they can't refuse."

Cameron groaned. "Enough with *The Godfather* references, already."

THIRTY-THREE

ZACH MORROW SLOWLY PACED around the wide area in the dirt road where the Suburban was parked. Up ahead the dirt lane went on, and it was an odd feeling, knowing an international boundary beckoned just a few yards up that road. He had crossed a fair number of international borders over the years. During most of those occasions, he had either been in, on, or under water, performing his duty for an allegedly grateful nation.

To the left of the parked Suburban was brush and saplings, and to the right was the road and a cleared area that looked like it had once been pastureland, though low-growth was slowly reclaiming it. He paused, took a deep breath, and found an odd sense of memory and nostalgia flowing though him. Ever since coming back to Turner, he had been focused on getting the job done—i.e., betraying Duncan and his friends and family so he could get his precious Federal bennies back—but something else had popped up during his few days there. It was seeing the old buildings downtown, the high school where he had practically drifted during those four years, and of course, most importantly, seeing Karen Crowley nee Delaney once again. He was under no illusions about his relationship with Karen. She was totally devoted to Duncan and their two children, and that was fine. But inside of him a small spark kindled, of that special and oh so warm late spring romance, where each had been the other's first.

He smiled at the thought. Duncan may have her forever, but Zach would always have been her first, and the thought cheered him. That was something, at least.

A whisper from the rear of the Suburban. "Hey, Zach, you want a drink?"

He came over, saw Luke Munce there, rummaging in a small cooler. Zach said, "What do you have?"

"Water, Coke, Diet Coke."

"I'll take a regular Coke."

A can was offered to him and he popped it open, sucking in the cold cola drink. Luke said, "It's not beer or a mixed drink, but I guess it'll do. Damn, this waiting, it sure does suck, doesn't it."

"It does," Zach said.

"You know, I'm still thinking about that night you took me and the other three guys on. You were a fucking whirlwind."

"If that's a compliment, thanks."

"Shit, I've been tossed around some, have done my share of tossing around. But it was like you weren't even thinking, like you were just doing, anticipating our moves and countermoves, like you were four or five steps ahead of us. Where the hell did you get experience like that? Military?"

"Sort of," Zach said. "Coast Guard, truth be told."

"Coast Guard?" Luke asked. "Thought those guys did search and rescue, boat safety inspections, stuff like that. Didn't know they were into hand-to-hand shit like the other night."

Zach said, "There's a special unit I belonged to. Pretty much still secret. You see, the Coast Guard, they're responsible for a lot of things on the water, from harbors to navigable waters. Somewhere along the line, somebody thought it'd be best if the Coast Guard had their own special guys to kick ass when the time came. That's the unit I was with."

"You see some heavy shit?"

"Yeah, though at the time, I thought it was just shit, didn't know if it was heavy, light, or skim."

Luke laughed at that. "So did you put your time in and get out, is that it?"

"Not really," Zach said. "I kicked the wrong ass and pissed off the wrong people. So I got tossed out of the Guard, no pay, no pension. Which is one of the reasons I'm here tonight, working for the Crowley brothers."

Luke put the cooler away. "Hell of a thing."

"Certainly is."

"But know this," Luke said. "You're one lucky guy, to be working for the Crowleys. First of all, they pay well, and second, they're so fucking loyal you can't believe it. Meaning, they trust you, they'll back you up a hundred percent, and then some. So you got that going for you, Zach. That should make you feel good."

Zach said, "You would think."

———

Brewster Flagg lowered his speed to nearly a crawl as he maneuvered down the increasingly narrow road. Branches and brush were whipping against the side windows and fenders of the cab, and he hated being closed in like this, with all of these trees pressing in against him. He didn't believe in spooks or ghosts or haunts, but he still didn't like the feeling of being trapped, for there was no place to turn around. It was like being stuck in a long dark tunnel with no easy way out.

He took a breath and whispered to himself, "Man up, buttercup." Frig, he'd been in tighter spots before, like back there in Arizona, after he wasted those three spics. That long walk back to the pickup truck with Chuck and Robbie was dicey because he didn't if either one of them was going to turn around and take him out. That didn't happen, so here he was.

He checked the odometer. Just a ways to go before he saw the pre-arranged signal. But all ahead of him was the long and narrow road. Where in hell was he supposed to go?

———

Duncan kept pace with his older brother, and even smiled at the old joke as they passed the cleared area. "Welcome to Canada," Cameron said. "Anything to declare?"

Putting on the voice of what might have been a Southern belle, Duncan replied, "I do declare that I'm about to break a number of laws in your fair land, suh."

They walked ahead about another ten yards or so before they stopped. An apparently impassable wall of brush and small trees were in front of them, as the road came to an abrupt end. There was an open area of night sky above them.

Cameron said, "So you're okay, then, with me heading out to California, eh?"

"Why not?"

Cameron carefully said, "Feel like I'm … betraying you, I guess. I mean, after that shitty summer, where everything collapsed, it was like, oh, I don't know. Things equaled out for the both of us. You didn't get to play baseball, I didn't go to college. Now I'm off west, to really do hands on stuff ... and you, well ... "

"Forget it."

"Still feel guilty about it."

Duncan said, "Enough, all right? No guilt necessary. It's all going to be squared away tonight, just you wait and see."

They both kept quiet and Cameron arched his head back and said, "My God, the stars are bright tonight."

"See anything interesting?"

"Every night's interesting, if you know where to look. Hey, there's a satellite, catch it."

Duncan tilted his head back as well, saw an unblinking dot of light race overhead. Years ago his brother had shown him how to spot satellites at night. For one thing, they were never red or green; that always marked aircraft. Secondly, they never blinked; again, that was the sign of aircraft. No, satellites were a steady little dot that moved gracefully and quickly before fading from view, and Cameron was always pleased to run up some computer program that would tell you—after you plugged in a location, date, and time— what that dot of light represented, either a bit of space debris, a weather satellite, or a communications outpost.

Duncan watched the little dot fly overhead in a break of the trees, until it was lost from view. A breeze came up, and he said, "So Cameron, where are they?"

"Who?"

"The aliens, that's who," Duncan said. "SETI, like you said. There are billions of stars out there, billions of galaxies, and you've told me that every month, more and more planets are being discovered around other stars. So where are the aliens? Why haven't we heard from them, or seen them?"

Cameron carefully said, "Some would say they've already been poking around."

Duncan said, "No, you're not getting off that lightly. No flying saucer tales, please. Looking for real evidence. With all those stars and planets out there, do you really think we're alone?"

"Not for a moment," Cameron replied. "But I'll tell you what I think, as scary as it is."

"Scary? What do you mean by that?"

Cameron said, "We like to think that for the most part, aliens are friendly and cuddly, like the movie *ET* or most *Star Trek* episodes. But look at reality. Man is on the top of the evolutionary food chain on this planet because he's mean, tough, and nasty. Chances are, so are any aliens out there who survived on their own worlds. Mean, tough, and nasty. We might be living in a rough neighborhood, where other alien races have decided it's for the best to keep their goddamn mouths shut, stop advertising their existence to meaner aliens out there. But we've decided to be fat, dumb, and happy by trying to contact the universe through our radio messages."

Duncan said, "You telling me there might be an alien death armada heading our way?"

His brother said, "No. Maybe an alien version of the State Police, coming here to clean things up. Just like the real State Police would do to us if they ever snooped around enough."

Duncan said, "So it'd be best for all of us, for you and me to step aside, and for Mother Earth to take a low profile as well."

"It's a goddamn perceptive thought now, isn't it."

Duncan was going to say something snappy when he heard the straining growl of a diesel truck approaching, traveling at a crawl.

"I think our alien has just arrived," Duncan said.

Cameron said, "Congrats on your discovery."

From a pocket on his Kevlar vest, Cameron pulled out an instrument that looked like a television remote, pointed it at the direction of the truck sound, and pressed a switch.

———

Brewster Flagg was driving the Peterbilt just barely above stalling speed, looking up at the narrow road and the thick trees, then looking down at the odometer, and looking up again. Damn his fucking cousin and his friends! He was at the meeting place! Where was the damn signal?

He looked to the right, out front, and to the left. He checked both sideview mirrors, and he was about to keep moving, thinking the odometer was wrong, or he was wrong, when a tiny amber light suddenly flared up to the left, and started blinking.

He had made it!

Brewster reached to his headlight switch, pulled it out, quickly illuminating the road ahead of him, and then he went back to parking lights.

But where was he to go?

Then the world next to him fell apart.

———

When Duncan and Cameron saw the brief flash of headlights through the brush and trees from the truck, they went to work. First, Duncan pressed the switch again, turning off the little flashing battery-powered amber light on the other side of the trees and brush. Weapons slung over their shoulders, they both knelt down at the side of the road, where something that looked like a tree stump was positioned.

The two brothers lifted up the tree stump, which was a heavy piece of plastic painted and carved to look like a stump. Underneath the plastic were a set of car batteries and a small electric motor. Duncan closed a switch and the motor whined into life. Up ahead, Cameron helped guide two sets of cables that suddenly lifted up and started dragging a wall of carefully entwined brush, trees, and branches that hid an intersecting dirt road.

With the wall moved to one side, a tractor-trailer truck was exposed, a half-sized shipping container hitched to the rear.

Duncan said, "Going to meet our business partner. Hope he's in a good mood."

Cameron said, "Tell you what, if I see you drop back with a round through your forehead, I'll make sure he'll live long enough to regret it."

"Always know I can count on you, big brother."

He took a breath, strode quickly to the side of the Peterbilt truck, its diesel engine grumbling, exhaust eddying. He took the red-lensed Maglite, lifted it up, and blinked it three times. The window rolled down.

"Yeah?" a Southern-accented voice called out.

Duncan recalled the phrase he had memorized some time ago. "What did Thomas Jefferson say about the tree of liberty?" he said in a loud voice, waiting.

He hoped he didn't have to wait long. In the meanwhile, hidden in his waistband, was a 10mm Glock semiautomatic pistol with something special.

———

After the long and smelly bus rides, passing through Customs, and now the grueling drive here, Brewster grinned with delight. He had made it. In two days it would be April 19th, and this truck would be in its target area. He wasn't sure what was back there—nerve gas, a dirty bomb, hell, maybe even the kind of bomb McVeigh had used—but all he cared was that he had done his job. He also didn't know who this man was, deep in the Canadian woods, with a red flashlight before him, but no matter. He was truly a patriot and fellow traveler.

Brewster finished the quote. "Jefferson said 'The tree of liberty must be refreshed from time to time with the blood of patriots and tyrants.'"

"So he did, so he did," the man said. "Glad to finally meet you, bud. Follow me down this road. Keep your lights off. When you see me and my companion flash our lights at you, come to a halt. Do you understand?"

"I do, I absolutely do," Brewster said with pride.

The man walked away, and with a companion, illuminated the dirt road to the left. He shifted the truck into first, swung the wheel, and went down the well-made dirt road.

———

When the truck grumbled in, Duncan started walking at a good clip back down the road, illuminating it as best as he could with his flashlight. His brother worked at putting the brush and tree barrier back, and as the truck slowly moved along, Cameron jogged past the truck, joining his brother.

"Looks good," Cameron said, raising his voice over the loud engine. "We should get this wrapped up in a few minutes."

Duncan said, "Yeah, you're right. Oh, by the way, I've got one more thing to tell you."

His brother said, "For Christ's sake, when are you going to stop with the goddamn surprises?"

Duncan said, "You know you love it. Puts spice in your life."

———

Francois Ouellette jerked forward as Sherry suddenly hit the brakes and murmured, "Shit."

"What's wrong?"

"He's gone."

"What do you mean, he's gone?"

Sherry said, "Lights are gone. Road is empty. Fuck, where did he go?"

Something cold and greasy seemed to fill his chest. He leaned forward, peering through the windshield. Through the dim light of the overhead moon, he saw the narrow road descending into the forest.

"What happened?" Francois demanded.

"His lights flickered. Then … shifted some. Then he was gone."

From behind them, Michael spoke up. "Gee, maybe instead of a spanking tonight, you'll get a bullet in your head."

Francois was going to say something and Sherry said, "Ooh, such hard words from the big man in the back seat. Tell you what, I'll step out now, toss the keys into the woods, and start walking away. Feel free to put a bullet in my head. Then see if you can get out of this wilderness alive when the temps drop and when you run out of gas 'cause you're lost, especially since there's no damn cellphone coverage down here."

Francois said, "Michael, do us all a favor and shut the fuck up. Sherry, now what?"

"Hold on. Stay here and I'll be right back."

She got out with a flashlight and started walking up the road, moving slow, stopping every now and then. Francois turned in his seat and said, "Michael, what the hell are you thinking?"

"Me? What I'm thinking is what a fucking wild goose chase this is, that's what I'm thinking. A total waste of time and resources. You don't know what's in that truck or why we're chasing it, except there's supposed to be something valuable in it. Big fucking deal. All you've managed to do is to lose four good guys and we should just cut our losses and go home. You know—"

The door to the Jeep Cherokee opened up. "They're sly, but so am I," Sherry said.

Francois's heart lightened. "What do you have?"

"I was walking up ahead and I heard a truck engine, off to the left, deep in the woods. Checked things out. There's a man-made barricade of trees and brush that got dragged out and dragged back in. If I can borrow your strong men, Francois, then we can catch up with them in five, ten minutes at the most. Is that okay?"

Francois could sense the tension coming from the rear seat, not only from Michael, but from Johnny and Phil as well. He had an idea what they were thinking: they were urban gangbangers, the hardest bike club in this part of North America. What the fuck were they doing in the middle of nowhere?

Following orders, Francois thought. Following *his* orders.

"Yeah, that's okay," Francois said. "Let's do it."

THIRTY-FOUR

In a cold, tiny hunting camp near the target area, Tanya Gibbs watched with quiet satisfaction as all these strong, big-armed men scurried around and planned and plotted, all under her direction. Surprisingly enough, the door to the camp was unlocked, meaning no wasted minutes breaking in or looking for a key. The men were clustered the middle of the camp's main room, where they had dragged in a wooden kitchen table. Lights burned and cast odd shadows as maps, radio frequencies, and weapons were examined, discussed, and considered.

Her driver Henry Wolfe stood in the corner, arms folded, keeping eye on the proceedings. The room was bare wooden walls and studs, with decorations consisting of stuffed deer and moose heads. Dirty and scuffed linoleum covered the floor, with a couple of threadbare rugs so old their patterns couldn't be discerned.

A whiteboard was set up on an easel, where a hand-drawn map in blue and black ink had been filled in. Henry caught her eye, made a slight shrug, as if to say he was glad he was observing and not participating. Next to him, communications gear had been set up on a rickety card table, with another State Police trooper manning the console.

Major Carl Kenyon, dressed in combat fatigues and SWAT gear, like nearly everyone else in the room, backed up from the map and held up a hand. "Guys, we're doing something that should take hours to prep, but we don't have the time. Peter, your deputy sheriffs?"

A sheriff from the Washington County Sheriff's Department pointed to areas on the topo map. "We're set up on trails we found, on either side of this main road that we're waiting on. Ready to provide flanking or blocking action where necessary."

"Sounds good," Carl said, wiping at a sweaty brow. "Tanya, any idea of the ETA of this trailer?"

"Approximately ten p.m.," she said. "Best I can do."

"Sounds screwy to me," he replied.

"Trust me, it's coming across, and it's coming across tonight," she said.

Carl shot her a look like he wouldn't trust her to tell him the correct year, but he kept his mouth shut. "Fine, Tanya. Since you've made it quite clear this is your operation, what are the rules of engagement?"

Tanya felt a thrill of anticipation race through her, knowing that she was in command, she was the lead, and that others higher up weren't going to be allowed to let this attack come through. She thought of the innocents out there, innocents who would still be alive and safe and breathing in the days ahead because of what she was about to do here tonight. And despite that anger and the hatred Carl was sending her way, she could tell he was stepping up to the proverbial plate like the true pro he was—ready to do battle against America's enemies.

No more victims, she thought. No more men or women jumping out of shattered, burning buildings, filled with terror and fear during the last confusing seconds of their lives.

No more Emilys.

"Rules of engagement," she said. "Neutralize that truck. Make sure it doesn't leave this border area once it crosses into New Hampshire."

"Very clear, Tanya," he said, his voice cold. "We now know what to do with the offending truck. But what about the driver of the truck? Or the people out there? What are your rules of engagement concerning them? Our state law is quite clear, in case you're interested. We're not to open fire unless there's a direct and deadly threat either to ourselves or to civilians. But since this is a Federal matter, it seems you hold the trump card."

She spoke slowly and clearly. "The people are to be seized and arrested if possible. If not, they are to be neutralized."

"Shot and killed, then," Carl said. The other state troopers and sheriff's deputies stood still and stayed silent, like they were youngsters watching Mom and Dad fight in public.

Tanya was quick to agree. "Shot and killed, then. Any other questions, or are you now satisfied?"

"Satisfied, no. Questions answered, yes. Looks like you Feds are overruling local laws. Again."

The trooper at the communications gear raised his voice. "Major, word coming in from Sullivan!"

"Put it on speaker," Carl said. Tanya stepped closer to the trooper. Sullivan was a sniper out in the woods, conducting surveillance on the suspected transit point, moving slowly through the forest, with another trooper accompanying him, serving as a backup observer.

A switch was turned on the communications gear, leading to a hiss from the small speakers. Carl picked up a handheld radio. "Sierra, this is TOC. Go."

Tanya looked to Henry, who mouthed the words, "Sierra is sniper. TOC is Tactical Operations Center."

"TOC, Sierra here," came a whisper. "Eyes on target. Have Chevy Suburban with New Hampshire plates in view. Registration is Thomas Ida Charles four-zero-three. Three male subjects. All male subjects carrying long rifles. No heavy truck in view. Go."

Carl looked around the group. Keyed his handheld. "Sierra, TOC. Maintain surveillance. Assault team moving into position. ETA of subject vehicle is approximately twenty-two hundred. Go."

"TOC, Sierra. Acknowledged."

Carl clipped the radio microphone to his vest, put a small headset to his thick right ear, then reached and picked up a Kevlar helmet with night-vision goggles attached to the brim. "Saddle up. We should be in the target area in about five minutes. From there, we wait until the truck comes into view. Guys, I don't have to make a pretty speech about what we're up against. More than ten years ago, in New York and D.C., and Pennsylvania, war came to our doorstep. Now it's here again, about to cross over, intent on doing us harm. But that truck is not going to pass by us, understand? That truck is not leaving here."

Tanya saw the grim faces of the men standing around, all of them in SWAT gear, all looking at Carl, save for one man—the health physicist from the state's Department of Public Health. His name was Kwasnick, he had a thick black moustache, dark hair, and a long nose. Dressed in khakis and a green L.L.Bean jacket, he sat in the corner, a handheld computer in his hand, idly playing a game.

Carl put on his helmet, fastened the chin strap. "Keep focused, stay calm, maintain radio discipline. Remember what's working in our favor: speed, surprise, and violence of action. Any questions?"

There were none.

"All right," Carl said. "Let's roll."

352

Tanya waited until he was distracted with a piece of gear. She walked over and said, "Major, a minute. I know time is of essence. I promise not to waste it."

Tanya could see the struggle in his eyes, and then he flicked his hand towards an open door. She followed him into a musky-smelling bedroom where wood paneling was pulling away from the wall studs. She closed the door and said, "Not open for negotiation. My driver and I, we're going to get comm gear, so we can listen in. No interference, no chatter, but we're not to be kept blind."

"Fair enough."

"I'm also following you in."

"Not a chance in hell."

She stepped closer, close enough to smell the sweat and cheap aftershave he was wearing. "Every chance in hell, Carl. Unless you want me to have a very intimate and revealing luncheon with the lovely and vanilla Mrs. Kenyon. Got that?"

His face reddened and she was certain that if they were truly alone, he would have punched her lights out. "You promised," he said. "Fucking bitch."

"Truest thing you've said tonight."

Then, surprising them both, she lifted herself up and kissed him on the cheek. "A great speech out there, Major. Very inspiring. If I peed standing up, I'm sure I'd have a boner. Now go out and get the bastards."

———

Francois Ouellette felt his palms moisten as Sherry maneuvered the Jeep Cherokee down the hidden road. Earlier he had sent out Michael, Johnny, and Phil to go where Sherry had heard the truck, and sure enough, there was a smart-looking barricade of tree trunks, branches and brush blocking the other road. The three of them had broken the barricade and tossed enough of it aside so the Cherokee could slide through.

Ahead he saw flickering red lights, the occasional flare of the tail-lights. Whispering, he said, "What's going on up there?"

Sherry whispered back, "Truck's moving slow. Looks like one or two guys with flashlights are serving as pathfinders, until they get to where they're going. Maybe another truck to take the cargo, maybe a refueling, maybe the cargo is going be unloaded and split up into other vehicles. Meanwhile, I'm keeping it nice and slow. That honking big diesel up there will drown out our engine noise."

Francois reached over, squeezed her thigh. He thought he heard her sigh with pleasure. Good. He said, "When you think they've stopped, then you stop, too. We'll head out. When you can, turn around so you're facing back the way we came. All right?"

"You got it, hon." He was about to say something snappy in return when she said, "Yeah, fuck, yeah."

The Cherokee stopped. She put it in park and shut the engine off.

"Showtime," she said. "Now go make momma proud."

Francois grinned, opened the door. After taking care of Crowley and his crew, this little piece next to him was going to be a great dessert.

———

Duncan turned around and, with his brother Cameron, flashed their lights at the approaching truck. It came to a halt about fifty feet from the Suburban. Duncan said, "Tell Nat we're going to need his services in about ninety seconds, all right?"

"Got it, bro. You going to be okay?"

"Just fine," he said. "Time for me to exercise my diplomatic skills. Wish me luck."

"Wish we were done, that's what I wish."

Duncan circled around the truck, feeling the heat coming off the radiator grille. Flashlight still in hand, he waved it up at the driver. The driver's side window rolled down. Duncan called up, "Hey, pal. Good job. Take a break and come on down. We've got some brews and a barbecue for you."

He waited, wondering what the driver would say. Peepers were calling out in the woods, and a wind came up, cooling his exposed skin. It was hot, wearing the Kevlar vest. The driver laughed. "Shit, that sounds great. I've been living on piss-poor coffee and crap they call sandwiches."

Duncan stepped back.

———

Brewster got out of the cab, nearly laughing with delight. He had made it! Had driven those tricky roads, took care of that snoopy darkie cop, and here he was, back in the States, ready to see this mission through. He was dreaming about the headlines and stories that would be breaking next week when this truck got to where it belonged.

He shook the man's hand, and said, "The name's Brewster Flagg. Can I ask you yours?"

"You may," the strong looking man replied. "But first, I have a message for you, from your cousin Troy, God bless him."

Brewster was surprised. His cousin, sending him a message?

"Really?" Brewster said. "What the hell did Troy have to say?"

"This," the man said, pulling a pistol out from behind his back.

Duncan took his 10mm Glock out—upon which he had earlier screwed in a tubular silencer—pressed it against the surprised man's left eye, and pulled the trigger. The pistol made a thick sound—silencers never worked like they did in movies and TV shows, they merely suppressed the sound— and the guy fell, the back of his head spewing out a fountain of blood.

Duncan unscrewed the silencer and put it in a mesh pocket on the side of his Kevlar. Another thing wrong about the movies: silencers could only be used once. A man was coming up the road and he turned, expecting to see Nat, his driver, approach, but it wasn't Nat. It was Zach.

"Duncan," Zach said urgently. "You've got a problem."

—————

The earplug was hurting her left ear, but Tanya kept it in place as she trotted up the dirt road, following a hunched-over Major Carl Kenyon, who was moving with his troops, if not into battle, at least into conflict. At the major's insistence, she was wearing a Kevlar vest and a helmet that kept on slipping off her head. At her own insistence, she was wearing a pair of night-vision goggles that gave her a narrow but clear-eyed view of the dirt road in front of her, in ghostly gray-green. The woods were all about her, dark woods, and she had flashes of memory of the terror that had flowed through her that night with the Girl Scouts, lost and fumbling around and oh so scared.

Tanya kept one hand on her head as they moved into the darkness, with Henry Wolfe beside her. Having Henry next to her was a comfort. She wasn't sure what Carl and the Staties would do if she got caught in the middle of a firefight or something similar, but she was pretty certain Henry would watch her back. Her feet hurt but she kept on moving, right up to the point when Carl held up his hand, halting the movement, as a whispered voice urgently came over the radio.

"TOC, this is Sierra," the sniper breathlessly reported. "Truck has arrived, has halted. Two targets to the right of the truck cab. Wait … looks like we have a shot fired … subject down. Repeat, shot fired, subject down."

———

Francois Ouellette moved quickly with his gang members flanking him. They had on Canadian Army night-vision gear that was obsolete but still worked, bullet-resistant vests, and each carried a Russian-made AK-47 semiautomatic rifle. As they had exited the Jeep Cherokee, Francois had said, "This is a straight smash and grab. We go in, hose anybody standing up, take care of business, and steal that fucking truck."

Moving his head slightly back and forth, back and forth, Francois saw the truck ahead of him, that blessed truck that had caused so many rough nights and busy days, days when he had been filled with rage at what happened to his four club members, sent here to settle accounts. Well, that fucking Granite Stater decided not to do business with the Iron Steeds, so they was about to bring the business to him.

Up ahead the driver's side door of the truck cab opened up, and the driver came out, stood down, and started talking to a man who approached him, carrying a rifle of sort slung on his back. Then the guy pulled out a pistol, and there was a bright flare of light against his goggles, nearly blinding him.

Next to him Michael frantically said, "Fuck, somebody just took a shot."

Francois was going to say something as Michael raised his AK-47.

———

It was the distant sound of an engine that finally made Zach move. Luke and Nat had been idly standing by the rear of the Chevy Suburban, whispering to each other, when Zach heard the sound of an aircraft engine, up there in the night sky, approaching them. Earlier he had seen dim red lights as the Crowley brothers had come back with the truck slowly following them. Lots of thoughts were crowding around in his mind. A hot and dark river in Sierra Leone. A plaintive voice—*Sir, can you help? Can you?* Collateral damage. There was always collateral damage. The sight of Karen, sitting on the couch, a gun to her head. The sights and sounds of Turner, after all these years. The young and attractive Tanya Gibbs, able to make him come here and do what she wanted him to do. Thinking of getting his Federal bennies and then leaving here and going back to ... what? A concrete slab with burnt timbers upon it, fifty acres of empty land, and no neighbors?

His brief phone calls to the older man. *Can't you do something? Can't you help?*

Zach made up his mind. To hell with it.

He walked up the road as Cameron approached him. "What's up?" the older Crowley asked.

"Need to see Duncan."

"Give him a minute," Cameron said, holding out an arm to block him. "He's busy with the driver."

"The driver? What's he doing with the driver?"

Cameron said, "He's sending him either to heaven or hell, depending on how God's feeling tonight. The little shit is a domestic terrorist, through and through, with lots of blood on his hands. Duncan made a deal with the guy setting up the shipment, as a side favor."

A muffled *thump*, a sudden flare of light by the truck cab.

"Who the hell asked for the favor? What guy?"

Cameron said, "The driver's cousin. Guess the driver was an embarrassment to the family name, killed one guy too many. Go on, now, looks like Duncan's got a free minute."

Zach shook his head, walked a few more yards to Duncan. He said in a loud whisper, "Duncan, you've got a problem."

"Hold on," Duncan said, walking toward him, blocking the view of what had just happened. The truck engine idled. Duncan came up, flashlight with red lens in his hand. "What problem? We've got to get moving here in a minute or two."

Zach took a deep breath. "Go. Leave the truck behind. Get the hell out of here."

"What the heck are you saying, Zach?"

"I'm saying the Feds know," he said quickly. "They're on their way now. Leave. Get your guys together and get the hell out of here. Go fade in the woods, start running, I'm sure they've got all the roads blocked. I'll stick behind and take the heat, keep them occupied as much as I can. But for Christ's sake, haul ass!"

Duncan's voice was edged with amazement. "How the hell do you know this?"

He grabbed Duncan's shoulder, like he was trying to force a stubborn child to listen to his words. "Damn it, because I fucking told them, I betrayed you! Now get your ass in gear and leave!"

Duncan broke free from his hand, just as automatic weapon fire erupted behind them.

Tanya heard the stuttering fire of weapons just as a voice from the radio screamed in her left ear, "Sierra to TOC! Shots fired! Shots fired! We've got shots fired from a secondary element, arriving behind the truck!"

Somebody tackled her to the ground and her helmet flew off. Her mouth tasted of dirt and a strap from the Kevlar vest was digging into her ribs. She tried to get up but a firm hand pushed her head down.

A voice in her right ear, the one without the radio earbud. "Ma'am, I've driven you, I've waited for you, I've worked at your pleasure, but this once, you're going to do what I fucking say. Keep your goddamn head down! We don't know who's shooting at what!"

"Let me go," she said. "I've got to get up there!"

"The fuck you do," Henry Wolfe said. "We're staying here until the shooting is over."

She fought against his grip on her neck, lost the fight, and then the radio traffic crackled in her left ear, one message right after another.

"Two, maybe three shooters behind the truck."

"Heavy automatic fire."

"Other shooters in front of the truck have opened fire."

"Permission to engage."

"Permission to engage."

"Permission to engage."

Carl Kenyon's voice, cutting through the chatter. "TOC to team members. Engage what? Sweet Jesus, what a goat fuck."

A second passed. Carl said, "Sierra, this is TOC."

"Sierra, go."

"Disable that truck. Repeat. Disable that truck."

"Rounds down range."

———

When the gunfire roared out from behind them, Duncan shoved Zach in his chest, pushing him back, tumbling him into a drainage ditch. Duncan dove in right after him, knee deep in mud. He unslung his H&K, noted the muzzle flashes up the road, heard the incoming rounds zip over head, *thunking* and *thopping* as they struck tree trunks, whistling as they went through thinner branches. Zach was next to him, breathing hard.

Duncan flipped the safety off on his weapon. "The Feds, they believe in shooting first, asking questions later?"

"Not in my line of work," Zach said, his weapon in hand as well. "Look, just retreat, get the hell out of here, I—"

Duncan raised up his weapon. "Yeah, you betrayed me. I knew you probably weren't straight, that first night at the pub, when you got in a fight with the pool players."

Awe in his voice, Zach said, "How the hell did you know?"

Another burst of gunfire, more sounds of rounds flying overhead and impacting. Duncan laughed. "Zach, I kept an eye on you that first night. Thought you looked familiar. I saw you order two pitchers of beer, get drunk, and get in a fight. But when you sat down later and talked to me, you were as sober as the proverbial judge. So you faked getting drunk. So you had something to accomplish. So congrats, mission accomplished."

There was real sorrow in Zach's voice. "Duncan, look, you can still get out of here and—"

"Stage is set, players have arrived, and it's time to do what has to be done," Duncan said. "All you can do is to run out or help me."

Duncan brought the stock of the H&K up to his shoulder, fired off two- and three-round bursts, aiming to where the muzzle flashes were bursting, up there on the road. He felt good at hearing a yelp.

Felt even better, seeing and hearing Zach open fire as well.

———

Francois was on one knee, firing off a few rounds, shifting, and then firing again. Around him Michael and Phil and Johnny were firing, but Jesus Christ on a crutch, where was their fucking fire discipline? They were going full auto, sending round after round at the truck, aiming high, and he screamed, "Fuck it, aim, you idiots, fucking aim!"

He fell to the ground, yelled as something heavy slammed into his back. Gunfire started opening up from the area by the truck, and a heavier, flatter weapon started firing one round after another.

His head hurt.

———

Tanya raised her head, just a bit, to see what she could see, which wasn't much. Brief flares of gunfire illuminating the truck and the road up a ways, where another group of people were firing automatic weapons. To the left was a hard report as the State Police

362

sniper called Sullivan started shooting, the nearby sound very loud. This is what combat must be like, she thought quickly, loud noises, confusion, hugging the ground, brief violent bits of gunfire lighting up the dark scenery. She squirmed, but Henry kept his grip fierce on the back of her neck. She thought about chewing him out when this whole mess was over, but when a bullet went whistling over her head, she almost pissed herself in fear.

All right, maybe a recommendation for promotion instead of a dressing down. That made much more sense.

The voice on the radio. "TOC, Woods."

"Go, TOC."

"Let's light up the joint. Send up a couple of parachute flares."

Up ahead, one of the silhouetted State Police troopers knelt down, and there was hollow *chunk*, and another *chunk*, and a burst of light as one and then a second parachute flare erupted into bright light.

———

Zach whirled as a man jumped into the drainage ditch next to them. It was Nat, the driver, breathing hard. "Duncan, I'm damn sorry to tell you this, but I can't drive that truck."

"What happened, Nat?" Duncan said, not moving his head, firing off a shot here and there.

"This happened," he said mournfully, raising up his right hand. Zach took in a breath. It was a bloody mess. "I got hit, Duncan, I'm really sorry, but I can't drive. Luke got hit, too. Round bounced off a piece of metal and hit his leg. He's bleeding pretty bad."

"Damn it," Duncan said, and Nat added, "But Cameron, he said he'd handle it."

Duncan whirled around. "Cameron is coming up here?"

"That's right," Nat said. "He told me to tell you that he was going to make it finally right by you. Said he was gonna drive that fucker out of here. Said he wasn't going to let this sweet deal get away."

Zach looked over at the dirt road, saw a figure dodging and racing up the opposite side, and Duncan screamed, "Cameron, get down! Get down! It's not worth it!"

"Sorry, bro!" his brother yelled back. "For once I'm not listening to you!"

The night sky lit up like noontime, more gunfire, and the running figure of his brother tumbled and fell.

———

Francois rolled over on his back, AK-47 torn out of his hands, heard Michael call out, "Hold your fire, hold your fire, hold your fire!"

As Michael knelt down next to him, he coughed, cleared his throat. "You … you fucker … what the hell are you doing?"

Michael said, "What I should have done a long time ago. You've lost your smarts man, chasing this truck like it was that fucking white whale. That's bad business, all around. Shit, we lost four guys in this stupid quest. But man …. you also made me cut my hair. You said I looked like a faggot. You think I was going to take that?"

Francois opened his mouth to say something, anything, but he couldn't say a word as the muzzle of Michael's AK-47 was shoved past his teeth and tongue. He choked and didn't hear anything more after that.

———

Duncan cried out, tried to run across the road, but hands grabbed him, dragged him back to the ditch. Zach was on top of him as the gunfire dribbled out and he tried to squirm free, and he shouted, "I've got to get to him, I've got to get to Cameron!"

"Not running across in the open like that!" Zach shouted back.

Duncan fought free and as he got up in the flickering light from the parachute flares overhead, there was splash of water as a heavy-set man jumped into the drainage ditch, an AK-47 pointed right at him, wearing combat gear, night-vision goggles around his neck, making him look like an alien warrior.

Duncan closed his eyes, opened them.

The man said quickly, "Know where Duncan Crowley is?"

"That's me," he said. The gunfire from up the road had halted.

The guy said, "I'm from the Iron Steeds."

"Figured so," Duncan said. "You Francois Ouellette?"

"Nope, Francois is over on the ground over there," the man said. "I'm the new president. Got one thing to say to you."

"Do it then," Cameron said. "Get it over with."

"Here's the thing. You up for a truce?"

"What?

"A truce. We bail out of here now, you can keep whatever the fuck's in that truck, and that's it."

Duncan said, "Sounds good to me."

"Then we're the fuck out of here. Good luck with whoever's over there shooting at you, man."

He turned and sloshed out of the ditch.

———

Zach looked behind them, knowing that Homeland Security and whoever else was out there was coming in hard. Then there was the sudden roaring noise of a helicopter engine, right overhead, followed by an intense beam of light that blinded him. He put a hand over his face, and it seemed the voice of God boomed down.

"Cease firing, cease firing, cease firing. This area is under control of Federal authorities. All personnel, including law enforcement, cease firing, cease firing, cease firing. Weapons are to be holstered or dropped to the ground immediately."

Zach dropped his H&K to the ground as a dark green Black Hawk helicopter roared in close, the backwash tossing up gravel and small branches. The wide beam of light panned across the ground, illuminating the truck, Nat sitting next to him wrapping a handkerchief around his hand, and what looked to be SWAT members down the road. Up the road, a Jeep Cherokee roared off, leaving behind a cloud of dust as the Iron Steeds members retreated north to Canada.

The light moved again, revealing the Suburban, coming back to the truck and the far side of the road, where a weeping Duncan rocked back and forth, holding the head of an unmoving Cameron in his lap.

THIRTY-FIVE

TANYA SHAKILY GOT UP, her driver Henry Wolfe next to her, a helicopter roaring overhead, its bright searchlight revealing everything in front her. Carl Kenyon was nearby as well, his CAR-15 slung on his back, his helmet off. The helicopter blew over again, the same message booming down from its loudspeakers, and then it shifted to the right.

Damn, damn, damn, she thought. Her boss Gordie was no doubt in that Black Hawk, having somehow found out the location and time of this smuggling op.

Well, there was still a chance to make it all work out.

"Carl!" she called out, then walked over to him. "I need that health physicist from the state up here, to examine the trailer."

The State Police major tossed his helmet to the ground. "You heard the man, whoever the hell he is. We're to stand down."

"No, we're to put weapons away. Nothing was said about staying put. I still have control of this operation, until I've been relieved."

Carl pointed to the whirling blades and flashing navigation lights of the Black Hawk helicopter as it descended to the stretch of pastureland to the right. "Looks like you're about to be relieved."

Tanya said, "Maybe so, but I want that HP guy up here right now, to examine the trailer."

Carl looked like he wished he hadn't received the earlier order about holstering weapons. Tanya was sure he was quite tempted to put a bullet through her forehead and blame friendly fire. Instead, he raised up his radio, murmured some words, and the HP guy emerged from the woods, escorted by another State Police trooper.

She pointed to the trailer, wondering how many minutes she had left to do what's right. "I want a scan of that trailer, pronto."

The HP guy shrugged. "That's what I'm here for."

He walked over, carrying a wide shoulder bag, and she fell in with him as State Police troopers advanced on the Suburban and quickly handcuffed one of the gunman. Up by the truck, two of the gunmen were on the right, one holding the other, and two more on the left were facedown, also handcuffed. It looked like the larger guy on the ground on the left was Zach Morrow. If so, as much as she wanted to talk to him, he could wait.

A dead man was on the ground by the driver's side, with a good chunk of his head missing. She looked away, but oddly enough, the HP guy walked on like everything here was a drill, made for his amusement. He gingerly stepped around the dead body and went to the rear of the trailer. Portable spotlights were being set up, and she saw smoke rising up from the shot-up radiator of the truck, noting the front tires were flat. Good shooting, at least, from the sniper.

Kwasnick, the health physicist, squatted on the ground, unzipped his bag. "Excuse me, could I have some light over here?"

Carl aimed a flashlight down at the bag. Tanya stood still. Her legs were frozen. She couldn't seem to catch her breath. It was all here. Right here in front of her. In the next minute or so, Emily's death would be avenged. All of her work, all of the gambles, all of her lies and violating procedures—it was all now coming to a head in the very next few seconds.

Failure. She did not allow herself to think of failure.

The health physicist worked on some dials and switches and then took up a probelike device, with a curled cord running from its base. He brought the probe up to the side of the truck and pressed a switch.

A red light started flashing.

A recorded voice came from his bag:

Gamma alert.

Gamma alert.

Gamma alert.

"Wow," Kwasnick said. "Whatever's in the truck, it's going right off the scale."

She clenched her fists. Tasted sweet victory. Emily, she thought. My dear Emily.

————

When it became apparent what he was doing, Duncan was allowed to keep holding his brother's shattered head in his lap. A state trooper stood away at respectful distance, CAR-15 pointed at him, as Duncan stroked his dead brother's forehead. From the way Cameron had tumbled, Duncan was sure he had been hit bad, probably fatally, but he had hoped he could get over here at the last moment, so Cameron wouldn't die alone.

But he had been too late. A round from either the bikers or the State Police had torn away his throat and he had instantly bled out.

In the nearby lights, Cameron's face was the color of dull paper, and Duncan murmured to his brother as his body cooled against him.

"Oh, Cam," he said softly. "You didn't have to prove a damn thing to me. You brave guy. Running up to the truck, all those bullets flying by. So damn brave. But you had nothing to prove to me. I never blamed you for the accident, for me not going to school, not getting into the majors …. It just happened. You and me … we stuck together. And you watched my back, and had my back, year after year … oh, Cam …. I'm so fucking sorry. Betrayals … I'm the one that betrayed you, Cam … oh, I'm so sorry …"

Someone stepped in front of him. He looked up at a state trooper, who said, "Someone needs to talk to you. Like now."

"I want a blanket."

"Now, no discussion, because—"

"Please. A blanket. This man … he's my brother. He's so damn cold. Then I'll come with you."

The trooper slowly nodded. "I understand. A blanket."

Duncan went back to gently stroking his dead brother's forehead.

———

Zach was lying down in mud and water, not wanting to think much of anything, when there was splashing about him. A voice from behind him. "Which one of you two fuckers is Zach Morrow?"

He raised his head above the mud. "I'm Zach Morrow."

"Hold on," the voice said. There was something tugging at his wrists, and then the handcuffs were undone. "Somebody wants to see you."

Zach got up, looked at the brightly lit scene about him, the dead truck, the Black Hawk helicopter off on the pasture, its rotors still turning.

"I'm sure," he said.

————

Duncan walked slowly over to an area by the Suburban, where more portable lights had been set up. Luke was on his side, being treated by two State Police troopers for the wound in his leg. There was also activity up by the truck, but he didn't care. An older man, dressed in a finely cut dark blue suit with white shirt and red necktie, stepped from around the side of the Suburban.

"Duncan Crowley," the old man said.

"Gordon Simpson," Duncan said.

The old man looked around and let out a breath. "Not what we expected, eh? Thought this would be a relatively quiet operation, without all this gunfire."

"My brother's dead."

Gordon shook his head. "My sympathies."

"Yeah, I'm sure."

"The other matter?" Gordon asked.

"The driver is down," Duncan said. "You can tell his cousin that he can sleep better at night, knowing his wayward relative is gone."

"One bit of good news, at least," he said.

"How did this go so wrong?" Duncan demanded.

Gordon sighed, his face wrinkled, old, fleshy. "From my shop, I'm afraid. Someone with burning ambition who didn't know her limits found out about the truck. She came in with all guns blazing."

Duncan said, "Is she going to be taken care of?"

Gordon ignored the question. "I'm afraid our earlier arrangement may have to be adjusted. There's been too much ... too much exposure tonight. I'm sure you'll understand."

Duncan looked over at the blanket-covered shape of his dead brother. "Don't be sure of that."

A woman came up, tugged Gordon's elbow. "Mr. Simpson? It looks like Miss Gibbs has reached the truck."

"Very good," he said. As he turned to walk away, the woman caught Duncan's eye, nodded, and joined her boss. It was Melanie Pope, the new police chief in Crowdin, confidential employee of the Department of Homeland Security. The one who had told him during that traffic stop that this trailer was coming across in two days.

―――――

Tanya stood at the rear of the truck, her heart nearly singing with joy. Twice she had the health physicist conduct another radiological survey, and both times, the words came back.

Gamma alert.

Gamma alert.

Gamma alert.

Now there was a metal step ladder at the rear of the trailer, and a state trooper with a bolt cutter standing on top of it. But she waited for Gordie to finally stumble over here and see what she had done. This had been her op, one she had taken control of from the very beginning, and once the trailer was opened, she imagined all the crow that managers higher up the food chain would have to eat. They had pooh-poohed this trailer and she had proven them wrong. Oh my, the headlines, the stories ... surely there was room over there in the pasture for Boston TV crews to come see this, the first bona fide interception of a nuclear device en route to the United States.

She had done it!

A flash of memory, of dear old famous Diana Dean of Customs. She had single-handily prevented disaster.

And now Tanya had joined her rank.

Gordie finally made his appearance, strolling over all relaxed, like he was on a Congressional junket or something. He had his wrinkled old hands in his coat pockets and even out here in the middle of the proverbial nowhere, he was dressed like he was going to lunch back in Boston at the recently reopened Locke-Ober.

"Tanya, it looks like quite the situation you have here," he said.

Pride and happiness at what she had accomplished thumped along in her chest. "One that I have quite in hand."

"How did this come about, then?"

"Earlier I had received intelligence that an attempt may be made to cross the border with a WME. I arranged a practice drill just in case the circumstances changed, which they did."

"I see. Let's see, would that be the Mextel trailer, missing from a storage facility at the St. Lawrence Seaway, suspected of containing a Weapon of Mass Effect?"

"The same."

She waited, expecting loud voices, fireworks, the whole enraged supervisor shtick, but he just nodded, pursed his lips and said, "I take it you attempted to inform me."

"I most certainly did. Via text and a phone message."

Gordon took one hand out, tugged at a long ear. "So what do you have?"

"A health physicist from the state of New Hampshire has detected gamma ray radiation from inside the truck," she said, trying to keep the triumph out of her voice. "He said it was off the scale."

She motioned to the state trooper with the bolt cutters, who leaned forward, worked the cutters, and with a loud *snap*, a length of chain was cut.

Gordon said, "Don't you think you should wait for the State Police bomb squad? Or perhaps a Federal NEST unit?"

"Bomb squad and Nuclear Emergency Search Team would take too long, Gordie. You know that. I think we should find out immediately what's in there."

Another tug of his ear. He sighed. "What can I say? It certainly looks like you have everything under control. Go ahead then."

Tanya moved the trooper aside, went up the step ladder, and opened the door. Never in her life had she ever been so excited, so filled with anticipation. It was like every past Christmas morning and birthday, wrapped up in this one minute.

"Light," she called out. "Somebody give me a damn light!"

A lit flashlight was put in her hand. Her mouth was dry, and her hand was shaking. But the light worked well enough, showing that the near half of the truck was empty. Up ahead were bundles of … cloth? She slowly stepped forward, flashed the light down. Plastic wrapped packages of cloth. She tore one open, pulled out a T-shirt. Blue, red, and white, promoting the Montreal Canadiens hockey team.

Damn.

She kicked the T-shirts away, saw a large cardboard box, easily five feet to a side. The T-shirts were just cover, that's all. On top of the box was a loose piece of tape. She tugged at and it ripped away, and she tore open the box, revealing—

Boxes upon boxes, piled upon each other.

Black & Decker smoke detectors.

Scores of them.

It was like the temperature inside of the truck had gone up twenty degrees, as if hidden infrared heat lamps had suddenly been switched on over her. She was sweating. She was flushed. Her mouth was so dry she felt like she had to chew her tongue to get it moistened.

Footsteps behind her. She whirled around, holding up the flashlight like a weapon, ready to crack it over the head of whoever was disturbing her.

Gordon Simpson, walking in, small flashlight in his hand. Beams from both of their lights reflected off the walls illuminated the interior of the truck.

He was smiling.

Smiling!

He pointed his own flashlight at the smoke detectors. "Funny thing about these smoke detectors, Tanya. Each one contains a tiny bit of Americium-241, which emits gamma radiation. One detector, eh, not that much. But a large number of smoke detectors, in one place, well, enough to make the surveillance equipment from a state health physicist go off the scale. Even if it is harmless."

Tanya stood there, like her feet had been spiked to the floor of the truck. She worked her mouth, felt it moisten. "Why?" she finally said, and she was humiliated at how squeaky her voice sounded.

Gordon shrugged. "This little confidential drill was set up weeks ago, on my orders, just to see what kind of parameters would be exploited by various domestic law enforcement agencies if word about this trailer was leaked out. First, to test security procedures. Second, to see what would happen if agencies and personnel received unauthorized classified information. When I learned that you had found about this drill and had come to the spectacularly wrong conclusion of what was happening, well, it was in my interest to let you take it for a ride. As I've said before, Tanya, I may not know the latest in technologies—

as you so graciously pointed out to me—but I know people. I know ambition. I know you."

She didn't know what to say. She felt like an insect pinned to a board. He went on. "Remember that GAO audit I was telling you about? Investigators from the GAO like to have trophies. Once an audit is completed, they don't like to go away empty-handed. So when they do leave, Tanya, their hands will be filled with your ass— an administrator who went so far off the reservation she ended up in the ocean."

The light in her hands wavered. She heard additional helicopters overhead, their searchlights illuminating everything she could see from the open end of the truck trailer. Gordie turned for a moment. "Ah, yes, right on schedule. Our so-called independent news media. Television stations from Portland and Boston, all here to record and report on your utter and complete disgrace."

Tanya's legs started quivering. Her mouth was so very, very dry. She now held her flashlight in two hands. "This doesn't make sense."

Gordie said, "Do go on."

"Doesn't make sense for all this effort and energy to humiliate and cripple me, an unknown government worker … Days ago you could have brought me into your office and fired me, with just cause. You didn't have to take it this far."

It suddenly came to her, something dark and blossoming inside, spreading out like an approaching and threatening thunderstorm. The trailer seemed to quake about her.

"This was never about me, was it," she finally said. "You're after my uncle. The senior senator from Ohio. Warren Gibbs. The presidential candidate."

Gordie stayed quiet, those reptile eyes of his unblinking. Her voice growing stronger, she said, "You bastards. You couldn't quite figure a way of kneecapping Senator Gibbs and driving him down in the polls.

So you did all this"—and she motioned the light so it illuminated the roof of the trailer—"to humiliate me, and by extension, my uncle."

Gordie shrugged. "I won't say that, but I'm sure others eventually will. They'll say both you and your uncle share the same paranoid vision of what we should do as a country, what the proper role of Homeland Security should be. It's going to be reported shortly that you, a mid-level government official, caused this enormous waste of resources and loss of life, acting irrationally and without proper authorization. Shortly thereafter, the names will be noted, and the dots will be connected. Like niece, like uncle."

"That's damn unfair and reckless, and you know it, Gordie."

"That's life and politics, and you know that, Tanya."

She closed her eyes for a moment as tears filled them, as the bitter taste of humiliation overpowered her. All this work and effort, long hours and harsh actions, all to avenge Emily and the thousands of other victims, and for what? Utter and complete disaster. Instead of a victory, she had ended up strengthening the same officials, the same close-minded politicians and bureaucrats who had allowed 9/11 to happen.

She opened her eyes. "Gordie … how could you have done this? How?"

Another slight shrug. "Your uncle wasn't playing the game, wasn't taking part in the proper narrative. There are people in power and influence who won't let that happen."

"What's the narrative, Gordie?" she said, bitterness in her voice

Her boss said, "It's been long enough since 9/11. We're no longer going to overreact to whatever terrorist threat may be out there, we're no longer going to profile people because of their religion and background. Homeland Security is going to do its job of worrying about immigration status and deportation arrangements and that's it. No increased surveillance, no paramilitary teams, and no rogue administrators doing what they feel. Obviously you haven't gotten the memo: The war on terror is over. We won. All that's left are small-time losers like the Boston Marathon bombers, acting on their own."

Tanya said, "I have another story, by God, and I'll say it."

Gordie smiled, his leathery skin stretching. "Go right ahead. The well-dressed men and women in those approaching helicopters know the narrative as well, and that's how they'll report it. Oh, they pretend they're independent and above it all, but they know their role. They don't want to lose access. Don't want to be off the team, off the story. So they'll report it the way we and their editors want it, and by this time next week, thanks to you, your uncle's campaign will collapse."

Tanya said, "I quit."

Gordie said, "Too late for that."

————

Zach was taken to the front of the Suburban. Luke's wounded leg was bandaged and he was sitting up, his hands cuffed behind him. Nat was sitting next to him, a temporary bandage on his hand. In front of the Suburban was Gordon Simpson, and he said, "Chief Morrow."

"Captain Simpson."

"Please," Gordon said, "I'm not on duty tonight. How are you, Zach?"

"Tired, disgusted, in the need of a hot shower." He pointed to the truck. "What was in there?"

"A collection of smoke detectors. Enough gamma source material to fool an initial examiner that a weapon of some sort was inside.

Enough material to tempt someone to break the rules, go rogue, not follow procedures."

Zach gestured again to the lights, the disabled truck, and the bodies. "A fake, then. So was this all necessary?"

"Meaning what?"

"I saw you talk to Duncan Crowley. It wasn't the first time you've met, was it."

"So?"

"So why was I here? Why did you recruit me before Tanya Gibbs popped into my life?"

Gordon said, "Belt and suspenders, Zach. Belt and suspenders. I wanted to make sure the outcome tonight was in my favor. If I had to use both you and Duncan Crowley, with neither one of you aware of the other, then that's what I did. No apologies."

"Didn't expect any."

"Then I won't apologize for this as well," Gordon went on. "Due to the … public nature of this operation, I'm not sure if our earlier arrangement can be honored. I'm sure you'll understand."

Zach said, "Being tossed over the side? I understand it all too well."

"Don't be so sarcastic."

"I'll be whatever I fucking please."

———

Duncan Crowley was now handcuffed, and he watched as his brother's body was placed in a metal litter to be hauled out in one of the helicopters that were joining the Black Hawk. There were so many floodlights being set up that when he tilted his head back, he could no longer see the stars Cameron had loved so much.

He started to weep.

Zach walked around as other helicopters landed near the Black Hawk. He was feeling that odd post-letdown that came after a mission was over, but instead of the usual sense of satisfaction and exhaustion after coming back in one piece, he felt out of place, insignificant, the sense of being a betrayer coursing through him. This mission was done, but there was no way he could call it a success.

He walked by the infamous trailer, saw someone sitting alone at the base of a pine tree.

Tanya Gibbs.

Zach went to her, and she looked up. From the lights illuminating the area, it was easy to make out her features and her appearance. The first time he had met her, a few days and a lifetime ago, she had looked about sixteen. Now she looked about twelve, defeated, and crushed. Her knees were pulled up to her chest and her hands were cupping her knees.

"Chief," she said.

"Miss Gibbs," he replied.

She kept on looking at him, and he said, "My apologies, Tanya. I betrayed you about five minutes after we met. Every day I informed Gordon Simpson that I was with you, assisting you in locating that trailer. It was a setup, and you were the target."

Tanya shook her head. "No, chief, I wasn't the target. My uncle was."

Zach felt like something off in the distance had blown up, something big, something important, that had just made the ground tremble. "I see. They're going to publicize your involvement in this fiasco. Connect you with your uncle. Disgracing you, disgracing him. That was the whole deal, wasn't it."

She rocked back and forth. "Some involvement. I haven't talked to my uncle in a couple of years. He's been too busy being senator."

Zach said, "When we first met, you said you had somebody who could help at the right moment. I thought you meant your uncle. Were you lying?"

Tanya said, "I wanted that trailer. I lied, I cheated, and I threatened people, all to do that. So, yeah. I lied. I betrayed you as well. No apologies, though. Never any apologies."

There were shouts out by the meadow, and Zach noted little cones of light as television crewman switched on their lamps and started trotting to the disabled truck and the knots of State Police and Homeland Security officers.

"So what now?" Zach asked.

"I'll tell you," Tanya said, her voice more firm. "You're an educated man, Chief. You love your history books. Tell me what happened to the armed forces of the United States between August 1945 and June 1951."

"What is this, *Jeopardy*?"

"In a way, yes it is. Most important *Jeopardy* game ever."

"A hell of a time and place to be playing a game."

"Humor me, Chief. Answer the damn question."

He didn't have to think about it too much. "The time between VJ Day and the invasion of South Korea. Our armed forces became a hollow shell. You had reservists and occupation troops from Japan, trying to fight off an invading army with surplus gear from World War II. For the first few months they got slaughtered."

The television crews got closer. "Thanks for the right answer," she said. "The war was over, budgets got cut, troops were sent home. We were victorious and why would there be another war?"

Some loud voices, coming closer. "So here we are," she said. "Bin Laden's dead, we're pulling out of Afghanistan and Iraq, Predator drones are paying whack-a-mole in the tribal regions, and those in power and influence think we've won. Meantime, in the real world, those who hate us will patiently do the prep work for the next year or two or five, and they'll come back and hit us hard. This time, it won't be hijacked aircraft. It might be hijacked nukes from Pakistan's strategic arsenal. Or black-market nukes from Russia. Or some bio-warfare agent cooked up in a lab. Whatever it is, I'm afraid living in big cities is going to be very, very unhealthy in the near future."

Zach wanted to stop hearing this sweet voice talking betrayal and destruction. He thought for a moment that she was crying but no, her face, as young as it looked, was now strong and defiant. He couldn't tear his gaze away from her.

Tanya rocked slightly back and forth. "Lucky you," she said. "You've got a nice small town to live in when hell pays us a visit again."

"Yeah," Zach said. "Lucky me."

THIRTY-SIX

In a visitor's room at the Washington County House of Corrections, Zach Morrow sat at a metal table across from Duncan Crowley, who was dressed in a bright orange jumpsuit. Duncan looked thinner and pale, and he was faintly smiling as Zach settled in.

Duncan said, "Pretty remote for a county prison, isn't it."

"Damn right," Zach said.

"Some of the guys who've been here for a while, they see what's beyond the fence, the bears, the coyotes, the moose. They told me that if they were out in the yard and the fence magically fell down, that they'd just sit there and wouldn't move. Wouldn't try to escape. Some of those guys are tough gang members from Nashua and Manchester who got caught up here in Washington County, but these woods at night scare the crap out of them."

"You doing all right?"

"As well as can be expected," Duncan said, his voice slightly raspy. "Though Karen has come in, checked out the menu, nearly had a fight with a supervisor. But damn, a man does love fried food. How are you doing?"

"A bit at loose ends. But I want you to tell me something."

"Gordon Simpson."

"Yeah."

Duncan put his hands on the dull metal table. "Cameron and I, we got an invitation some months ago, to look at some distressed properties up in Lake Palmer. It was going to be an expensive retreat for ex-government types, Europeans with disposable income, that sort of thing. But the invite was a scam. Gordon Simpson wanted me far away from home, in a private meeting."

"How did he get to you?"

"Feds are sly and creative creatures when they want to be. There's been a secret surveillance program going on along the northern border for years, using Predator drones. My import-export business got tracked and recorded, numerous times. Usually Homeland Security doesn't care about such stuff, but Gordon told me state officials and other agencies had gotten wind of what Homeland Security had found out about me. Gordon's deal was pretty straightforward. If I helped get that trailer across as part of a clandestine drill, then he promised me one very large get-out-of-jail free card and a generous compensation package. So I took the deal."

"And the driver? The one you shot?"

"A disgraced and violent former member of the Tea Party, recruited to drive the truck across the border, make the drill that much more realistic. Official story, deep in the records, is that he was shot trying to escape. Unofficial story, I was asked to take care of him as a favor for Gordon Simpson and a Mexican construction big-shot who's been very cooperative with Homeland Security when it comes to southern border issues. Seems the driver shot the Mexican's son a few months ago, who was running a smuggling operation in Arizona."

Zach shook his head. "Hell of a story. What about Cameron? What did he know?"

Duncan's face darkened, and he paused for a moment, like he was trying to catch his breath. He swallowed hard. "No, not old Cam. He only knew part of it ... I should have told them the whole thing, but that was key to the deal. Me, and me alone. Nobody else. Cam ... Looks like he was caught in the crossfire."

Zach thought. "Collateral damage."

"Eh?"

"We were all caught in the crossfire, Duncan."

"Probably so," he said. "Your sorry tale, then?"

"Gordon was a captain in the Naval Reserves," Zach said. "Met him a couple of times over the years during my deployments. Plus he knew my father, back in the days when he was in politics. When I got cashiered, I contacted him to see if he could help me out. He came back with a deal, too. To help a rogue administrator in his department named Tanya Gibbs. I was to cooperate with her, go along with her demands, see where it took us. Make a phone call every day to his private line, pretending to be one pissed-off ex-Coast Guardsmen, but actually letting him know I was on the job. That way, if other agencies were listening in, it would seem that I was just a pissed-off vet."

"That's it? Just to go after one woman?"

Zach said, "You must be missing the news stuck in here. Thing is, her uncle's a senator from Ohio. Running for president. The usual suspects are trying to hang this fiasco and his niece around his neck, drag him down. Might just work in the end."

"Christ, that's something," Duncan said. "What happened to that Tanya woman?"

"Last I heard, she went back to Boston, found her office belongings piled in a cardboard box on the sidewalk. Then she just dropped out."

Duncan said, "That Gordon Simpson, one hell of a deal maker. But he's backing out of the deal he made with me. Extenuating circumstances and all that. So here I am, in jail, awaiting trial."

"For what?"

"Officially, for a variety of illegal activities, from smuggling T-shirts and smoke detectors to unauthorized weapons discharging in a state forest preserve, that sort of thing. Unofficially, I'm here because the State Police are very pissed off about how they got roped into this fiasco. Somebody has to take the fall and it's going to be me."

Zach said, "Gordie's backed out with me as well, because of all the gunfire and bodies littered around. It was supposed to be a quiet little op ending in trapping a woman who was making Gordon's life miserable. You were there; definitely wasn't quiet."

"Sweet understatement."

"Yeah. So my discharge status remains unchanged. No back pay, no pension, no medical coverage. Looks like Gordon remains a member in good standing of the government. No deal too small to remain unbroken."

"Heck of a thing, ain't it," Duncan said. "But we'll get by, just you wait and see. I've got some plans ahead."

"You do?" Zach said. "Funny thing, I saw in the *Union Leader* the other day about a series of mysterious barn fires in Washington County. What was going on? Doing some spring cleaning?"

"Let's just say I have a very lovely and dedicated wife who knows what to do in emergencies. Any large pool of potential evidence out there against me just got drained."

"State fire marshal's office?"

Duncan said, "They're so overworked, they often just follow the lead of the fire chief in the area. So these barn fires will all be considered accidental. Funny things can happen up in the north, hunh?"

"Speaking of funny things," Zach said carefully. "The first day after that fight in the Flight Deck, you took me on a little tour. Brought me up to that deer butchering shed, just before your cell-phone rang from Karen."

"I remember."

"So what were you going to do to me in that shed? Go after me with pliers? Jumper cables? Or just appeal to my better nature?"

"I was suspicious," Duncan said. "No excuse, no apologies. I wanted to make sure who you were. If you were from the State Police, the Attorney General's office, the FBI, well, it would have gotten interesting. But when you did what you did later that day … you could have had a US Marshal's Office badge tattooed on your chest and I wasn't going to do anything against you, Zach."

"Fair enough," he said.

Duncan looked around the tiny room. "So what do you do next?"

"Not sure. My employment options are pretty narrow."

"Then come work for me."

"What?"

Duncan said, "I'm going to be here for a while, but not as long as the state wants. I have a number of legitimate businesses that need oversight. Karen is wonderful, but she's busy with her hair shop and the kids. So what do you think?"

"I know shit about business."

"You'll learn. It'll pay well. It also has one other advantage, Zach. You'll be back home."

"Home is Purmort."

"From what I heard, Purmort is empty acreage with a burnt-out double-wide resting on a concrete slab."

Zach looked at Duncan and his calm face, and said, "I'll certainly think about it, that's for sure."

"Fair enough."

Zach pushed his chair back and said, "What did you mean earlier, about having some plans ahead?"

"I just do, that's all," Duncan said. "Some plans to make it right for me, make it right for you."

"Must be one hell of plan."

"That's what I'm good at, most times. Making plans and seeing them through."

"Glad to hear it," Zach said. Thinking carefully, he said, "I also have a plan or two myself for Gordon Simpson, if yours don't work out."

"In what way?"

"My duffel bags are still at your house. If you know what I mean." Zach looked into Duncan's calm eyes, knowing his old classmate knew exactly what was meant: Zach's collection of weapons, from the pen disguised as a knife to an Israeli submachine gun. With all that had gone on before, Zach would not allow one more betrayal. It would be against the law, of course, but he was beyond that now.

Duncan slowly nodded. "You sure do remind me of Cam. He was always in favor of taking a more direct approach. Thought diplomacy meant leaving no bloodstains behind. But before you do an imitation of a one-man blitzkrieg, see how I make out. All right?"

"You got it."

Duncan said, "Now, you think about my job offer, all right?"

"I will," Zach said, getting up from the chair.

"But one more thing," Duncan cautioned. "I know about you and Karen, back in high school. You keep your hands off of her, all right?"

Zach turned, to hide his smile. "You can count on it."

———

As Duncan was being led back to his holding cell, the day supervisor for his housing unit approached the male corrections officer escorting him and said, "Ronnie, I'll take him back."

"You got it, Gail."

The day supervisor was a heavy-set woman named Mooney, closing in on three hundred pounds, who had very short black hair and a collection of stud earrings in both ears. The uniform was black trousers and light blue uniform shirt. She clasped Duncan's upper arm with her strong hand and said, "Finally, the famous Duncan Crowley of Washington County, in my hand and wearing prison orange."

"Glad I'm making your day," he said.

"Oh, you know it," she said, her fingers pushing hard into his bicep. She nearly dragged him down a corridor, floor polished and shiny, and she unexpectedly stopped at an office door. From her keychain, she unlocked the door, and shoved him into an empty office. Duncan nearly stumbled and he turned as she stood in the doorway.

"Duncan Crowley?"

"Still here," he said.

She gestured with her right hand. "Phone's on the desk. Dial nine to get an outside line. Won't be overheard like every other inmate phone call from here. Best I can do is to give you five minutes. I also made sure nobody listened in on your visitor."

"Thanks so much."

Mooney stepped out and before she closed the door, she said, "You did good for my neighbor Mrs. Ziff a couple of weeks ago. It's nice to know she and her kids won't freeze this winter."

"Glad to help."

He went to the office phone, dialed nine, and then dialed a Boston-based number. It was picked up the first ring.

"Simpson."

Duncan started in. "Gordon, I know your first reaction is to hang up, but do hold on. This is the situation. You may think you know me, and know Zach Morrow, but you don't know enough. For example, ever hear of Hubert Conan?"

"I can't say I have. I'm about to go into a meeting."

"Hubert is my wife's uncle. He's a correspondent for the *Union Leader* newspaper up here. Before that, he used to be a reporter for the *New York Times*. Still has a fair number of contacts down there, at the old Gray Lady."

Duncan waited, hearing the old man's breathing on the other side of the phone. He waited, and waited, and said, "Gee, looks like you're not going to hang up after all. So this is what's going to happen. You make it good for me and Zach Morrow, or I'm going to have a fascinating discussion with Uncle Hubert about what really happened up in the north woods a few nights ago. Now, it doesn't have to happen tonight, or tomorrow, but it will happen."

He waited some more. Gordon sighed. "Talk to me tomorrow, at this same time. We'll see what we can do."

"That sounds fine," Duncan said, smiling as Gordon hung up on him. Tomorrow, ah tomorrow. This was going to result in some very delicate negotiations, but Duncan looked forward to it.

Negotiating on behalf of family and the ones he cared for, those who were overlooked and ignored, was something Duncan Crowley lived for.

THIRTY-SEVEN

ZACH MORROW PULLED HIS F-150 pickup truck onto the side of Route 115 by Gibson's Hill, looking down once again upon the town of Turner. Thought about his first eighteen years there, and recalled the last few days, where he was welcomed back, where he seemed to fit in, to belong.

Thought some about spending a lot more time here over the next decade or two, finding the idea unexpectedly filling him with sweet anticipation. Running businesses. Finding a place to live. Challenges all. But would it be as hard as swimming for a mile or two at night, or being shot at, or running ops that would never ever appear in the history books?

A car approached, pulled in behind him. It was a white GM sedan, one of the numerous rental hordes that could be picked up at any airport across the country. He looked on in surprise as the driver stepped out.

It was Tanya Gibbs.

She offered a hesitant smile. He smiled right back at her. She looked different. Her hair was trimmed, and she had on a short black leather jacket, black skirt above the knees, and she looked pretty good. She didn't look like a teenage girl who had stolen her father's car for Take Your Daughter to Work Day. She looked like a young professional woman.

"Miss Gibbs," he said.

"Please, Chief," she said. "I'm no longer working for Homeland Security. So it's Tanya."

Zach nodded. "So call me Zach. How in the world did you find me?"

She smiled again, wider and more sincere, and strolled over to the front of his truck. She had good legs. Damn, she had fine legs. Tanya went to the left fender, squatted down, her fine butt outlined in the tight skirt, and reached up to the wheel well. In a moment or two, she came out with a thin metal box, with an antenna trailing.

Zach laughed. "Two tracers instead of one. Very thorough."

Tanya turned and tossed it into a nearby ditch. "Not thorough enough."

She moved to him and he said, "So now I know why you found me. But why? Considering what I did to you … I'm surprised."

A stray breeze brought a scent of lilac to him. "Last time we chatted, I told you that big cities weren't going to be healthy places over the next few years. Haven't changed my mind. So here I am. I was hoping you could show me what small-town life is all about. If you're interested. Considering all that went on before, if you're not, I understand."

Zach looked at her eyes, saw something missing. There was no desperate drive there, no fear of overlooking something important. What was there was a hunger, a desire for something quiet, peaceful, out of the way. Something he was looking for as well.

He didn't hesitate.

"Yes," he said. "I'm interested."

She put her hands in her leather coat, nodded, like she couldn't find the right words. Zach came to her, put his hands on her shoulders, looked at her expectant eyes, kissed her forehead. "I think I'd enjoy it as well."

"Me, too," Tanya said, leaning into him. The two of them stood like that for a few sweet seconds, then she said, "They won, didn't they. You were seeking something, I was seeking something, but in the end, the all-powerful, the all-reaching *they*… victory belonged to them. Not us."

He found he enjoyed her being next to him. "Depends how you define victory, I guess. Right now, I don't care."

"Me either."

He kissed her forehead again, she squeezed his rough hand, and they went back to their own vehicles.

Zach shifted his old truck back into drive and headed down into Turner, followed by a small white car that was offering something special. Once again, he passed that metal sign announcing he was on the Montgomery Morrow Memorial Highway.

He paid the sign no heed.

He was finally going home.

Daily Threat Assessment Task Force Teleconference Call
April 22nd

Homeland Security representative: "Before we go over today's agenda, I just want to welcome our new FBI representative, Special Agent Wendell Blake. Wendell, glad to have you here."

FBI representative: "Happy to be here."

State Department representative: "Welcome aboard."

FBI: "Thanks."

Homeland Security: "If I can speak out of turn for a moment, Wendell, I truly hope you turn out be a real team player. Nothing personal against your predecessor, you understand, but in these sessions, we all need to pull together in the correct direction. We don't need someone tossing sand in the gears. No offense, you understand."

FBI: "None taken."

State Department: "So what happened to Tom?"

FBI: "Transferred to Boise."

CIA: "What, the Siberia station not available?"

[[[Laughter]]]

Homeland Security: "Very well, let's move on. Wendell, do you have anything you want to add to today's agenda?"

FBI: "Not really, Gordon. All's quiet."

Homeland Security: "Good."

ABOUT THE AUTHOR

Brendan DuBois of New Hampshire is the award-winning author of 17 novels and more than 150 short stories.

His short fiction has appeared in *Playboy, Ellery Queen's Mystery Magazine, Alfred Hitchcock's Mystery Magazine, The Magazine of Fantasy & Science Fiction, The Saturday Evening Post*, and numerous anthologies including *The Best American Mystery Stories of the Century*, published in 2000, as well as the *The Best American Noir of the Century*, published in 2010.

His stories have twice won him the Shamus Award from the Private Eye Writers of America, and have also earned him three Edgar Allan Poe Award nominations from the Mystery Writers of America. DuBois has won two Barry Awards and an Al Blanchard Crime Fiction Award and is also a *Jeopardy!* gameshow champion.

Visit his website at www.BrendanDuBois.com.

www.MidnightInkBooks.com

From the gritty streets of New York City to sacred tombs in the Middle East, it's always midnight somewhere. Join us online at any hour for fresh new voices in mystery fiction.

At midnightinkbooks.com you'll also find our author blog, new and upcoming books, events, book club questions, excerpts, mystery resources, and more.

ᵀᴹ MIDNIGHT INK

MIDNIGHT INK ORDERING INFORMATION

Order Online:
• Visit our website www.midnightinkbooks.com, select your books, and order them on our secure server.

Order by Phone:
• Call toll-free within the U.S. and Canada at
1-888-NITE-INK (1-888-648-3465)
• We accept VISA, MasterCard, and American Express

Order by Mail:
Send the full price of your order (MN residents add 6.875% sales tax) in U.S. funds, plus postage & handling to:

Midnight Ink
2143 Wooddale Drive
Woodbury, MN 55125-2989

Postage & Handling:

Standard (U.S. & Canada). If your order is:
$25.00 and under, add $4.00
$25.01 and over, FREE STANDARD SHIPPING

AK, HI, PR: $16.00 for one book plus $2.00 for each additional book.

International Orders (airmail only):
$16.00 for one book plus $3.00 for each additional book